SWORD OF DESTINY

ANDRZEJ SAPKOWSKI

Translated by David French

First published in Great Britain in 2015
by Gollancz
An imprint of the Orion Publishing Group
Carmelite House, 50 Victoria Embankment, London EC4Y 0DZ
An Hachette UK Company

This edition published in Great Britain in 2016 by Gollancz

025

Originally published as *Miecz przeznaczenia*

Published by arrangement with Literary Agency 'Agence de l'Est'

A CIP catalogue record for this book is available
from the British Library

ISBN 978 1 473 21154 4

Typeset by Input Data Services Ltd, Bridgwater, Somerset

Printed and bound by Clays Ltd, Elcograf S.p.A.

The Orion Publishing Group's policy is to use papers that
are natural, renewable and recyclable products and made from
wood grown in sustainable forests. The logging and manufacturing
processes are expected to conform to the environmental
regulations of the country of origin.

www.gollancz.co.uk
www.orionbooks.co.uk

By Andrzej Sapkowski from Gollancz:

The Witcher

CONTENTS

THE BOUNDS OF REASON

I

'He won't get out of there, I'm telling you,' the pockmarked man said, shaking his head with conviction. 'It's been an hour and a quarter since he went down. That's the end of 'im.'

The townspeople, crammed among the ruins, stared in silence at the black hole gaping in the debris, at the rubble-strewn opening. A fat man in a yellow jerkin shifted from one foot to the other, cleared his throat and took off his crumpled biretta.

'Let's wait a little longer,' he said, wiping the sweat from his thinning eyebrows.

'For what?' the spotty-faced man snarled. 'Have you forgotten, Alderman, that a basilisk is lurking in that there dungeon? No one who goes in there comes out. Haven't enough people perished? Why wait?'

'But we struck a deal,' the fat man muttered hesitantly. 'This just isn't right.'

'We made a deal with a living man, Alderman,' said the spotty-faced man's companion, a giant in a leather butcher's apron. 'And now he's dead, sure as eggs is eggs. It was plain from the start he was heading to his doom, just like the others. Why, he even went in without a looking glass, taking only a sword. And you can't kill a basilisk without a looking glass, everyone knows that.'

'You've saved yourself a shilling, Alderman,' the spotty-faced man added. 'For there's no one to pay for the basilisk. So get off home nice and easy. And we'll take the sorcerer's horse and chattels. Shame to let goods go to waste.'

1

'Aye,' the butcher said. 'A sturdy mare, and saddlebags nicely stuffed. Let's take a peek at what's inside.'

'This isn't right. What are you doing?'

'Quiet, Alderman, and stay out of this, or you're in for a hiding,' the spotty-faced man warned.

'Sturdy mare,' the butcher repeated.

'Leave that horse alone, comrade.'

The butcher turned slowly towards the newcomer, who had appeared from a recess in the wall, and the people gathered around the entrance to the dungeon.

The stranger had thick, curly, chestnut hair. He was wearing a dark brown tunic over a padded coat and high riding boots. And he was not carrying a weapon.

'Move away from the horse,' he repeated, smiling venomously. 'What is this? Another man's horse, saddlebags and property, and you can't take your watery little eyes off them, can't wait to get your scabby mitts on them? Is that fitting behaviour?'

The spotty-faced man, slowly sliding a hand under his coat, glanced at the butcher. The butcher nodded, and beckoned towards a part of the crowd, from which stepped two stocky men with close-cropped hair. They were holding clubs of the kind used to stun animals in a slaughterhouse.

'Who are you,' the spotty-faced man asked, still holding his hand inside his coat, 'to tell us what is right and what is not?'

'That is not your concern, comrade.'

'You carry no weapon.'

''Tis true.' The stranger smiled even more venomously. 'I do not.'

'That's too bad.' The spotty-faced man removed his hand – and with it a long knife – from inside his coat. 'It is very unfortunate that you do not.'

The butcher also drew a knife, as long as a cutlass. The other two men stepped forward, raising their clubs.

'I have no need,' the stranger said, remaining where he stood. 'My weapons follow me.'

Two young women came out from behind the ruins, treading

with soft, sure steps. The crowd immediately parted, then stepped back and thinned out.

The two women grinned, flashing their teeth and narrowing their eyes, from whose corners broad, tattooed stripes ran towards their ears. The muscles of their powerful thighs were visible beneath lynx skins wrapped around their hips, and on their sinuous arms, naked above their mail gloves. Sabre hilts stuck up behind their shoulders, which were also protected by chainmail.

Slowly, very slowly, the spotty-faced man bent his knees and dropped his knife on the ground.

A rattle of stones and a scraping sound echoed from the hole in the rubble, and then two hands, clinging to the jagged edge of the wall, emerged from the darkness. After the hands then appeared, in turn, a head of white hair streaked with brick dust, a pale face, and a sword hilt projecting above the shoulders. The crowd murmured.

The white-haired man reached down to haul a grotesque shape from the hole; a bizarre bulk smeared in blood-soaked dust. Holding the creature by its long, reptilian tail, he threw it without a word at the fat Alderman's feet. He sprang back, tripping against a collapsed fragment of wall, and looked at the curved, birdlike beak, webbed wings and the hooked talons on the scaly feet. At the swollen dewlap, once crimson, now a dirty russet. And at the glazed, sunken eyes.

'There's your basilisk,' the white-haired man said, brushing the dust from his trousers, 'as agreed. Now my two hundred lintars, if you please. Honest lintars, not too clipped. I'll check them, you can count on it.'

The Alderman drew out a pouch with trembling hands. The white-haired man looked around, and then fixed his gaze for a moment on the spotty-faced man and the knife lying by his foot. He looked at the man in the dark brown tunic and at the young women in the lynx skins.

'As usual,' he said, taking the pouch from the Alderman's trembling hands, 'I risk my neck for you for a paltry sum, and in the meantime you go after my things. You never change; a pox on the lot of you.'

'Haven't been touched,' the butcher muttered, moving back. The

3

men with the clubs had melted into the crowd long before. 'Your things haven't been touched, sir.'

'That pleases me greatly,' the white-haired man smiled. At the sight of the smile burgeoning on his pale face, like a wound bursting, the small crowd began to quickly disperse. 'And for that reason, friend, you shall also remain untouched. Go in peace. But make haste.'

The spotty-faced man was also retreating. The spots on his white face were unpleasantly conspicuous.

'Hey, stop there,' the man in the dark brown tunic said to him. 'You've forgotten something.'

'What is that . . . sir?'

'You drew a knife on me.'

The taller of the women suddenly swayed, legs planted widely apart, and twisted her hips. Her sabre, which no one saw her draw, hissed sharply through the air. The spotty-faced man's head flew upwards in an arc and fell into the gaping opening to the dungeon. His body toppled stiffly and heavily, like a tree being felled, among the crushed bricks. The crowd let out a scream. The second woman, hand on her sword hilt, whirled around nimbly, protecting her partner's back. Needlessly. The crowd, stumbling and falling over on the rubble, fled towards the town as fast as they could. The Alderman loped at the front with impressive strides, outdistancing the huge butcher by only a few yards.

'An excellent stroke,' the white-haired man commented coldly, shielding his eyes from the sun with a black-gloved hand. 'An excellent stroke from a Zerrikanian sabre. I bow before the skill and beauty of the free warriors. I'm Geralt of Rivia.'

'And I,' the stranger in the dark brown tunic pointed at the faded coat of arms on the front of his garment, depicting three black birds sitting in a row in the centre of a uniformly gold field, 'am Borch, also known as Three Jackdaws. And these are my girls, Téa and Véa. That's what I call them, because you'll twist your tongue on their right names. They are both, as you correctly surmised, Zerrikanian.'

'Thanks to them, it appears, I still have my horse and belongings. I thank you, warriors. My thanks to you too, sir.'

4

'Three Jackdaws. And you can drop the "sir". Does anything detain you in this little town, Geralt of Rivia?'

'Quite the opposite.'

'Excellent. I have a proposal. Not far from here, at the crossroads on the road to the river port, is an inn. It's called the Pensive Dragon. The vittals there have no equal in these parts. I'm heading there with food and lodging in mind. It would be my honour should you choose to keep me company.'

'Borch.' The white-haired man turned around from his horse and looked into the stranger's bright eyes. 'I wouldn't want anything left unclear between us. I'm a witcher.'

'I guessed as much. But you said it as you might have said "I'm a leper".'

'There are those,' Geralt said slowly, 'who prefer the company of lepers to that of a witcher.'

'There are also those,' Three Jackdaws laughed, 'who prefer sheep to girls. Ah, well, one can only sympathise with the former and the latter. I repeat my proposal.'

Geralt took off his glove and shook the hand being proffered.

'I accept, glad to have made your acquaintance.'

'Then let us go, for I hunger.'

II

The innkeeper wiped the rough table top with a cloth, bowed and smiled. Two of his front teeth were missing.

'Right, then . . . ' Three Jackdaws looked up for a while at the blackened ceiling and the spiders dancing about beneath it.

'First . . . First, beer. To save your legs, an entire keg. And to go with the beer . . . What do you propose with the beer, comrade?'

'Cheese?' risked the innkeeper.

'No,' Borch grimaced. 'We'll have cheese for dessert. We want something sour and spicy with the beer.'

'At your service,' the innkeeper smiled even more broadly. His two front teeth were not the only ones he lacked. 'Elvers with garlic in olive oil and green pepper pods in vinegar or marinated . . . '

'Very well. We'll take both. And then that soup I once ate here, with diverse molluscs, little fish and other tasty morsels floating in it.'

'Log drivers' soup?'

'The very same. And then roast lamb with onions. And then three-score crayfish. Throw as much dill into the pot as you can. After that, sheep's cheese and lettuce. And then we'll see.'

'At your service. Is that for everyone? I mean, four times?'

The taller Zerrikanian shook her head, patting herself knowingly on her waist, which was now hugged by a tight, linen blouse.

'I forgot.' Three Jackdaws winked at Geralt. 'The girls are watching their figures. Lamb just for the two of us, innkeeper. Serve the beer right now, with those elvers. No, wait a while, so they don't go cold. We didn't come here to stuff ourselves, but simply to spend some time in conversation.'

'Very good.' The innkeeper bowed once more.

'Prudence is a matter of import in your profession. Give me your hand, comrade.'

Gold coins jingled. The innkeeper opened his gap-toothed mouth to the limit.

'That is not an advance,' Three Jackdaws announced, 'it is a bonus. And now hurry off to the kitchen, good fellow.'

It was warm in the snug. Geralt unbuckled his belt, took off his tunic and rolled up his shirtsleeves.

'I see,' he said, 'that you aren't troubled by a shortage of funds. Do you live on the privileges of a knightly estate?'

'Partially,' Three Jackdaws smiled, without offering further details.

They dealt quickly with the elvers and a quarter of the keg. Neither of the two Zerrikanians stinted on the beer, and soon were both in visible good humour. They were whispering something to each other. Véa, the taller one, suddenly burst out in throaty laughter.

'Are the warriors versed in the Common Speech?' Geralt asked quietly, sneaking a sideways glance at them.

'Poorly. And they are not garrulous. For which they deserve credit. How do you find the soup, Geralt?'

'Mmm.'

'Let us drink.'

'Mmm.'

'Geralt,' Three Jackdaws began, putting aside his spoon and hiccoughing in a dignified manner, 'I wish to return, for a moment, to the conversation we had on the road. I understand that you, a witcher, wander from one end of the world to the other, and should you come across a monster along the way, you kill it. And you earn money doing that. Does that describe the witcher's trade?'

'More or less.'

'And does it ever happen that someone specifically summons you somewhere? On a special commission, let's say. Then what? You go and carry it out?'

'That depends on who asks me and why.'

'And for how much?'

'That too,' the Witcher shrugged. 'Prices are going up, and one has to live, as a sorceress acquaintance of mine used to say.'

'Quite a selective approach; very practical, I'd say. But at the root of it lies some idea, Geralt. The conflict between the forces of Order and the forces of Chaos, as a sorcerer acquaintance of mine used to say. I imagine that you carry out your mission, defending people from Evil, always and everywhere. Without distinction. You stand on a clearly defined side of the palisade.'

'The forces of Order, the forces of Chaos. Awfully high-flown words, Borch. You desperately want to position me on one side of the palisade in a conflict, which is generally thought to be perennial, began long before us and will endure long after we've gone. On which side does the farrier, shoeing horses, stand? Or our innkeeper, hurrying here with a cauldron of lamb? What, in your opinion, defines the border between Chaos and Order?'

'A very simple thing,' said Three Jackdaws, and looked him straight in the eye. 'That which represents Chaos is menace, is the aggressive side. While Order is the side being threatened, in need of protection. In need of a defender. But let us drink. And make a start on the lamb.'

'Rightly said.'

The Zerrikanians, watching their figures, were taking a break from eating, time they spent drinking more quickly. Véa, leaning over on her companion's shoulder, whispered something again, brushing the table top with her plait. Téa, the shorter of the two, laughed loudly, cheerfully narrowing her tattooed eyelids.

'Yes,' Borch said, picking a bone clean. 'Let us continue our talk, if you will. I understand you aren't keen on being placed on either side. You do your job.'

'That's correct.'

'But you cannot escape the conflict between Chaos and Order. Although it was your comparison, you are not a farrier. I've seen you work. You go down into a dungeon among some ruins and come out with a slaughtered basilisk. There is, comrade, a difference between shoeing horses and killing basilisks. You said that if the payment is fair, you'll hurry to the end of the world and dispatch the monster you're asked to. Let's say a fierce dragon is wreaking havoc on a—'

8

'Bad example,' Geralt interrupted. 'You see, right away you've mixed up Chaos and Order. Because I do not kill dragons; and they, without doubt, represent Chaos.'

'How so?' Three Jackdaws licked his fingers. 'Well, I never! After all, among all monsters, dragons are probably the most bestial, the cruellest and fiercest. The most revolting of reptiles. They attack people, breathe fire and carry off, you know, virgins. There's no shortage of tales like that. It can't be that you, a witcher, don't have a few dragons on your trophy list.'

'I don't hunt dragons,' Geralt said dryly. 'I hunt forktails, for sure. And dracolizards. And flying drakes. But not true dragons; the green, the black or the red. Take note, please.'

'You astonish me,' Three Jackdaws said. 'Very well, I've taken note. In any case, that's enough about dragons for the moment, I see something red on the horizon and it is surely our crayfish. Let us drink!'

Their teeth crunched through the red shells, and they sucked out the white flesh. The salt water, stinging painfully, trickled down over their wrists. Borch poured the beer, by now scraping the ladle across the bottom of the keg. The Zerrikanians were even more cheerful, the two of them looking around the inn and smiling ominously. The Witcher was convinced they were searching out an opportunity for a brawl. Three Jackdaws must also have noticed, because he suddenly shook a crayfish he was holding by the tail at them. The women giggled and Téa pouted her lips for a kiss and winked. Combined with her tattooed face, this made for a gruesome sight.

'They are as savage as wildcats,' Three Jackdaws murmured to Geralt. 'They need watching. With them, comrade, suddenly – before you know it – the floor's covered in guts. But they're worth every penny. If you knew what they're capable of . . . '

'I know,' Geralt nodded. 'You couldn't find a better escort. Zerrikanians are born warriors, trained to fight from childhood.'

'I didn't mean that.' Borch spat a crayfish claw onto the table. 'I meant what they're like in bed.'

Geralt glanced anxiously at the women. They both smiled. Véa reached for the dish with a swift, almost imperceptible movement.

9

Looking at the Witcher through narrowed eyes, she bit open a shell with a crack. Her lips glistened with the salt water. Three Jackdaws belched loudly.

'And so, Geralt,' he said. 'You don't hunt dragons; neither green nor any other colour. I've made a note of it. And why, may I ask, only those three colours?'

'Four, to be precise.'

'You mentioned three.'

'Dragons interest you, Borch. For any particular reason?'

'No. Pure curiosity.'

'Aha. Well, about those colours: it's customary to define true dragons like that, although they are not precise terms. Green dragons, the most common, are actually greyish, like ordinary dracolizards. Red dragons are in fact reddish or brick-red. It's customary to call the large dark brown ones "black". White dragons are the rarest. I've never seen one. They occur in the distant North. Reputedly.'

'Interesting. And do you know what other dragons I've also heard about?'

'I do,' Geralt sipped his beer. 'The same ones I've heard about. Golden dragons. There are no such creatures.'

'On what grounds do you claim that? Because you've never seen one? Apparently, you haven't seen a white one either.'

'That's not the point. Beyond the seas, in Ofir and Zangvebar, there are white horses with black stripes. I haven't seen them, but I know they exist. But golden dragons are mythical creatures. Fabled. Like the phoenix, let's say. There are no phoenixes or golden dragons.'

Véa, leaning on her elbows, looked at him curiously.

'You must know what you're talking about, you're a witcher,' Borch ladled beer from the keg, 'but I think that every myth, every fable, must have some roots. Something lies among those roots.'

'It does,' Geralt confirmed. 'Most often a dream, a wish, a desire, a yearning. Faith that there are no limits to possibility. And occasionally chance.'

'Precisely, chance. Perhaps there once was a golden dragon, an accidental, unique mutation?'

'If there were, it met the fate of all mutants.' The Witcher turned his head away. 'It differed too much to endure.'

'Ha,' Three Jackdaws said, 'now you are denying the laws of nature, Geralt. My sorcerer acquaintance was wont to say that every being has its own continuation in nature and survives in some way or another. The end of one is the beginning of another, there are no limits to possibility; or at least nature doesn't know any.'

'Your sorcerer acquaintance was a great optimist. But he failed to take one thing into consideration: a mistake committed by nature. Or by those who trifle with it. Golden dragons and other similar mutants, were they to exist, couldn't survive. For a very natural limit of possibilities prevents it.'

'What limit is that?'

'Mutants,' the muscles in Geralt's jaw twitched violently, 'mutants are sterile, Borch. Only in fables survives what cannot survive in nature. Only myths and fables do not know the limits of possibility.'

Three Jackdaws said nothing. Geralt looked at the Zerrikanians, at their faces, suddenly grown serious. Véa unexpectedly leant over towards him and put a hard, muscular arm around his neck. He felt her lips, wet from beer, on his cheek.

'They like you,' Three Jackdaws said slowly. 'Well, I'll be damned, they like you.'

'What's strange about that?' the Witcher smiled sadly.

'Nothing. But we must drink to it. Innkeeper. Another keg!'

'Take it easy. A pitcher at most.'

'Two pitchers!' Three Jackdaws yelled. 'Téa, I have to go out for a while.'

The Zerrikanian stood up, took her sabre from the bench and swept the room with a wistful gaze. Although previously, as the Witcher had observed, several pairs of eyes had lit up greedily at the sight of Borch's bulging purse, no one seemed in a hurry to go after him as he staggered slightly towards the door to the courtyard. Téa shrugged, following her employer.

'What is your real name?' Geralt asked the one who had remained at the table. Véa flashed her white teeth. Her blouse was very loosely

11

laced, almost to the limits of possibility. The Witcher had no doubt it was intentionally provocative.

'Alvéaenerle.'

'Pretty.' The Witcher was sure the Zerrikanian would purse her lips and wink at him. He was not mistaken.

'Véa?'

'Mm?'

'Why do you ride with Borch? You, free warriors? Would you mind telling me?'

'Mm.'

'Mm, what?'

'He is . . . ' the Zerrikanian, frowning, searched for the words. 'He is . . . the most . . . beautiful.'

The Witcher nodded. Not for the first time, the criteria by which women judged the attractiveness of men remained a mystery to him.

Three Jackdaws lurched back into the snug fastening his trousers, and issued loud instructions to the innkeeper. Téa, walking two steps behind him, feigning boredom, looked around the inn, and the merchants and log drivers carefully avoided her gaze. Véa was sucking the contents from another crayfish, and continually throwing the Witcher meaningful glances.

'I've ordered us an eel each, baked this time,' Three Jackdaws sat down heavily, his unfastened belt clinking. 'I struggled with those crayfish and seem to have worked up an appetite. And I've organised a bed for you, Geralt. There's no sense in you roaming around tonight. We can still amuse ourselves. Here's to you, girls!'

'*Vessekheal*,' Véa said, saluting him with her beaker. Téa winked and stretched; and her bosom, contrary to Geralt's expectations, did not split the front of her blouse.

'Let's make merry!' Three Jackdaws leant across the table and slapped Téa on the backside. 'Let's make merry, Witcher. Hey, landlord! Over here!'

The innkeeper scuttled briskly over, wiping his hands on his apron.

'Could you lay your hands on a tub? The kind you launder clothes in, sturdy and large?'

'How large, sir?'

'For four people.'

'For . . . four . . . ' the innkeeper opened his mouth.

'For four,' Three Jackdaws confirmed, drawing a full purse from his pocket.

'I could.' The innkeeper licked his lips.

'Splendid,' Borch laughed. 'Have it carried upstairs to my room and filled with hot water. With all speed, comrade. And have beer brought there too. Three pitchers.'

The Zerrikanians giggled and winked at the same time.

'Which one do you prefer?' Three Jackdaws asked. 'Eh? Geralt?'

The Witcher scratched the back of his head.

'I know it's difficult to choose,' said Three Jackdaws, understandingly. 'I occasionally have difficulty myself. Never mind, we'll give it some thought in the tub. Hey, girls. Help me up the stairs!'

III

There was a barrier on the bridge. The way was barred by a long, solid beam set on wooden trestles. In front and behind it stood halberdiers in studded leather coats and mail hoods. A purple banner bearing the emblem of a silver gryphon fluttered lazily above the barrier.

'What the devil?' Three Jackdaws said in surprise, approaching at a walk. 'Is there no way through?'

'Got a safe-conduct?' the nearest halberdier asked, without taking the stick he was chewing, either from hunger or to kill time, from his mouth.

'Safe-conduct? What is it, the plague? Or war, perhaps? On whose orders do you obstruct the way?'

'Those of King Niedamir, Lord of Caingorn,' the guardsman replied, shifting the stick to the other side of his mouth and pointing at the banner. 'Without a safe-conduct you can't go up.'

'Some sort of idiocy,' Geralt said in a tired voice. 'This isn't Caingorn, but Barefield's territory. Barefield, not Caingorn, levies tolls from the bridges on the Braa. What has Niedamir to do with it?'

'Don't ask me,' the guard said, spitting out his stick. 'Not my business. I'm here to check safe-conducts. If you want, talk to our decurion.'

'And where might he be?'

'He's basking in the sun over there, behind the toll collector's lodgings,' the halberdier said, looking not at Geralt but at the naked thighs of the Zerrikanians, who were stretching languidly in their saddles.

Behind the toll collector's cottage sat a guard on a pile of dry logs, drawing a woman in the sand with the end of his halberd. It was actually a certain part of a woman, seen from an unusual perspective. Beside him, a slim man with a fanciful plum bonnet pulled down over his eyes, adorned with a silver buckle and a long, twitching heron's feather, was reclining, gently plucking the strings of a lute.

Geralt knew that bonnet and that feather, which were famed from the Buina to the Yaruga, known in manor houses, fortresses, inns, taverns and whorehouses. Particularly whorehouses.

'Dandelion!'

'Geralt the Witcher!' A pair of cheerful cornflower-blue eyes shone from under the bonnet, now shoved back on his head. 'Well, I never! You're here too? You don't have a safe-conduct by any chance?'

'What's everyone's problem with this safe-conduct?' The Witcher dismounted. 'What's happening here, Dandelion? We wanted to cross the Braa, myself and this knight, Borch Three Jackdaws, and our escort. And we cannot, it appears.'

'I can't either,' Dandelion stood up, took off his bonnet and bowed to the Zerrikanians with exaggerated courtesy. 'They don't want to let me cross either. This decurion here won't let *me*, Dandelion, the most celebrated minstrel and poet within a thousand miles, through, although he's also an artist, as you can see.'

'I won't let anyone cross without a safe-conduct,' the decurion said resolutely, at which he completed his drawing with a final detail, prodding the end of his halberd shaft in the sand.

'No matter,' the Witcher said. 'We'll ride along the left bank. The road to Hengfors is longer that way, but needs must.'

'To Hengfors?' the bard said, surprised. 'Aren't you following Niedamir, Geralt? And the dragon?'

'What dragon?' Three Jackdaws asked with interest.

'You don't know? You really don't know? Oh, I shall have to tell you everything, gentlemen. I'm waiting here, in any case; perhaps someone who knows me will come with a safe-conduct and let me join them. Please be seated.'

'Just a moment,' Three Jackdaws said. 'The sun is almost a quarter to the noontide and I have an awful thirst. We cannot talk on an empty stomach. Téa, Véa, head back to the town at a trot and buy a keg.'

'I like the cut of your jib, sire . . .'

'Borch, also known as Three Jackdaws.'

'Dandelion, also known as the Unparalleled. By certain girls.'

'Talk, Dandelion,' the Witcher said impatiently. 'We aren't going to loiter around here till evening.'

The bard seized the fingerboard of his lute and plucked the strings vigorously.

'How would you prefer it, in verse or in normal speech?'

'Normal speech.'

'As you please,' Dandelion said, not putting his lute down. 'Listen then, noble gentlemen, to what occurred a week ago near the free town of Barefield. 'Twas thus, that at the crack of dawn, when the rising sun had barely tinged pink the shrouds of mist hanging pendent above the meadows—'

'It was supposed to be normal speech,' Geralt reminded him.

'Isn't it? Very well, very well. I understand. Concise, without metaphors. A dragon alighted on the pastures outside Barefield.'

'Oh, come on,' the Witcher said. 'It doesn't seem very likely to me. No one has seen a dragon in these parts for years. Wasn't it just a common or garden dracolizard? Dracolizard specimens can occasionally be as large as—'

'Don't insult me, Witcher. I know what I'm talking about. I saw it. As luck would have it I was at the market in Barefield and saw it all with my own eyes. The ballad's composed, but you didn't want—'

'Go on. Was it big?'

'The length of three horses. No taller than a horse at the withers, but much fatter. Sand grey.'

'In other words, green.'

'Yes. It swooped down unexpectedly, flew right into a flock of sheep, scattered the shepherds, did for about a dozen beasts, devoured four of them and flew away.'

'Flew away . . .' Geralt shook his head. 'And that was all?'

'No. Because it came again the next day, this time nearer to the town. It swooped down on a knot of women washing their linen on

16

the banks of the Braa. And how they bolted, old friend! I've never laughed so much. Then the dragon circled Barefield a couple of times and flew towards the pastures, where it fell on the sheep again. Only then did the chaos and confusion begin, because few had believed the herdsmen before. The mayor called out the town constabulary and the guilds, but before they could form up, the plebs took matters into their own hands and did for it.'

'How?'

'In a forceful peasant manner. The local master cobbler, a certain Sheepbagger, came up with a way of dealing with the brute. They killed a sheep, stuffed it full of hellebore, deadly nightshade, poison parsley, brimstone and cobbler's tar. Just to be sure, the local apothecary poured in two quarts of his concoction for carbuncles, and the priest from the temple of Kreve said prayers over the carcass. Then they stood the poisoned sheep among the flock, held up by a stake. If truth be told, no one believed the dragon would be lured by that shit, which stank to high heaven, but reality surpassed our expectations. Ignoring the living and bleating baa-lambs, the reptile swallowed the bait and the stake.'

'And what then? Go on, Dandelion.'

'What do you think I'm doing? I am telling you. Listen to what happened next. In less time than a skilled man needs to unlace a woman's corset, the dragon suddenly began to roar and vent smoke from its front and rear ends. It turned somersaults, tried to take off, and then collapsed and lay still. Two volunteers set off to check whether the poisoned reptile was still breathing. It was the local gravedigger and the town halfwit, the fruit of the union between the retarded daughter of a woodcutter and a squad of hired pikemen who marched through Barefield at the time of Warlord Nelumbo's rebellion.'

'Now you're lying, Dandelion.'

'Not lying, just embellishing, and there's a difference.'

'Not much of one. Speak on, we're wasting time.'

'Well then, as I was saying, the gravedigger and the doughty idiot set off as scouts. Afterwards, we built them a small, but pleasing, burial mound.'

'Aha,' Borch said, 'that means the dragon was still alive.'

'And how,' Dandelion said cheerfully. 'It was alive. But it was so weak it didn't devour either the gravedigger or the halfwit, it just lapped up their blood. And then, to general consternation, it flew away, taking flight with some difficulty. Every furlong it fell with a clatter and then rose again. It walked occasionally, dragging its back legs. Some courageous individuals followed it, keeping it in view. And do you know what?'

'Speak, Dandelion.'

'The dragon disappeared among the ravines of the Kestrel Mountains, near the source of the Braa, and hid in the caves there.'

'Now everything's clear,' Geralt said. 'The dragon has probably lived in those caves for centuries, in a state of torpor. I've heard of cases like that. And his treasure hoard must be there too. Now I know why they're blocking the bridge. Someone wants to get his greedy hands on the treasure. And that someone is Niedamir of Caingorn.'

'Exactly,' the troubadour confirmed. 'The whole of Barefield is fair seething for that reason, because they claim that the dragon and its hoard belongs to them. But they hesitate to cross Niedamir. Niedamir's a young whelp, who hasn't started shaving, but he's already proved it doesn't pay to fall foul of him. And he wants that dragon, like the very devil, which is why he's reacted so fast.'

'Wants the treasure, you mean.'

'Actually, more the dragon than the treasure. For you see, Niedamir has his eye on the kingdom of Malleore. A princess, of a – so to speak – beddable age was left there after the sudden and odd death of the prince. The noblemen of Malleore look on Niedamir and the other suitors with reluctance, for they know that the new ruler will keep them on a short leash – unlike the callow princess. So they dug up some dusty old prophecy saying that the mitre and the lass's hand belong to the man who vanquishes the dragon. Because no one had seen a dragon there for ages, they thought they were safe. Niedamir, of course, laughed at the legend, took Malleore by force, and that was that, but when the news of the Barefield dragon got out, he realised he could hoist the Malleore nobility by their own petard. If he showed up there clutching the dragon's head, the people would greet him like a monarch sent by the gods, and the noblemen wouldn't dare breathe a word. Does it surprise you, then, that he rushed after the dragon like a scalded cat? Particularly since it's dead on its feet? For him it's a real godsend, a stroke of luck, by thunder.'

'And he's shut the competition out.'

'So it would appear. And the people of Barefield. Except that he sent riders with safe-conducts throughout the countryside. They're for the ones who are supposed to actually kill the dragon, because Niedamir himself is in no hurry to walk into a cave wielding a sword. In a flash he drafted in the most renowned dragon slayers. You probably know most of them, Geralt.'

'Possibly. Who has turned up?'

'Eyck of Denesle, to begin with.'

'Damn . . . ' the Witcher whistled softly. 'The pious and virtuous Eyck, a knight without flaw or blemish, in person.'

'Do you know him, Geralt?' Borch asked. 'Is he really the scourge of dragons?'

'Not just dragons. Eyck is a match for any monster. He's even killed manticores and gryphons. He's dispatched a few dragons, so I've heard. He's good. But he spoils my business, the swine, because he doesn't take any money for it. Who else, Dandelion?'

'The Crinfrid Reavers.'

'Well, that's the dragon done for. Even if it has recovered. That trio are a good team. They fight pretty dirty, but they're effective. They've wiped out all the dracolizards and forktails in Redania, not to mention three red and one black dragon which they also dispatched, and that's no mean feat. Is that everybody?'

'No. Six dwarves under the command of Yarpen Zigrin have joined in.'

'I don't know him.'

'But you *have* heard of the dragon Ocvist from Quartz Mountain?'

'Yes. And I saw some gemstones from its hoard. There were sapphires of remarkable colour and diamonds as large as cherries.'

'Well, know you that because Yarpen Zigrin and his dwarves did for Ocvist. A ballad was composed about it, but it was lousy because it wasn't one of mine. You've missed nothing if you haven't heard it.'

'Is that everybody?'

'Yes. Not counting you. You claim not to know about the dragon. Who knows, perhaps that's true? But now you do. Well?'

'Nothing. That dragon doesn't interest me.'

'Hah! Very crafty, Geralt. Because you don't have a safe-conduct anyway.'

'The dragon doesn't interest me, I told you. But what about you, Dandelion? What draws you here?'

'The usual,' the troubadour shrugged. 'I need to be near the action and the excitement. Everyone will be talking about the fight with the dragon. Of course, I could compose a ballad based on reports, but it'll sound different sung by someone who saw the fight with his own eyes.'

'Fight?' Three Jackdaws laughed. 'More like some kind of pig-sticking or a carcass being quartered. I'm listening and I'm astounded. Celebrated warriors rushing here as fast as they can to finish off a half-dead dragon, poisoned by a peasant. It makes me want to laugh and vomit.'

'You're wrong,' Geralt said. 'If the dragon hasn't expired from the poison, its constitution has probably already fought it off and it's back at full strength. It actually doesn't make much difference. The Crinfrid Reavers will kill it anyway, but it'll put up a fight, if you want to know.'

'So you're betting on the Reavers, Geralt?'

'Naturally.'

'Don't be so sure.' The artistic guard, who had been silent up to then, spoke up. 'A dragon is a magical creature and you can't kill it any other way than with spells. If anybody can deal with it then it's that sorceress who rode through yesterday.'

'Who was that?' Geralt cocked his head.

'A sorceress,' the guard repeated, 'I told you.'

'Did she give her name?'

'She did, but I've forgotten it. She had a safe-conduct. She was young, comely, in her own way, but those eyes . . . You know how it is, sire. You come over all cold when they look at you.'

'Know anything about this, Dandelion? Who could it be?'

'No,' the bard grimaced. 'Young, comely and "those eyes". Some help that is. They're all like that. Not one of them that I know – and I know plenty – looks older than twenty-five, thirty; though some of them, I've heard, can recall the times when the forest soughed as far as where Novigrad stands today. Anyway, what are elixirs and mandrake for? And they also sprinkle mandrake in their eyes to make them shine. As women will.'

'Was her hair red?' the Witcher asked.

'No, sire,' the decurion said. 'Coal-black.'

'And her horse, what colour was it? Chestnut with a white star?'

'No. Black, like her hair. Well, gentlemen, I'm telling you, she'll kill the dragon. A dragon's a job for a sorcerer. Human strength isn't enough against it.'

'I wonder what the cobbler Sheepbagger would have to say about that,' Dandelion laughed. 'If he'd had something stronger to hand than hellebore and deadly nightshade the dragon's skin would be drying on the Barefield stockade, the ballad would be ready, and I wouldn't be fading in this sun . . .'

'Why exactly didn't Niedamir take you with him?' Geralt asked, looking askance at the poet. 'You were in Barefield when he set off, after all. Could it be that the king doesn't like artists? How come you're fading here, instead of strumming an air by the royal stirrups?'

'The cause was a certain young widow,' Dandelion said dejectedly. 'The hell with it. I tarried, and the next day Niedamir and the others were already over the river. They even took that Sheepbagger with them and some scouts from the Barefield constabulary; they just forgot about me. I've explained it to the decurion, but he keeps repeating—'

'If there's a safe-conduct, I let you through,' the halberdier said dispassionately, relieving himself on the wall of the toll collector's cottage. 'If there isn't, I don't let you through. I've got me orders—'

'Oh,' Three Jackdaws interrupted him, 'the girls are returning with the beer.'

'And they aren't alone,' Dandelion added, standing up. 'Look at that horse. Big as a dragon.'

The Zerrikanians galloped up from the birch wood, flanking a rider sitting on a large, restless warhorse.

The Witcher also stood up.

The rider was wearing a long, purple, velvet kaftan with silver braid and a short coat trimmed with sable fur. Sitting erect in the saddle, he looked imperiously down at them. Geralt knew that kind of look. And was not fond of it.

'Greetings, gentlemen. I am Dorregaray,' the rider introduced himself, dismounting slowly and with dignity. 'Master Dorregaray. Sorcerer.'

'Master Geralt. Witcher.'

'Master Dandelion. Poet.'

'Borch, also known as Three Jackdaws. And my girls, who are removing the bung from that keg, you have already met, Master Dorregaray.'

'That is so, indeed,' the sorcerer said without a smile. 'We exchanged bows, I and the beautiful warriors from Zerrikania.'

'Well then, cheers,' Dandelion distributed the leather cups brought by Véa. 'Drink with us, Master Sorcerer. My Lord Borch, shall I also serve the decurion?'

'Of course. Join us, soldier.'

'I presume,' the sorcerer said, after taking a small, distinguished sip, 'that the same purpose has brought you gentlemen to the barrier on the bridge, as it has me?'

'If you have the dragon in mind, Master Dorregaray,' Dandelion said, 'that is so, indeed. I want to be there and compose a ballad. Unfortunately, that decurion there, clearly a fellow without refinement, doesn't want to let me through. He demands a safe-conduct.'

'I beg your pardon,' the halberdier said, draining his cup and smacking his lips. 'I've been ordered on pain of death not to let anyone through without a safe-conduct. And I'm told the whole of Barefield has already gathered with wagons, and plans to head up after the dragon. I have my orders—'

'Your orders, soldier,' Dorregaray frowned, 'apply to the rabble, who might hinder; trollops, who might spread debauchery and foul sicknesses; thieves, scum and rabble. But not to me.'

'I won't let anyone through without a safe-conduct,' the decurion glowered, 'I swear—'

'Don't swear,' Three Jackdaws interrupted him. 'Better to have another drink. Téa, pour this stout-hearted soldier a beer. And let us be seated, gentlemen. Drinking standing up, in a rush and without due reverence, does not become the nobility.'

They sat down on logs around the keg. The halberdier, newly raised to nobility, blushed with pleasure.

'Drink, brave centurion,' Three Jackdaws urged.

'But I am a decurion, not a centurion,' the halberdier said, blushing even more intensely.

'But you will be a centurion, for certain,' Borch grinned. 'You're an astute fellow, you'll be promoted in no time.'

Dorregaray, declining a refill, turned towards Geralt.

'People are still talking about the basilisk in town, Witcher, sir, and you now have your eye on the dragon, I see,' he said softly. 'I wonder whether you're so short of money, or whether you murder endangered creatures for the simple pleasure of it.'

'Curious interest,' Geralt answered, 'coming from someone who is rushing not to be late for the butchering of a dragon, in order to knock out its teeth, so crucial, after all, in the making of magical cures and elixirs. Is it true, sorcerer, sir, that the best ones are those removed from a living dragon?'

'Are you certain that is why I am going there?'

'I am. But someone has already beaten you to it, Dorregaray. A female companion of yours has already gone through with a safe-conduct, which you don't have. She is black-haired, if that's of any interest to you.'

'On a black horse?'

'Apparently.'

'Yennefer,' Dorregaray said, glumly. Unnoticed by anybody, the Witcher twitched.

A silence fell, broken only by the belching of the future centurion.

'Nobody . . . without a safe-conduct . . . '

'Will two hundred lintars suffice?' Geralt calmly took from his pocket the purse received from the fat Alderman.

'Ah, Geralt,' Three Jackdaws smiled mysteriously, 'so you—'

'My apologies, Borch. I'm sorry, but I won't ride with you to Hengfors. Another time perhaps. Perhaps we'll meet again.'

'I have no interest in going to Hengfors,' Three Jackdaws said slowly. 'Not at all, Geralt.'

'Put away that purse, sire,' the future centurion said menacingly, 'that's sheer bribery. I won't even let you through for three hundred.'

'And for five hundred?' Borch took out his pouch. 'Put away that purse, Geralt. I'll pay the toll. This has begun to amuse me. Five hundred, soldier, sir. One hundred a piece, counting my girls as one gorgeous item. What?'

'Oh dear, oh dear,' the future centurion said, distressed, stowing Borch's pouch away under his jacket. 'What will I tell the king?'

'Tell him,' Dorregaray said, straightening up and removing an ornate ivory wand from his belt, 'that you were overcome by fear when you saw it.'

'Saw what, sire?'

The sorcerer flourished his wand and shouted an incantation. A pine tree on the riverbank burst into flames. In one moment the entire tree was engulfed from top to bottom in a blaze of fire.

'To horse!' cried Dandelion, springing up and slinging his lute across his back. 'To horse, gentlemen! And ladies!'

'Raise the barrier!' the rich decurion with a good chance of becoming a centurion shouted to the halberdiers.

On the bridge, beyond the barrier, Véa reined in her horse. It skittered, hooves thudding on the planking. The woman, tossing her plaits, screamed piercingly.

24

'That's right, Véa!' Three Jackdaws shouted back. 'Onwards, my lords. To horse! We'll ride in the Zerrikanian fashion, with a thundering and a yelling!'

IV

'Well, just look,' said the oldest of the Reavers, Boholt, massive and burly, like the trunk of an old oak tree. 'So Niedamir didn't chase you away, my good sirs, though I was certain he would. But it's not for us paupers to question royal commands. Join us by the campfire. Make yourselves a pallet, boys. And between you and me, Witcher, what did you talk to the king about?'

'About nothing,' Geralt said, making himself comfortable by leaning back against his saddle, which he had dragged over beside the fire. 'He didn't even come out of his tent to talk to us. He just sent that flunky of his, what's his name . . . '

'Gyllenstiern,' said Yarpen Zigrin, a stocky, bearded dwarf, who was rolling a huge resinous tree stump he had dragged from the undergrowth into the fire. 'Pompous upstart. Fat hog. When we joined the hunt he came over, nose stuck up towards the heavens, pooh-pooh, "remember, you dwarves", he says, "who's in command, who you have to obey, King Niedamir gives the orders here and his word is law" and so on. I stood and listened and I thought to myself, I'll have my lads knock him to the ground and I'll piss all over his cape. But I dropped the idea, you know, because word would get around again that dwarves are nasty, that they're aggressive, that they're whoresons and it's impossible to live with them in . . . what the hell was it? . . . harmonium, or whatever it is. And right away there'd be another pogrom somewhere, in some little town or other. So I just listened politely and nodded.'

'It looks like that's all Lord Gyllenstiern knows,' Geralt said, 'because he said the same to us and all we did was nod too.'

'And I reckon,' the second Reaver said, spreading a blanket over a pile of brushwood, 'it was a bad thing Niedamir didn't chase you away. Doesn't bear thinking how many people are after this dragon.

Swarms of them. It's not a hunting expedition no more, it's a funeral procession. I need elbow room when I'm fighting.'

'Come off it, Gar,' Boholt said, 'the more the merrier. What, never hunted a dragon before? There's always a swarm of people behind a dragon, a noisy rabble, a veritable bordello on wheels. But when the reptile shows up, guess who's left standing in the field. Us, that's who.'

Boholt was silent for a moment, took a long draw from a large, wicker-bound demijohn, blew his nose loudly and coughed.

'Another thing,' he continued. 'In practice it's often only after the dragon's been killed that the merrymaking and bloodletting begins and the heads start rolling. It's only when the treasure's being shared out that the hunters go for each others' throats. Right, Geralt? Oi? Am I right? Witcher, I'm talking to you.'

'I'm aware of cases like that,' Geralt concurred dryly.

'Aware, you say. No doubt from hearsay, because I can't say I've ever heard of you stalking a dragon. Never in all my born days have I heard of a witcher hunting dragons. Which makes it all the stranger you're here.'

'True,' drawled Kennet, also known as Beanpole, the youngest Reaver. 'That's strange. And we—'

'Wait, Beanpole, I'm talking,' Boholt cut in, 'and besides, I don't plan to talk for too long. Anyway, the Witcher knows what I'm on about. I know him and he knows me, and up to now we haven't got in each other's way and we probably never will. See, lads, if I wanted to disrupt the Witcher's work or snatch the loot from under his nose, the Witcher would waste no time slashing me with that witcher razor of his, and he'd be within his rights. Agreed?'

No one seconded or challenged this. There was nothing to suggest that Boholt cared either way.

'Aye,' he continued, 'the more the merrier, as I said. And the Witcher may prove useful to the company. It's wild and deserted round here, and should a frightener, or ilyocoris, or a striga, jump out at us, there might be trouble. But if Geralt's standing by there won't be any trouble, because that's his speciality. But dragons aren't his speciality. Right?'

Once more no one seconded or challenged this.

'Lord Three Jackdaws is with Geralt,' continued Boholt, handing the demijohn to Yarpen, 'and that's enough of a guarantee for me. So who's bothering you, Gar, Beanpole? Can't be Dandelion, can it?'

'Dandelion,' Yarpen Zigrin said, passing the demijohn to the bard, 'always tags along whenever something interesting's happening and everybody knows he doesn't interfere, doesn't help and won't slow the march down. Bit like a burr on a dog's tail. Right, boys?'

The 'boys' – stocky, bearded dwarves – cackled, shaking their beards. Dandelion pushed his bonnet back and drank from the demijohn.

'Oooh, bloody hell,' he groaned, gasping for air. 'It takes your voice away. What was it distilled from, scorpions?'

'There's one thing irking me, Geralt,' Beanpole said, taking the demijohn from the minstrel, 'and that's you bringing that sorcerer along. We can hardly move for sorcerers.'

'That's true,' the dwarf butted in. 'Beanpole's right. We need that Dorregaray like a pig needs a saddle. For some time now we've had our very own witch, the noble Yennefer. Ugh.' He spat her name.

'Yes indeed,' Boholt said, scratching himself on his bull neck, from which a moment earlier he had unfastened a leather collar, bristling with steel studs. 'There are too many sorcerers here, gentlemen. Two too many, to be precise. And they're a sight too thick with our Niedamir. Just look, we're under the stars around a fire, and they, gentlemen, are in the warm, plotting in the royal tent, the cunning foxes. Niedamir, the witch, the wizard and Gyllenstiern. And Yennefer's the worst. And do you want to know what they're plotting? How to cheat us, that's what.'

'And stuffing themselves with venison,' Beanpole interjected gloomily. 'And what did we eat? Marmot! And what's a marmot, I ask you? A rat, nothing else. So what have we eaten? Rat!'

'Never mind,' Gar said, 'We'll soon be sampling dragon's tail. There's nothing like dragon's tail, roasted over charcoal.'

'Yennefer,' Boholt went on, 'is a foul, nasty, mouthy bint. Not like your lasses, Lord Borch. They are quiet and agreeable, just look, they've sat down by the horses, they're sharpening their sabres. I walked past, said something witty, they smiled and showed their little teeth. Yes, I'm glad they're here, not like Yennefer, all she does is scheme and scheme. And I tell you, we have to watch out, because we'll end up with shit all from our agreement.'

'What agreement, Boholt?'

'Well, Yarpen, do we tell the Witcher?'

'Ain't got nothing against it,' the dwarf answered.

'There's no more booze,' Beanpole interjected, turning the demijohn upside down.

'Get some then. You're the youngest, m'lord. The agreement was our idea, Geralt, because we aren't hirelings or paid servants, and we won't be having Niedamir send us after that dragon and then toss a few pieces of gold in our direction. The truth is we'll cope with that dragon without Niedamir, but Niedamir won't cope without us. So it's clear from that who's worth more and whose share should be bigger. And we put the case fairly – whoever takes on the dragon in mortal combat and bests it takes half of the treasure hoard. Niedamir, by virtue of his birthright and title, takes a quarter, in any event. And the rest, provided they help, will share the remaining quarter between themselves, equally. What do you think about that?'

'And what does Niedamir think about it?'

'He said neither yes nor no. But he'd better not put up a fight, the whippersnapper. I told you, he won't take on the dragon himself, he has to count on experts, which means us, the Reavers, and Yarpen and his lads. We, and no one else, will meet the dragon at a sword's length. The rest, including the sorcerers, if they give honest assistance, will share a quarter of the treasure among themselves.'

'Who do you include in the rest, apart from the sorcerers?' Dandelion asked with interest.

'Certainly not buskers and poetasters,' Yarpen Zigrin cackled. 'We include those who put in some work with a battle-axe, not a lute.'

'Aha,' Three Jackdaws said, looking up at the starry sky. 'And how will the cobbler Sheepbagger and his rabble be contributing?'

Yarpen Zigrin spat into the campfire, muttering something in dwarven.

'The constabulary from Barefield know these bloody mountains and will act as guides,' Boholt said softly, 'hence it will be fair to allow them a share of the spoils. It's a slightly different matter with the cobbler. You see, it will go ill if the peasantry become convinced that when a dragon shows up in the land, instead of sending for professionals, they can casually poison it and go back to humping wenches in the long grass. If such a practice became widespread, we'd probably have to start begging. Yes?'

'That's right,' Yarpen added. 'For which reason, I tell you, something bad ought to befall that cobbler, before the bastard passes into legend.'

'If it's meant to befall him, it'll befall him,' Gar said with conviction. 'Leave it to me.'

'And Dandelion,' the dwarf took up, 'will blacken his name in a ballad, make him look a fool. So that he'll suffer shame and dishonour, for generations to come.'

'You've forgotten about one thing,' Geralt said. 'There's one person here who could throw a spoke in the wheel. Who won't assent to any divisions or agreements. I mean Eyck of Denesle. Have you talked to him?'

'What about?' Boholt said, grinding his teeth, using a stout stick to move the logs around in the campfire. 'You won't get anywhere with Eyck, Geralt. He knows nothing about business.'

'As we rode up to your camp,' Three Jackdaws said, 'we met him. He was kneeling on the rocks, in full armour, staring at the sky.'

'He's always doing that,' Beanpole said. 'He's meditating, or saying his prayers. He says he must, because he has orders from the gods to protect people from evil.'

'Back home in Crinfrid,' Boholt muttered, 'we keep people like that on a chain in the cowshed, and give them a piece of coal so they can draw outlandish pictures on the walls. But that's enough gossip about my neighbours, we're talking business.'

A petite, young woman with black hair held tightly by a gold hairnet, wrapped in a woollen cloak, noiselessly entered the circle of light.

'What reeks so much round here?' Yarpen Zigrin asked, pretending not to see her. 'Not brimstone, is it?'

'No,' Boholt, glancing to the side and sniffing pointedly, 'it's musk or some other scent.'

'No, it has to be . . . ' the dwarf grimaced. 'Oh! Why it's the noble Madam Yennefer! Welcome, welcome.'

The sorceress's eyes slowly swept over the company, her shining eyes coming to rest for a while on the Witcher. Geralt smiled faintly.

'May I join you?'

'But of course, good lady,' Boholt said and hiccoughed. 'Sit down here, on the saddle. Move your arse, Kennet, and give the noble sorceress the saddle.'

'From what I hear, you're talking business, gentlemen.' Yennefer sat down, stretching out her shapely, black-stockinged legs in front of her. 'Without me?'

'We didn't dare,' Yarpen Zigrin said, 'trouble such an important personage.'

'If would be better, Yarpen' – Yennefer narrowed her eyes, turning her head towards the dwarf – 'if you kept quiet. From the very first day you've been treating me as if I were nothing but air, so please continue, don't let me bother you. Because it doesn't bother me either.'

'Really, m'lady,' Yarpen's smile revealed uneven teeth. 'May I be infested by ticks, if I haven't been treating you better than the air. I've been known, for example, to spoil the air, which there's no way I'd dare to do in your presence.'

The bearded 'boys' roared with thunderous laughter, but fell silent immediately at the sight of the blue glow which suddenly enveloped the sorceress.

'One more word and you'll end as spoiled air, Yarpen,' Yennefer said in a voice with a metallic edge, 'and a black stain on the grass.'

'Indeed,' Boholt cleared his throat, relieving the silence that had fallen. 'Quiet, Zigrin. Let's hear what Madam Yennefer has to say to us. She just complained that we're talking about business without her. From which I conclude she has some kind of offer for us. Let's hear, my lords, what kind of offer it is. As long as she doesn't suggest killing the dragon by herself, using spells.'

'And what if I do?' Yennefer raised her head. 'Don't think it's possible, Boholt?'

'It might be possible. But it's not profitable, because you'd be certain to demand half the dragon's hoard.'

'At least half,' the sorceress said coldly.

'Well, you see for yourself there's no profit in it for us. We, my lady, are poor warriors, and if the loot passes us by, hunger will come beckoning. We live on sorrel and pigweed . . .'

'Only once in a blue moon do we manage to catch a marmot,' Yarpen Zigrin interrupted in a sombre voice.

'. . . we drink spring water,' Boholt took a swig from the demijohn and shuddered slightly. 'There's no choice for us, Madam Yennefer. It's either loot, or freeze to death in the winter huddled against a fence. For inns cost money.'

'Beer does too,' Gar added.

'And dirty strumpets,' Beanpole said, daydreaming.

'Which is why,' Boholt said, looking up at the sky, 'we will kill the dragon, by ourselves, without spells and without your help.'

'Are you certain about that? Just remember there are limits to what is possible, Boholt.'

'Perhaps there are, but I've never come across them. No, m'lady. I repeat, we'll kill the dragon ourselves, without any spells.'

'Particularly,' Yarpen Zigrin added, 'since spells surely have their own limits, which, unlike our own, we don't know.'

'Did you come up with that yourself?' Yennefer asked slowly. 'Or did someone put you up to it? Does the presence of the Witcher in this select company give you the right to such brazenness?'

'No,' Boholt replied, looking at Geralt, who seemed to be dozing, stretched out lazily on a blanket with his saddle beneath his head, 'the Witcher has nothing to do with it. Listen, noble Yennefer. We put forward a proposition to the king, but he hasn't honoured us with an answer. We're patient, we'll wait till the morning. Should the king agree to a settlement, we ride on together. If not, we go back.'

'Us too,' the dwarf snarled.

'There won't be any bargaining,' Boholt continued. 'Take it or leave it. Repeat our words to Niedamir, Madam Yennefer. And I'll tell you; a deal's also good for you and for Dorregaray, if you come to an agreement with him. We don't need the dragon's carcass, mark you, we'll take but the tail. And the rest is yours, you can have whatever you want. We won't stint you with the teeth or the brain; we'll keep nothing that you need for sorcery.'

'Of course,' Yarpen Zigrin added, chuckling, 'the carrion will be for you, sorcerers, no one will take it from you. Unless some other vultures do.'

Yennefer stood up, throwing her cloak over her shoulder.

'Niedamir won't wait until morning,' she said sharply. 'He has agreed to your conditions already. Against mine and Dorregaray's advice, mark you.'

'Niedamir,' Boholt slowly drawled, 'is displaying astonishing wisdom for one so young. To me, Madam Yennefer, wisdom includes the ability to turn a deaf ear to foolish or insincere advice.'

Yarpen Zigrin snorted into his beard.

'You'll be singing a different tune,' the sorceress put her hands on her hips, 'when the dragon lacerates and perforates you and shatters your shinbones. You'll be licking my shoes and begging for help. As usual. How well, oh, how very well do I know your sort. I know you so well it makes me sick.'

She turned away and disappeared into the gloom, without saying goodbye.

'In my day,' Yarpen Zigrin said, 'sorceresses stayed in their towers, read learned books and stirred cauldrons. They didn't get under warriors' feet, didn't interfere in our business. And didn't wiggle their bottoms in front of a fellow.'

'Frankly speaking, she can wiggle all she likes,' Dandelion said, tuning his lute. 'Right, Geralt? Geralt? Hey, where's the Witcher?'

'What do we care?' Boholt muttered, throwing another log on the fire. 'He went somewhere. Perhaps he had to relieve himself, my lord. It's his business.'

'That's right,' the bard agreed and strummed the strings. 'Shall I sing you something?'

'Sing, dammit,' Yarpen Zigrin said and spat. 'But don't be thinking, Dandelion, that I'll give you as much as a shilling for your bleating. It's not the royal court, son.'

'I can see that,' the troubadour nodded.

V

'Yennefer.'

She turned around, as though surprised, though the Witcher was in doubt she had heard his steps well before. She placed a small wooden pail on the floor, straightened up and brushed aside some hair which had freed itself from her golden hairnet and fell in curls onto her shoulders.

'Geralt.'

She was wearing just two colours, as usual: black and white. Black hair, long, black eyelashes forcing one to guess the colour of the eyes concealed beneath them. A black skirt and a short, black tunic with a white fur collar. A white blouse of the sheerest linen. On her neck a black velvet ribbon adorned with an obsidian star bestrewn with tiny diamonds.

'You haven't changed at all.'

'Neither have you,' she sneered. 'And in both cases it is equally normal. Or, if you prefer, equally abnormal. In any case, the mention of it, though it may not be a bad way to begin the conversation, is meaningless. Am I right?'

'You are,' he nodded, looking to one side, towards Niedamir's tent and the fires of the royal bowmen obscured by the dark shapes of wagons. From the more distant campfire floated Dandelion's sonorous voice singing *The Stars above the Path*, one of his most popular romantic ballads.

'Well, now that we have the preliminaries out of the way,' the sorceress said, 'I wonder what's coming next'.

'You see, Yennefer—'

'I see,' she interrupted sharply, 'But I don't understand. Why did you come here, Geralt? Surely not because of the dragon? I presume nothing has changed in that regard?'

'No. Nothing's changed.'

'Why, then, I pray, have you joined the party?'

'If I said that it was because of you, would you believe me?'

She looked at him in silence, and there was something in her flashing eyes which Geralt did not like.

'I believe you, why not?' she finally said. 'Men like to meet their former lovers, like to relive memories. They like to imagine that erstwhile erotic ecstasies give them some kind of perpetual ownership of their partner. It enhances their self-importance. You are no exception. In spite of everything.'

'Nevertheless,' he smiled, 'you're right, Yennefer. The sight of you makes me feel wonderful. In other words, I'm glad to see you.'

'And is that all? Well, let's say I'm also glad. Having said that, I wish you goodnight. I am retiring for the night, as you can see. Before that I intend to bathe and I usually get undressed to perform that activity. Withdraw, then, in order graciously to assure me a minimum of discretion.'

'Yen,' he held his hands out to her.

'Don't call me that!' she hissed furiously, springing back, blue and red sparks streaming from her extended fingers. 'And if you touch me I'll scorch your eyes out, you bastard.'

The Witcher moved back. The sorceress, somewhat calmer, brushed her hair aside once again and stood before him with her fists resting on her hips.

'What did you think, Geralt? That we'd have a nice, cheerful gossip, that we'd reminisce about the old days? That perhaps at the end of our chat we'd get onto a wagon and make love on the sheepskins, just like that, for old times' sake? Did you?'

Geralt, not certain if the sorceress was magically reading his mind or had only guessed right, kept silent, smiling wryly.

'Those four years left their mark, Geralt. I'm over it now, which is the only reason why I didn't spit in your eyes during today's encounter. But don't let my civility deceive you.'

'Yennefer . . .'

'Be quiet! I gave you more than I've ever given any other man, you scoundrel. I don't know, myself, why I gave it to you. And you

. . . Oh, no, my dear. I'm not a slut or an elf-woman met by chance in the forest, who can be discarded in the morning, walked out on without being woken, with a posy of violets left on the table. Who can be made a mockery of. Beware! Utter a single word and you will regret it!'

Geralt did not utter a single word, correctly sensing the anger seething in Yennefer.

The sorceress once again brushed aside some unruly locks and looked him in the eyes, from close up.

'We've met, that's too bad,' she said softly. 'But we shall not make a spectacle of ourselves for everybody. We shall save face. We'll pretend to be good friends. But don't be mistaken, Geralt. There is nothing between us now. Nothing, understood? And be glad of it, because it means I have now abandoned the plans which, until recently I still harboured regarding you. But that in no way means I've forgiven you. I shall never forgive you, Witcher. Never.'

She turned around suddenly, seized the pail, spraying water around, and disappeared behind a wagon.

Geralt chased away a mosquito whining above his ear and slowly walked back towards the campfire, where Dandelion's performance was being rewarded with half-hearted applause. He looked up at the dark blue sky above the black, serrated saw blade of the mountain peaks. He felt like bursting out laughing. He did not know why.

VI

'Careful up there! Take heed!' Boholt called, turning around on the coachman's seat to look back towards the column. 'Closer to the rocks! Take heed!'

The wagons trundled along, bouncing on stones. The wagoners swore, lashing the horses with their reins and leaning out. They glanced anxiously to see if the wheels were sufficiently far from the edge of the ravine, along which ran a narrow, uneven road. Below, at the bottom of the chasm, the waters of the River Braa foamed white among the boulders.

Geralt reined back his horse, pressing himself against the rock wall, which was covered with sparse brown moss and white lichen. He let the Reavers' wagon overtake him. Beanpole galloped up from the head of the column where he had been leading the cavalcade with the Barefield scouts.

'Right!' he shouted, 'With a will! It widens out up ahead!'

King Niedamir and Gyllenstiern, both on horseback, accompanied by several mounted bowmen, came alongside Geralt. Behind them rattled the wagons of the royal caravan. Even further back trundled the dwarves' wagon, driven by Yarpen Zigrin, who was yelling relentlessly.

Niedamir, a very thin, freckled youngster in a white sheepskin jacket, passed the Witcher, casting him a haughty, though distinctly bored, look. Gyllenstiern straightened up and reined in his horse.

'Over here, Witcher, sir,' he said overbearingly.

'Yes?' Geralt jabbed his mare with his heels, and rode slowly over to the chancellor, behind the caravan. He was astonished that, in spite of having such an impressive paunch, Gyllenstiern preferred horseback to a comfortable ride in a wagon.

'Yesterday,' Gyllenstiern said, gently tugging his gold-studded reins, and throwing a turquoise cape off his shoulder, 'yesterday you said the dragon does not interest you. What does interest you then, Witcher, sir? Why do you ride with us?'

'It's a free country, chancellor.'

'For the moment. But in this cortege, my dear Geralt, everyone should know his place. And the role he is to fulfil, according to the will of King Niedamir. Do you comprehend that?'

'What are you driving at, my dear Gyllenstiern?'

'I shall tell you. I've heard that it has recently become tiresome to negotiate with you witchers. The thing is that, whenever a witcher is shown a monster to be killed, the witcher, rather than take his sword and slaughter it, begins to ponder whether it is right, whether it is transgressing the limits of what is possible, whether it is not contrary to the code and whether the monster really *is* a monster, as though it wasn't clear at first glance. It seems to me that you are simply doing too well. In my day, witchers didn't have two pennies to rub together, just two stinking boots. They didn't question, they slaughtered what they were ordered to, whether it was a werewolf, a dragon or a tax collector. All that counted was a clean cut. So, Geralt?'

'Do you have a job for me, Gyllenstiern?' the Witcher asked coldly. 'If so, tell me what. I'll think it over. But if you don't, there's no sense wasting our breath, is there?'

'Job?' the chancellor sighed. 'No, I don't. This all concerns a dragon, and that clearly transgresses your limits, Witcher. So I prefer the Reavers. I merely wanted to alert you. Warn you. King Niedamir and I may tolerate the whims of witchers and their classification of monsters into good and bad, but we do not wish to hear about them, much less see them effected in our presence. Don't meddle in royal matters, Witcher. And don't consort with Dorregaray.'

'I am not accustomed to consorting with sorcerers. Why such an inference?'

'Dorregaray,' Gyllenstiern said, 'surpasses even witchers with his whims. He does not stop at categorising monsters into good and bad. He considers them all good.'

'That's overstating the case somewhat.'

'Clearly. But he defends his views with astonishing obstinacy. I truly would not be surprised if something befell him. And the fact he joined us keeping such curious company—'

'I am not Dorregaray's companion. And neither is he mine.'

'Don't interrupt. The company is strange. A witcher crawling with scruples like a fox's pelt with fleas. A sorcerer spouting druidic humbug about equilibrium in nature. The silent knight Borch Three Jackdaws and his escort from Zerrikania, where – as is generally known – sacrifices are made before the image of a dragon. And suddenly they all join in the hunt. Strange, isn't it?'

'If you insist, then yes it is.'

'Know then,' the chancellor said, 'that the most mysterious problems find – as experience proves – the simplest solutions. Don't compel me, Witcher, to use them.'

'I don't understand.'

'Oh, but you do. Thank you for the conversation, Geralt.'

Geralt stopped. Gyllenstiern urged his horse on and joined the king, catching up with the caravan. Eyck of Denesle rode alongside wearing a quilted kaftan of light-coloured leather marked with the impressions of a breastplate, pulling a packhorse laden with a suit of armour, a uniformly silver shield and a powerful lance. Geralt greeted him by raising his hand, but the knight errant turned his head to the side, tightening his thin lips, and spurred his horse on.

'He isn't keen on you,' Dorregaray said, riding over. 'Eh, Geralt?'

'Clearly.'

'Competition, isn't it? The two of you have similar occupations. Except that Eyck is an idealist, and you are a professional. A minor difference, particularly for the ones you kill.'

'Don't compare me to Eyck, Dorregaray. The devil knows who you wrong with that comparison, him or me, but don't compare us.'

'As you wish. To me, frankly speaking, you are equally loathsome.'

'Thank you.'

'Don't mention it,' the sorcerer patted the neck of his horse, which had been scared by all the yelling from Yarpen and his dwarves. 'To me, Witcher, calling killing a vocation is loathsome, low and nonsensical. Our world is in equilibrium. The annihilation, the killing, of any creatures that inhabit this world upsets that equilibrium. And a lack of equilibrium brings closer extinction; extinction and the end of the world as we know it.'

'A druidic theory,' Geralt pronounced. 'I know it. An old hierophant expounded it to me once, back in Rivia. Two days after our conversation he was torn apart by wererats. It was impossible to prove any upset in equilibrium.'

'The world, I repeat,' Dorregaray glanced at him indifferently, 'is in equilibrium. Natural equilibrium. Every species has its own natural enemies, every one is the natural enemy of other species. That also includes humans. The extermination of the natural enemies of humans, which you dedicate yourself to, and which one can begin to observe, threatens the degeneration of the race.'

'Do you know what, sorcerer?' Geralt said, annoyed. 'One day, take yourself to a mother whose child has been devoured by a basilisk, and tell her she ought to be glad, because thanks to that the human race has escaped degeneration. See what she says to you.'

'A good argument, Witcher,' Yennefer said, riding up to them on her large, black horse. 'And you, Dorregaray, be careful what you say.'

'I'm not accustomed to concealing my views.'

Yennefer rode between them. The Witcher noticed that the golden hairnet had been replaced by a rolled up white kerchief.

'Start concealing them as quickly as possible, Dorregaray,' she said, 'especially before Niedamir and the Reavers, who already suspect you plan to interfere in the killing of the dragon. As long as you only talk, they treat you like a harmless maniac. If, however, you try to start anything they'll break your neck before you manage to let out a sigh.'

The sorcerer smiled contemptuously and condescendingly.

'And besides,' Yennefer continued, 'by expressing those views you damage the solemnity of our profession and vocation.'

'How so?'

'You can apply your theory to all sorts of creatures and vermin,

41

Dorregaray. But not to dragons. For dragons are the natural, greatest enemies of man. And I do not refer to the degeneration of the human race, but to its survival. In order to survive, one has to crush one's enemies, enemies which might prevent that survival.'

'Dragons aren't man's enemies,' Geralt broke in. The sorceress looked at him and smiled. But only with her lips.

'In that matter,' she said, 'leave the judging to us *humans*. Your role, Witcher, is not to judge. It's to get a job done.'

'Like a programmed, servile golem?'

'That was your comparison, not mine,' Yennefer replied coldly. 'But, well, it's apt.'

'Yennefer,' Dorregaray said, 'for a woman of your education and age you are coming out with some astonishing tripe. Why is it that dragons have been promoted in your eyes to become the foremost enemies of man? Why not other – a hundredfold more dangerous – creatures, those that have a hundredfold more victims on their consciences than dragons? Why not hirikkas, forktails, manticores, amphisbaenas or gryphons? Why not wolves?'

'I'll tell you why not. The advantage of men over other races and species, the fight for their due place in nature, for living space, can only be won when nomadism, wandering from place to place in search of sustenance in accordance with nature's calendar, is finally eliminated. Otherwise the proper rhythm of reproduction will not be achieved, since human children are dependent for too long. Only a woman safe and secure behind town walls or in a stronghold can bear children according to the proper rhythm, which means once a year. Fecundity, Dorregaray, is growth, is the condition for survival and domination. And now we come to dragons. Only a dragon, and no other monster, can threaten a town or stronghold. Were dragons not to be wiped out, people would – for their own safety – disperse, instead of cleaving together, because dragon's fire in a densely populated settlement is a nightmare, means hundreds of victims, and terrible destruction. That is why dragons must be utterly wiped out, Dorregaray.'

Dorregaray looked at her with a strange smile on his face.

'Do you know what, Yennefer, I wouldn't like to see the day your idea of the dominance of man comes about, when people like you will occupy their due place in nature. Fortunately, it will never come to that. You would rather poison or slaughter each other, expire from typhoid fever and typhus, because it is filth and lice – and not dragons – which threaten your splendid cities, where women are delivered of children once a year, but where only one new-born baby in ten lives longer than ten days. Yes, Yennefer, fecundity, fecundity and once again fecundity. So take up bearing children, my dear; it's the most natural pursuit for you. It will occupy the time you are currently fruitlessly wasting on dreaming up nonsense. Farewell.'

Urging on his horse, the sorcerer galloped off towards the head of the column. Geralt, having glanced at Yennefer's pale, furiously twisted face, began to feel sorry for him in advance. He knew what this was about. Yennefer, like most sorceresses, was barren. But unlike most sorceresses she bemoaned the fact and reacted with genuine rage at the mention of it. Dorregaray certainly knew that. But he probably did not know how vengeful she was.

'He's in trouble,' she hissed. 'Oh, yes. Beware, Geralt. Don't think that when the time comes and you don't show good sense, I'll protect you.'

'Never fear,' he smiled. 'We – and I mean witchers and servile golems – always act sensibly. Since the limits within which we operate are clearly and explicitly demarcated.'

'Well, I never,' Yennefer said, looking at him, still pale. 'You're taking umbrage like a tart whose lack of chastity has been pointed out to her. You're a witcher, you can't change that. Your vocation . . .'

'That's enough about vocations, Yen, because it's beginning to make me queasy.'

'I told you not to call me that. And I'm not especially bothered about your queasiness. Nor any other reactions in your limited witcher's range of reactions.'

'Nevertheless, you'll see some of them if you don't stop plying me with tales about lofty missions and the fight between good and evil. And about dragons; the dreadful enemies of the human tribe. I know better.'

'Oh, yes?' The sorceress narrowed her eyes. 'And what do you know, Witcher?'

'Only,' Geralt said, ignoring the sudden warning vibration of the medallion around his neck, 'that if dragons didn't have treasure hoards, not a soul would be interested in them; and certainly not sorcerers. Isn't it interesting that whenever a dragon is being hunted, some sorcerer closely linked to the Goldsmiths' Guild is always hanging around. Just like you. And later, although a deal of gemstones ought to end up on the market, it never happens and their price doesn't go down. So don't talk to me about vocation and the fight for the survival of the race. I know you too well, have known you too long.'

'Too long,' she repeated, sneering malevolently. 'Unfortunately. But don't think you know me well, you whore's son. Dammit, how stupid I've been . . . Oh, go to hell! I can't stand the sight of you!'

She screamed, yanked her horse's reins and galloped fiercely ahead. The Witcher reined back his mount, and let through the wagon of dwarves, yelling, cursing and whistling through bone pipes. Among them, sprawled on some sacks of oats, lay Dandelion, plucking his lute.

'Hey!' roared Yarpen Zigrin, who was sitting on the box, pointing at Yennefer. 'There's something black on the trail! I wonder what it is? It looks like a nag!'

'Without doubt!' Dandelion shouted, shoving his plum bonnet back, 'It's a nag! Riding a gelding! Astounding!'

The beards of Yarpen's boys shook in general laughter. Yennefer pretended not to hear.

Geralt reined back his horse again and let Niedamir's mounted bowmen through. Borch was riding slowly some distance beyond them, and the Zerrikanians brought up the rear just behind him. Geralt waited for them to catch up and led his mare alongside Borch's horse. They rode on in silence.

'Witcher,' Three Jackdaws suddenly said, 'I want to ask you a question.'

'Ask it.'

'Why don't you turn back?'

The Witcher looked at him in silence for a moment.

'Do you really want to know?'

'Yes, I do,' Three Jackdaws said, turning his face towards Geralt.

'I'm riding with them because I'm a servile golem. Because I'm a wisp of oakum blown by the wind along the highway. Tell me, where should I go? And for what? At least here some people have gathered with whom I have something to talk about. People who don't break off their conversations when I approach. People who, though they may not like me, say it to my face, and don't throw stones from behind a fence. I'm riding with them for the same reason I rode with you to the log drivers' inn. Because it's all the same to me. I don't have a goal to head towards. I don't have a destination at the end of the road.'

Three Jackdaws cleared his throat.

'There's a destination at the end of every road. Everybody has one. Even you, although you like to think you're somehow different.'

'Now I'll ask you a question.'

'Ask it.'

'Do you have a destination at the end of the road?'

'I do.'

'Lucky for you.'

'It is not a matter of luck, Geralt. It is a matter of what you believe in and what you serve. No one ought to know that better than . . . than a witcher.'

'I keep hearing about goals today,' Geralt sighed. 'Niedamir's aim is to seize Malleore. Eyck of Denesle's calling is to protect people from dragons. Dorregaray feels obligated to something quite the opposite. Yennefer, by virtue of certain changes which her body was subjected to, cannot fulfil her wishes and is terribly undecided. Dammit, only the Reavers and the dwarves don't feel a calling, and simply want to line their pockets. Perhaps that's why I'm so drawn to them?'

'You aren't drawn to them, Geralt of Rivia. I'm neither blind nor deaf. It wasn't at the sound of their name you pulled out that pouch. But I surmise . . .'

45

'There's no need to surmise,' the Witcher said, without anger.

'I apologise.'

'There's no need to apologise.'

They reined back their horses just in time, in order not to ride into the column of bowmen from Caingorn which had suddenly been called to a halt.

'What has happened?' Geralt stood up in his stirrups. 'Why have we stopped?'

'I don't know.' Borch turned his head away. Véa, her face strangely contorted, uttered a few quick words.

'I'll ride up to the front,' the Witcher said, 'to see what's going on.'

'Stay here.'

'Why?'

Three Jackdaws was silent for a moment, eyes fixed on the ground.

'Why?' Geralt repeated.

'Go,' Borch said. 'Perhaps it'll be better that way.'

'What'll be better?'

'Go.'

The bridge connecting the two edges of the chasm looked sound. It was built from thick, pine timbers and supported on a quadrangular pier, against which the current crashed and roared in long strands of foam.

'Hey, Beanpole!' yelled Boholt, who was driving the wagon. 'Why've you stopped?'

'I don't know if the bridge will hold.'

'Why are we taking this road?' Gyllenstiern asked, riding over. 'It's not to my liking to take the wagons across the bridge. Hey, cobbler! Why are you leading us this way, and not by the trail? The trail continues on towards the west, doesn't it?'

The heroic poisoner of Barefield approached, removing his sheepskin cap. He looked ridiculous, dressed up in an old-fashioned half-armour probably hammered out during the reign of King Sambuk, pulled down tightly over a shepherd's smock.

'The road's shorter this way, Your Majesty,' he said, not to the chancellor, but directly to Niedamir, whose face still expressed thoroughly excruciated boredom.

'How is that?' Gyllenstiern asked, frowning. Niedamir did not even grace the cobbler with a more attentive glance.

'Them's,' Sheepbagger said, indicating the three notched peaks towering over the surrounding area, 'is Chiava, Great Kestrel and Harbinger's Fang. The trail leads toward the ruins of the old stronghold, and skirts around Chiava from the north, beyond the river's source. But we can shorten the way by takin' the bridge. We'll pass through the gorge and onto the plain 'tween the mountains. And if we don't find no sign of the dragon there, we'll continue on eastwards, we'll search the ravines. And even further eastward there are flat pastures, where there's a straight road to Caingorn, towards your lands, sire.'

'And where, Sheepbagger, did you acquire such knowledge about these mountains?' Boholt asked. 'At your cobbler's last?'

'No, sir. I herded sheep here as a young 'un.'

'And that bridge won't give way?' Boholt stood up on the box, and looked downwards at the foaming river. 'That must be a drop of forty fathoms.'

'It'll 'old, sir.'

'What's a bridge doing in this wilderness anyhow?'

'That there bridge,' Sheepbagger said, 'was built by trolls in the olden days, and whoever came this way had to pay them a pretty penny. But since folk seldom came this way the trolls were reduced to beggary. But the bridge remains.'

'I repeat,' Gyllenstiern said irately. 'We have wagons with tackle and provender, and we may become bogged down in the wilderness. Is it not better to take the trail?'

'We could take the trail,' the cobbler shrugged, 'but it's longer that way. And the king said 'e'd give 'is earteeth to get to that dragon soon.'

'Eyeteeth,' the chancellor corrected him.

'Have it your way, eyeteeth,' Sheepbagger agreed. 'But it's still quicker by the bridge.'

'Right, let's go, Sheepbagger,' Boholt decided. 'Forge ahead, you and your men. We have a custom of letting the most valiant through first.'

'No more than one wagon at a time,' Gyllenstiern warned.

'Right,' Boholt lashed his horses and the wagon rumbled onto the bridge's timbers. 'Follow us, Beanpole! Make sure the wheels are rolling smoothly!'

Geralt reined back his horse, his way barred by Niedamir's bowmen in their purple and gold tunics, crowded on the stone bridgehead.

The Witcher's mare snorted.

The earth shuddered. The mountains trembled, the jagged edge of the rock wall beside them became blurred against the sky, and the wall itself suddenly spoke with a dull, but audible rumbling.

'Look out!' Boholt yelled, now on the other side of the bridge. 'Look out, there!'

The first, small stones pattered and rattled down the spasmodically shuddering rock wall. Geralt watched as part of the road they had followed, very rapidly widening into a yawning, black crack, broke off and plunged into the chasm with a thunderous clatter.

'To horse!' Gyllenstiern yelled. 'Your Majesty! To the other side!'

Niedamir, head buried in his horse's mane, charged onto the bridge, and Gyllenstiern and several bowmen leapt after him. Behind them, the royal wagon with its flapping gryphon banner rumbled onto the creaking timbers.

'It's a landslide! Get out of the way!' Yarpen Zigrin bellowed from behind, lashing his horses' rumps, overtaking Niedamir's second wagon and jostling the bowmen. 'Out of the way, Witcher! Out of the way!'

Eyck of Denesle, stiff and erect, galloped beside the dwarves' wagon. Were it not for his deathly pale face and mouth contorted in a quivering grimace, one might have thought the knight errant had not noticed the stones and boulders falling onto the trail. Further back, someone in the group of bowmen screamed wildly and horses whinnied.

Geralt tugged at the reins and spurred his horse, as right in front of him the earth boiled from the boulders cascading down. The dwarves' wagon rattled over the stones. Just before the bridge it jumped up and landed with a crack on its side, onto a broken axle. A wheel bounced off the railing and plunged downwards into the spume.

The Witcher's mare, lacerated by sharp shards of stone, reared up. Geralt tried to dismount, but caught his boot buckle in the stirrup and fell to the side, onto the trail. His mare neighed and dashed ahead, straight towards the bridge, dancing over the chasm. The dwarves ran across the bridge yelling and cursing.

'Hurry, Geralt!' Dandelion yelled, running behind him and looking back.

'Jump on, Witcher!' Dorregaray called, threshing about in the saddle, struggling to control his terrified horse.

Further back, behind them, the entire road was engulfed in a cloud of dust stirred up by falling rocks, shattering Niedamir's wagons. The Witcher seized the straps of the sorcerer's saddle bags. He heard a cry.

Yennefer had fallen with her horse, rolled to the side, away from the wildly kicking hooves, and flattened herself to the ground, shielding her head with her arms. The Witcher let go of the saddle, ran towards her, diving into the deluge of stones and leaping across the rift opening under his feet. Yennefer, yanked by the arm, got up onto her knees. Her eyes were wide open and the trickle of blood running down from her cut brow had already reached her ear.

'Stand up, Yen!'

'Geralt! Look out!'

An enormous, flat block of stone, scraping against the side of the rock wall with a grinding, clattering sound, slid down and plummeted towards them. Geralt dropped, shielding the sorceress with his body. At the very same moment the block exploded, bursting into a billion fragments, which rained down on them, stinging like wasps.

'Quick!' Dorregaray cried. Brandishing his wand atop the skittering horse, he blasted more boulders which were tumbling down from the cliff into dust. 'Onto the bridge, Witcher!'

Yennefer waved a hand, bending her fingers and shrieking incomprehensibly. As the stones came into contact with the bluish hemisphere which had suddenly materialised above their heads they vaporised like drops of water falling on red-hot metal.

'Onto the bridge, Geralt!' the sorceress yelled. 'Stay close to me!'

They ran, following Dorregaray and several fleeing bowmen. The bridge rocked and creaked, the timbers bending in all directions as it flung them from railing to railing.

'Quick!'

The bridge suddenly slumped with a piercing, penetrating crack, and the half they had just crossed broke off, tumbling with a clatter into the gulf, taking the dwarves' wagon with it, which shattered against the rocky teeth to the sound of the horses' frantic whinnying. The part they were now standing on was still intact, but Geralt suddenly realised they were now running upwards across a rapidly tilting slope. Yennefer panted a curse.

'Get down, Yen! Hang on!'

The rest of the bridge grated, cracked and sagged into a ramp. They fell with it, digging their fingers into the cracks between the timbers. Yennefer could not hold on. She squealed like a little girl and dropped. Geralt, hanging on with one hand, drew a dagger, plunged the blade between the timbers and seized the haft in both hands. His elbow joints creaked as Yennefer tugged him down, suspended by the belt and scabbard slung across his back. The bridge made a cracking noise again and tilted even more, almost vertically.

'Yen,' the Witcher grunted. 'Do something . . . Cast a bloody spell!'

'How can I?' he heard a furious, muffled snarl. 'I'm hanging on!'

'Free one of your hands!'

'I can't . . .'

'Hey!' Dandelion yelled from above. 'Can you hold on? Hey!'

Geralt did not deign to reply.

'Throw down a rope!' Dandelion bellowed. 'Quickly, dammit!'

The Reavers, the dwarves and Gyllenstiern appeared beside the troubadour. Geralt heard Boholt's quiet words.

'Wait, busker. She'll soon fall. Then we'll pull the Witcher up.'

50

Yennefer hissed like a viper, writhing and suspended from Geralt's back. His belt dug painfully into his chest.

'Yen? Can you find a hold? Using your legs? Can you do anything with your legs?'

'Yes,' she groaned. 'Swing them around.'

Geralt looked down at the river seething and swirling among the sharp rocks, against which some bridge timbers, a horse and a body in the bright colours of Caingorn were bumping. Beyond the rocks, in the emerald, transparent maelstrom, he saw the tapered bodies of large trout, languidly moving in the current.

'Can you hold on, Yen?'

'Just about . . . yes . . . '

'Heave yourself up. You have to get a foothold . . . '

'I . . . can't . . . '

'Throw down a rope!' Dandelion yelled. 'Have you all gone mad? They'll both fall!'

'Perhaps that's not so bad?' Gyllenstiern wondered, out of sight.

The bridge creaked and sagged even more. Geralt's fingers, gripping the hilt of his dagger, began to go numb.

'Yen . . . '

'Shut up . . . and stop wriggling about . . . '

'Yen?'

'Don't call me that . . . '

'Can you hold on?'

'No,' she said coldly. She was no longer struggling, but simply hanging from his back; a lifeless, inert weight.

'Yen?'

'Shut up.'

'Yen. Forgive me.'

'No. Never.'

Something crept downwards over the timbers. Swiftly. Like a snake. A rope, emanating with a cold glow, twisting and curling, as though alive, searched for and found Geralt's neck with its moving tip, slid under his armpits, and ravelled itself into a loose knot. The sorceress beneath him moaned, sucking in air. He was certain she would start sobbing. He was mistaken.

'Careful!' Dandelion shouted from above. 'We're pulling you up! Gar! Kennet! Pull them up! Heave!'

A tug, the painful, constricting tension of the taut rope. Yennefer sighed heavily. They quickly travelled upwards, bellies scraping against the coarse timbers.

At the top, Yennefer was the first to stand up.

'We saved but one wagon from the entire caravan, Your Majesty,' Gyllenstiern said, 'not counting the Reavers' wagon. Seven bowmen remain from the troop. There's no longer a road on the far side of the chasm, just scree and a smooth wall, as far as the breach permits one to look. We know not if anyone survived of those who remained when the bridge collapsed.'

Niedamir did not answer. Eyck of Denesle, standing erect, stood before the king, staring at him with shining, feverish eyes.

'The ire of the gods is hounding us,' he said, raising his arms. 'We have sinned, King Niedamir. It was a sacred expedition, an expedition against evil. For the dragon is evil, yes, each dragon is evil incarnate. I do not pass by evil indifferently, I crush it beneath my foot . . . Annihilate it. Just as the gods and the Holy Book demand.'

'What is he drivelling on about?' Boholt asked, frowning.

'I don't know,' Geralt said, adjusting his mare's harness. 'I didn't understand a single word.'

'Be quiet,' Dandelion said, 'I'm trying to remember it, perhaps I'll be able to use it if I can get it to rhyme.'

'The Holy Book says,' Eyck said, now yelling loudly, 'that the serpent, the foul dragon, with seven heads and ten horns, will come forth from the abyss! And on his back will sit a woman in purple and scarlet, and a golden goblet will be in her hand, and on her forehead will be written the sign of all and ultimate whoredom!'

'I know her!' Dandelion said, delighted. 'It's Cilia, the wife of the Alderman of Sommerhalder!'

'Quieten down, poet, sir,' Gyllenstiern said. 'And you, O knight from Denesle, speak more plainly, if you would.'

'One should act against evil, O King,' Eyck called, 'with a pure heart and conscience, with head raised! But who do we see here? Dwarves, who are pagans, are born in the darkness and bow down before dark forces! Blasphemous sorcerers, usurping divine laws, powers and privileges! A witcher, who is an odious aberration, an accursed, unnatural creature. Are you surprised that a punishment has befallen us? King Niedamir! We have reached the limits of possibility! Divine grace is being sorely tested. I call you, king, to purge the filth from our ranks, before—'

'Not a word about me,' Dandelion interjected woefully. 'Not a mention of poets. And I try so hard.'

Geralt smiled at Yarpen Zigrin, who with slow movements was stroking the blade of his battle-axe, which was stuck into his belt. The dwarf, amused, grinned. Yennefer turned away ostentatiously, pretending that her skirt, torn up to her hip, distressed her more than Eyck's words.

'I think you were exaggerating a little, Sir Eyck,' Dorregaray said sharply, 'although no doubt for noble reasons. I regard the making known of your views about sorcerers, dwarves and witchers as quite unnecessary. Although, I think, we have all become accustomed to such opinions, it is neither polite, nor chivalrous, Sir Eyck. And it is utterly incomprehensible after you, and no one else, ran and used a magical, elven rope to save a witcher and a sorceress whose lives were in danger. I conclude from what you say that you should rather have been praying for them to fall.'

'Dammit,' Geralt whispered to Dandelion. 'Did he throw us that rope? Eyck? Not Dorregaray?'

'No,' the bard muttered. 'Eyck it was, indeed.'

Geralt shook his head in disbelief. Yennefer cursed under her breath and straightened up.

'Sir Eyck,' she said with a smile that anyone other than Geralt might have taken as pleasant and friendly. 'Why was that? I'm blasphemous, but you save my life?'

'You are a lady, Madam Yennefer,' the knight bowed stiffly. 'And your comely and honest face permits me to believe that you will one day renounce this accursed sorcery.'

Boholt snorted.

'I thank you, sir knight,' Yennefer said dryly, 'and the Witcher Geralt also thanks you. Thank him, Geralt.'

'I'd rather drop dead,' the Witcher sighed, disarmingly frank. 'What exactly should I thank him for? I'm an odious aberration, and my uncomely face does not augur any hope for an improvement. Sir Eyck hauled me out of the chasm by accident, simply because I was tightly clutching the comely damsel. Had I been hanging there alone, Eyck would not have lifted a finger. I'm not mistaken, am I, sir knight?'

'You are mistaken, Geralt, sir,' the knight errant replied calmly. 'I never refuse anybody in need of help. Even a witcher.'

'Thank him, Geralt. And apologise,' the sorceress said sharply, 'otherwise you will be confirming that, at least with regard to you, Eyck was quite right. You are unable to coexist with people. Because you are different. Your participation in this expedition is a mistake. A nonsensical purpose brought you here. Thus it would be sensible to leave the party. I think you understand that now. And if not, it's time you did.'

'What purpose are you talking about, madam?' Gyllenstiern cut in. The sorceress looked at him, but did not answer. Dandelion and Yarpen Zigrin smiled meaningfully at each other, but so that the sorceress would not notice.

The Witcher looked into Yennefer's eyes. They were cold.

'I apologise and thank you, O knight of Denesle,' he bowed. 'I thank everybody here present. For the swift rescue offered at once. I heard, as I hung there, how you were all raring to help. I ask everybody here present for forgiveness. With the exception of the noble Yennefer, whom I thank, but ask for nothing. Farewell. The dregs leave the company of their own free will. Because these dregs have had enough of you. Goodbye, Dandelion.'

'Hey, Geralt,' Boholt called, 'don't pout like a maiden, don't make a mountain out of a molehill. To hell with—'

'Look out everyoooone!'

Sheepbagger and several members of the Barefield constabulary, who had been sent ahead to reconnoitre, were running back from the narrow opening to the gorge.

'What is it? Why's he bellowing like that?' Gar lifted his head up.

'Good people . . . Your . . . Excellencies . . . ' the cobbler panted.

'Get it out, man,' Gyllenstiern said, hooking his thumbs into his golden belt.

'A dragon! There's a dragon there!'

'Where?'

'Beyond the gorge . . . On level ground . . . Sire, he . . . '

'To horse!' Gyllenstiern ordered.

'Gar!' Boholt yelled, 'onto the wagon! Beanpole, get mounted and follow me!'

'Look lively, lads!' Yarpen Zigrin roared. 'Look lively, by thunder!'

'Hey, wait for me!' Dandelion slung his lute over his shoulder. 'Geralt! Take me with you!'

'Jump on!'

The gorge ended in a mound of light-coloured rocks, which gradually thinned out, creating an irregular ring. Beyond them the ground descended gently into a grassy, undulating mountain pasture, enclosed on all sides by limestone walls, gaping with thousands of openings. Three narrow canyons, the mouths of dried-up streams, opened out onto the pasture.

Boholt, the first to gallop to the barrier of rocks, suddenly reined in his horse and stood up in his stirrups.

'Oh, hell,' he said. 'Oh, bloody hell. It . . . it can't be!'

'What?' Dorregaray asked, riding up. Beside him Yennefer, dismounting from the Reavers' wagon, pressed her chest against the rocky block, peeped out, moved back and rubbed her eyes.

'What? What is it?' Dandelion shouted, leaning out from behind Geralt's back. 'What is it, Boholt?'

'That dragon . . . is golden.'

No further than a hundred paces from the gorge's rocky entrance from which they had emerged, on the road to the northward-leading canyon, on a gently curving, low hill, sat the creature. It was sitting, arching its long, slender neck in a smooth curve, inclining its narrow head onto its domed chest, wrapping its tail around its extended front feet.

56

There was something inexpressibly graceful in the creature and the way it was sitting; something feline, something that contradicted its clearly reptilian origins. But it was also undeniably reptilian. For the creature was covered in distinctly outlined scales, which shone with a glaring blaze of bright, yellow gold. For the creature sitting on the hillock was golden; golden from the tips of its talons, dug into the ground, to the end of its long tail, which was moving very gently among the thistles growing on the hill. Looking at them with its large, golden eyes, the creature unfurled its broad, golden, bat-like wings and remained motionless, demanding to be admired.

'A golden dragon,' Dorregaray whispered. 'It's impossible . . . A living fable!'

'There's no such thing as a bloody golden dragon,' Gar pronounced and spat. 'I know what I'm talking about.'

'Then what's sitting on that hillock?' Dandelion asked pointedly.

'It's some kind of trickery.'

'An illusion.'

'It is not an illusion,' Yennefer said.

'It's a golden dragon,' Gyllenstiern said. 'An absolutely genuine, golden dragon.'

'Golden dragons only exist in fables!'

'Stop that, all of you,' Boholt suddenly broke in. 'There's no point getting worked up. Any blockhead can see it's a golden dragon. And what difference does it make, my lords, if it's golden, lapis lazuli, shit-coloured or chequered? It's not that big, we'll sort it out in no time. Beanpole, Gar, clear the debris off the wagon and get the gear out. What's the difference if it's golden or not?'

'There is a difference, Boholt,' Beanpole said. 'And a vital one. That isn't the dragon we're stalking. Not the one that was poisoned outside Barefield, which is now sitting in its cave on a pile of ore and jewels. That one's just sitting on its arse. What bloody use is it to us?'

'That dragon is golden, Kennet,' Yarpen Zigrin snarled. 'Have you ever seen anything like it? Don't you understand? We'll get more for its hide than we would for a normal treasure hoard.'

'And without flooding the market with precious stones,' Yennefer added, smiling unpleasantly. 'Yarpen's right. The agreement is still binding. Quite something to divide up, isn't it?'

'Hey, Boholt?' Gar shouted from the wagon, where he was clattering amongst the tackle. 'What shall we equip ourselves and the horses with? What could that golden reptile belch, hey? Fire? Acid? Steam?'

'Haven't got an effing clue,' Boholt said, sounding worried. 'Hey, sorcerers! Anything in the fables about golden dragons, about how to kill them?'

'How do you kill them? The usual way!' Sheepbagger suddenly shouted. 'No point pondering, give us an animal. We'll stuff it full of something poisonous and feed it to the reptile, and good riddance.'

Dorregaray looked askance at the cobbler, Boholt spat, and Dandelion turned his head away with a grimace of disgust. Yarpen Zigrin smiled repulsively, hands on hips.

'Wha' you looking at?' Sheepbagger asked. 'Let's get to work, we have to decide what to stuff the carcass with so the reptile quickly perishes. It 'as to be something which is extremely toxic, poisonous or rotten.'

'Aha,' the dwarf spoke, still smiling. 'Well, what's poisonous, foul and stinks? Do you know what, Sheepbagger? Looks like it's you.'

'What?'

'You bloody heard. Get lost, bodger, out of my sight.'

'Lord Dorregaray,' Boholt said, walking over to the sorcerer. 'Make yourself useful. Call to mind some fables and tales. What do you know about golden dragons?'

The sorcerer smiled, straightening up self-importantly.

'What do I know about golden dragons, you ask? Not much, but enough.'

'We're listening.'

'Then listen and listen attentively. Over there, before us, sits a golden dragon. A living legend, possibly the last and only creature of its kind to have survived your murderous frenzy. One doesn't kill legends. I, Dorregaray, will not allow you to touch that dragon. Is that understood? You can get packed, fasten your saddlebags and go home.'

Geralt was convinced an uproar would ensue. He was mistaken.

'Noble sorcerer, sir,' Gyllenstiern's voice interrupted the silence. 'Heed what and to whom you speak. King Niedamir may order you, Dorregaray, to fasten your saddlebags and go to hell. But not the other way around. Is that clear?'

'No,' the sorcerer said proudly, 'it is not. For I am Master Dorregaray, and will not be ordered around by someone whose kingdom encompasses an area visible from the height of the palisade on a mangy, filthy, stinking stronghold. Do you know, Lord Gyllenstiern, that were I to speak a charm and wave my hand, you would change into a cowpat, and your underage king into something ineffably worse? Is *that* clear?'

Gyllenstiern did not manage to answer, for Boholt walked up to Dorregaray, caught him by the shoulder and pulled him around to face him. Gar and Beanpole, silent and grim, appeared from behind Boholt.

'Just listen, magician, sir,' the enormous Reaver said. 'Before you wave that hand, listen to me. I could spend a long time explaining what I would do with your prohibitions, your fables and your foolish chatter. But I have no wish to. Let this suffice as my answer.'

Boholt placed a finger against his nose and from a short distance ejected the contents onto the toes of the sorcerer's boots.

Dorregaray blanched, but did not move. He saw – as everyone did – the morning star mace on a cubit-long shaft hanging low at Gar's side. He knew – as everyone did – that the time he needed to cast a spell was incomparably longer than the time Gar needed to smash his head to pieces.

'Very well,' Boholt said. 'And now move nicely out of the way, your lordship. And should the desire to open your gob occur to you, quickly shove a bunch of grass into it. Because if I hear you whining again, I'll give you something to remember me by.'

Boholt turned away and rubbed his hands.

'Right, Gar, Beanpole, let's get to work, because that reptile won't hang around forever.'

'Doesn't seem to be planning on going anywhere,' Dandelion said, looking at the foreground. 'Look at it.'

The golden dragon on the hill yawned, lifted its head, waved its wings and lashed the ground with its tail.

'King Niedamir and you, knights!' it yelled with a roar like a brass trumpet. 'I am the dragon Villentretenmerth! As I see, the landslide which I – though I say it, as shouldn't – sent down on your heads did not completely stop you. You have come this far. As you know, there are only three ways out of this valley. East, towards Barefield, and west, towards Caingorn. And you may use those roads. You will not take the northern gorge, gentlemen, because I, Villentretenmerth, forbid you. However, if anyone does not wish to respect my injunction, I challenge him to fight an honourable, knightly duel. With conventional weapons, without spells, without breathing fire. A fight to the utter capitulation of one of the sides. I await an answer through your herald, as custom dictates!'

Everyone stood with their mouths open wide.

'It can talk!' Boholt panted. 'Remarkable!'

'Not only that, but very intelligently,' Yarpen Zigrin said. 'Anyone know what a confessional weapon is?'

'An ordinary, non-magical one,' Yennefer said frowning. 'But something else puzzles me. With a forked tongue it's not capable of articulated speech. The rogue is using telepathy! Be careful, it works in both directions. It can read your thoughts.'

'Has it gone completely barmy, or what?' Kennet Beanpole said, annoyed. 'An honourable duel? With a stupid reptile? Not a chance! We'll attack him together! There's strength in numbers!'

'No.'

They looked around.

Eyck of Denesle, already mounted in full armour, with his lance set by his stirrup, looked much better than he had on foot. His feverish eyes blazed from beneath his raised visor and his face was pale.

'No, Kennet, sir,' the knight repeated. 'Unless it is over my dead body. I will not permit knightly honour to be insulted in my presence. Whomsoever dares to violate the principles of this honourable duel . . .'

Eyck was talking louder and louder. His exalted voice was cracking and he was trembling with excitement.

' . . . whomsoever affronts honour, also affronts me, and his or my blood will be shed on this tired earth. The beast calls for a duel? Very well! Let the herald trumpet my name! May divine judgement decide! On the dragon's side is the power of fang and talon and infernal fury, and on my side . . . '

'What a moron,' Yarpen Zigrin muttered.

' . . . on my side righteousness, faith, the tears of virgins, whom this reptile—'

'That's enough, Eyck, you make me want to puke!' Boholt yelled. 'Go on, to the lists! Don't talk, set about that dragon!'

'Hey, Boholt, wait,' one of the dwarves, tugging on his beard, suddenly said. 'Forgotten about the agreement? If Eyck lays low the serpent, he'll take half . . . '

'Eyck won't take anything,' Boholt grinned. 'I know him. He'll be happy if Dandelion writes a song about him.'

'Silence!' Gyllenstiern declared. 'Let it be. Against the dragon will ride out the virtuous knight errant, Eyck of Denesle, fighting in the colours of Caingorn as the lance and sword of King Niedamir. That is the kingly will!'

'There you have it,' Yarpen Zigrin gnashed his teeth. 'The lance and sword of Niedamir. The Caingorn kinglet has fixed us. What now?'

'Nothing,' Boholt spat. 'I reckon you don't want to cross Eyck, Yarpen? He talks nonsense, but if he's already mounted his horse and roused himself, better get out of his way. Let him go, dammit, and sort the dragon out. And then we'll see.'

'Who shall be the herald?' Dandelion asked. 'The dragon wanted a herald. Maybe me?'

'No. We don't need a song, Dandelion,' Boholt frowned. 'Yarpen Zigrin can be the herald. He's got a voice like a bull.'

'Very well, no bother,' Yarpen said. 'Bring me a flag-bearer with a banner so that everything is as it should be.'

'Just talk politely, dwarf, sir. And courteously,' Gyllenstiern cautioned.

'Don't learn me how to talk,' the dwarf proudly stuck out his belly. 'I was sent on diplomatic missions when you lot were still knee-high to a grasshopper.'

The dragon continued to sit patiently on the hillock, waving its tail cheerfully. The dwarf clambered up onto the largest boulder, hawked and spat.

'Hey, you there!' he yelled, putting his hands on his hips. 'You fucking dragon, you! Listen to what the herald has to say! That means me! The first one to take you on honourably will be the meandering knight, Eyck of Denesle! And he will stick his lance in your paunch, according to the holy custom, to your confusion, and to the joy of poor virgins and King Niedamir! It will be a fair fight and honourable, breathing fire is not allowed, and you may only lambast the other confessionally, until the other gives up the ghost or expires! Which we sincerely wish on you! Understood, dragon?'

The dragon yawned, flapped its wings, and then, flattening itself to the ground, quickly descended from the hillock to level ground.

'I have understood, noble herald!' it yelled back. 'Then may the virtuous Eyck of Denesle enter the fray. I am ready!'

'What a pantomime,' Boholt spat, following Eyck with a grim expression, as he walked his horse over the barrier of boulders. 'A ruddy barrel of laughs . . . '

'Shut your yap, Boholt,' Dandelion shouted, rubbing his hands. 'Look, Eyck is preparing to charge! It'll be a bloody beautiful ballad!'

'Hurrah! Long live Eyck!' someone shouted from Niedamir's troop of bowmen.

'And I,' Sheepbagger said gloomily, 'would still have stuffed him full of brimstone, just to be certain.'

Eyck, already in the field, saluted the dragon with his upraised lance, slammed down his visor and struck his horse with his spurs.

'Well, well,' the dwarf said. 'He may be stupid, but he knows how to charge. Look at him go!'

Eyck, lent forward, braced in the saddle, lowered his lance at full gallop. The dragon, contrary to Geralt's expectations, did not leap aside, did not move in a semicircle, but, flattened to the ground, rushed straight at the attacking knight.

'Hit him! Hit him, Eyck!' Yarpen yelled.

Eyck, although in full gallop, did not strike headlong, straight ahead. At the last moment he nimbly changed direction, shifting the lance over his horse's head. Flashing past the dragon, he thrust with all his might, standing up in the stirrups. Everybody shouted in unison. Geralt did not join in with the choir.

The dragon evaded the blow with a delicate, agile, graceful turn and, coiling like a living, golden ribbon, as quick as lightning, but softly, catlike, reached a foot beneath the horse's belly. The horse squealed, jerking its croup high up, and the knight rocked in the saddle, but did not release his lance. Just as the horse was about to hit the ground snout first, the dragon swept Eyck from the saddle with a fierce swipe of his clawed foot. Everybody saw his breastplate spinning upwards and everybody heard the clanking and thudding with which the knight fell onto the ground.

The dragon, sitting on its haunches, pinned the horse with a foot, and lowered its toothy jaws. The horse squealed shrilly, struggled and then was quiet.

In the silence that fell everybody heard the deep voice of the dragon Villentretenmerth.

'The doughty Eyck of Denesle may now be taken from the battle-field, for he is incapable of fighting any longer. Next, please.'

'Oh, fuck,' Yarpen Zigrin said in the silence that followed.

VIII

'Both legs,' Yennefer said wiping her hands on a linen cloth, 'and probably something with his spine. The armour on his back is dented as though he'd been hit by a pile driver. He injured his legs with his own lance. He won't be mounting a horse for some time. If he ever mounts one again.'

'Professional hazard,' Geralt muttered. The sorceress frowned.

'Is that all you have to say?'

'And what else would you like to hear, Yennefer?'

'That dragon is unbelievably fast, Geralt. Too fast for a *man* to fight it.'

'I understand. No, Yen. Not me.'

'Principles,' the sorceress smiled spitefully, 'or ordinary, commonplace fear? The only human feeling that wasn't eradicated in you?'

'One and the other,' the Witcher agreed dispassionately. 'What difference does it make?'

'Precisely,' Yennefer came closer. 'None. Principles may be broken, fear can be overcome. Kill that dragon, Geralt. For me.'

'For you?'

'For me. I want that dragon, Geralt. In one piece. I want to have him all for myself.'

'So cast a spell and kill it.'

'No. You kill it. And I'll use my spells to hold back the Reavers and the others so they don't interfere.'

'You'll kill them, Yennefer.'

'Since when has that ever bothered you? You take care of the dragon, I'll deal with the people.'

'Yennefer,' the Witcher said coldly, 'I don't understand. What do you want with that dragon? Does the yellowness of its scales dazzle you to that degree? You don't suffer from poverty, after all. You have numerous sources of income; you're famous. What are you about? Just don't talk about a calling, I beg you.'

Yennefer was silent, then finally, twisting her lips, aimed a powerful kick at a stone lying in the grass.

'There's someone who can help me, Geralt. Apparently, it's . . . you know what I'm talking about . . . Apparently it isn't irreversible. There's a chance. I could still have . . . Do you understand?'

'I do.'

'It's a complex operation, costly. But in exchange for a golden dragon . . . Geralt?'

The Witcher remained silent.

'When we were hanging on the bridge,' the sorcereress said, 'you asked me for something. I'll meet your request. In spite of everything.'

The Witcher smiled sadly and touched the obsidian star on Yennefer's neck with his index finger.

'It's too late, Yen. We aren't hanging now. It's stopped mattering to me. In spite of everything.'

He expected the worst: a cascade of fire, lightning, a smack in the face, abuse, curses. He was surprised just to see the suppressed trembling of her lips. Yennefer slowly turned away. Geralt regretted his words. He regretted the emotion which had engendered them. The limit of possibility overstepped, now snapped like a lute string. He looked at Dandelion and saw the troubadour quickly turn his head away and avoid his gaze.

'Well, we've got the issue of knightly honour out of the way, my lords,' Boholt called, now dressed in armour and standing before Niedamir, who was still sitting on a stone with an unvarying expression of boredom on his face. 'Knightly honour is lying there, groaning softly. It was a lousy idea, Lord Gyllenstiern, to send out Eyck as your knight and vassal. I wouldn't dream of pointing the finger, but I know whom Eyck can thank for his broken pins. Yes, I swear, we've killed two birds with one stone. One was a lunatic, insanely reviving the legends of how a bold knight defeats a dragon in a duel. And the other a swindler, who wanted to make money from it. Do you know who I'm talking about, Gyllenstiern, what? Good. And now our move. Now the dragon is ours. Now we, the Reavers, will sort out that dragon. But by ourselves.'

'And the agreement, Boholt?' the chancellor drawled. 'What about the agreement?'

'I don't give a shit about the agreement.'

'This is outrageous! This is lese-majesty!' Gyllenstiern stamped his foot. 'King Niedamir—'

'What about the king?' Boholt yelled, resting on an enormous, two-handed sword. 'Perhaps the king will personally decide to take on the dragon by himself? Or perhaps you, his faithful chancellor, will squeeze your belly into a suit of armour and go into battle? Why not, please do, we'll wait, my lord. You had your chance, Gyllenstiern. Had Eyck mortally lanced the dragon, you would have taken it in its entirety, nothing would have been left to us because we hadn't helped, not one golden scale on its back. But it's too late now. Open your eyes. There's no one to fight under Caingorn's colours. You won't find another chump like Eyck.'

'That's not true!' the cobbler Sheepbagger said, hurrying to the king, who was still busy watching a point on the horizon of interest only to him. 'O King! Just wait a little, and our men from Barefield will be arriving, they'll be 'ere any moment! To hell with the cock-sure nobility, chase them away! You'll see who is really brave, who is strong in deed, and not just in word!'

'Shut your trap,' Boholt said calmly, wiping a spot of rust from his breastplate. 'Shut your trap, peasant, because if you don't I'll shut it so hard I'll shove your teeth down your throat.'

Sheepbagger, seeing Kennet and Gar approaching, quickly backed away and hid among the Barefield constables.

'King!' Gyllenstiern called. 'O King, what do you command?'

The expression of boredom suddenly vanished from Niedamir's face. The underage monarch wrinkled his freckly nose and stood up.

'What do I command?' he said in a shrill voice. 'You've finally asked, Gyllenstiern, rather than decide for me and speak for me and on my behalf? I'm very pleased. And may it thus remain,

Gyllenstiern. From this moment you will be silent and listen to my orders. Here is the first of them. Muster the men and order Eyck of Denesle be placed on a wagon. We're going back to Caingorn.'

'But sire—'

'Not a word, Gyllenstiern. Madam Yennefer, noble lords, I bid you farewell. I've lost some time on this expedition, but have gained much. I have learned a great deal. Thank you for your words, Madam Yennefer, Master Dorregaray, Sir Boholt. And thank you for your silence, Sir Geralt.'

'O King,' Gyllenstiern said. 'What do you mean? The dragon is in our grasp. It's there for the taking. King, your dream . . . '

'My dream,' Niedamir repeated pensively. 'I do not have it yet. And should I stay here . . . Then I might never have it.'

'But Malleore? And the hand of the princess?' The chancellor waved his arms, not giving up. 'And the throne? King, the people there will acknowledge you as . . . '

'I don't give a shit about the people there, as Sir Boholt would say,' Niedamir laughed. 'The throne of Malleore is mine anyway, because in Caingorn I have three hundred armoured troops and fifteen hundred foot soldiers against their thousand crappy spearmen. Do they acknowledge me? They will have to. I'll keep hanging, beheading and dismembering until they do. And their princess is a fat goose and to hell with her hand, I only need her womb. Let her bear me an heir, and then I'll poison her anyway. Using Master Sheepbagger's method. That's enough chatter, Gyllenstiern. Set about carrying out my orders.'

'Indeed,' Dandelion whispered to Geralt, 'he has learned a great deal.'

'A great deal,' Geralt confirmed, looking at the hillock where the golden dragon, with its triangular head lowered, was licking something grey-green sitting in the grass beside it with its forked, scarlet tongue. 'But I wouldn't like to be his subject, Dandelion.'

'And what do you think will happen now?'

The Witcher looked calmly at the tiny, grey-green creature, fluttering its bat-like wings beside the golden talons of the stooping dragon.

'And what's your opinion about all this, Dandelion? What do you think?'

'What does it matter what I think? I'm a poet, Geralt. Does my opinion matter at all?'

'Yes it does.'

'Well I'll tell you then. When I see a reptile, Geralt, a viper, let's say, or some other serpent, it gives me the creeps, the vileness disgusts and terrifies me. But that dragon . . . '

'Yeah?'

'It . . . it's pretty, Geralt.'

'Thank you, Dandelion.'

'What for?'

Geralt turned his head away, and with a slow movement reached for the buckle of his belt, which crossed his chest diagonally, and shortened it by two holes. He lifted his right hand to check if his sword hilt was positioned correctly. Dandelion looked on with eyes wide open.

'Geralt! Do you plan to . . . ?'

'Yes,' the Witcher said calmly, 'there is a limit to what I can accept as possible. I've had enough of all this. Are you going with Niedamir or staying, Dandelion?'

The troubadour leaned over, placed his lute beneath a stone cautiously and with great care and then straightened up.

'I'm staying. What did you say? The limits of possibility? I'm bagging that as the title of a ballad.'

'It could be your last one, Dandelion.'

'Geralt?'

'Mm?'

'Don't kill it . . . Can you not?'

'A sword is a sword, Dandelion. Once drawn . . . '

'Please try.'

'I will.'

Dorregaray chuckled, turned towards Yennefer and the Reavers, and pointed at the receding royal caravan.

'Over there,' he said, 'King Niedamir is leaving. He no longer gives orders through Gyllenstiern's mouth. He is departing, having demonstrated good sense. I'm glad you're here, Dandelion. I suggest you begin composing a ballad.'

'What about?'

'About,' the sorcerer drew his wand from his coat, 'Master Dorregaray, sorcerer, chasing back home the rabble who wanted to use vulgar methods to kill the last golden dragon left in the world. Don't move, Boholt! Yarpen, hands off your battle-axe! Don't move a muscle, Yennefer! Off you go, good-for-nothings, follow the king, like good little boys. Be off, mount your horses or wagons. I warn you that if anybody makes a false move all that will remain of him will be a burning smell and a bit of fused sand. I am serious.'

'Dorregaray!' Yennefer hissed.

'My lord sorcerer,' Boholt said conciliatorily. 'Is this any way to act—'

'Be quiet, Boholt. I told you not to touch that dragon. Fables are not to be killed. About-turn and scram.'

Yennefer's hand suddenly shot forward, and the ground around Dorregaray exploded in blue flame, seething in a dust cloud of torn turf and grit.

The sorcerer staggered, encircled by fire. Gar leaped forward and struck him in the face with the heel of his hand. Dorregaray fell to the ground, a bolt of red lightning shooting from his wand and harmlessly zapping out among the rocks. Beanpole sprang at him from the other side, kicked the sorcerer to the ground, and took a backswing to repeat the blow. Geralt fell among them, pushed Beanpole away, drew his sword and thrust flat, aiming between the breastplate and the spaulder. He was thwarted by Boholt, who parried the blow with the broad blade of his two-handed sword. Dandelion tried to trip Gar, but ineffectively; Gar clung to the bard's rainbow-hued jerkin and thumped him between the eyes with his fist. Yarpen Zigrin, leaping from behind, tripped Dandelion, hitting him behind his knees with the haft of a hatchet.

Geralt spun into a pirouette, evading Boholt's sword, and jabbed at the onrushing Beanpole, tearing off his iron bracer. Beanpole leaped back, tripped and fell over. Boholt grunted and whirled

69

his sword like a scythe. Geralt jumped over the whistling blade, slammed the hilt of his sword into Boholt's breastplate, fended him off, and thrust, aiming for his cheek. Boholt, realising he could not parry with his heavy sword, threw himself backwards, falling on his back. The Witcher leaped at him and at that moment felt the earth fall away from under his rapidly numbing feet. He saw the horizon going from horizontal to vertical. Vainly trying to form a protective Sign with his fingers, he fell heavily onto the ground on his side, his sword slipping from his numb hand. There was a pounding and a buzzing in his ears.

'Tie them up before the spell stops working,' Yennefer said, somewhere above and very far away. 'All three of them.'

Dorregaray and Geralt, befuddled and paralysed, allowed themselves to be bound and tethered to a wagon, silently and without resisting. Dandelion fought and cursed, so he received a punch in the face before he was tied to the wagon.

'Why tie 'em up, traitors, sons of dogs?' Sheepbagger said, walking over. 'They should be clubbed to death at once and be done with it.'

'You're a son yourself, and not a dog's,' Yarpen Zigrin said, 'Don't insult dogs here. Scram, you heel.'

'You're awfully brave,' Sheepbagger snapped. 'We'll see if you're brave enough when my comrades arrive from Barefield. They'll be here any moment. You'll . . . '

Yarpen, twisting with surprising agility considering his build, whacked Sheepbagger over the head with his hatchet. Gar, standing alongside, gave him a kick for good measure. Sheepbagger flew a few feet through the air and fell nose-first in the grass.

'You'll be sorry!' he yelled, crawling on all fours. 'I'll fix . . . '

'Lads!' Yarpen Zigrin roared. 'Kick the cobbler in the cobblers! Grab 'im, Gar!'

Sheepbagger did not wait. He sprang up and dashed towards the eastern canyon. The Barefield trackers followed him, cringing. The dwarves, cackling, sent a hail of stones after them.

'The air's freshened up already,' Yarpen laughed. 'Right, Boholt, let's get down to the dragon.'

'Hold on,' Yennefer raised a hand. 'The only thing you're getting down to is the bottom of the valley. Be gone, all of you.'

'Excuse me?' Boholt bent over, his eyes blazing ominously. 'What did you say, Most Honourable Madam Witch?'

'Follow that cobbler,' Yennefer repeated. 'All of you. I'll deal with the dragon myself. Using unconventional weapons. And you can thank me as you leave. Had it not been for me you would have tasted the Witcher's sword. Come now, quickly, Boholt, before I lose my temper. I warn you that I know a spell which can make you all geldings. I just have to raise my hand.'

'Is that so?' Boholt drawled. 'My patience has reached its limits. I won't be made a fool of. Beanpole, unhook the shaft from the cart. I feel I'll also be needing unconventional weapons. Someone is soon going to get a damn good thrashing, my lords. I won't point the finger, but a certain hideous witch is going to get a bloody sound hiding.'

'Just try, Boholt. You'll brighten up my day.'

'Why, Yennefer?' the dwarf asked reproachfully.

'Perhaps I simply don't like sharing, Yarpen?'

'Well now,' Yarpen Zigrin smiled. 'That's profoundly human. So human it's almost dwarven. It's nice to see familiar qualities in a sorceress. Because I don't like sharing, either, Yennefer.'

He hunched into a short, very rapid backswing. A steel ball, appearing out of his pocket as if from nowhere, whirred through the air and smacked Yennefer right in the forehead. Before the sorceress had time to come to her senses, she was suspended in the air, being held up by Beanpole and Gar, and Yarpen was binding her ankles with twine. Yennefer screamed furiously, but one of Yarpen's boys threw the wagon's reins over her head from behind and pulled them tight, the leather strap digging into her open mouth, stifling her cries.

'Well, Yennefer,' Boholt said as he walked over, 'how do you plan to turn me into a gelding now? When you can't move a hand?'

He tore the collar of her coat and then ripped and wrenched open her blouse. Yennefer shrieked, choked by the reins.

'I don't have the time now,' Boholt said, groping her shamelessly to the cackling of the dwarves, 'but wait a little while, witch. Once we've sorted out the dragon, we'll make merry. Tie her firmly to the wheel, boys. Both little hands to the rim, so she won't be able to lift a finger. And no one's to bloody touch her yet, my lords. We'll sort the order out depending on who does a good job on the dragon.'

'Beware, Boholt,' Geralt, arms tied, said, softly, calmly and ominously. 'I'll follow you to the ends of the world.'

'You surprise me,' the Reaver replied, just as calmly. 'In your place I'd keep mum. I know you, and I know I have to take your threat seriously. I won't have a choice. You might not come out of this alive, Witcher. We'll return to this matter. Gar, Beanpole, to horse.'

'What bad luck,' Dandelion snapped. 'Why the hell did I get mixed up in this?'

Dorregaray, lowering his head, watched the thick drops of blood slowly dripping from his nose onto his belly.

'Would you stop staring!' the sorceress screamed at Geralt. She was writhing like a snake in her bonds, vainly trying to conceal her exposed charms. The Witcher obediently turned his head away. Dandelion did not.

'You must have used an entire barrel of mandrake elixir on what I can see, Yennefer,' the bard laughed. 'Your skin's like a sixteen-year-old's, dammit.'

'Shut your trap, whore's son!' the sorceress bellowed.

'How old are you, actually, Yennefer?' Dandelion asked, not giving up. 'Two hundred? Well, a hundred and fifty, let's say. And you're behaving like . . . '

Yennefer twisted her neck and spat at him, but was wide of the mark.

'Yen,' the Witcher said reproachfully, wiping his spit-covered ear on his shoulder.

'I wish he would stop staring!'

'Not on your life,' Dandelion said, without taking his eyes off the bedraggled sorceress. 'I'm here because of her. They may slit our throats, but at least I'll die happy.'

72

'Shut up, Dandelion,' the Witcher said.

'I have no intention of so doing. In fact I plan to compose the Ballad of the Two Tits. Please don't interfere.'

'Dandelion,' Dorregaray sniffed through his bloody nose. 'Be serious.'

'I am being bloody serious.'

The dwarves heaved Boholt up into the saddle. He was heavy and squat from the armour and the leather pads he was wearing. Gar and Beanpole were already mounted, holding huge, two-handed swords across their saddles.

'Right,' Boholt rasped, 'let's have at him.'

'Oh, no,' said a deep voice, sounding like a brass trumpet. 'I have come to you!'

From beyond the ring of boulders emerged a long snout shimmering with gold, a slender neck armed with a row of triangular, serrated projections and, behind, taloned feet. The evil, reptilian eyes, with their vertical pupils, peered from beneath horned eyelids.

'I was tired of waiting in the open,' the dragon Villentretenmerth said, looking around, 'so I came myself. Fewer and fewer challengers, I see.'

Boholt held the reins in his teeth and a longsword two-handed.

'Thas nuff,' he said indistinctly, holding the strap in his teeth. 'Stah an fight, heptile!'

'I am,' the dragon said, arching its back and lifting its tail insultingly.

Boholt looked around. Gar and Beanpole slowly, almost ostentatiously, calmly, flanked the dragon. Yarpen Zigrin and his boys waited behind, holding battle-axes.

'Aaaargh!' Boholt roared, striking his horse hard with his heels and lifting his sword.

The dragon curled up, flattened itself to the ground and struck with its tail from above and behind, like a scorpion, hitting not Boholt, but Gar, who was attacking from the side. Gar fell over with his horse amid a clanking, screaming and neighing tumult. Boholt, charging at a gallop, struck with a terrible blow, but the dragon nimbly dodged the wide blade. The momentum of the gallop carried Boholt alongside the dragon's body. The dragon twisted, standing on its hind legs, and clawed Beanpole, tearing open his horse's belly and the rider's thigh with a single slash. Boholt, leaning far out from the saddle, managed to steer his horse around, pulling the reins with his teeth, and attacked once more.

The dragon lashed its tail over the dwarves rushing towards it, knocking them all over, and then lunged at Boholt, en route – seemingly in passing – stamping vigorously on Beanpole, who was trying to get up. Boholt, jerking his head around, tried to steer his galloping horse, but the dragon was infinitely quicker and more agile. Cunningly stealing up on Boholt from the left in order to obstruct his swing, it struck with a taloned foot. The horse reared up and lurched over to one side. Boholt flew from the saddle, losing his sword and helmet, tumbling backwards onto the ground, banging his head against a rock.

'Run for it, lads! Up the hill!' Yarpen Zigrin bellowed, outshouting the screams of Gar, who was pinned down by his horse. Beards fluttering, the dwarves dashed towards the rocks at a speed that belied their short legs. The dragon did not give chase. It sat calmly and looked around. Gar was thrashing and screaming beneath the horse. Boholt lay motionless. Beanpole was crawling towards the rocks, sideways, like a huge, iron crab.

'Staggering,' Dorregaray whispered. 'Staggering . . . '

'Hey!' Dandelion struggled in his bonds, making the wagon shake. 'What is it? Over there! Look!'

A great cloud of dust could be seen on the eastern side of the gorge, and shouting, rattling and the tramping of hooves quickly reached them. The dragon extended its neck to look.

Three large wagons full of armed men rolled onto the plain. Splitting up, they began to surround the dragon.

'It's . . . Dammit, it's the constabulary and guilds from Barefield!' Dandelion called. 'They came around by the source of the Braa! Yes, it's them! Look, it's Sheepbagger, there, at the front!'

The dragon lowered its head and gently pushed a small, green-greyish, mewling creature towards the wagon. Then it struck the ground with its tail, roared loudly and shot like an arrow towards the encounter with the men of Barefield.

'What is it?' Yennefer asked, 'That little thing? Crawling around in the grass? Geralt?'

'It's what the dragon was protecting from us,' the Witcher said. 'That's what hatched some time ago in the cave, over there in the northern canyon. It's the dragonling from the egg of the dragon that Sheepbagger poisoned.'

The dragonling, stumbling and dragging its bulging belly across the ground, scurried unsteadily over to the wagon, squealed, stood on its hind legs, stretched out its little wings, and then without a second's thought clung to the sorceress's side. Yennefer, with an extremely queer look on her face, sighed loudly.

'It likes you,' Geralt murmured.

'He's young, but he ain't stupid,' Dandelion twisting in his fetters, grinned. 'Look where he's stuck his snout. I'd like to be in his shoes, dammit. Hey, little one, run away! That's Yennefer! Terror of dragons! And witchers. Well, at least one witcher—'

'Quiet, Dandelion,' Dorregaray shouted. 'Look over there, on the battlefield! They've got him, a pox on them!'

The Barefield wagons, rumbling like war chariots, raced towards the attacking dragon.

'Smack 'im!' Sheepbagger yelled, hanging on to the wagoner's back. 'Smack 'im, kinsmen, anywhere and anyhow! Don't hold back!'

The dragon nimbly eluded the first advancing wagon, flashing with scythe blades, forks and spears, but ended up between the next two, from which a huge double fishing net pulled by straps dropped onto it. The dragon, fully enmeshed, fell down, rolled over, curled up in a ball, and spread its legs. The net tore to shreds with a sharp rending noise. More nets were thrown onto it from the first wagon, which had managed to turn around, this time utterly entangling the dragon. The two other wagons also turned back, dashed towards the dragon, rattling and bouncing over bumps.

'You're caught in the net, you carp!' Sheepbagger bawled. 'And we'll soon scale you!'

The dragon roared and belched a cloud of steam into the sky. The Barefield constables rushed towards him, spilling out of the wagons. The dragon bellowed again, desperately, with a thundering roar.

From the northern canyon came a reply, a high-pitched, battle cry.

Out from the gorge, straining forward in a frenzied gallop, blonde plaits streaming, whistling piercingly, surrounded by the flickering flashes of sabres, charged . . .

'The Zerrikanians!' the Witcher shouted, helplessly tugging at the ropes.

'Oh, shit!' Dandelion chimed in. 'Geralt! Do you understand?'

The Zerrikanians rode through the throng like hot knives through a barrel of butter, scattering their path with massacred corpses, and then leaped from their horses in full flight, to stand beside the dragon struggling in the net. The first of the onrushing constables immediately lost his head. The second aimed a blow with his pitchfork at Véa, but the Zerrikanian, holding her sabre in both hands, upside down, with the tip pointing towards the ground, slashed him open from crotch to sternum. The others beat a hurried retreat.

'To the wagons!' Sheepbagger yelled. 'To the wagons, kinsmen! We'll crush them under the wagons!'

'Geralt!' Yennefer suddenly shouted, pulling up her bound legs and pushing them with a sudden thrust under the wagon, beneath the arms of the Witcher, which were bound and twisted behind him. 'The Igni Sign! Make it! Can you feel the rope? Cast the bloody thing!'

'Without looking?' Geralt groaned. 'I'll burn you, Yen!'

'Make the Sign! I can take it!'

He obeyed, and felt a tingling in his fingers, which were forming the Igni Sign just above the sorceress's bound ankles. Yennefer turned her head away, biting down on her coat collar and stifling a moan. The dragonling, squealing, beat its wings beside her.

'Yen!'

'Make it!' she bellowed.

Her bonds gave way in an instant, as the disgusting, nauseating odour of charred skin became unbearable. Dorregaray uttered a strange noise and fainted, suspended by his fetters from the wagon wheel.

The sorceress, wincing with the pain, straightened up, lifting her now free leg. She screamed in a furious voice, full of pain and rage. The medallion on Geralt's neck jerked as though it were alive. Yennefer straightened her thigh, waved her foot towards the charging wagons of the Barefield constabulary, and shouted out a spell. The air crackled and gave off the smell of ozone.

'O, ye Gods,' Dandelion wailed in admiration. 'What a ballad this will be, Yennefer!'

The spell, cast by her shapely little foot, was not totally effective. The first wagon – and everything on it – took on the yellow colour of a kingcup, which the Barefield soldiers in the frenzy of battle did not even notice. It did better with the second wagon, whose entire crew were transformed into huge, rough-skinned frogs, which hopped around in all directions, croaking comically. The wagon, now bereft of a driver, tipped over and fell apart. The horses, neighing hysterically, fled into the distance, dragging the broken shaft behind them.

Yennefer bit her lip and waved her leg in the air again. The kingcup-yellow wagon suddenly dissolved into kingcup-yellow smoke to the sound of lively musical tones drifting down from above, and its entire crew flopped onto the grass, stupefied, forming a picturesque heap. The wheels of the third wagon went from round to square and the result was instant. The horses reared up, the wagon crashed over, and the Barefield constabulary were tipped out and thrown onto the ground. Yennefer, now driven by pure vindictiveness, flourished a leg ferociously and yelled out a spell, transforming the Barefielders randomly into turtles, geese, woodlice, flamingos and stripy piglets. The Zerrikanians expertly and methodically finished off the rest.

The dragon, having finally torn the nets to shreds, leaped up, flapped its wings, roared and hurtled, as straight as a ramrod, after the unharmed and fleeing Sheepbagger. Sheepbagger was dashing like a stag, but the dragon was faster. Geralt, seeing the gaping jaws and razor-sharp flashing teeth, turned his head away. He heard a gruesome scream and a revolting crunching sound. Dandelion gave a stifled shout. Yennefer, her face as white as a sheet, bent over double, turned to one side and vomited under the wagon.

A silence fell, interrupted only by the occasional gaggling, croaking and squealing of the remains of the Barefield constabulary.

Véa, smiling unpleasantly, stood over Yennefer, legs wide apart. The Zerrikanian raised her sabre. Yennefer, pale, raised a leg.

'No,' said Borch, also known as Three Jackdaws, who was sitting on a stone. In his lap he was holding the dragonling, peaceful and content.

'We aren't going to kill Madam Yennefer,' the dragon Villentretenmerth repeated. 'It is over. What is more, we are grateful to Madam Yennefer for her invaluable assistance. Release them, Véa.'

'Do you understand, Geralt?' Dandelion whispered, chafing feeling into his numb arms. 'Do you understand? There's an ancient ballad about a golden dragon. A golden dragon can . . .'

'Can assume any form it wishes,' Geralt muttered, 'even that of a human. I've heard that too. But I didn't believe it.'

'Yarpen Zigrin, sir!' Villentretenmerth called to the dwarf, who was hanging onto a vertical rock twenty ells above the ground. 'What are you looking for there? Marmots? Not your favourite dish, if memory serves me. Climb down and busy yourself with the Reavers. They need help. There won't be any more killing. Of anybody.'

Dandelion, casting anxious glances at the Zerrikanians, who were vigilantly patrolling the battlefield, was still trying to revive the unconscious Dorregaray. Geralt was dressing Yennefer's scorched ankles and rubbing ointment into them. The sorceress was hissing with pain and mumbling spells.

Having completed his task, the Witcher stood up.

'Stay here,' he said. 'I have to talk to him.'

Yennefer stood up, wincing.

'I'm going with you, Geralt,' she said, linking her arm in his. 'May I? Please, Geralt.'

'With me, Yen? I thought . . .'

'Don't think,' she pressed herself against his arm.

'Yen?'

'It's alright, Geralt.'

He looked into her eyes, which were warm. As they used to be. He lowered his head and kissed her lips; hot, soft and willing. As they used to be.

They walked over. Yennefer, held up by Geralt, curtsied low, as though before a king, holding her dress in her fingertips.

'Three Jack . . . Villentretenmerth . . . ' the Witcher said.

'My name, when freely translated into your language, means Three Black Birds,' the dragon said. The dragonling, little claws digging into his forearm, arched its back to be stroked.

'Chaos and Order,' Villentretenmerth smiled. 'Do you remember, Geralt? Chaos is aggression, Order is protection against it. It's worth rushing to the ends of the world, to oppose aggression and evil, isn't it, Witcher? Particularly, as you said, when the pay is fair. And this time it was. It was the treasure hoard of the she-dragon Myrgtabrakke, the one poisoned outside Barefield. She summoned me to help her, to stop the evil threatening her. Myrgtabrakke flew away soon after Eyck of Denesle was removed from the battlefield. She had sufficient time, while you were talking and quarrelling. But she left me her treasure as my payment.'

The dragonling squealed and flapped its little wings.

'So you . . . '

'That is right,' the dragon interrupted. 'Well, it's the times we live in. For some time, creatures, which you usually call monsters, have been feeling more and more under threat from people. They can no longer cope by themselves. They need a Defender. Some kind of . . . witcher.'

'And the destination . . . The goal at the end of the road?'

'This is it,' Villentretenmerth lifted his forearm. The dragonling squealed in alarm. 'I've just attained it. Owing to him I shall survive, Geralt of Rivia, I shall prove there are no limits of possibility. One day, you will also find such a purpose, Witcher. Even those who are different can survive. Farewell, Geralt. Farewell, Yennefer.'

The sorceress, grasping the Witcher's arm more firmly, curtsied again.

Villentretenmerth stood up and looked at her, and his expression was very serious.

'Forgive me my frankness and forthrightness, Yennefer. It is written all over your faces, I don't even have to try to read your thoughts. You were made for each other, you and the Witcher. But nothing will come of it. Nothing. I'm sorry.'

'I know,' Yennefer blanched slightly. 'I know, Villentretenmerth. But I would also like to believe there are no limits of possibility. Or at least I would like to believe that they are still very far away.'

Véa walked over, touched Geralt's shoulder, and quickly uttered a few words. The dragon laughed.

'Geralt, Véa says she will long remember the tub at the Pensive Dragon. She hopes we'll meet again some day.'

'What?' Yennefer answered, narrowing her eyes.

'Nothing,' the Witcher said quickly, 'Villentretenmerth . . . '

'Yes, Geralt of Rivia?'

'You can assume any form. Any that you wish.'

'Indeed.'

'Why then, a man? Why Borch with three black birds on his coat of arms?'

The dragon smiled cheerfully.

'I don't know, Geralt, in what circumstances the distant ancestors of our races encountered one another for the first time. But the fact is that for dragons, there is nothing more repugnant than man. Man arouses instinctive, irrational disgust in a dragon. With me it's different. To me you're . . . likeable. Farewell.'

It was not a gradual, blurred transformation, or a hazy, pulsating trembling as with an illusion. It was as sudden as the blink of an eye. Where a second before had stood a curly-haired knight in a tunic decorated with three black birds, now sat a golden dragon, gracefully extending its long, slender neck. Inclining its head, the dragon spread its wings, dazzlingly gold in the sunshine. Yennefer sighed loudly.

Véa, already mounted beside Téa, waved.

'Véa,' the Witcher said, 'you were right.'

'Hm?'

'He is the most beautiful.'

A SHARD OF ICE

I

The dead sheep, swollen and bloated, its stiff legs pointing towards the sky, moved. Geralt, crouching by the wall, slowly drew his sword, careful not to let the blade grate against the scabbard. Ten paces from him, a pile of refuse suddenly arched up and heaved. The Witcher straightened and jumped before the wave of stench emanating from the disturbed midden reached him.

A tentacle ending in a rounded, tapering protuberance, bristling with spikes, suddenly shot out from under the rubbish, hurtling out towards him at incredible speed. The Witcher landed surely on the remains of a broken piece of furniture tottering on a pile of rotten vegetables, swayed, regained his balance, and slashed the tentacle with a short blow of his sword, cutting off the tentacular club. He sprang back at once, but this time slipped from the boards and sank up to his thighs in the boggy midden.

The rubbish heap erupted, throwing up viscous, foul-smelling slime, fragments of pots, rotten rags and pale threads of sauerkraut, and from beneath it all burst an enormous, bulbous body, as deformed as a grotesque potato, lashing the air with three tentacles and the stump of a fourth.

Geralt, trapped and immobilised, struck with a broad twist of his hips, smoothly hacking off another tentacle. The remaining two, as thick as tree boughs, fell on him with force, plunging him more deeply into the waste. The body glided towards him, ploughing into the midden like a barrel being dragged along. He saw the hideous, bulbous shape snap open, gaping with a wide maw full of large, lumpish teeth.

He let the tentacles encircle his waist, pull him with a squelch from the stinking slime and drag him towards the body, now boring into the refuse heap with circular movements. The toothed maw snapped savagely and ferociously. Having been dragged close to the dreadful jaws, the Witcher struck with his sword, two-handed, the blade biting smoothly and easily. The obnoxious, sweetish odour took his breath away. The monster hissed and shuddered, and the tentacles released their grip, flapping convulsively in the air. Geralt, bogged down in the refuse, slashed again, backhanded, the blade repulsively crunching and grating on the bared teeth. The creature gurgled and drooped, but immediately swelled, hissing, vomiting putrid slime over the Witcher. Keeping his balance with strenuous movements of his legs, still stuck in the muck, Geralt broke free and lunged forward, cleaving the refuse with his chest like a swimmer moving through water, and struck with all his strength from above, powerfully bearing down on the blade as it cut into the body, between the weakly glowing eyes. The monster groaned, flapped around, unfolding onto the pile of muck like a punctured bladder, emitting palpable, warm gusts of stench. The tentacles twitched and writhed among the rubbish.

The Witcher clambered out of the treacly slime and stood on slippery but hard ground. He felt something sticky and revolting which had got into his boot crawling over his calf. To the well, he thought, wash it off, wash off all the repulsiveness as soon as possible. Wash myself. The creature's tentacles flapped on the refuse one last time, sloppy and wet, and then stopped moving.

A star fell, a brief flash of lightning illuminating the black firmament, flecked with unmoving dots of light. The Witcher made no wish.

He was breathing heavily, wheezing, and feeling the effects of the elixirs he had drunk before the fight wearing off. The gigantic heap of rubbish and waste piled up against the town walls, descending steeply towards the glistening ribbon of the river, looked pretty and alluring in the starlight. The Witcher spat.

The monster was dead, now part of the midden where it had dwelled.

Another star fell.

'A garbage heap,' the Witcher said with effort. 'Muck, filth and shit.'

II

'You reek, Geralt,' Yennefer grimaced, not turning from the mirror, where she was cleaning off the colouring from her eyelids and eyelashes. 'Take a bath.'

'There's no water,' he said, looking into the tub.

'We shall remedy that,' the sorceress stood up and threw the window open. 'Do you prefer sea water or fresh water?'

'Sea water, for a change.'

Yennefer spread her arms vigorously and shouted a spell, making a brief, intricate movement with her hands. Suddenly a sharp, wet coldness blew in through the open window, the shutters juddered, and a green cloud gushed into the room with a hiss, billowing in an irregular sphere. The tub foamed with water, rippling turbulently, banging against the edges and splashing onto the floor. The sorceress sat down and resumed her previously interrupted activity.

'How did it go?' she asked. 'What was it, on the midden?'

'A zeugl, as I suspected,' Geralt said, pulling off his boots, discarding his clothes and lowering a foot into the tub. 'Bloody hell, Yen, that's cold. Can't you heat the water?'

'No,' the sorceress, moving her face towards the looking glass and instilling something into her eye using a thin glass rod. 'That spell is bloody wearying and makes me feel sick. And the cold will do you good after the elixirs.'

Geralt did not argue. There was absolutely no point arguing with Yennefer.

'Did the zeugl cause you any problems?' The sorceress dipped the rod into a vial and dropped something into her other eye, twisting her lips comically.

'Not particularly.'

From outside the open window there was a thud, the sharp crack of wood breaking and an inarticulate voice, tunelessly and incoherently repeating the chorus of a popular, obscene song.

'A zeugl,' said the sorceress as she reached for another vial from the impressive collection on the table, and removed the cork from it. The fragrance of lilac and gooseberries filled the room. 'Well, well. Even in a town it's easy for a witcher to find work, you don't have to roam through the wilds at all. You know, Istredd maintains it's becoming a general rule. The place of every creature from the forests and swamps that becomes extinct is occupied by something else, some new mutation, adapted to the artificial environment created by people.'

As usual, Geralt winced at the mention of Istredd. He was beginning to be sick of Yennefer's admiration for Istredd's brilliance. Even if Istredd was right.

'Istredd is right,' Yennefer continued, applying the lilac-and-gooseberry perfumed something to her cheeks and eyelids. 'Look for yourself; pseudorats in sewers and cellars, zeugls in rubbish dumps, neocorises in polluted moats and sewers, taggirs in millponds. It's virtually symbiosis, don't you think?'

And ghouls in cemeteries, devouring corpses the day after the funeral, he thought, rinsing off the soap. Total symbiosis.

'Yes,' the sorceress put aside the vials and jars, 'witchers can be kept busy in towns, too. I think one day you'll settle in a city for good, Geralt.'

I'd rather drop dead, he thought. But he did not say it aloud. Contradicting Yennefer, as he knew, inevitably led to a fight, and a fight with Yennefer was not the safest thing.

'Have you finished, Geralt?'

'Yes.'

'Get out of the tub.'

Without getting up, Yennefer carelessly waved a hand and uttered a spell. The water from the tub – including everything which had spilled onto the floor or was dripping from Geralt – gathered itself with a swoosh into a translucent sphere and whistled through the window. He heard a loud splash.

'A pox on you, whoresons!' an infuriated yell rang out from below. 'Have you nowhere to pour away your piss? I bloody hope you're eaten alive by lice, catch the ruddy pox and croak!'

The sorceress closed the window.

'Dammit, Yen,' the Witcher chuckled. 'You could have chucked the water somewhere else.'

'I could have,' she purred, 'but I didn't feel like it.'

She took the oil lamp from the table and walked over to him. The white nightdress clinging to her body as she moved made her tremendously appealing. More so than if she were naked, he thought.

'I want to look you over,' she said, 'the zeugl might have injured you.'

'It didn't. I would have felt it.'

'After the elixirs? Don't be ridiculous. After the elixirs you wouldn't even have felt an open fracture, until the protruding bones started snagging on hedges. And there might have been anything on the zeugl, including tetanus and cadaveric poison. If anything happens there's still time for counter-measures. Turn around.'

He felt the soft warmth of the lamp's flame on his body and the occasional brushing of her hair.

'Everything seems to be in order,' she said. 'Lie down before the elixirs knock you off your feet. Those mixtures are devilishly dangerous. They'll destroy you in the end.'

'I have to take them before I fight.'

Yennefer did not answer. She sat down at the looking glass once more and slowly combed her black, curly, shimmering locks. She always combed her hair before going to bed. Geralt found it peculiar, but he adored watching her doing it. He suspected Yennefer was aware of it.

He suddenly felt very cold, and the elixirs indeed jolted him, numbed the nape of his neck and swirled around the bottom of his stomach in vortices of nausea. He cursed under his breath and fell heavily onto the bed, without taking his eyes off Yennefer.

A movement in the corner of the chamber caught his attention. A smallish, pitch-black bird sat on a set of antlers nailed crookedly to the wall and festooned in cobwebs.

Glancing sideways, it looked at the Witcher with a yellow, fixed eye.

'What's that, Yen? How did it get here?'

'What?' Yennefer turned her head. 'Oh, that. It's a kestrel.'

'A kestrel? Kestrels are rufous and speckled, and that one's black.'

'It's an enchanted kestrel. I made it.'

'What for?'

'I need it,' she cut him off. Geralt did not ask any more questions, knowing that Yennefer would not answer.

'Are you seeing Istredd tomorrow?'

The sorceress moved the vials to the edge of the table, put her comb into a small box and closed the side panels of the looking glass.

'Yes. First thing. Why?'

'Nothing.'

She lay down beside him, without snuffing out the lamp. She never doused lights; she could not bear to fall asleep in the dark. Whether an oil lamp, a lantern, or a candle, it had to burn right down. Always. One more foible. Yennefer had a remarkable number of foibles.

'Yen?'

'Uh-huh?'

'When are we leaving?'

'Don't be tedious,' she tugged the eiderdown sharply. 'We've only been here three days, and you've asked that question at least thirty times. I've told you, I have things to deal with.'

'With Istredd?'

'Yes,'

He sighed and embraced her, not concealing his intentions.

'Hey,' she whispered. 'You've taken elixirs . . .'

'What of it?'

'Nothing,' she giggled like a schoolgirl, cuddling up to him, arching her body and lifting herself to allow her nightdress to slip off. As usual, the delight in her nakedness coursed in a shudder down his back and tingled in his fingers as they touched her skin. His lips touched her breasts, rounded and delicate, with nipples so pale they were visible only by their contours. He entwined his fingers in her hair, her lilac-and-gooseberry perfumed hair.

She succumbed to his caresses, purring like a cat, rubbing her bent knee against his hip.

It rapidly turned out – as usual – that he had overestimated his stamina regarding the witcher elixirs, had forgotten about their disagreeable effects on his body. But perhaps it's not the elixirs, he thought, perhaps it's exhaustion brought on by fighting, risks, danger and death? Exhaustion, which has simply become routine? But my body, even though artificially enhanced, doesn't succumb to routine. It reacts naturally. Just not when it's supposed to. Dammit.

But Yennefer, as usual, was not discouraged by a mere trifle. He felt her touch him, heard her purr right by his ear. As usual, he involuntarily pondered over the colossal number of occasions she must have used that most practical of spells. And then he stopped pondering.

As usual it was anything but ordinary.

He looked at her mouth, at its corners, twitching in an unwitting smile. He knew that smile well, it always seemed to him more one of triumph than of happiness. He had never asked her about it. He knew she would not answer.

The black kestrel sitting on the antlers beat its wings and snapped its curved beak. Yennefer turned her head away and sighed. Very sadly.

'Yen?'

'It's nothing, Geralt,' she said, kissing him. 'It's nothing.'

The oil lamp glimmered and flickered. A mouse was scratching in the wall, and a deathwatch beetle in the dresser clicked softly, rhythmically and monotonously.

'Yen?'

'Mhm?'

'Let's get away. I feel bad here. This town has an awful effect on me.'

She turned over on her side, ran a hand across his cheek, brushing some strands of hair away. Her fingers travelled downwards, touching the coarse scars marking the side of his neck.

'Do you know what the name of this town means? Aedd Gynvael?'

'No. Is it in the elven speech?'

'Yes. It means a shard of ice.'

'Somehow, it doesn't suit this lousy dump.'

'Among the elves,' the sorceress whispered pensively, 'there is a legend about a Winter Queen who travels the land during snowstorms in a sleigh drawn by white horses. As she rides, she casts hard, sharp, tiny shards of ice around her, and woe betide anyone whose eye or heart is pierced by one of them. That person is then lost. No longer will anything gladden them; they find anything that doesn't have the whiteness of snow ugly, obnoxious, repugnant. They will not find peace, will abandon everything, and will set off after the Queen, in pursuit of their dream and love. Naturally, they will never find it and will die of longing. Apparently here, in this town, something like that happened in times long gone. It's a beautiful legend, isn't it?'

'Elves can couch everything in pretty words,' he muttered drowsily, running his lips over her shoulder. 'It's not a legend at all, Yen. It's a pretty description of the hideous phenomenon that is the Wild Hunt, the curse of several regions. An inexplicable, collective madness, compelling people to join a spectral cavalcade rushing across the sky. I've seen it. Indeed, it often occurs during the winter. I was offered rather good money to put an end to that blight, but I didn't take it. There's no way of dealing with the Wild Hunt . . .'

'Witcher,' she whispered, kissing his cheek, 'there's no romance in you. And I . . . I like elven legends, they are so captivating. What a pity humans don't have any legends like that. Perhaps one day they will? Perhaps they'll create some? But what would human legends deal with? All around, wherever one looks, there's greyness and dullness. Even things which begin beautifully lead swiftly to boredom and dreariness, to that human ritual, that wearisome rhythm called life. Oh, Geralt, it's not easy being a sorceress, but comparing it to mundane, human existence . . . Geralt?' She laid her head on his chest, which was rising and falling with slow breathing.

'Sleep,' she whispered. 'Sleep, Witcher.'

III

The town was having a bad effect on him.

Since first thing that morning everything was spoiling his mood, making him dejected and angry. Everything. It annoyed him that he had overslept, so the morning had become to all intents and purposes the afternoon. He was irritated by the absence of Yennefer, who had left before he woke up.

She must have been in a hurry, because the paraphernalia she usually neatly put away in boxes was lying on the table, randomly strewn like dice cast by a soothsayer performing a prophecy ritual. Brushes made from delicate horsehair: the large ones used for powdering her face, the smaller ones which she used to apply lipstick to her mouth, and the utterly tiny ones for the henna she used to dye her eyelashes. Pencils and sticks for her eyelids and eyebrows. Delicate silver tweezers and spoons. Small jars and bottles made of porcelain and milky glass, containing, as he knew, elixirs and balms with ingredients as banal as soot, goose grease and carrot juice, and as menacingly mysterious as mandrake, antimony, belladonna, cannabis, dragon's blood and the concentrated venom of the giant scorpion. And above all of that, all around, in the air, the fragrance of lilac and gooseberry, the scent she always used.

She was present in those objects. She was present in the fragrance. But she was not there.

He went downstairs, feeling anxiety and anger welling up in him. About everything.

He was annoyed by the cold, congealed scrambled egg he was served for breakfast by the innkeeper, who tore himself away for a moment from groping a girl in the kitchen. He was annoyed that the girl was no more than twelve years old. And had tears in her eyes.

The warm, spring weather and cheerful chatter of the vibrant streets did not improve Geralt's mood. He still did not enjoy being in Aedd Gynvael, a small town which he deemed to be a nasty parody of all the small towns he knew; it was grotesquely noisier, dirtier, more oppressive and more irritating.

He could still smell the faint stench of the midden on his clothes and in his hair. He decided to go to the bathhouse.

In the bathhouse, he was annoyed by the expression of the attendant, looking at his witcher medallion and his sword lying on the edge of the tub. He was annoyed by the fact that the attendant did not offer him a whore. He had no intention of availing himself of one, but in bathhouses everybody was offered them, so he was annoyed by the exception being made for him.

When he left, smelling strongly of lye ash soap, his mood had not improved, and Aedd Gynvael was no more attractive. There was still nothing there that he could find to like. The Witcher did not like the piles of sloppy manure filling the narrow streets. He did not like the beggars squatting against the wall of the temple. He did not like the crooked writing on the wall reading: 'ELVES TO THE RESERVATION!'.

He was not allowed to enter the castle; instead they sent him to speak to the mayor in the merchants' guild. That annoyed him. He was also annoyed when the dean of the guild, an elf, ordered him to search for the mayor in the market place, looking at him with a curious contempt and superiority for someone who was about to be sent to a reservation.

The market place was teeming with people; it was full of stalls, carts, wagons, horses, oxen and flies. On a platform stood a pillory with a criminal being showered by the throng in mud and dung. The criminal, with admirable composure, showered his tormentors with vile abuse, making little effort to raise his voice.

For Geralt, who possessed considerable refinement, the mayor's reason for being among this clamour was absolutely clear. The visiting merchants from caravans included bribes in their prices, and thus had to give someone the bribes. The mayor, well aware of this custom, would appear, to ensure that the merchants would not have to go to any trouble.

The place from which he officiated was marked by a dirty-blue canopy supported on poles. Beneath it stood a table besieged by vociferous applicants. Mayor Herbolth sat behind the table, displaying on his faded face scorn and disdain to all and sundry.

'Hey! Where might you be going?'

Geralt slowly turned his head. He instantly suppressed the anger he felt inside, overcame his annoyance and froze into a cold, hard shard of ice. He could not allow himself to become emotional. The man who stopped him had hair as yellow as oriole feathers and the same colour eyebrows over pale, empty eyes. His slim, long-fingered hands were resting on a belt made from chunky brass plates, weighed down by a sword, mace and two daggers.

'Aha,' the man said. 'I know you. The Witcher, isn't it? To see Herbolth?'

Geralt nodded, watching the man's hands the whole time. He knew it would be dangerous to take his eyes off them.

'I've heard of you, the bane of monsters,' said the yellow-haired man, also vigilantly observing Geralt's hands. 'Although I don't think we've ever met, you must also have heard of me. I'm Ivo Mirce. But everyone calls me Cicada.'

The Witcher nodded to indicate he had heard of him. He also knew the price that had been offered for Cicada's head in Vizima, Caelf and Vattweir. Had he been asked his opinion he would have said it was a low price. But he had not been asked.

'Very well,' Cicada said. 'The mayor, from what I know, is waiting for you. You may go on. But you leave your sword, friend. I'm paid here, mark you, to make sure etiquette is observed. No one is allowed to approach Herbolth with a weapon. Understood?'

Geralt shrugged indifferently, unfastened his belt, wrapped it around the scabbard and handed the sword to Cicada. Cicada raised the corners of his mouth in a smile.

'Well, well,' he said. 'How meek, not a word of protest. I knew the rumours about you were exaggerated. I'd like you to ask for my sword one day; then you'd see my answer.'

'Hi, Cicada!' the mayor called, getting up. 'Let him through! Come here, Lord Geralt, look lively, greetings to you. Step aside, my dear merchants, leave us for a moment. Your business dealings must yield to issues of greater note for the town. Submit your entreaties to my secretary!'

The sham geniality of the greeting did not deceive Geralt. He knew it served exclusively as a bargaining ploy. The merchants were being given time to worry whether their bribes were sufficiently high.

'I'll wager Cicada tried to provoke you,' Herbolth said, raising his hand nonchalantly in response to the Witcher's equally nonchalant nod. 'Don't fret about it. Cicada only draws his weapon when ordered to. True, it's not especially to his liking, but while I pay him he has to obey, or he'll be out on his ear, back on the highway. Don't fret about it.'

'Why the hell do you need someone like Cicada, mayor? Is it so dangerous here?'

'It's not dangerous, because I'm paying Cicada,' Herbolth laughed. 'His fame goes before him and that suits me well. You see, Aedd Gynvael and the other towns in the Dogbane valley fall under the authority of the viceroys of Rakverelin. And in recent times the viceroys have changed with every season. No one knows why they keep changing, because anyway every second one is a half-elf or quarter-elf; accursed blood and race. Everything bad is the fault of the elves.'

Geralt did not add that it was also the fault of the carters, because the joke, although well-known, did not amuse everybody.

'Every new viceroy,' Herbolth continued in a huff, 'begins by removing the castellans and mayors of the old regime, in order to give his friends and relations jobs. But after what Cicada once did to the emissaries of a certain viceroy, no one tries to unseat me from my position any more and I'm the oldest mayor of the oldest regime. Which one, I can't even remember. Well, but we're sitting here chin-wagging, and we need to get on, as my late first wife was wont to say. Let's get to the point. What kind of creature had infested our muck heap?'

'A zeugl.'

'First time I've ever heard of anything like that. I trust it's dead?'

'It is.'

'How much will it cost the town treasury? Seventy?'

'A hundred.'

'Oh, really, Witcher, sir! You must have been drinking hemlock! A hundred marks for killing a lousy worm that burrowed into a pile of shit?'

'Worm or no worm, mayor, it devoured eight people, as you said yourself.'

'People? I like that! The brute, so I am informed, ate old Zakorek, who was famous for never being sober, one old bag from up near the castle and several children of the ferryman Sulirad, which wasn't discovered very quickly, because Sulirad himself doesn't know how many children he has. He produces them too quickly to count them. People, my hat! Eighty.'

'Had I not killed the zeugl, it would soon have devoured somebody more important. The apothecary, let us say. And then where would you get your chancre ointment from? One hundred.'

'A hundred marks is a good deal of money. I don't know if I'd give that much for a nine-headed hydra. Eighty-five.'

'A hundred, Mayor Herbolth. Mark that although it wasn't a nine-headed hydra, no local man, including the celebrated Cicada, was capable of dealing with the zeugl.'

'Because no local man is accustomed to slopping around in dung and refuse. This is my last word: ninety.'

'A hundred.'

'Ninety-five, by all the demons and devils!'

'Agreed.'

'Well, now,' Herbolth said, smiling broadly, 'that's settled. Do you always bargain so famously, Witcher?'

'No,' Geralt did not smile. 'Seldom, actually. But I wanted to give you the pleasure, mayor.'

'And you did, a pox on you,' Herbolth cackled. 'Hey, Peregrib! Over here! Give me the ledger and a purse and count me out ninety marks at once.'

'It was supposed to be ninety-five.'

'What about the tax?'

The Witcher swore softly. The mayor applied his sprawling mark to the receipt and then poked around in his ear with the clean end of the quill.

'I trust things'll be quiet on the muck heap now? Hey, Witcher?'

'Ought to be. There was only one zeugl. Though there is a chance it managed to reproduce. Zeugls are hermaphroditic, like snails.'

'What poppycock is that?' Herbolth asked, looking askance at him. 'You need two to reproduce, I mean a male and a female. What, do those zeugls hatch like fleas or mice, from the rotten straw in a palliasse? Every dimwit knows there aren't he-mice and she-mice, that they're all identical and hatch out of themselves from rotten straw.'

'And snails hatch from wet leaves,' secretary Peregrib interjected, still busy piling up coins.

'Everyone knows,' Geralt concurred, smiling cheerfully. 'There aren't he-snails and she-snails. There are only leaves. And anyone who thinks differently is mistaken.'

'Enough,' the mayor interrupted, looking at him suspiciously. 'I've heard enough about vermin. I asked whether anything might hatch from the muck heap, so be so gracious as to answer, clearly and concisely.'

'In a month or so the midden ought to be inspected, ideally using dogs. Young zeugls aren't dangerous.'

'Couldn't you do it, Witcher? We can come to agreement about payment.'

'No,' Geralt said, taking the money from Peregrib's hands. 'I have no intention of being stuck in your charming town for even a week, quite less a month.'

'Fascinating, what you're telling me.' Herbolth smiled wryly, looking him straight in the eye. 'Fascinating, indeed. Because I think you'll be staying here longer.'

'You think wrong, mayor.'

'Really? You came here with that black-haired witch, what was it again, I forget . . . Guinevere, wasn't it? You've taken lodgings with her at The Sturgeon. In a single chamber, they say.'

'And what of it?'

'Well, whenever she comes to Aedd Gynvael, she does not leave so quickly. It's not the first time she's been here.'

Peregrib smiled broadly, gap-toothed and meaningfully. Herbolth continued to look Geralt in the eye, without smiling. Geralt also smiled, as hideously as he could.

'Actually, I don't know anything,' the mayor looked away and bored his heel into the ground. 'And it interests me as much as dog's filth. But the wizard Istredd is an important figure here, mark you. Indispensable to this municipality. Invaluable, I'd say. People hold him in high regard, locals and outsiders, too. We don't stick our noses in his sorcery and especially not in his other matters.'

'Wisely, perhaps,' the Witcher agreed. 'And where does he live, if I may ask?'

'You don't know? Oh, it's right there, do you see that house? That tall, white one stuck between the storehouse and the armoury like, if you'll pardon the expression, a candle between two arsecheeks. But you won't find him there now. Not long ago, Istredd dug something up by the southern embankment and is now burrowing around there like a mole. And he's put some men to work on the excavation. I went over there and asked politely, why, master, are you digging holes like a child, folk are beginning to laugh. What is in that ground there? And he looks at me like I'm some sort of pillock and says: "History". What do you mean, history? I asks. And he goes: "The history of humanity. Answers to questions. To the question of what there was, and the question of what there will be". There was fuck-all here, I says to that, except green fields, bushes and werewolves, before they built the town. And what there will be depends on who they appoint viceroy in Rakverelin; some lousy half-elf again. And there's no history in the ground, there's nothing there, except possibly worms, if someone's fond of angling. Do you think he listened? Fat chance. He's still digging. So if you want to see him, go to the southern embankment.'

'Oh, come on, mayor,' Peregrib snorted. ''E's at 'ome now. Why would 'e want to be at the diggings, when he's . . .'

Herbolth glanced at him menacingly. Peregrib bent over and

cleared his throat, shuffling his feet. The Witcher, still smiling unpleasantly, crossed his arms on his chest.

'Yes, hem, hem,' the mayor coughed. 'Who knows, perhaps Istredd really is at home. After all, what does it . . .'

'Farewell, mayor,' Geralt said, not even bothering with an imitation of a bow. 'I wish you a good day.'

He went over to Cicada, who was coming out to meet him, his weapons clinking. Without a word he held out his hand for his sword, which Cicada was holding in the crook of his elbow. Cicada stepped back.

'In a hurry, Witcher?'

'Yes.'

'I've examined your sword.'

Geralt shot a look at him which, with the best will in the world, could not have been described as warm.

'That's quite something,' he nodded. 'Not many have. And even fewer could boast about it.'

'Ho, ho.' Cicada flashed his teeth. 'That sounded so menacing it's given me the shivers. It's always interested me, Witcher, why people are so afraid of you. And now I think I know.'

'I'm in a hurry, Cicada. Hand over the sword, it you don't mind.'

'Smoke in the eyes, Witcher, nothing but smoke. You witchers frighten people like a beekeeper frightens his bees with smoke and stench, with your stony faces, with all your talk and those rumours, which you probably spread about yourselves. And the bees run from the smoke, foolish things, instead of shoving their stings in the witcher's arse, which will swell up like any other. They say you can't feel like people can. That's lies. If one of you was properly stabbed, you'd feel it.'

'Have you finished?'

'Yes,' Cicada said, handing him back his sword. 'Know what interests me, Witcher?'

'Yes. Bees.'

'No. I was wondering if you was to enter an alley with a sword from one side and me from the other, who would come out the other side? I reckon it's worth a wager.'

'Why are you goading me, Cicada? Looking for a fight? What's it about?'

'Nothing. It just intrigues me how much truth there is in what folk say. That you're so good in a fight, you witchers, because there's no heart, soul, mercy or conscience in you. And that suffices? Because they say the same about me, for example. And not without reason. So I'm terribly interested which of us, after going into that alley, would come out of it alive. What? Worth a wager? What do you think?'

'I said I'm in a hurry. I'm not going to waste time on your nonsense. And I'm not accustomed to betting. But if you ever decide to hinder me walking down an alley, take my advice, Cicada, think about it first.'

'Smoke,' Cicada smiled. 'Smoke in the eyes, Witcher. Nothing more. To the next time. Who knows, maybe in some alley?'

'Who knows.'

IV

'We'll be able to talk freely here. Sit down, Geralt.'

What was most conspicuous about the workshop was the impressive number of books; they took up most of the space in the large chamber. Bulky tomes filled the bookcases on the walls, weighed down shelves, and were piled high on chests and cabinets. The Witcher judged that they must have cost a fortune. Of course, neither was there any shortage of other typical elements of décor: a stuffed crocodile, dried porcupine fish hanging from the ceiling, a dusty skeleton, and a huge collection of jars full of alcohol containing, it seemed, every conceivable abomination: centipedes, spiders, serpents, toads, and also countless human and non-human parts, mainly entrails. There was even a homunculus, or something that resembled a homunculus, but might just as likely have been a smoked new-born baby.

The collection made no impression on Geralt, who had lived with Yennefer in Vengerberg for six months, and Yennefer had a yet more fascinating collection, even including a phallus of exceptional proportions, allegedly that of a mountain troll. She also possessed a very expertly stuffed unicorn, on whose back she liked to make love. Geralt was of the opinion that if there existed a place less suitable for having sex it was probably only the back of a live unicorn. Unlike him, who considered his bed a luxury and valued all the possible uses of that marvellous piece of furniture, Yennefer was capable of being extremely extravagant. Geralt recalled some pleasant moments spent with the sorceress on a sloping roof, in a tree hollow full of rotten wood, on a balcony (someone else's, to boot), on the railing of a bridge, in a wobbly boat on a rushing river and levitating thirty fathoms above the earth. But the unicorn was the worst. One happy day, however, the dummy broke beneath him, split and fell apart, supplying much amusement.

'What amuses you so much, Witcher?' Istredd asked, sitting down behind a long table overlaid with a considerable quantity of mouldy skulls, bones and rusty ironware.

'Whenever I see things like that,' the Witcher said, sitting down opposite the sorceror, pointing at the array of jars, 'I wonder whether you really can't make magic without all that stomach-turning ghastliness.'

'It's a matter of taste,' the sorcerer said, 'and also of habit. What disgusts one person, somehow doesn't bother another. And what, Geralt, repels you? I wonder what might disgust someone, who, as I've heard, is capable of standing up to his neck in dung and filth? Please do not treat that question as insulting or provocative. I am genuinely fascinated to learn what might trigger a feeling of repugnance in a witcher.'

'Does this jar, by any chance, contain the menstrual blood of an undefiled virgin, Istredd? Well it disgusts me when I picture you, a serious sorcerer, with a phial in your hand, trying to obtain that precious liquid, drop by drop, kneeling, so to speak, at the very source.'

'Touché,' Istredd said, smiling. 'I refer, naturally, to your cutting wit, because as regards the jar's contents, you were wide of the mark.'

'But you do use blood occasionally, don't you? You can't even contemplate some spells, I've heard, without the blood of a virgin, ideally one killed by a lightning bolt from a clear sky during a full moon. In what way, one wonders, is that blood better than that of an old strumpet, who fell, drunk, from a palisade?'

'In no way,' the sorcerer agreed, a pleasant smile playing on his lips. 'But if it became common knowledge that that role could actually be played just as easily by hog's blood, which is much easier to obtain, then the rabble would begin experimenting with spells. But if it means the rabble having to gather and use virgin's blood, dragon's tears, white tarantula's venom, decoction of severed babies' hands or a corpse exhumed at midnight, many would think again.'

They were silent. Istredd, apparently deep in thought, tapped his fingernails on a cracked, browned skull, which lacked its lower jaw, and ran his index finger over the serrated edge of a hole gaping in the temporal bone. Geralt observed him unobtrusively. He wondered how old the sorcerer might be. He knew that the more talented among them were capable of curbing the ageing process permanently and at any age they chose. Men preferred a mature age, suggesting knowledge and experience, for reasons of reputation and prestige. Women, like Yennefer, were concerned less with prestige and more with attractiveness. Istredd looked no older than a well-earned, robust forty. He had straight, slightly grizzled, shoulder-length hair and numerous wrinkles on his forehead, around his mouth and at the corners of his eyelids. Geralt did not know whether the profundity and wisdom in his benign, grey eyes were natural or brought on by charms. A moment later he concluded that it made no difference.

'Istredd,' he interrupted the awkward silence, 'I came here because I wanted to see Yennefer. Even though she isn't here, you invited me inside. To talk. About what? About the rabble trying to break your monopoly on the use of magic? I know you include me among that rabble. That's nothing new to me. For a while I had the impression you would turn out to be different to your confreres, who have often entered into serious conversations with me, in order just to inform me that they don't like me.'

'I have no intention of apologising to you for my – as you call them – confreres,' the sorcerer answered calmly. 'I understand them for, just like them, in order to gain any level of proficiency at sorcery, I had to apply myself seriously. While still a mere stripling, when my peers were running around fields with bows, fishing or playing odds and evens, I was poring over manuscripts. My bones and joints ached from the stone floor in the tower – in the summer, of course, because in the winter the enamel on my teeth cracked. I would cough from the dust on old scrolls and books until my eyes bulged from their sockets, and my master, old Roedskilde, never passed up an opportunity to flog me with a knout, clearly believing that without it I would not achieve satisfactory progress in my studies. I didn't enjoy soldiering or wenching or drinking during the years when all those pleasures taste the best.'

'Poor thing,' the Witcher grimaced. 'Indeed, it brings a tear to my eye.'

'Why the sarcasm? I'm trying to explain why sorcerers aren't fond of village quacks, charmers, healers, wise women and witchers. Call it what you will, even simple envy, but here lies the cause of the animosity. It annoys us when we see magic – a craft we were taught to treat as an elite art, a privilege of the few and a sacred mystery – in the hands of laymen and dilettantes. Even if it is shoddy, pitiable, derisory magic. That is why my confreres don't like you. Incidentally, I don't like you either.'

Geralt had had enough of the discussion, of pussyfooting around, of the feeling of anxiety which was crawling over the nape of his neck and his back like a snail. He looked straight into Istredd's eyes and gripped the edge of the table.

'It's about Yennefer, isn't it?'

The sorcerer lifted his head, but continued to tap the skull on the table with his fingernails.

'I commend your perspicacity,' he said, steadily returning the Witcher's gaze. 'My congratulations. Yes, it's about Yennefer.'

Geralt was silent. Once, years ago, many, many years ago, as a young witcher, he had been waiting to ambush a manticore. And he sensed the manticore approaching. He did not see or hear it. He sensed it. He had never forgotten that feeling. And now he felt exactly the same.

'Your perspicacity,' the sorcerer went on, 'will save us a great deal of the time we would have wasted on further fudging. And this way the issue is out in the open.'

Geralt did not comment.

'My close acquaintance with Yennefer,' Istredd continued, 'goes back a long way, Witcher. For a long time it was an acquaintance without commitment, based on longer or shorter, more or less regular periods of time together. This kind of noncommittal partnership is widely practised among members of our profession. It's just that it suddenly stopped suiting me. I determined to propose to her that she remain with me permanently.'

'How did she respond?'

'That she would think it over. I gave her time to do so. I know it is not an easy decision for her.'

'Why are you telling me this, Istredd? What drives you, apart from this admirable – but astonishing – candour, so rarely seen among members of your profession? What lies behind it?'

'Prosaicness,' the sorcerer sighed. 'For, you see, your presence hinders Yennefer in making a decision. I thus request you to remove yourself. To vanish from her life, to stop interfering. In short: that you get the hell out of here. Ideally quietly and without saying good-bye, which, as she confided in me, you are wont to do.'

'Indeed,' Geralt smiled affectedly, 'your blunt sincerity astonishes me more and more. I might have expected anything, but not such a request. Don't you think that instead of asking me, you ought rather to leap out and blast me with ball lightning? You'd be rid of the obstacle and there'd just be a little soot to scrape off the wall. An easier – and more reliable – method. Because, you see, a request can be declined, but ball lightning can't be.'

'I do not countenance the possibility of your refusing.'

'Why not? Would this strange request be nothing but a warning preceding the lightning bolt or some other cheerful spell? Or is this request to be supported by some weighty arguments? Or a sum which would stupefy an avaricious witcher? How much do you intend to pay me to get out of the path leading to your happiness?'

The sorcerer stopped tapping the skull, placed his hand on it and clenched his fingers around it. Geralt noticed his knuckles whitening.

'I did not mean to insult you with an offer of that kind,' he said. 'I had no intention of doing so. But . . . if . . . Geralt, I *am* a sorcerer, and not the worst. I wouldn't dream of feigning omnipotence here, but I could grant many of your wishes, should you wish to voice them. Some of them as easily as this.'

He waved a hand, carelessly, as though chasing away a mosquito. The space above the table suddenly teemed with fabulously coloured Apollo butterflies.

'My wish, Istredd,' the Witcher drawled, shooing away the insects fluttering in front of his face, 'is for you to stop pushing in between me and Yennefer. I don't care much about the propositions

106

you're offering her. You could have proposed to her when she was with you. Long ago. Because then was then, and now is now. Now she's with me. You want me to get out of the way, make things easy for you? I decline. Not only will I not help you, but I'll hinder you, as well as my modest abilities allow. As you see, I'm your equal in candour.'

'You have no right to refuse me. Not you.'

'What do you take me for, Istredd?'

The sorcerer looked him in the eye and leaned across the table.

'A fleeting romance. A passing fascination, at best a whim, an adventure, of which Yenna has had hundreds, because Yenna loves to play with emotions; she's impulsive and unpredictable in her whims. That's what I take you for, since having exchanged a few words with you I've rejected the theory that she treats you entirely as an object. And, believe me, that happens with her quite often.'

'You misunderstood the question.'

'You're mistaken; I didn't. But I'm intentionally talking solely about Yenna's emotions. For you are a witcher and you cannot experience any emotions. You do not want to agree to my request, because you think she matters to you, you think she . . . Geralt, you're only with her because she wants it, and you'll only be with her as long as she wants it. And what you feel is a projection of her emotions, the interest she shows in you. By all the demons of the Netherworld, Geralt, you aren't a child; you know what you are. You're a mutant. Don't understand me wrongly. I don't say it to insult you or show you contempt. I merely state a fact. You're a mutant, and one of the basic traits of your mutation is utter insensitivity to emotions. You were created like that, in order to do your job. Do you understand? You cannot feel anything. What you take for emotion is cellular, somatic memory, if you know what those words mean.'

'It so happens I do.'

'All the better. Then listen. I'm asking you for something which I can ask of a witcher, but which I couldn't ask of a man. I am being frank with a witcher; with a man I couldn't afford to be frank. Geralt, I want to give Yenna understanding and stability, affection and happiness. Could you, hand on heart, pledge the same? No, you couldn't. Those are meaningless words to you. You trail after Yenna like a child, enjoying the momentary affection she shows you. Like a stray cat that everyone throws stones at, you purr, contented, because here is someone who's not afraid to stroke you. Do you understand what I mean? Oh, I know you understand. You aren't a fool, that's plain. You see yourself that you have no right to refuse me if I ask politely.'

'I have the same right to refuse as you have to ask,' Geralt drawled, 'and in the process they cancel each other out. So we return to the starting point, and that point is this: Yen, clearly not caring about my mutation and its consequences, is with me right now. You proposed to her, that's your right. She said she'd think it over? That's her right. Do you have the impression I'm hindering her in taking a decision? That she's hesitating? That I'm the cause of her hesitation? Well, that's my right. If she's hesitating, she clearly has reason for doing so. I must be giving her something, though perhaps the word is absent from the witcher dictionary.'

'Listen—'

'No. You listen to me. She used to be with you, you say? Who knows, perhaps it wasn't me but you who was the fleeting romance, a caprice, a victim of those uncontrolled emotions so typical of her. Istredd, I cannot even rule out her treatment of you as completely objectionable. That, my dear sorcerer, cannot be ruled out just on the basis of a conversation. In this case, it seems to me, the object may be more relevant than eloquence.'

Istredd did not even flinch, he did not even clench his jaw. Geralt admired his self-control. Nonetheless the lengthening silence seemed to indicate that the blow had struck home.

'You're playing with words,' the sorcerer said finally. 'You're becoming intoxicated with them. You try to substitute words for normal, human feelings, which you do not have. Your words don't express feelings, they are only sounds, like those that skull emits when you tap it. For you are just as empty as this skull. You have no right—'

'Enough,' Geralt interrupted harshly, perhaps even a little too harshly. 'Stop stubbornly denying me rights. I've had enough of it, do you hear? I told you our rights are equal. No, dammit, mine are greater.'

'Really?' the sorcerer said, paling somewhat, which caused Geralt unspeakable pleasure. 'For what reason?'

The Witcher wondered for a moment and decided to finish him off.

'For the reason,' he shot back, 'that last night she made love with me, and not with you.'

Istredd pulled the skull closer to himself and stroked it. His hand, to Geralt's dismay, did not even twitch.

'Does that, in your opinion, give you any rights?'

'Only one. The right to draw a few conclusions.'

'Ah,' the sorcerer said slowly. 'Very well. As you wish. She made love with *me* this morning. Draw your own conclusions, you have the right. I already have.'

The silence lasted a long time. Geralt desperately searched for words. He found none. None at all.

'This conversation is pointless,' he finally said, getting up, angry at himself, because it sounded blunt and stupid. 'I'm going.'

'Go to hell,' Istredd said, equally bluntly, not looking at him.

V

When she entered he was lying on the bed fully dressed, with his hands under his head.

He pretended to be looking at the ceiling. He looked at her.

Yennefer slowly closed the door behind her. She was ravishing.

How ravishing she is, he thought. Everything about her is ravishing. And menacing. Those colours of hers; that contrast of black and white. Beauty and menace. Her raven-black, natural curls. Her cheekbones, pronounced, emphasising a wrinkle, which her smile – if she deigned to smile – created beside her mouth, wonderfully narrow and pale beneath her lipstick. Her eyebrows, wonderfully irregular, when she washed off the kohl that outlined them during the day. Her nose, exquisitely too long. Her delicate hands, wonderfully nervous, restless and adroit. Her waist, willowy and slender, emphasised by an excessively tightened belt. Slim legs, setting in motion the flowing shapes of her black skirt. Ravishing.

She sat down at the table without a word, resting her chin on clasped hands.

'Very well, let's begin,' she said. 'This growing, dramatic silence is too banal for me. Let's sort this out. Get out of bed and stop staring at the ceiling looking upset. The situation is idiotic enough and there's no point making it any more idiotic. Get up, I said.'

He got up obediently, without hesitation, and sat astride the stool opposite her. She did not avoid his gaze. He might have expected that.

'As I said, let's sort it out and sort it out quickly. In order not to put you in an awkward situation, I'll answer any questions at once. You don't even have to ask them. Yes, it's true that when I came with you to Aedd Gynvael I was coming to meet Istredd and I knew

110

I would go to bed with him. I didn't expect it to come out, that you'd boast about it to each other. I know how you feel now and I'm sorry about that. But no, I don't feel guilty.'

He said nothing.

Yennefer shook her head, her shining, black locks cascading from her shoulders.

'Geralt, say something.'

'He . . .' The Witcher cleared his throat, 'he calls you Yenna.'

'Yes,' she said, not lowering her eyes, 'and I call him Val. It's his first name. Istredd is a nickname. I've known him for years. He's very dear to me. Don't look at me like that. You're also dear to me. And that's the whole problem.'

'Are you considering accepting his proposal?'

'For your information, I am. I told you, we've known each other for years. For . . . many years. We share common interests, goals and ambitions. We understand each other wordlessly. He can give me support, and – who knows – perhaps there'll come a day when I'll need it. And above all . . . he . . . he loves me. I think.'

'I won't stand in your way, Yen.'

She tossed her head and her violet eyes flashed with blue fire.

'In my way? Don't you understand anything, you idiot? If you'd been in my way, if you were bothering me, I'd have got rid of the obstacle in the blink of an eye, I'd have teleported you to the end of Cape Bremervoord or transported you to the land of Hann in a whirlwind. With a bit of effort I'd have embedded you in a piece of quartz and put you in the garden in a bed of peonies. I could have purged your brain such that you would have forgotten who I was and what my name was. I could have done all that had I felt like it. But I could also have simply said: "It was agreeable, farewell". I could have quietly taken flight, as you once did when you fled my house in Vengerberg.'

'Don't shout, Yen, don't be aggressive. And don't drag up that story from Vengerberg, we swore not to go back to it, after all. I don't bear a grudge against you, Yen, I'm not reproaching you, am I? I know you can't be judged by ordinary standards. And the fact that I'm saddened . . . the fact that I know I'm losing you . . . is cellular memory. The atavistic remnants of feelings in a mutant purged of emotion—'

'I can't stand it when you talk like that!' she exploded. 'I can't bear it when you use that word. Don't ever use it again in my presence. Never!'

'Does it change the fact? After all, I *am* a mutant.'

'There is no fact. Don't utter that word in front of me.'

The black kestrel sitting on the stag's antlers flapped its wings and scratched the perch with its talons. Geralt glanced at the bird, at its motionless, yellow eye. Once again, Yennefer rested her chin on clasped hands.

'Yen.'

'Yes, Geralt.'

'You promised to answer my questions. Questions I don't even have to ask. One remains; the most important. The one I've never asked you. Which I've been afraid to ask. Answer it.'

'I'm incapable of it, Geralt,' she said firmly.

'I don't believe you, Yen. I know you too well.'

'No one can know a sorceress well.'

'Answer my question, Yen.'

'My answer is: I don't know. But what kind of answer is that?'

They were silent. The din from the street had diminished, calmed down.

The sun setting in the west blazed through the slits of the shutters and pierced the chamber with slanting beams of light.

'Aedd Gynvael,' the Witcher muttered. 'A shard of ice . . . I felt it. I knew this town . . . was hostile to me. Evil.'

'Aedd Gynvael,' she repeated slowly. 'The sleigh of the Elf Queen. Why? Why, Geralt?'

'I'm travelling with you, Yen, because the harness of my sleigh got entangled, caught up in your runners. And a blizzard is all around me. And a frost. It's cold.'

'Warmth would melt the shard of ice in you, the shard I stabbed you with,' she whispered. 'Then the spell would be broken and you would see me as I really am.'

'Then lash your white horses, Yen. May they race north, where a thaw never sets in. I hope it never sets in. I want to get to your ice castle as quickly as I can.'

'That castle doesn't exist,' Yennefer said, her mouth twitching. She grimaced. 'It's a symbol. And our sleigh ride is the pursuit of a dream which is unattainable. For I, the Elf Queen, desire warmth. That is my secret. Which is why, every year, my sleigh carries me amidst a blizzard through some little town and every year someone dazzled by my spell gets their harness caught in my runners. Every year. Every year someone new. Endlessly. Because the warmth I so desire at the same time blights the spell, blights the magic and the charm. My sweetheart, stabbed with that little icy star, suddenly becomes an ordinary nobody. And I become, in his thawed out eyes, no better than all the other . . . mortal women . . .'

'And from under the unblemished whiteness emerges spring,' he said. 'Emerges Aedd Gynvael, an ugly little town with a beautiful name. Aedd Gynvael and its muck heap, that enormous, stinking pile of garbage which I have to enter, because they pay me to, because I was created to enter filth which fills other people with disgust and revulsion. I was deprived of the ability to feel so I wouldn't be able to feel how dreadfully vile is that vileness, so I wouldn't retreat from it, wouldn't run horror-stricken from it. Yes, I was stripped of feelings. But not utterly. Whoever did it made a botch of it, Yen.'

They were silent. The black kestrel rustled its feathers, unfurling and folding its wings.

'Geralt . . .'

'Yes, Yen.'

'Now you answer my question. The question I've never asked you. The one I've always feared. I won't ask you it this time, either, but answer it. Because . . . because I greatly desire to hear your answer. It's the one word, the only word you've never told me. Utter it, Geralt. Please.'

'I cannot, Yen.'

'Why not?'

'You don't know?' he smiled sadly. 'My answer would just be a word. A word which doesn't express a feeling, doesn't express an emotion, because I'm bereft of them. A word which would be 'nothing but the sound made when you strike a cold, empty skull.'

She looked at him in silence. Her eyes, wide open, assumed an ardent violet colour. 'No, Geralt,' she said, 'that's not the truth. Or perhaps it is, but not the whole truth. You aren't bereft of feeling. Now I see it. Now I know you . . .'

She was silent.

'Complete the sentence, Yen. You've decided. Don't lie. I know you. I can see it in your eyes.'

She did not lower her eyes. He knew.

'Yen,' he whispered.

'Give me your hand,' she said.

She took his hand between hers and at once he felt a tingling and the pulsing of blood in the veins of his forearm. Yennefer whispered a spell in a serene, measured voice, but he saw the beads of sweat which the effort caused to stipple her pale forehead, saw her pupils dilate in pain.

Releasing his arm, she extended her hands, and moved them, smoothing an invisible shape with tender strokes, slowly, from top to bottom. The air between her fingers began to congeal and become turbid, swell and pulsate like smoke.

He watched in fascination. Creational magic – considered the most elevated accomplishment among sorcerers – always fascinated him, much more than illusions or transformational magic. Yes, Istredd was right, he thought. In comparison with this kind of magic my Signs just look ridiculous.

The form of a bird, as black as coal, slowly materialised between Yennefer's hands, which were trembling with effort. The sorceress' fingers gently stroked the ruffled feathers, the small, flattened head and curved beak. One more hypnotically fluid, delicate movement and a black kestrel, turning its head, cried loudly. Its twin, still sitting motionless on the antlers, gave an answering cry.

'Two kestrels,' Geralt said softly. 'Two black kestrels, created by magic. I presume you need them both.'

'You presume right,' she said with effort. 'I need them both. I was wrong to believe one would suffice. How wrong I was, Geralt. To what an error the vanity of the Ice Queen, convinced of her omnipotence, has brought me. For there are some . . . things . . . which there is no way of obtaining, even by magic. And there are gifts which may not be accepted, if one is unable to . . . reciprocate them . . . with something equally precious. Otherwise such a gift will slip through the fingers, melt like a shard of ice gripped in the hand. Then only regret, the sense of loss and hurt will remain . . .'

'Yen—'

'I am a sorceress, Geralt . . . The power over matter which I possess is a gift. A reciprocated gift. For it I paid . . . with everything I possessed. Nothing remained.'

He said nothing. The sorceress wiped her forehead with a trembling hand.

'I was mistaken,' she repeated. 'But I shall correct my mistake. Emotions and feelings . . .'

She touched the black kestrel's head. The bird fluffed up its feathers and silently opened its curved beak.

'Emotions, whims and lies, fascinations and games. Feelings and their absence. Gifts, which may not be accepted. Lies and truth. What is truth? The negation of lies? Or the statement of a fact? And if the fact is a lie, what then is the truth? Who is full of feelings which torment him, and who is the empty carapace of a cold skull? Who? What is truth, Geralt? What is the essence of truth?'

'I don't know, Yen. Tell me.'

'No,' she said and lowered her eyes. For the first time. He had never seen her do that before. Never.

'No,' she repeated. 'I cannot, Geralt. I cannot tell you that. That bird, begotten from the touch of your hand, will tell you. Bird? What is the essence of truth?'

'Truth,' the kestrel said, 'is a shard of ice.'

VI

Although it seemed to him he was roaming the streets aimlessly and purposelessly, he suddenly found himself at the southern wall, by the excavations, among the network of trenches criss-crossing the ruins by the stone wall and wandering in zigzags among the exposed squares of ancient foundations.

Istredd was there. Dressed in a smock with rolled-up sleeves and high boots, he was shouting instructions to his servants, who were digging with hoes into the coloured stripes of earth, clay and charcoal which made up the walls of the excavation. Alongside, on planks, lay blackened bones, shards of pots and other objects; unidentifiable, corroded and gnarled into rusty lumps.

The sorcerer noticed him immediately. After giving the workers some loud instructions, he jumped out of the trench, and walked over, wiping his hands on his britches.

'Yes? What is it?' he asked bluntly.

The Witcher, standing in front of him without moving, did not answer. The servants, pretending to work, watched them attentively, whispering among themselves.

'You're almost bursting with hatred.' Istredd grimaced. 'What is it, I asked? Have you decided? Where's Yenna? I hope she—'

'Don't hope too much, Istredd.'

'Oho,' the sorcerer said. 'What do I hear in your voice? Is it what I sense it is?'

'And what is it you sense?'

Istredd placed his fists on his hips and looked at the Witcher provocatively.

'Let's not deceive ourselves, Geralt,' he said. 'I hate you and you hate me. You insulted me by saying that Yennefer . . . you know what. I came back with a similar insult. You're in my way and I'm in your way. Let's solve this like men. I don't see any other solution. That's why you've come here, isn't it?'

'Yes,' Geralt said, rubbing his forehead. 'That's right, Istredd. That's why I came here. Undeniably.'

'Indeed. It cannot go on like this. Only today did I learn that for several years Yenna has been circulating between us like a rag ball. First she's with me, then she's with you. She runs from me to look for you, then the other way around. The others she's with during the breaks don't count. Only we two count. This can't go on. There are two of us, but only one can remain.'

'Yes,' Geralt repeated, without removing his hand from his forehead. 'Yes . . . You're right.'

'In our conceit,' the sorcerer continued, 'we thought that Yenna would, without hesitation, choose the better man. Neither of us was in any doubt as to who that was. In the end, we started to argue over her favours like whipsters, and like foolish whipsters understood what those favours were and what they meant. I suppose that, like me, you've thought it through and know how mistaken the two of us were. Yenna, Geralt, hasn't the slightest intention of choosing between us, were we even to assume she's capable of choosing. Well, we'll have to decide for her. For I wouldn't dream of sharing Yenna with anyone, and the fact that you're here says the same about you. We, Geralt, simply know her too well. While there are two of us neither of us can be certain. There can only be one. That's the truth, isn't it?'

'It is,' the Witcher said, moving his numb lips with difficulty. 'The truth is a shard of ice . . .'

'What?'

'Nothing.'

'What's the matter with you? Are you infirm or in your cups? Or perhaps stuffed full of witcher herbs?'

'There's nothing wrong with me. I've . . . I've got something in my eye. Istredd, there can only be one. Yes, that's why I came here. Undeniably.'

'I knew,' the sorcerer said. 'I knew you'd come. As a matter of fact, I'm going to be frank with you. You anticipated my plans.'

'Ball lightning?' the Witcher asked, smiling wanly. Istredd frowned.

'Perhaps,' he said. 'Perhaps there'll be ball lightning. But definitely not shot from around the corner. Honourably, face to face. You're a witcher; that evens things out. Very well, decide when and where.'

Geralt pondered. And decided.

'That little square . . . he pointed. 'I passed through it . . .'

'I know. There's a well there called the Green Key.'

'By the well then. Yes indeed. By the well . . . Tomorrow, two hours after sunup.'

'Very well. I shall be on time.'

They stood still for a moment, not looking at each other. The sorcerer finally muttered something to himself, kicked a lump of clay and crushed it under his heel.

'Geralt?'

'What?'

'Do you feel foolish, by any chance?'

'Yes, I do,' the Witcher reluctantly admitted.

'That's a relief,' Istredd muttered. 'Because I feel like an utter dolt. I never expected I'd ever have to fight a witcher to the death over a woman.'

'I know how you feel, Istredd.'

'Well . . .' the sorcerer smiled affectedly. 'The fact that it's come to this, that I've decided to do something so utterly against my nature, proves that . . . that it has to be done.'

'I know, Istredd.'

'Needless to say, you know that whichever of us survives will have to flee at once and hide from Yenna at the end of the world?'

'I do.'

'And needless to say you count on being able to go back to her when she simmers down?'

'Of course.'

118

'It's all settled then,' the sorcerer said, and made to turn away, but after a moment's hesitation held out his hand to him. 'Till tomorrow, Geralt.'

'Till tomorrow,' the Witcher said, shaking his hand. 'Till tomorrow, Istredd.'

VII

'Hey, Witcher!'

Geralt looked up from the table, on which he had been absent-mindedly sketching fanciful squiggles in the spilled beer.

'It was hard to find you,' Mayor Herbolth said, sitting down and moving aside the jugs and beer mugs. 'They said in the inn that you'd moved out to the stables, but I only found a horse and some bundles of clothes there. And you're here . . . This is probably the most disreputable inn in the entire town. Only the worst scum comes here. What are you doing?'

'Drinking.'

'I can see that. I wanted to converse with you. Are you sober?'

'As a child.'

'I'm pleased.'

'What is it you want, Herbolth? As you can see, I'm busy,' Geralt smiled at the wench who was putting another jug on the table.

'There's a rumour doing the rounds,' the mayor said, frowning, 'that you and our sorcerer plan to kill each other.'

'That's our business. His and mine. Don't interfere.'

'No, it isn't your business,' Herbolth countered. 'We need Istredd, we can't afford another sorcerer.'

'Go to the temple and pray for his victory, then.'

'Don't scoff,' the mayor snapped, 'and don't be a smart-arse, you vagrant. By the Gods, if I didn't know that the sorcerer would never forgive me, I would have thrown you into the dungeons, right at the very bottom, or dragged you beyond the town behind two horses, or ordered Cicada to stick you like a pig. But, alas, Istredd has a thing about honour and wouldn't have excused me it. I know you wouldn't forgive me, either.'

'It's turned out marvellously,' the Witcher said, draining another mug and spitting out a straw which had fallen into it. 'I'm a lucky fellow, amn't I. Is that all?'

'No,' Herbolth said, taking a full purse out from under his coat. 'Here is a hundred marks, Witcher. Take it and get out of Aedd Gynvael. Get out of here, at once if possible, but in any case before sunrise. I told you we can't afford another sorcerer, and I won't let ours risk his neck in a duel with someone like you, for a stupid reason, because of some—'

He broke off, without finishing, although the Witcher did not even flinch.

'Take your hideous face away, Herbolth,' Geralt said. 'And stick your hundred marks up your arse. Go away, because the sight of you makes me sick. A little longer and I'll cover you in puke from your cap to your toes.'

The mayor put away the purse and put both hands on the table.

'If that's how you want it,' he said. 'I tried to let you leave of your own free will, but it's up to you. Fight, cut each other up, burn each other, tear each other to pieces for that slut, who spreads her legs for anyone who wants her. I think Istredd will give you such a thrashing, you thug, that only your boots will be left, and if not, I'll catch you before his body cools off and break all your bones on the wheel. I won't leave a single part of you intact, you—'

He did not manage to remove his hands from the table, the Witcher's movement was so swift. The arm which shot out from under the table was a blur in front of the mayor's eyes and a dagger lodged with a thud between his fingers.

'Perhaps,' the Witcher whispered, clenching his fist on the dagger's haft, and staring into Herbolth's face, from which the blood had drained, 'perhaps Istredd will kill me. But if not . . . Then I'll leave, and don't try to stop me, you vile scum, if you don't want the streets of your filthy town to foam with blood. Now get out of here.'

'Mayor. What's going on here? Hey, you—'

'Calm down, Cicada,' Herbolth said, slowly withdrawing his hand, cautiously sliding it across the table, as far as possible from the dagger's blade. 'It's nothing. Nothing.'

Cicada returned his half-drawn sword to its scabbard. Geralt did not look at him. He did not look at the mayor as he left the inn, shielded by Cicada from the staggering log drivers and carters. A small man with a ratty face and piercing, black eyes sitting a few tables away was watching him.

I'm annoyed, he realised in amazement. My hands are trembling. Really, my hands are trembling. It's astonishing what's happening to me. Could it mean that . . .?

Yes, he thought, looking at the little man with the ratty face. I think so.

I'll have to, he thought.

How cold it is . . .

He got up.

He smiled as he looked at the small man. Then he drew aside the front of his jacket, took two coins from the full purse and threw them on the table. The coins clinked. One of them rolled across the table and struck the dagger's blade, still stuck into the polished wood.

VIII

The blow fell unexpectedly, the club swished softly in the darkness, so fast that the Witcher only just managed to protect his head by instinctively raising an arm, and only just managed to cushion the blow by lithely twisting his body. He sprang aside, dropping on one knee, somersaulted, landed on his feet, felt a movement of the air yielding before another swing of the club, evaded the blow with a nimble pirouette, spinning between the two shapes closing in on him in the dark, and reached above his right shoulder. For his sword.

His sword was not there.

Nothing can take these reactions from me, he thought, leaping smoothly aside. Routine? Cellular memory? I'm a mutant, I react like a mutant, he thought, dropping to one knee again, dodging a blow, and reaching into his boot for his dagger. There was no dagger.

He smiled wryly and was hit on the head with a club. A light blazed in his eyes and the pain shot down to his fingertips. He fell, relaxing, still smiling.

Somebody flopped onto him, pressing him against the ground. Somebody else ripped the purse from his belt. His eye caught sight of a knife flashing. The one kneeling on his chest tore open his jerkin at the neck, seized the chain and pulled out his medallion. And immediately let go of it.

'By Baal-Zebuth,' Geralt heard somebody pant. 'It's a witcher . . . A real bruiser . . .'

The other swore, breathing heavily.

'He didn't have a sword . . . O Gods, save us from the Evil . . . Let's scarper, Radgast! Don't touch him.'

For a moment the moon shone through a wispy cloud. Geralt saw just above him a gaunt, ratty face and small, black, shining eyes. He heard the other man's loud footsteps fading away, vanishing into an alleyway reeking of cats and burnt fat.

The small man with the ratty face slowly removed his knee from Geralt's chest.

'Next time . . .' Geralt heard the clear whisper, 'next time you feel like killing yourself, Witcher, don't drag other people into it. Just hang yourself in the stable from your reins.'

It must have rained during the night.

Geralt walked out in front of the stable, wiping his eyes, combing the straw from his hair with his fingers. The rising sun glistened on the wet roofs, gleamed gold in the puddles. The Witcher spat. He still had a nasty taste in his mouth and the lump on his head throbbed with a dull ache.

A scrawny black cat sat on a rail in front of the stable, licking a paw intently.

'Here, kitty, kitty,' the Witcher said. The cat stopped what it was doing and looked at him malevolently, flattened its ears and hissed, baring its little fangs.

'I know,' Geralt nodded. 'I don't like you either. I'm only joking.'

He pulled tight the loosened buckles and clasps of his jerkin with unhurried movements, smoothed down the creases in his clothing, and made sure it did not hinder his freedom of movement at any point. He slung his sword across his back and adjusted the position of the hilt above his right shoulder. He tied a leather band around his forehead, pulling his hair back behind his ears. He pulled on long combat gloves, bristling with short, conical silver spikes.

He glanced up at the sun once more, his pupils narrowing into vertical slits. A glorious day, he thought. A glorious day for a fight.

He sighed, spat and walked slowly down the narrow road, beside walls giving off the pungent, penetrating aroma of wet plaster and lime mortar.

'Hey, freak!'

He looked around. Cicada, flanked by three suspicious-looking, armed individuals, sat on a heap of timbers piled up beside the embankment. He rose, stretched and walked into the middle of the alley, carefully avoiding the puddles.

'Where you going?' he asked, placing his slender hands on his belt, weighed down with weapons.

'None of your business.'

'Just to be clear, I don't give a tinker's cuss about the mayor, the sorcerer or this whole shitty town,' Cicada said, slowly emphasising the words. 'This is about you, Witcher. You won't make it to the end of this alley. Hear me? I want to find out how good a fighter you are. The matter's tormenting me. Stop, I said.'

'Get out of my way.'

'Stop!' Cicada yelled, placing a hand on his sword hilt. 'Didn't you hear what I said? We're going to fight! I'm challenging you! We'll soon see who's the better man!'

Geralt shrugged without slowing down.

'I'm challenging you to fight! Do you hear me, mutant?' Cicada shouted, barring his way again. 'What are you waiting for? Draw your weapon! What, got cold feet? Or perhaps you're nothing more than one of those other fools who's humped that witch of yours, like Istredd?'

Geralt walked on, forcing Cicada to retreat, to walk clumsily backwards. The individuals with Cicada got up from the pile of timbers and followed them, although they hung back a little way off. Geralt heard the mud squelching beneath their boots.

'I challenge you!' Cicada repeated, blanching and flushing by turns. 'Do you hear me, you witcher pox? What else do I have to do to you? Spit in your ugly face?'

'Go ahead and spit.'

Cicada stopped and indeed took a breath, pursing his lips to spit. He was watching the Witcher's eyes, not his hands, and that was a mistake. Geralt, still not slowing down, struck him very fast, without a backswing, just flexing from the knees, his fist encased in the spiked glove. He punched Cicada right in the mouth, straight in his twisted lips. They split, exploding like mashed cherries. The Witcher crouched and struck once again, in the same place, this time from a short backswing, feeling the fury spilling from him with the force and the momentum. Cicada, whirling around with one foot in the mud and the other in the air, spat blood and splashed onto his back into a puddle. The Witcher, hearing behind him the hiss of a sword blade in the scabbard, stopped and turned sinuously around, his hand on his sword hilt.

'Well,' he said in a voice trembling with anger, 'be my guests.'

The one who had drawn the sword looked him in the eyes. Briefly. Then he averted his gaze. The others began to fall back. First slowly, then more and more quickly. Hearing it, the man with the sword also stepped back, noiselessly moving his lips. The furthest away of them turned and ran, splattering mud. The others froze to the spot, not attempting to come closer.

Cicada turned over in the mud and dragged himself up on his elbows. He mumbled, hawked and spat out something white amid a lot of red. As Geralt passed he casually kicked him in the face, shattering his cheekbone, and sending him splashing into the puddle again.

He walked on without looking back.

Istredd was already by the well and stood leaning against it, against the wooden cover, green with moss. He had a sword in his belt. A magnificent, light, Terganian sword with a half-basket hilt, the metal-fitted end of the scabbard resting against the shining leg of a riding boot. A black bird with ruffled feathers sat on the sorcerer's shoulder.

It was a kestrel.

'You're here, Witcher,' Istredd said, proffering the kestrel a gloved hand and gently and cautiously setting the bird down on the canopy of the well.

'Yes, I am, Istredd.'

'I hadn't expected you to come. I thought you'd leave town.'

'I didn't.'

The sorcerer laughed loudly and freely, throwing his head back.

'She wanted . . . she wanted to save us,' he said. 'Both of us. Never mind, Geralt. Let's cross swords. Only one of us can remain.'

'Do you mean to fight with a sword?'

'Does that surprise you? After all, you do. Come on, have at you.'

'Why, Istredd? Why with swords and not with magic?'

The sorcerer blanched and his mouth twitched anxiously.

'Have at you, I said!' he shouted. 'This is not the time for questions; that time has passed! Now is the time for deeds!'

'I want to know,' Geralt said slowly. 'I want to know why with swords. I want to know why you have a black kestrel and where it came from. I have the right to know. I have the right to know the truth, Istredd.'

'The truth?' the sorcerer repeated bitterly. 'Yes, perhaps you have. Perhaps you have. Our rights are equal. The kestrel, you ask? It came at dawn, wet from the rain. It brought a letter. A very short one, I know it by heart. "Farewell, Val. Forgive me. There are gifts which one may not accept, and there is nothing in me I could repay you with. And that is the truth, Val. Truth is a shard of ice". Well, Geralt? Are you satisfied? Have you availed yourself of your right?'

The Witcher slowly nodded.

'Good,' Istredd said. 'Now I shall avail myself of mine. Because I don't acknowledge that letter. Without her, I cannot . . . I prefer to . . . Have at you, dammit!'

He crouched over and drew his sword with a swift, lithe movement, demonstrating his expertise. The kestrel cried.

The Witcher stood motionless, his arms hanging at his sides.

'What are you waiting for?' the sorcerer barked.

Geralt slowly raised his head, looked at him for a moment and then turned on his heel.

'No, Istredd,' he said quietly. 'Farewell.'

'What do you bloody mean?'

Geralt stopped.

'Istredd,' he said over his shoulder. 'Don't drag other people into your suicide. If you must, hang yourself in the stable from your reins.'

'Geralt!' the sorcerer screamed, and his voice suddenly cracked, jarring the ear with a false, wrong note. 'I'm not giving up! She won't run away from me! I'll follow her to Vengerberg, I'll follow her to the end of the world. I'll find her! I'll never give her up! Know that!'

'Farewell, Istredd.'

He walked off into the alley, without turning back at all. He walked, paying no attention to the people quickly getting out of his way, or to the hurried slamming of doors and shutters. He did not notice anybody or anything.

He was thinking about the letter waiting for him in the inn.

He speeded up. He knew that a black kestrel, wet from the rain, holding a letter in its curved beak, was waiting for him on the bed-head. He wanted to read the letter as soon as possible.

Even though he knew what was in it.

ETERNAL FLAME

I

'You pig! You plague-stricken warbler! You trickster!'

Geralt, his interest piqued, led his mare around the corner of the alleyway. Before he located the source of the screams, a deep, stickily glassy clink joined them. A large jar of cherry preserve, thought the Witcher. A jar of cherry preserve makes that noise when you throw it at somebody from a great height or with great force. He remembered it well. When he lived with Yennefer she would occasionally throw jars of preserve at him in anger. Jars she had received from clients. Yennefer had no idea how to make preserve – her magic was fallible in that respect.

A large group of onlookers had formed around the corner, outside a narrow, pink-painted cottage. A young, fair-haired woman in a nightdress was standing on a tiny balcony decorated with flowers, just beneath the steep eaves of the roof. Bending a plump, fleshy arm, visible beneath the frills of her nightdress, the woman hurled down a chipped flowerpot.

A slim man in a plum bonnet with a white feather jumped aside like a scalded cat, and the flowerpot crashed onto the ground just in front of him, shattering into pieces.

'Please, Vespula!' the man in the bonnet shouted, 'Don't lend credence to the gossip! I was faithful to you, may I perish if it is not true!'

'You bastard! You son of the Devil! You wretch!' the plump blonde yelled and went back into the house, no doubt in search of further missiles.

'Hey, Dandelion,' called the Witcher, leading his resisting and snorting mare onto the battlefield. 'How are you? What's going on?'

'Nothing special,' said the troubadour, grinning. 'The usual. Greetings, Geralt. What are you doing here? Bloody hell, look out!'

A tin cup whistled through the air and bounced off the cobbles with a clang. Dandelion picked it up, looked at it and threw it in the gutter.

'Take those rags,' the blonde woman screamed, the frills on her plump breasts swaying gracefully, 'and get out of my sight! Don't set foot here again, you bastard!'

'These aren't mine,' Dandelion said in astonishment, taking a pair of men's trousers with odd-coloured legs from the ground. 'I've never had trousers like these in my life.'

'Get out! I don't want to see you anymore! You . . . you . . . Do you know what you're like in bed? Pathetic! Pathetic, do you hear! Do you hear, everybody?'

Another flowerpot whistled down, a dried stalk that had grown out of it flapping. Dandelion barely managed to dodge. Following the flowerpot, a copper cauldron of at least two and a half gallons came spinning down. The crowd of onlookers standing a safe distance away from the cannonade reeled with laughter. The more active and unprincipled jokers among them applauded and incited the blonde to further action.

'She doesn't have a crossbow in the house, does she?' the Witcher asked anxiously.

'It can't be ruled out,' said the poet, lifting his head up towards the balcony. 'She has a load of junk in there. Did you see those trousers?'

'Perhaps we ought to get out of here? You can come back when she calms down.'

'Hell no,' Dandelion grimaced. 'I shall never go back to a house from which calumny and copper pots are showered on me. I consider this fickle relationship over. Let's just wait till she throws my . . . Oh, mother, no! Vespula! My lute!'

He lunged forward, arms outstretched, stumbled, fell and caught the instrument at the last moment, just above the cobbles. The lute spoke plaintively and melodiously.

'Phew,' sighed the bard, springing up, 'I've got it. It's fine, Geralt, we can go now. Admittedly my cloak with the marten collar is still there, but too bad, let it be my grievance. Knowing her she won't throw the cloak down.

'You lying sloven!' the blonde screamed and spat copiously from the balcony. 'You vagrant! You croaking pheasant!'

'What's the matter with her? What have you been up to, Dandelion?'

'Nothing unusual,' the troubadour shrugged. 'She demands monogamy, like they all do, and then throws another man's trousers at a fellow. Did you hear what she was screaming about me? By the Gods, I also know some women who decline their favours more prettily than she gives hers, but I don't shout about it from the rooftops. Let's go.'

'Where do you suggest we go?'

'Are you serious? The temple of the Eternal Fire? Let's drop into the Spear Blade. I have to calm my nerves.'

Without protest, the Witcher led his mare after Dandelion, who had headed off briskly into a narrow lane. The troubadour tightened the pegs of his lute as he strode, strummed the strings to test them, and played a deep, resounding chord.

The air bears autumn's cool scent
Our words seized by an icy gust
Your tears have my heart rent
But all is gone and part we must.

He broke off, waving cheerfully at two maids who were passing, carrying baskets of vegetables. The girls giggled.

'What brings you to Novigrad, Geralt?'

'Fitting out. A harness, some tackle. And a new jacket.' The Witcher pulled down the creaking, fresh-smelling leather. 'How do you like it, Dandelion?'

'You don't keep up with the fashion,' the bard grimaced, brushing a chicken feather from his gleaming, cornflower-blue kaftan with puffed sleeves and a serrated collar. 'Oh, I'm glad we've met. Here in Novigrad, the capital of the world, the centre and cradle of culture. *Here* a cultured man can live life to the full.'

'Let's live it one lane further on,' suggested Geralt, glancing at a tramp who had squatted down and was defecating, eyes bulging, in an alleyway.

'Your constant sarcasm is becoming annoying,' Dandelion said, grimacing again. 'Novigrad, I tell you, is the capital of the world. Almost thirty thousand dwellers, Geralt, not counting travellers; just imagine! Brick houses, cobbled main streets, a seaport, stores, shops, four watermills, slaughterhouses, sawmills, a large manufactory making beautiful slippers, and every conceivable guild and trade. A mint, eight banks and nineteen pawnbrokers. A castle and guardhouse to take the breath away. And diversions: a scaffold, a gallows with a drop, thirty-five taverns, a theatre, a menagerie, a market and a dozen whorehouses. And I can't remember how many temples, but plenty. Oh, and the women, Geralt; bathed, coiffured and fragrant; those satins, velvets and silks, those whalebones and ribbons . . . Oh, Geralt! The rhymes pour out by themselves:

Around your house, now white from frost
Sparkles ice on the pond and marsh
Your longing eyes grieve what is lost
But naught can change this parting harsh . . .

'A new ballad?'

'Aye. I'll call it *Winter*. But it's not ready yet, I can't finish it. Vespula's made me completely jittery and the rhymes won't come together. Ah, Geralt, I forgot to ask, how is it with you and Yennefer?'

'It isn't.'

'I understand.'

'No you bloody don't. Is it far to this tavern?'

'Just round the corner. Ah, here we are. Can you see the sign?'

'Yes, I can.'

'My sincere and humble greetings!' Dandelion flashed a smile at the wench sweeping the steps. 'Has anyone ever told you, my lady, that you are gorgeous?'

The wench flushed and gripped her broom tightly. For a moment Geralt thought she would whack the troubadour with the handle. He was mistaken. The wench smiled engagingly and fluttered her eyelashes. Dandelion, as usual, paid absolutely no attention.

'Greetings to one and all! Good day!' he bellowed, entering the tavern and plucking the lute strings hard with his thumb. 'Master Dandelion, the most renowned poet in this land, has visited your tawdry establishment, landlord! For he has a will to drink beer! Do you mark the honour I do you, swindler?'

'I do,' said the innkeeper morosely, leaning forward over the bar. 'I'm content to see you, minstrel, sir. I see that your word is indeed your bond. After all, you promised to stop by first thing to pay for yesterday's exploits. And I – just imagine – presumed you were lying, as usual. I swear I am ashamed.'

'There is no need to feel shame, my good man,' the troubadour said light-heartedly, 'for I have no money. We shall converse about that later.'

'No,' the innkeeper said coldly. 'We shall converse about it right away. Your credit has finished, my lord poet. No one befools me twice in a row.'

Dandelion hung up his lute on a hook protruding from the wall, sat down at a table, took off his bonnet and pensively stroked the egret's feather pinned to it.

'Do you have any funds, Geralt?' he asked with hope in his voice.

'No, I don't. Everything I had went on the jacket.'

'That is ill, that is ill,' Dandelion sighed. 'There's not a bloody soul to stand a round. Innkeeper, why is it so empty here today?'

'It's too early for ordinary drinkers. And the journeymen masons who are repairing the temple have already been and returned to the scaffolding, taking their master with them.'

'And there's no one, no one at all?'

'No one aside from the honourable merchant Biberveldt, who is breaking his fast in the large snug.'

'Dainty's here?' Dandelion said, pleased. 'You should have said at once. Come to the snug, Geralt. Do you know the halfling, Dainty Biberveldt?'

'No.'

'Never mind. You can make his acquaintance. Ah!' the troubadour called, heading towards the snug. 'I smell from the east a whiff and hint of onion soup, pleasing to my nostrils. Peekaboo! It's us! Surprise!'

A chubby-cheeked, curly-haired halfling in a pistachio-green waistcoat was sitting at the table in the centre of the chamber, beside a post decorated with garlands of garlic and bunches of herbs. In his left hand he held a wooden spoon and in his right an earthenware bowl. At the sight of Dandelion and Geralt, the halfling froze and opened his mouth, and his large nut-brown eyes widened in fear.

'What cheer, Dainty?' Dandelion said, blithely waving his bonnet. The halfling did not move or close his mouth. His hand, Geralt noticed, was trembling a little, and the long strips of boiled onion hanging from the spoon were swinging like a pendulum.

'Gggreetings ... gggreetings, Dandelion,' he stammered and swallowed loudly.

'Do you have the hiccoughs? Would you like me to frighten you? Look out: your wife's been seen on the turnpike! She'll be here soon. Gardenia Biberveldt in person! Ha, ha, ha!'

'You really are an ass, Dandelion,' the halfling said reproachfully.

Dandelion laughed brightly again, simultaneously playing two complicated chords on his lute.

'Well you have an exceptionally stupid expression on your face, and you're goggling at us as though we had horns and tails. Perhaps you're afraid of the Witcher? What? Perhaps you think halfling season has begun? Perhaps—'

'Stop it,' Geralt snapped, unable to stay quiet, and walked over to the table. 'Forgive us, friend. Dandelion has experienced a serious personal tragedy, and he still hasn't got over it. He's trying to mask his sorrow, dejection and disgrace by being witty.'

'Don't tell me,' the halfling said, finally slurping up the contents of the spoon. 'Let me guess. Vespula has finally thrown you out on your ear? What, Dandelion?'

'I don't engage in conversations on sensitive subjects with individuals who drink and gorge themselves while their friends stand,' the troubadour said, and then sat down without waiting. The half-ling scooped up a spoon of soup and licked off the threads of cheese hanging from it.

'Right you are,' he said glumly. 'So, be my guests. Sit you down, and help yourselves. Would you like some onion potage?'

'In principle I don't dine at such an early hour,' Dandelion said, putting on airs, 'but very well. Just not on an empty stomach. I say, landlord! Beer, if you please! And swiftly!'

A lass with an impressive, thick plait reaching her hips brought them mugs and bowls of soup. Geralt, observing her round, downy face, thought that she would have a pretty mouth if she remembered to keep it closed.

'Forest dryad!' Dandelion cried, seizing the girl's arm and kissing her on her open palm. 'Sylph! Fairy! O, Divine creature, with eyes like azure lakes! Thou art as exquisite as the morn, and the shape of thy parted lips are enticingly . . .'

'Give him some beer, quick,' Dainty groaned. 'Or it'll end in disaster.'

'No, it won't, no, it won't,' the bard assured him. 'Right, Geralt? You'd be hard pressed to find more composed men than we two. I, dear sir, am a poet and a musician, and music soothes the savage breast. And the Witcher here present is menacing only to monsters. I present Geralt of Rivia, the terror of strigas, werewolves and sundry vileness. You've surely heard of Geralt, Dainty?'

'Yes, I have,' the halfling said, glowering suspiciously at the Witcher. 'What . . . What brings you to Novigrad, sir? Have some dreadful monsters been sighted here? Have you been . . . hem, hem . . . commissioned?'

'No,' smiled the Witcher, 'I'm here for my own amusement.'

'Oh,' Dainty said, nervously wriggling his hirsute feet, which were dangling half a cubit above the floor, 'that's good . . .'

'What's good?' Dandelion asked, swallowing a spoonful of soup and sipping some beer. 'Do you plan to support us, Biberveldt? In our amusements, I mean? Excellent. We intend to get tipsy, here, in the Spear Blade. And then we plan to repair to the Passiflora, a very dear and high-class den of iniquity, where we may treat ourselves to a half-blood she-elf, and who knows, maybe even a pure-blood she-elf. Nonetheless, we need a sponsor.'

'What do you mean?'

'Someone to pay the bills.'

'As I thought,' Dainty muttered. 'I'm sorry. Firstly, I've arranged several business meetings. Secondly, I don't have the funds to sponsor such diversions. Thirdly, they only admit humans to the Passiflora.'

'What are we, then, short-eared owls? Oh, I understand? They don't admit halflings. That's true. You're right, Dainty. This is Novigrad. The capital of the world.'

'Right then . . .' the halfling said, still looking at the Witcher and twisting his mouth strangely. 'I'll be off. I'm due to be—'

The door to the chamber opened with a bang and in rushed . . .

Dainty Biberveldt.

'O, ye Gods!' Dandelion yelled.

The halfling standing in the doorway in no way differed from the halfling sitting at the table, if one were to disregard the fact that the one at the table was clean and the one in the doorway was dirty, dishevelled and haggard.

'Got you, you bitch's tail!' the dirty halfling roared, lunging at the table. 'You thief!'

His clean twin leaped to his feet, overturning his stool and knocking the dishes from the table. Geralt reacted instinctively and very quickly. Seizing his scabbarded sword from the table, he lashed Biberveldt on the nape of his neck with the heavy belt. The halfling tumbled onto the floor, rolled over, dived between Dandelion's legs and scrambled towards the door on all fours, his arms and legs suddenly lengthening like a spider's. Seeing this the dirty Dainty Biberveldt swore, howled and jumped out of the way, slamming his back into the wooden wall. Geralt threw aside the scabbard and kicked the stool out of the way, darting after him. The clean Dainty Biberveldt – now utterly dissimilar apart from the colour of his waistcoat – cleared the threshold like a grasshopper and hurtled into the common bar, colliding with the lass with the half-open mouth. Seeing his long limbs and melted, grotesque physiognomy, the lass opened her mouth to its full extent and uttered an ear-splitting scream. Geralt, taking advantage of the loss of momentum caused by the collision, caught up with the creature in the centre of the chamber and knocked it to the ground with a deft kick behind the knee.

'Don't move a muscle, chum,' he hissed through clenched teeth, holding the point of his sword to the oddity's throat. 'Don't budge.'

'What's going on here?' the innkeeper yelled, running over clutching a spade handle. 'What's this all about? Guard! Detchka, run and get the guard!'

'No!' the creature wailed, flattening itself against the floor and deforming itself even more. 'Have mercy, nooooo!'

'Don't call them!' the dirty halfling echoed, rushing out of the snug. 'Grab that girl, Dandelion!'

The troubadour caught the screaming Detchka, carefully choosing the places to seize her by. Detchka squealed and crouched on the floor by his legs.

'Calm down, innkeeper,' Dainty Biberveldt panted. 'It's a private matter, we won't call out the guard. I'll pay for any damage.'

'There isn't any damage,' the innkeeper said level-headedly, looking around.

'But there will be,' the plump halfling said, gnashing his teeth, 'because I'm going to thrash him. And properly. I'm going to thrash him cruelly, at length and frenziedly, and then everything here will be broken.'

The long-limbed and spread-out caricature of Dainty Biberveldt flattened on the floor snivelled pathetically.

'Nothing doing,' the innkeeper said coldly, squinting and raising the spade handle a little. 'Thrash it in the street or in the yard, sir, not here. And I'm calling the guard. Needs must, it is my duty. Forsooth . . . it's some kind of monster!'

'Innkeeper, sir,' Geralt said calmly, not relieving the pressure on the freak's neck, 'keep your head. No one is going to destroy anything, there won't be any damage. The situation is under control. I'm a witcher, and as you can see, I have the monster in my grasp. And because, indeed, it does look like a private matter, we'll calmly sort it out here in the snug. Release the girl, Dandelion, and come here. I have a silver chain in my bag. Take it out and tie the arms of this gentleman securely, around the elbows behind its back. Don't move, chum.'

The creature whimpered softly.

'Very well, Geralt,' Dandelion said, 'I've tied it up. Let's go to the snug. And you, landlord, what are you standing there for? I ordered beer. And when I order beer, you're to keep serving me until I shout "Water".'

Geralt pushed the tied-up creature towards the snug and roughly sat him down by the post. Dainty Biberveldt also sat down and looked at him in disgust.

'It's monstrous, the way it looks,' he said. 'Just like a pile of fermenting dough. Look at its nose, Dandelion, it'll fall off any second, gorblimey. And its ears are like my mother-in-law's just before her funeral. Ugh!'

'Hold hard, hold hard,' Dandelion muttered. 'Are you Biberveldt? Yes, you are, without doubt. But whatever's sitting by that post was you a moment ago. If I'm not mistaken. Geralt! Everybody's watching you. You're a witcher. What the bloody hell is going on here? What is it?'

'It's a mimic.'

'You're a mimic yourself,' the creature said in a guttural voice, swinging its nose. 'I am not a mimic, I'm a doppler, and my name is Tellico Lunngrevink Letorte. Penstock for short. My close friends call me Dudu.'

'I'll give you Dudu, you whoreson!' Dainty yelled, aiming a punch at him. 'Where are my horses? You thief!'

'Gentlemen,' the innkeeper cautioned them, entering with a jug and a handful of beer mugs, 'you promised things would be peaceful.'

'Ah, beer,' the halfling sighed. 'Oh, but I'm damned thirsty. And hungry!'

'I could do with a drink, too,' Tellico Lunngrevink Letorte declared gurglingly. He was totally ignored.

'What is it?' the innkeeper asked, contemplating the creature, who at the sight of the beer stuck its long tongue out beyond sagging, doughy lips. 'What is it, gentlemen?'

'A mimic,' the Witcher repeated, heedless of the faces the monster was making. 'It actually has many names. A changeling, shapeshifter, vexling, or fetch. Or a doppler, as it called itself.'

'A vexling!' the innkeeper yelled. 'Here, in Novigrad? In my inn? Swiftly, we must call the guard! And the priests! Or it will be on my head . . .'

'Easy does it,' Dainty Biberveldt rasped, hurriedly finishing off Dandelion's soup from a bowl which by some miracle had not been spilled. 'There'll be time to call anyone we need. But later. This scoundrel robbed me and I have no intention of handing it over to the local law before recovering my property. I know you Novigradians – and your judges. I might get a tenth, nothing more.'

'Have mercy,' the doppler whimpered plaintively. 'Don't hand me over to humans! Do you know what they do to the likes of me?'

'Naturally we do,' the innkeeper nodded. 'The priests perform exorcisms on any vexling they catch. Then they tie it up with a stick between its knees and cover it thickly with clay mixed with iron filings, roll it into a ball, and bake it in a fire until the clay hardens into brick. At least that's what used to be done years ago, when these monsters occurred more often.'

'A barbaric custom. Human indeed,' Dainty, said, grimacing and pushing the now empty bowl away, 'but perhaps it is a just penalty for banditry and thievery. Well, talk, you good-for-nothing, where are my horses? Quickly, before I stretch that nose of yours between your legs and shove it up your backside! Where are my horses, I said.'

'I've . . . I've sold them,' Tellico Lunngrevink Letorte stammered, and his sagging ears suddenly curled up into balls resembling tiny cauliflowers.

'Sold them! Did you hear that?' the halfling cried, frothing at the mouth. 'It sold my horses!'

'Of course,' Dandelion said. 'It had time to. It's been here for three days. For the last three days you've . . . I mean, it's . . . Dammit, Dainty, does that mean—'

'Of course that's what it means!' the merchant yelled, stamping his hairy feet. 'It robbed me on the road, a day's ride from the city! It came here as me, get it? And sold my horses! I'll kill it! I'll strangle it with my bare hands!'

'Tell us how it happened, Mr Biberveldt.'

'Geralt of Rivia, if I'm not mistaken? The Witcher?'

Geralt nodded in reply.

'That's a stroke of luck,' the halfling said. 'I'm Dainty Biberveldt of Knotgrass Meadow. Farmer, stock breeder and merchant. Call me Dainty, Geralt.'

'Say on, Dainty.'

'Very well, it was like this. Me and my ostlers were driving my horses to be sold at the market in Devil's Ford. We had our last stop a day's ride from the city. We overnighted, having first dealt with a small cask of burnt caramel vodka. I woke up in the middle of the night feeling like my bladder was about to burst, got off the wagon, and I thought to myself I'll take a look at what the nags are doing in the meadow. I walk out, fog thick as buggery, I look and suddenly someone's coming. Who goes there? I ask. He says nothing. I walk up closer and see . . . myself. Like in a looking glass. I think I oughtn't to have drunk that bloody moonshine, accursed spirit. And this one here – for that's what it was – ups and conks me on the noggin! I saw stars and went arse over tit. The next day I woke up in a bloody thicket, with a lump like a cucumber on my head, and not a soul in sight, not a sign of our camp, either. I wandered the whole day before I finally found the trail. Two days I trudged, eating roots and raw mushrooms. And in the meantime that . . . that lousy Dudulico, or whatever it was, has ridden to Novigrad as me and flogged my horses! I'll get the bloody . . . And I'll thrash my ostlers! I'll give each one a hundred lashes on his bare arse, the cretins! Not to recognise their own guvnor, to let themselves be outwitted like that! Numbskulls, imbeciles, sots . . .'

'Don't be too hard on them, Dainty,' Geralt said. 'They didn't have a chance. A mimic copies so exactly there's no way of distinguishing it from the original – I mean, from its chosen victim. Have you never heard of mimics?'

'Some. But I thought it was all fiction.'

'Well it isn't. All a doppler has to do is observe its victim closely in order to quickly and unerringly adapt to the necessary material structure. I would point out that it's not an illusion, but a complete, precise transformation. To the minutest detail. How a mimic does it, no one knows. Sorcerers suspect the same component of the blood is at work here as with lycanthropy, but I think it's either something totally different or a thousandfold more powerful. After all, a were-wolf has only two – at most three – different forms, while a doppler can transform into anything it wants to, as long as the body mass more or less tallies.'

'Body mass?'

'Well, he won't turn into a mastodon. Or a mouse.'

'I understand. And the chain you've bound him up in, what's that about?'

'It's silver. It's lethal to a lycanthrope, but as you see, for a mimic it merely stops the transmutations. That's why it's sitting here in its own form.'

The doppler pursed its glutinous lips and glowered at the Witcher with an evil expression in its dull eyes, which had already lost the hazel colour of the halfling's irises and were now yellow.

'I'm glad it's sitting, cheeky bastard,' Dainty snarled. 'Just to think it even stopped here, at the Blade, where I customarily lodge! It already thinks it's me!'

Dandelion nodded.

'Dainty,' he said, 'It *was* you. I've been meeting it here for three days now. It looked like you and spoke like you. And when it came to standing a round, it was as tight as you. Possibly even tighter.'

'That last point doesn't worry me,' the halfling said, 'because per-haps I'll recover some of my money. It disgusts me to touch it. Take the purse off it, Dandelion, and check what's inside. There ought to be plenty, if that horse thief really did sell my nags.'

'How many horses did you have, Dainty?'

'A dozen.'

'Calculating according to world prices,' the troubadour said, look-ing into the purse, 'what's here would just about buy a single horse,

143

if you chanced upon an old, foundered one. Calculating according to Novigradian prices, there's enough for two goats, three at most.'

The merchant said nothing, but looked as though he were about to cry. Tellico Lunngrevink Letorte hung his nose down low, and his lower lip even lower, after which he began to softly gurgle.

'In a word,' the halfling finally sighed, 'I've been robbed and ruined by a creature whose existence I previously didn't believe in. That's what you call bad luck.'

'That about sums it up,' the Witcher said, casting a glance at the doppler huddled on the stool. 'I was also convinced that mimics had been wiped out long ago. In the past, so I've heard, plenty of them used to live in the nearby forests and on the plateau. But their ability to mimic seriously worried the first settlers and they began to hunt them. Quite effectively. Almost all of them were quickly exterminated.'

'And lucky for us,' the innkeeper said, spitting onto the floor. 'I swear on the Eternal Fire, I prefer a dragon or a demon, which is always a dragon or a demon. You know where you are with them. But werewolfery, all those transmutations and metamorphoses, that hideous, demonic practice, trickery and the treacherous deceit conjured up by those hideous creatures, will be the detriment and undoing of people! I tell you, let's call the guard and into the fire with this repugnance!'

'Geralt?' Dandelion asked curiously. 'I'd be glad to hear an expert's opinion. Are these mimics really so dangerous and aggressive?'

'Their ability to mimic,' the Witcher said, 'is an attribute which serves as defence rather than aggression. I haven't heard of—'

'A pox on it,' Dainty interrupted angrily, slamming his fist down on the table. 'If thumping a fellow in the head and plundering him isn't aggression, I don't know what it is. Stop being clever. The matter is simple; I was waylaid and robbed, not just of my hard-earned property, but also of my own form. I demand compensation, and I shall not rest—'

'The guard, we must call the guard,' the innkeeper said. 'And we should summon the priests! And burn that monster, that non-human!'

144

'Give over, landlord,' the halfling said, raising his head. 'You're becoming a bore with that guard of yours. I would like to point out that that non-human hasn't harmed anybody else, only me. And incidentally, I'm also a non-human.'

'Don't be ridiculous, Mr Biberveldt,' the innkeeper laughed nervously. 'What are you and what is that? You're not far off being a man, and that's a monster. It astonishes me that you're sitting there so calmly, Witcher, sir. What's your trade, if you'll pardon me? It's your job to kill monsters, isn't it?'

'Monsters,' Geralt said coldly, 'but not the members of intelligent races.'

'Come, come, sir,' the innkeeper said. 'That's a bit of an exaggeration.'

'Indeed,' Dandelion cut in, 'you've overstepped the mark, Geralt, with that "intelligent race". Just take a look at it.'

Tellico Lunngrevink Letorte, indeed, did not resemble a member of an intelligent race at that moment. He resembled a puppet made of mud and flour, looking at the Witcher with a beseeching look in its dull, yellow eyes. Neither were the snuffling sounds being emitted from its nose – which now reached the table – consistent with a member of an intelligent race.

'Enough of this empty bullshit!' Dainty Biberveldt suddenly roared. 'There's nothing to argue about! The only thing that counts is my horses and my loss! Do you hear, you bloody slippery jack, you? Who did you sell my nags to? What did you do with the money? Tell me now, before I kick you black and blue and flay you alive!'

Detchka, opening the door slightly, stuck her flaxen-haired head into the chamber.

'We have visitors, father,' she whispered. 'Journeymen masons from the scaffolding and others. I'm serving them, but don't shout so loudly in here, because they're beginning to look funny at the snug.'

'By the Eternal Fire!' the innkeeper said in horror, looking at the molten doppler. 'If someone looks in and sees it . . . Oh, it'll look bad. If we aren't to call the guard, then . . . Witcher, sir! If it really is a vexling, tell it to change into something decent, as a disguise, like. Just for now.'

'That's right,' Dainty said. 'Have him change into something, Geralt.'

'Into whom?' the doppler suddenly gurgled. 'I can only take on a form I've had a good look at. Which of you shall I turn into?'

'Not me,' the innkeeper said hurriedly.

'Nor me,' Dandelion snorted. 'Anyway, it wouldn't be any disguise. Everybody knows me, so the sight of two Dandelions at one table would cause a bigger sensation than the one here in person.'

'It would be the same with me,' Geralt smiled. 'That leaves you, Dainty. And it's turned out well. Don't be offended, but you know yourself that people have difficulty distinguishing one halfling from another.'

The merchant did not ponder this for long.

'Very well,' he said. 'Let it be. Take the chain off him, Witcher. Right then, turn yourself into me, O intelligent race.'

After the chain had been removed the doppler rubbed its doughy hands together, felt its nose and stared goggle-eyed at the halfling. The sagging skin on its face tightened up and acquired colour. Its nose shrank and drew in with a dull, squelching sound, and curly hair sprouted on its bald pate. Now it was Dainty's turn to goggle, the innkeeper opened his mouth in mute astonishment and Dandelion heaved a sigh and groaned.

The last thing to change was the colour of its eyes.

The second Dainty Biberveldt cleared its throat, reached across the table, seized the first Dainty Biberveldt's beer mug and greedily pressed its mouth to it.

'It can't be, it can't be,' Dandelion said softly. 'Just look, he's been copied exactly. They're indistinguishable. Down to the last detail. This time even the mosquito bites and stains on its britches . . . Yes, on its britches! Geralt, not even sorcerers can manage that! Feel it, it's real wool, that's no illusion! Extraordinary! How does it do it?'

'No one knows,' the Witcher muttered. 'It doesn't, either. I said it has the complete ability for the free transformation of material structure, but it is an organic, instinctive ability . . .'

'But the britches . . . What has it made the britches out of? And the waistcoat?'

'That's its own adapted skin. I don't think it'd be happy to give up those trousers. Anyway, they'd immediately lose the properties of wool—'

'Pity,' Dainty said, showing cunning, 'because I was just wondering whether to make it change a bucket of matter into a bucket of gold.'

The doppler, now a faithful copy of the halfling, lounged comfortably and grinned broadly, clearly glad to be the centre of interest. It was sitting in an identical pose to Dainty, swinging its hairy feet the same way.

'You know plenty about dopplers, Geralt,' it said, then took a swig from the mug, smacked its lips and belched. 'Plenty, indeed.'

'Ye Gods, its voice and mannerisms are also Biberveldt's,' Dandelion said. 'Haven't any of you got a bit of red silk thread? We ought to mark it, dammit, because there might be trouble.'

'Come on, Dandelion,' the first Dainty Biberveldt said indignantly. 'Surely you won't mistake it for me? The differences are clear at . . .'

'. . . first glance,' the second Dainty Biberveldt completed the sentence and belched again gracefully. 'Indeed, in order to be mistaken you'd have to be more stupid than a mare's arse.'

'Didn't I say?' Dandelion whispered in amazement. 'It thinks and talks like Biberveldt. They're indistinguishable . . .'

'An exaggeration,' the halfling said, pouting. 'A gross exaggeration.'

'No,' Geralt rebutted. 'It's not an exaggeration. Believe it or not, but at this moment it *is* you, Dainty. In some unknown way the doppler also precisely copies its victim's mentality.'

'Mental what?'

'The mind's properties, the character, feelings, thoughts. The soul. Which would confirm what most sorcerers and all priests would deny. That the soul is also matter.'

'Blasphemy!' The innkeeper gasped.

'And poppycock,' Dainty Biberveldt said firmly. 'Don't tell

147

stories, Witcher. The mind's properties, I like that. Copying some-one's nose and britches is one thing, but someone's mind is no bloody mean feat. I'll prove it to you now. If that lousy doppler had copied my merchant's mind he wouldn't have sold the horses in Novigrad, where there's no market for them; he would have ridden to the horse fair in Devil's Ford where they're sold to the highest bidder. You don't lose money there—'

'Well actually, you do.' The doppler imitated the halfling's offended expression and snorted characteristically. 'First of all, the prices at the auctions in Devil's Ford are coming down, because the merchants are fixing the bidding. And in addition you have to pay the auctioneer's commission.'

'Don't teach me how to trade, you prat,' Biberveldt said indig-nantly. 'I would have taken ninety or a hundred a piece in Devil's Ford. And how much did you get off those Novigradian chancers?'

'A hundred and thirty,' the doppler replied.

'You're lying, you rascal.'

'I am not. I drove the horses straight to the port, sir, and found a foreign fur trader. Furriers don't use oxen when they assemble their caravans, because oxen are too slow. Furs are light, but costly, so one needs to travel swiftly. There's no market for horses in Novigrad, so neither are there any horses. I had the only available ones, so I could name my price. Simple—'

'Don't teach me, I said!' Dainty yelled, flushing red. 'Very well, you made a killing. So where's the money?'

'I reinvested it,' Tellico said proudly, imitating the halfling's typ-ical raking of his fingers through his thick mop of hair. 'Money, Mr Dainty, has to circulate, and business has to be kept moving.'

'Be careful I don't wring your neck! Tell me what you did with the cash you made on the horses.'

'I told you. I sank it into goods.'

'What goods? What did you buy, you freak?'

'Co . . . cochineal,' the doppler stuttered, and then enumerated quickly: 'A thousand bushels of cochineal, sixty-two hundredweight of mimosa bark, fifty-five gallons of rose oil, twenty-three barrels of cod liver oil, six hundred earthenware bowls and eighty pounds of beeswax. I bought the cod liver oil very cheaply, incidentally, because it was a little rancid. Oh, yes, I almost forgot. I also bought a hundred cubits of cotton string.'

A long – very long – silence fell.

'Cod liver oil,' Dainty finally said, enunciating each word very slowly. 'Cotton string. Rose oil. I must be dreaming. Yes, it's a nightmare. You can buy anything in Novigrad, every precious and everyday thing, and this moron here spends my money on shit. Pretending to be me. I'm finished, my money's lost, my merchant's reputation is lost. No, I've had enough of this. Lend me your sword, Geralt. I'll cut him to shreds here and now.'

The door to the chamber creaked open.

'The merchant Biberveldt!' crowed an individual in a purple toga which hung on his emaciated frame as though on a stick. He had a hat on his head shaped like an upturned chamber pot. 'Is the merchant Biberveldt here?'

'Yes,' the two halflings answered in unison.

The next moment, one of the Dainty Biberveldts flung the contents of the mug in the Witcher's face, deftly kicked the stool from under Dandelion and slipped under the table towards the door, knocking over the individual in the ridiculous hat on the way.

'Fire! Help!' it yelled, rushing out towards the common chamber. 'Murder! Calamity!'

Geralt, shaking off the beer froth, rushed after him, but the second Biberveldt, who was also tearing towards the door, slipped on the sawdust and fell in front of him. The two of them fell over, right on the threshold. Dandelion, clambering out from under the table, cursed hideously.

'Assaaault!' yelled the skinny individual, entangled in his purple toga, from the floor. 'Rooobberrrryyyy! Criminals!

Geralt rolled over the halfling and rushed into the main chamber, to see the doppler – jostling the drinkers – running out into the street. He rushed after him, only to run into a resilient but hard wall of men barring his way. He managed to knock one of them over, smeared with clay and stinking of beer, but others held him fast in the iron grip of powerful hands. He fought furiously, but heard the dry report of snapping thread and rending leather, and the sleeve become loose under his right armpit. The Witcher swore and stopped struggling.

'We 'ave 'im!' the masons yelled. 'We've got the robber! What do we do now, master?'

'Lime!' the master bellowed, raising his head from the table and looking around with unseeing eyes.

'Guaaard!' the purple one yelled, crawling from the chamber on all fours. 'An official has been assaulted! Guard! It will be the gallows for you, villain!'

'We 'ave 'im!' the masons shouted. 'We 'ave 'im, sir!'

'That's not him!' the individual in the toga bellowed, 'Catch the scoundrel! After him!'

'Who?'

'Biberveldt, the halfling! After him, give chase! To the dungeons with him!'

'Hold on a moment,' Dainty said, emerging from the snug. 'What's it all about, Mr Schwann? Don't drag my name through the mud. And don't sound the alarm, there's no need.'

Schwann was silent and looked at the halfling in astonishment. Dandelion emerged from the chamber, bonnet at an angle, examining his lute. The masons, whispering among themselves, finally released Geralt. The Witcher, although absolutely furious, limited himself to spitting copiously on the floor.

'Merchant Biberveldt!' Schwann crowed, narrowing his myopic eyes. 'What is the meaning of this? An assault on a municipal official may cost you dearly . . . Who was that? That halfling, who bolted?'

'My cousin,' Dainty said quickly. 'A distant cousin . . .'

'Yes, yes,' Dandelion agreed, swiftly backing him up and feeling in his element. 'Biberveldt's distant cousin. Known as Nutcase-Biberveldt. The black sheep of the family. When he was a child he fell into a well. A dried-up well. But unfortunately the pail hit him directly on his head. He's usually peaceful, it's just that the colour purple infuriates him. But there's nothing to worry about, because he's calmed by the sight of red hairs on a lady's loins. That's why he rushed straight to Passiflora. I tell you, Mr Schwann—'

'That's enough, Dandelion,' the Witcher hissed. 'Shut up, dammit.'

Schwann pulled his toga down, brushed the sawdust off it and straightened up, assuming a haughty air.

'Now, then,' he said. 'Heed your relatives more attentively, merchant Biberveldt, because as you well know, you are responsible. Were I to lodge a complaint . . . But I cannot afford the time. I am here, Biberveldt, on official business. On behalf of the municipal authorities I summon you to pay tax.'

'Eh?'

'Tax,' the official repeated, and pouted his lips in a grimace probably copied from someone much more important. 'What are you doing? Been infected by your cousin? If you make a profit, you have to pay taxes. Or you'll have to do time in the dungeon.'

'Me?' Dainty roared. 'Me, make a profit? All I have is losses, for fuck's sake! I—'

'Careful, Biberveldt,' the Witcher hissed, while Dandelion kicked the halfling furtively in his hairy shin. The halfling coughed.

'Of course,' he said, struggling to put a smile on his chubby face, 'of course, Mr Schwann. If you make a profit, you have to pay taxes. High profits, high taxes. And the other way around, I'd say.'

'It is not for me to judge your business, sir,' the official said, making a sour face. He sat down at the table, removing from the fathomless depths of his toga an abacus and a scroll of parchment, which he unrolled on the table, first wiping it with a sleeve. 'It is my job to count up and collect. Now, then . . . Let us reckon this up . . . That will be . . . hmmm . . . Two down, carry the one . . . Now, then . . . one thousand five hundred and fifty-three crowns and twenty pennies.

A hushed wheeze escaped Dainty Biberveldt's lips. The masons muttered in astonishment. The innkeeper dropped a bowl. Dandelion gasped.

'Very well. Goodbye, lads,' the halfling said bitterly. 'If anybody asks; I'm in the dungeon.'

151

II

'By tomorrow at noon,' Dainty groaned. 'And that whoreson, that Schwann, damn him, the repulsive creep, could have extended it. Over fifteen hundred crowns. How am I to come by that kind of coin by tomorrow? I'm finished, ruined, I'll rot in the dungeons! Don't let's sit here, dammit, let's catch that bastard doppler, I tell you! We have to catch it!'

The three of them were sitting on the marble sill of a disused fountain, occupying the centre of a small square among sumptuous, but extremely tasteless, merchants' townhouses. The water in the fountain was green and dreadfully dirty, and the golden ides swimming among the refuse worked their gills hard and gulped in air from the surface through open mouths. Dandelion and the halfling were chewing some fritters which the troubadour had swiped from a stall they had just passed.

'In your shoes,' the bard said, 'I'd forget about catching it and start looking around for somebody to borrow the money off. What will you get from catching the doppler? Perhaps you think Schwann will accept it as an equivalent?'

'You're a fool, Dandelion. When I catch the doppler, I'll get my money back.'

'What money? Everything he had in that purse went on covering the damage and a bribe for Schwann. It didn't have any more.'

'Dandelion,' the halfling grimaced. 'You may know something about poetry, but in business matters, forgive me, you're a total blockhead. Did you hear how much tax Schwann is charging me? And what do you pay tax on? Hey? On what?'

'On everything,' the poet stated. 'I even pay tax on singing. And they don't give a monkey's about my explanations that I was only singing from an inner need.'

'You're a fool, I said. In business you pay taxes on profits. On profits. Dandelion! Do you comprehend? That rascal of a doppler impersonated me and made some business transactions – fraudulent ones, no doubt. And made money on them! It made a profit! And I'll have to pay tax, and probably cover the debts of that scoundrel, if it has run up any debts! And if I don't pay it off, I'm going to the dungeons, they'll brand me with a red-hot iron in public and send me to the mines! A pox on it!'

'Ha,' Dandelion said cheerfully. 'So you don't have a choice, Dainty. You'll have to flee the city in secret. Know what? I have an idea. We'll wrap you up in a sheepskin. You can pass through the gate calling: "I'm a little baa-lamb, baa, baa". No one will recognise you.'

'Dandelion,' the halfling said glumly. 'Shut up or I'll kick you. Geralt?'

'What, Dainty?'

'Will *you* help me catch the doppler?'

'Listen,' the Witcher said, still trying in vain to sew up his torn jacket sleeve, 'this is Novigrad. A population of thirty thousand: humans, dwarves, half-elves, halflings and gnomes, and probably as many out-of-towners again. How do you mean to find someone in this rabbit warren?'

Dainty swallowed a fritter and licked his fingers.

'And magic, Geralt? Those witcher spells of yours, about which so many tales circulate?'

'A doppler is only magically detectable in its own form, and it doesn't walk down the street in it. And even if it did, magic would be no use, because there are plenty of weak sorcerers' signals all around. Every second house has a magical lock on the door and three quarters of the people wear amulets, of all kinds: against thieves, fleas and food poisoning. Too many to count.'

Dandelion ran his fingers over the lute's fingerboard and strummed the strings.

'Spring will return, with warm rain perfumed!' he sang. 'No, that's no good. Spring will return, the sun— No, dammit. It's just not coming. Not at all . . .'

'Stop squawking,' the halfling snapped. 'You're getting on my nerves.'

Dandelion threw the ides the rest of his fritter and spat into the fountain.

'Look,' he said. 'Golden fish. It's said that they grant wishes.'

'Those ones are red,' Dainty observed.

'Never mind, it's a trifle. Dammit, there are three of us, and they grant three wishes. That works out at one each. What, Dainty? Wouldn't you wish for the fish to pay the tax for you?'

'Of course. And apart from that for something to fall from the sky and whack the doppler on the noggin. And also—'

'Stop, stop. We also have our wishes. I'd like the fish to supply me with an ending for my ballad. And you, Geralt?'

'Get off my back, Dandelion.'

'Don't spoil the game, Witcher. Tell us what you'd wish for.'

The Witcher got up.

'I would wish,' he murmured, 'that the fact we're being surrounded would turn out to be a misunderstanding.'

From an alleyway opposite the fountain emerged four individuals dressed in black, wearing round, leather caps, heading slowly towards them. Dainty swore softly and looked around.

Another four men came out of a street behind their backs. They did not come any closer and, having positioned themselves, stood blocking the street. They were holding strange looking discs resembling coiled ropes. The Witcher looked around and moved his shoulders, adjusting the sword slung across his back. Dandelion groaned.

From behind the backs of the individuals in black emerged a small man in a white kaftan and a short, grey cape. The gold chain on his neck sparkled to the rhythm of his steps, flashing yellow.

'Chappelle . . .' Dandelion groaned. 'It's Chappelle . . .'

The individuals in black behind them moved slowly towards the fountain. The Witcher reached for his sword.

'No, Geralt,' Dandelion whispered, moving closer to him. 'For the Gods' sake, don't draw your weapon. It's the temple guard. If we resist we won't leave Novigrad alive. Don't touch your sword.'

The man in the white kaftan walked swiftly towards them. The individuals in black followed him, surrounding the fountain at a march, and occupied strategic, carefully chosen positions. Geralt observed them vigilantly, crouching slightly. The strange discs they were holding were not – as he had first thought – ordinary whips. They were lamias.

The man in the white kaftan approached them.

'Geralt,' the bard whispered. 'By all the Gods, keep calm—'

'I won't let them touch me,' the Witcher muttered. 'I won't let them touch me, whoever they are. Be careful, Dandelion . . . When it starts, you two flee, as fast as you can. I'll keep them busy . . . for some time . . .'

Dandelion did not answer. Slinging the lute over one shoulder, he bowed low before the man in the white kaftan, which was ornately embroidered with gold and silver threads in an intricate, mosaic pattern.

'Venerable Chappelle . . .'

The man addressed as Chappelle stopped and swept them with his gaze. His eyes, Geralt noticed, were frost-cold and the colour of steel. His forehead was pale, beaded unhealthily with sweat and his cheeks were flushed with irregular, red blotches.

'Mr Dainty Biberveldt, merchant,' he said. 'The talented Dandelion. And Geralt of Rivia, a representative of the oh-so rare witcher's profession. A reunion of old friends? Here, in Novigrad?'

None of them answered.

'I consider it highly regrettable,' Chappelle continued, 'that a report has been submitted about you.'

Dandelion blanched slightly and the halfling's teeth chattered. The Witcher was not looking at Chappelle. He did not take his eyes off the weapons of the men in leather caps surrounding the fountain. In most of the countries known to Geralt the production and possession of spiked lamias, also called Mayhenian scourges, were strictly prohibited. Novigrad was no exception. Geralt had seen people struck in the face by a lamia. He would never forget those faces.

'The keeper of the Spear Blade inn,' Chappelle continued, 'had

155

the audacity to accuse you gentlemen of collusion with a demon, a monster, known as a changeling or a vexling.'

None of them answered. Chappelle folded his arms on his chest and looked at them coldly.

'I felt obliged to forewarn you of that report. I shall also inform you that the above-mentioned innkeeper has been imprisoned in the dungeons. There is a suspicion that he was raving under the influence of beer or vodka. Astonishing what people will concoct. Firstly, there are no such things as vexlings. It is a fabrication of superstitious peasants.'

No one commented on this.

'Secondly, what vexling would dare to approach a witcher,' Chappelle smiled, 'and not be killed at once? Am I right? The innkeeper's accusation would thus be ludicrous, were it not for one vital detail.'

Chappelle nodded, pausing dramatically. The Witcher heard Dainty slowly exhaling a large lungful of air.

'Yes, a certain, vital detail,' Chappelle repeated. 'Namely, we are facing heresy and sacrilegious blasphemy here. For it is a well-known fact that no vexling, absolutely no vexling, nor any other monster, could even approach the walls of Novigrad, because here, in nineteen temples, burns the Eternal Fire, whose sacred power protects the city. Whoever says that he saw a vexling at the Spear Blade, a stone's throw from the chief altar of the Eternal Fire, is a blasphemous heretic and will have to retract his claim. Should he not want to, he shall be assisted by the power and means, which, trust me, I keep close at hand in the dungeons. Thus, as you can see, there is nothing to be concerned about.'

The expressions on the faces of Dandelion and the halfling showed emphatically that they both thought differently.

'There is absolutely nothing to be concerned about,' Chappelle repeated. 'You may leave Novigrad without let or hindrance. I will not detain you. I do have to insist, gentlemen, however, that you do not broadcast the lamentable fabrications of the innkeeper, that you do not discuss this incident openly. Statements calling into question the divine power of the Eternal Fire, irrespective of the intention, we, the humble servants of the temple, would have to treat as heresy, with all due consequences. Your personal religious convictions, whatever they might be, and however I respect them, are of no significance. Believe in what you will. I am tolerant while somebody venerates the Eternal Fire and does not blaspheme against it. But should they blaspheme, I shall order them burnt at the stake, and that is that. Everybody in Novigrad is equal before the law. And the law applies equally to everybody; anyone who blasphemes against the Eternal Fire perishes at the stake, and their property is confiscate. But enough of that. I repeat; you may pass through the gates of Novigrad without hindrance. Ideally . . .'

Chappelle smiled slightly, sucked in his cheeks in a cunning grimace, and his eyes swept the square. The few passers-by observing the incident quickened their step and rapidly turned their heads away.

'. . . ideally,' Chappelle finished, 'ideally with immediate effect. Forthwith. Obviously, with regard to the honourable merchant Biberveldt, that "forthwith" means "forthwith, having settled all fiscal affairs". Thank you for the time you have given me.'

Dainty turned away, mouth moving noiselessly. The Witcher had no doubt that the noiseless word had been 'whoreson'. Dandelion lowered his head, smiling foolishly.

'My dear Witcher,' Chappelle suddenly said, 'a word in private, if you would.'

Geralt approached and Chappelle gently extended an arm. If he touches my elbow, I'll strike him, the Witcher thought. I'll strike him, whatever happens.

Chappelle did not touch Geralt's elbow.

'My dear Witcher,' he said quietly, turning his back on the others, 'I am aware that some cities, unlike Novigrad, are deprived of the divine protection of the Eternal Fire. Let us then suppose that a creature similar to a vexling was prowling in one of those cities. I wonder how much you would charge in that case for undertaking to catch a vexling alive?'

'I don't hire myself out to hunt monsters in crowded cities,' the Witcher shrugged. 'An innocent bystander might suffer harm.'

'Are you so concerned about the fate of innocent bystanders?'

'Yes, I am. Because I am usually held responsible for their fate. And have to cope with the consequences.'

'I understand. And would not your concern for the fate of innocent bystanders be in inverse proportion to the fee?'

'It would not.'

'I do not greatly like your tone, Witcher. But no matter, I understand what you hint at by it. You are hinting that you do not want to do . . . what I would ask you to do, making the size of the fee meaningless. And the form of the fee?'

'I do not understand.'

'Come, come.'

'I mean it.'

'Purely theoretically,' Chappelle said, quietly, calmly, without any anger or menace in his voice, 'it might be possible that the fee for your services would be a guarantee that you and your friends would leave this— leave the theoretical city alive. What then?'

'It is impossible,' the Witcher said, smiling hideously, 'to answer that question theoretically. The situation you are discussing, Reverend Chappelle, would have to be dealt with in practice. I am in no hurry to do so, but if the necessity arises . . . If there proves to be no other choice . . . I am prepared to go through with it.'

'Ha, perhaps you are right,' Chappelle answered dispassionately. 'Too much theory. As concerns practice, I see that there will be no collaboration. A good thing, perhaps? In any case, I cherish the hope that it will not be a cause for conflict between us.'

'I also cherish that hope.'

'Then may that hope burn in us, Geralt of Rivia. Do you know what the Eternal Fire is? A flame that never goes out, a symbol of permanence, a way leading through the gloom, a harbinger of progress, of a better tomorrow. The Eternal Fire, Geralt, is hope. For everybody, everybody without exception. For if something exists that embraces us all . . . you, me . . . others . . . then that something is precisely hope. Remember that. It was a pleasure to meet you, Witcher.'

Geralt bowed stiffly, saying nothing. Chappelle looked at him for a moment, then turned about energetically and marched through the small square, without looking around at his escort. The men armed with the lamias fell in behind him, forming up into a well-ordered column.

'Oh, mother of mine,' Dandelion whimpered, timidly watching the departing men, 'but we were lucky. If that is the end of it. If they don't collar us right away—'

'Calm down,' the Witcher said, 'and stop whining. Nothing happened, after all.'

'Do you know who that was, Geralt?'

'No.'

'That was Chappelle, minister for security affairs. The Novigrad secret service is subordinate to the temple. Chappelle is not a priest but the eminence grise to the hierarch, the most powerful and most dangerous man in the city. Everybody, even the Council and the guilds, shake in their shoes before him, because he's a first-rate bastard, Geralt, drunk on power, like a spider drunk on fly's blood. It's common knowledge – though not discussed openly in the city – what he's capable of. People vanishing without trace. Falsified accusations, torture, assassinations, terror, blackmail and plain plunder. Extortion, swindles and fraud. By the Gods, you've landed us in a pretty mess, Biberveldt.'

'Give it a rest, Dandelion,' Dainty snapped. 'It's not that you have to be afraid of anything. No one ever touches a troubadour. For unfathomable reasons you are inviolable.'

'In Novigrad,' Dandelion whined, still pale, 'an inviolable poet may still fall beneath a speeding wagon, be fatally poisoned by a fish, or accidentally drown in a moat. Chappelle specialises in mishaps of that nature. I consider the fact that he talked to us at all something exceptional. One thing is certain, he didn't do it without a reason. He's up to something. You'll see, they'll soon embroil us in something, clap us in irons and drag us off to be tortured with the sanction of the law. That's how things are done here!'

'There is quite some truth,' the halfling said to Geralt, 'in what he says. We must watch out. It's astonishing that that scoundrel Chappelle hasn't keeled over yet. For years they've been saying he's

159

sick, that his heart will give out, and everybody's waiting for him to croak . . .'

'Be quiet, Biberveldt,' the troubadour hissed apprehensively, looking around, 'because somebody's bound to be listening. Look how everybody's staring at us. Let's get out of here, I'm telling you. And I suggest we treat seriously what Chappelle told us about the doppler. I, for example, have never seen a doppler in my life, and if it comes to it I'll swear as much before the Eternal Fire.'

'Look,' the halfling suddenly said. 'Somebody is running towards us.'

'Let's flee!' Dandelion howled.

'Calm yourself, calm yourself,' Dainty grinned and combed his mop of hair with his fingers. 'I know him. It's Muskrat, a local merchant, the Guild's treasurer. We've done business together. Hey, look at the expression on his face! As though he's shat his britches. Hey, Muskrat, are you looking for me?'

'I swear by the Eternal Fire,' Muskrat panted, pushing back a fox fur cap and wiping his forehead with his sleeve, 'I was certain they'd drag you off to the barbican. It's truly a miracle. I'm astonished—'

'It's nice of you,' the halfling sneeringly interrupted, 'to be astonished. You'll delight us even more if you tell us why.'

'Don't play dumb, Biberveldt,' Muskrat frowned. 'The whole city already knows the profit you made on the cochineal. Everybody's talking about it already and it has clearly reached the hierarch and Chappelle. How cunning you are, how craftily you benefited from what happened in Poviss.'

'What are you blathering about, Muskrat?'

'Ye Gods, would you stop trying to play the innocent, Dainty? Did you buy that cochineal? For a song, at ten-forty a bushel? Yes, you did. Taking advantage of the meagre demand you paid with a backed bill, without paying out a penny of cash. And what happened? In the course of a day you palmed off the entire cargo at four times the price, for cash on the table. Perhaps you'll have the cheek to say it was an accident, a stroke of luck? That when buying the cochineal you knew nothing about the coup in Poviss?'

'The what? What are you talking about?'

'There was a coup in Poviss!' Muskrat yelled. 'And one of those, you know . . . levorutions! King Rhyd was overthrown and now the Thyssenid clan is in power! Rhyd's court, the nobility and the army wore blue, and the weaving mills there only bought indigo. But the colour of the Thyssenids is scarlet, so the price of indigo went down, and cochineal's gone up, and then it came out that you, Biberveldt, had the only available cargo in your grasp! Ha!'

Dainty fell silent and looked distressed.

'Crafty, Biberveldt, must be said,' Muskrat continued. 'And you didn't tell anybody anything, not even your friends. If you'd let on, we might both have made a profit, might even have set up a joint factory. But you preferred to act alone, softly-softly. Your choice; but don't count on me any longer either. On the Eternal Fire, it's true that every halfling is a selfish bastard and a whoreson. Vimme Vivaldi never gives me a backed bill; and you? On the spot. Because you're one tribe, you damned inhumans, you poxy halflings and dwarves. Damn the lot of you!'

Muskrat spat, turned on his heel and walked off. Dainty, lost in thought, scratched his head until his mop of hair crunched.

'Something's dawning on me, boys,' he said at last. 'Now I know what needs to be done. Let's go to the bank. If anyone can make head or tail of all this, that someone is the banker friend of mine, Vimme Vivaldi.'

III

'I imagined the bank differently,' Dandelion whispered, looking around the room. 'Where do they keep the money, Geralt?'

'The Devil only knows,' the Witcher answered quietly, hiding his torn jacket sleeve. 'In the cellars, perhaps?'

'Not a chance. I've had a look around. There aren't any cellars here.'

'They must keep it in the loft then.'

'Would you come to my office, gentlemen?' Vimme Vivaldi asked.

Young men and dwarves of indiscernible age sitting at long tables were busy covering sheets of parchment with columns of figures and letters. All of them – without exception – were hunched over, with the tips of their tongues sticking out. The work, the Witcher judged, was fiendishly monotonous, but seemed to preoccupy the staff utterly. In the corner, on a low stool, sat an elderly, beggarly-looking man busy sharpening quills. He was making hard work of it.

The banker carefully closed the door to the office, stroked his long, white, well-groomed beard, spotted here and there with ink, and straightened a claret-coloured velvet jerkin stretched over a prominent belly.

'You know, Dandelion, sir,' he said, sitting down at an enormous, mahogany table, piled with parchments, 'I imagined you quite differently. And I know your songs, I know them, I've heard them. About Princess Vanda, who drowned in the River Duppie, because no one wanted her. And about the kingfisher that fell into a privy—'

'They aren't mine,' Dandelion flushed in fury. 'I've never written anything like that!'

'Ah. I'm sorry then.'

'Perhaps we could get to the point?' Dainty cut in. 'Time is short, and you're talking nonsense. I'm in grave difficulties, Vimme.'

'I was afraid of that,' the dwarf nodded. 'As you recall, I warned you, Biberveldt. I told you three days ago not to sink any resources into that rancid cod liver oil. What if it was cheap? It is not the nominal price that is important, but the size of the profit on resale. The same applies to the rose oil and the wax, and those earthenware bowls. What possessed you, Dainty, to buy that shit, and in hard cash to boot, rather than judiciously pay with a letter of credit or by draft? I told you that storage costs in Novigrad are devilishly high; in the course of two weeks they will surpass the value of those goods threefold. But you—'

'Yes,' the halfling quietly groaned. 'Tell me, Vivaldi. What did I do?'

'But you told me not to worry, that you would sell everything in the course of twenty-four hours. And now you come and declare that you are in trouble, smiling foolishly and disarmingly all the while. But it's not selling, is it? And costs are rising, what? Ha, that's not good, not good. How am I to get you out of it, Dainty? Had you at least insured that junk, I would have sent one of the clerks at once to quietly torch the store. No, my dear, the only thing to be done is to approach the matter philosophically, and say to oneself: "Fuck this for a game of soldiers". This is business; you win some, you lose some. What kind of profit was it anyway, that cod liver oil, wax and rose oil? Risible. Let us talk about serious business. Tell me if I should sell the mimosa bark yet, because the offers have begun to stabilise at five and five-sixths.'

'Hey?'

'Are you deaf?' the banker frowned. 'The last offer was exactly five and five-sixths. You came back, I hope, to close the deal? You won't get seven, anyhow, Dainty.'

'I came back?'

Vivaldi stroked his beard and picked some crumbs of fruit cake from it.

'You were here an hour since,' he said calmly, 'with instructions to hold out for seven. A sevenfold increase on the price you paid is two crowns five-and-forty pennies a pound. That is too high, Dainty, even for such a perfectly timed market. The tanneries will already have reached agreement and they will solidly stick to the price. I'm absolutely certain—'

The door to the office opened and something in a green felt cap and a coat of dappled coney fur girded with hempen twine rushed in.

'Merchant Sulimir is offering two crowns fifteen!' it squealed.

'Six and one-sixth,' Vivaldi swiftly calculated. 'What do we do, Dainty?'

'Sell!' the halfling yelled. 'A six-fold profit, and you're still bloody wondering?'

Another something in a yellow cap and a mantle resembling an old sack dashed into the office. Like the first something, it was about two cubits tall.

'Merchant Biberveldt instructs not to sell for below seven!' it shouted, wiped its nose on its sleeve and ran out.

'Aha,' the dwarf said after a long silence. 'One Biberveldt orders us to sell, and another Biberveldt orders us to wait. An interesting situation. What do we do, Dainty? Do you set about explaining at once, or do we wait until a third Biberveldt orders us to load the bark onto galleys and ship it to the Land of the Cynocephali? Hey?'

'What is that?' Dandelion stammered, pointing at the something in a green cap still standing in the doorway. 'What the bloody hell is it?'

'A young gnome,' Geralt said.

'Undoubtedly,' Vivaldi confirmed coldly. 'It is not an old troll. Anyway, it's not important what it is. Very well, Dainty, if you please.'

'Vimme,' the halfling said. 'If you don't mind. Don't ask questions. Something awful has happened. Just accept that I, Dainty Biberveldt of Knotgrass Meadow, an honest merchant, do not have a clue what's happening. Tell me everything, in detail. The events of the last three days. Please, Vimme.'

'Curious,' the dwarf said. 'Well, for the commission I take I have to grant the wishes of the client, whatever they might be. So listen. You came rushing in here three days ago, out of breath, gave me a deposit of a thousand crowns and demanded an endorsement on

164

a bill amounting to two thousand five hundred and twenty, to the bearer. I gave you that endorsement.'

'Without a guaranty?'

'Correct. I like you, Dainty.'

'Go on, Vimme.'

'The next day you rushed in with a bang and a clatter, demanding that I issue a letter of credit on a bank in Vizima. For the considerable sum of three thousand five hundred crowns. The beneficiary was to be, if I remember rightly, a certain Ther Lukokian, alias Truffle. Well, I issued that letter of credit.'

'Without a guaranty,' the halfling said hopefully.

'My affection for you, Biberveldt,' the banker said, 'ceases at around three thousand crowns. This time I took from you a written obligation that in the event of insolvency the mill would be mine.'

'What mill?'

'That of your father-in-law, Arno Hardbottom, in Knotgrass Meadow.'

'I'm not going home,' Dainty declared glumly, but determinedly. 'I'll sign on to a ship and become a pirate.'

Vimme Vivaldi scratched an ear and looked at him suspiciously.

'Oh, come on,' he said, 'you took that obligation and tore it up almost right away. You are solvent. No small wonder, with profits like that—'

'Profits?'

'That's right, I forgot,' muttered the dwarf. 'I was meant not to be surprised by anything. You made a good profit on the cochineal, Biberveldt. Because, you see, there was a coup in Poviss—'

'I already know,' the dwarf interrupted. 'Indigo's gone down and cochineal's gone up. And I made a profit. Is that true, Vimme?'

'Yes, it is. You have in my safe keeping six thousand three hundred and forty-six crowns and eighty pennies. Net, after deducting my commission and tax.'

'You paid the tax for me?'

'What else would I do?' Vivaldi said in astonishment. 'After all, you were here an hour ago and told me to pay it. The clerk has already delivered the entire sum to city hall. Something around fifteen hundred, because the sale of the horses was, of course, included in it.'

The door opened with a bang and something in a very dirty cap came running in.

'Two crowns thirty!' it shouted. 'Merchant Hazelquist!'

'Don't sell!' Dainty called. 'We'll wait for a better price! Be gone, back to the market with the both of you!'

The two gnomes caught some coppers thrown to them by the dwarf, and disappeared.

'Right . . . Where was I?' Vivaldi wondered, playing with a huge, strangely-formed amethyst crystal serving as a paperweight. 'Aha, with the cochineal bought with a bill of exchange. And you needed the letter of credit I mentioned to purchase a large cargo of mimosa bark. You bought a deal of it, but quite cheaply, for thirty-five pennies a pound, from a Zangwebarian factor, that Truffle, or perhaps Morel. The galley sailed into port yesterday. And then it all began.'

'I can imagine,' Dainty groaned.

'What is mimosa bark needed for?' Dandelion blurted out.

'Nothing,' the halfling muttered dismally. 'Unfortunately.'

'Mimosa bark, poet, sir,' the dwarf explained, 'is an agent used for tanning hides.'

'If somebody was so stupid,' Dainty interrupted, 'as to buy mimosa bark from beyond the seas, when oak bark can be bought in Temeria for next to nothing . . .'

'And here is the nub of the matter,' Vivaldi said, 'because in Temeria the druids have just announced that if the destruction of oaks is not stopped immediately they will afflict the land with a plague of hornets and rats. The druids are being supported by the dryads, and the king there is fond of dryads. In short: since yesterday there has been a total embargo on Temerian oak, for which reason mimosa is going up. Your information was accurate, Dainty.'

A stamping was heard from the chambers beyond the room, and then the something in a green cap came running into the office, out of breath.

'The honourable merchant Sulimir . . .' the gnome panted, 'has instructed me to repeat that merchant Biberveldt, the halfling, is

166

a reckless, bristly swine, a profiteer and charlatan, and that he, Sulimir, hopes that Biberveldt gets the mange. He'll give two crowns forty-four and that is his last word.'

'Sell,' the halfling blurted out. 'Go on, shorty, run off and accept it. Count it up, Vimme.'

Vivaldi reached beneath some scrolls of parchment and took out a dwarven abacus, a veritable marvel. Unlike abacuses used by humans, the dwarven one was shaped like a small openwork pyramid. Vivaldi's abacus, though, was made of gold wires, over which slid angular beads of ruby, emerald, onyx and black agate, which fitted into each other. The dwarf slid the gemstones upwards, downwards and sideways for some time, with quick, deft movements of his plump finger.

'That will be . . . hmm, hmm . . . Minus the costs and my commission . . . Minus tax . . . Yes. Fifteen thousand six hundred and twenty-two crowns and five-and-twenty pennies. Not bad.'

'If I've reckoned correctly,' Dainty Biberveldt said slowly, 'all together, net, then I ought to have in my account . . .'

'Precisely twenty-one thousand nine hundred and sixty-nine crowns and five pennies. Not bad.'

'Not bad?' Dandelion roared. 'Not bad? You could buy a large village or a small castle for that! I've never, ever, seen that much money at one time!'

'I haven't either,' the halfling said. 'But simmer down, Dandelion. It so happens that no one has seen that money yet, and it isn't certain if anyone ever will.'

'Hey, Biberveldt,' the dwarf snorted. 'Why such gloomy thoughts? Sulimir will pay in cash or by a bill of exchange, and Sulimir's bills are reliable. What then, is the matter? Are you afraid of losing on that stinking cod liver oil and wax? With profits like that you'll cover the losses with ease . . .'

'That's not the point.'

'So what *is* the point?'

Dainty coughed, and lowered his curly mop.

'Vimme,' he said, eyes fixed on the floor. 'Chappelle is snooping around me.'

The banker clicked his tongue.

'Very bad,' he drawled. 'But it was to be expected. You see, Biberveldt, the information you used when carrying out the transactions does not just have commercial significance, but also political. No one knew what was happening in Poviss and Temeria – Chappelle included – and Chappelle likes to be the first to know. So now, as you can imagine, he is wracking his brains about how you knew. And I think he has guessed. Because I think I've also worked it out.'

'That's fascinating.'

Vivaldi swept his eyes over Dandelion and Geralt, and wrinkled his snub nose.

'Fascinating? I'll tell you what's fascinating; your party, Dainty,' he said. 'A troubadour, a witcher and a merchant. Congratulations. Master Dandelion shows up here and there, even at royal courts, and no doubt keeps his ears open. And the Witcher? A bodyguard? Someone to frighten debtors?'

'Hasty conclusions, Mr Vivaldi,' Geralt said coldly. 'We are not partners.'

'And I,' Dandelion said, flushing, 'do not eavesdrop anywhere. I'm a poet, not a spy!'

'People say all sorts of things,' the dwarf grimaced. '*All* sorts of things, Master Dandelion.'

'Lies!' the troubadour yelled. 'Damned lies!'

'Very well, I believe you, I believe you. I just don't know if Chappelle will believe it. But who knows, perhaps it will all blow over. I tell you, Biberveldt, that Chappelle has changed a lot since his last attack of apoplexy. Perhaps the fear of death looked him in the arse and forced him to think things over? I swear, he is not the same Chappelle. He seems to have become courteous, rational, composed and . . . and somehow honest.'

'Get away,' the halfling said. 'Chappelle, honest? Courteous? Impossible.'

'I'm telling you how it is,' Vivaldi replied. 'And how it is, is what I'm telling you. What is more, now the temple is facing another problem: namely the Eternal Fire.'

'What do you mean?'

168

'The Eternal Fire, as it's known, is supposed to burn everywhere. Altars dedicated to that fire are going to be built everywhere, all over the city. A huge number of altars. Don't ask me for details, Dainty, I am not very familiar with human superstitions. But I know that all the priests, and Chappelle also, are concerned about almost nothing else but those altars and that fire. Great preparations are being made. Taxes will be going up, that is certain.'

'Yes,' Dainty said. 'Cold comfort, but—'

The door to the office opened again and the Witcher recognised the something in a green cap and coney fur coat.

'Merchant Biberveldt,' it announced, 'instructs to buy more pots, should they run out. Price no object.'

'Excellent,' the halfling smiled, and his smile called to mind the twisted face of a furious wildcat. 'We will buy huge quantities of pots; Mr Biberveldt's wish is our command. What else shall we buy more of? Cabbage? Wood tar? Iron rakes?'

'Furthermore,' the something in the fur coat croaked, 'merchant Biberveldt requests thirty crowns in cash, because he has to pay a bribe, eat something and drink some beer, and three miscreants stole his purse in the Spear Blade.'

'Oh. Three miscreants,' Dainty said in a slow, drawling voice. 'Yes, this city seems to be full of miscreants. And where, if one may ask, is the Honourable Merchant Biberveldt at this very moment?'

'Where else would he be,' the something said, sniffing, 'than at the Western Market?'

'Vimme,' Dainty said malevolently, 'don't ask questions, but find me a stout, robust stick from somewhere. I'm going to the Western Market, but I can't go without a stick. There are too many miscreants and thieves there.'

'A stick, you say? Of course. But, Dainty, I'd like to know something, because it is preying on me. I was supposed not to ask any questions, but I shall make a guess, and you can either confirm or deny it. All right?'

'Guess away.'

'That rancid cod liver oil, that oil, that wax and those bowls, that bloody twine, it was all a tactical gambit, wasn't it? You wanted

169

to distract the competition's attention from the cochineal and the mimosa, didn't you? To stir up confusion on the market? Hey, Dainty?'

The door opened suddenly and something without a cap ran in.

'Sorrel reports that everything is ready!' it yelled shrilly. 'And asks if he should start pouring.'

'Yes, he should!' the halfling bellowed. 'At once!'

'By the red beard of old Rhundurin!' Vimme Vivaldi bellowed, as soon as the gnome had shut the door. 'I don't understand anything! What is happening here? Pour what? Into what?'

'I have no idea,' Dainty admitted. 'But, Vimme, the wheels of business must be oiled.'

IV

Pushing through the crowd with difficulty, Geralt emerged right in front of a stall laden with copper skillets, pots and frying pans, sparkling in the rays of the twilight sun. Behind the stall stood a red-bearded dwarf in an olive-green hood and heavy sealskin boots. The dwarf's face bore an expression of visible dislike; to be precise he looked as though any moment he intended to spit on the female customer sifting through the goods. The customer's breast was heaving, she was shaking her golden curls and was besetting the dwarf with a ceaseless and chaotic flow of words.

The customer was none other than Vespula, known to Geralt as the thrower of missiles. Without waiting for her to recognise him, he melted swiftly back into the crowd.

The Western Market was bustling with life and getting through the crowd was like forcing one's way through a hawthorn bush. Every now and then something caught on his sleeves and trouser legs; at times it was children who had lost their mothers while they were dragging their fathers away from the beer tent, at others it was spies from the guardhouse, at others shady vendors of caps of invisibility, aphrodisiacs and bawdy scenes carved in cedar wood. Geralt stopped smiling and began to swear, making judicious use of his elbows.

He heard the sound of a lute and a familiar peal of laughter. The sounds drifted from a fabulously coloured stall, decorated with the sign: 'Buy your wonders, amulets and fish bait here'.

'Has anyone ever told you, madam, that you are gorgeous?' Dandelion yelled, sitting on the stall and waving his legs cheerfully. 'No? It cannot be possible! This is a city of blind men, nothing but a city of blind men. Come, good folk! Who would hear a ballad of love? Whoever would be moved and enriched spiritually, let him toss a coin into the hat. What are you shoving your way in for, you bastard? Keep your pennies for beggars, and don't insult an artist like me with copper. Perhaps *I* could forgive you, but art never could!'

'Dandelion,' Geralt said, approaching. 'I thought we had split up to search for the doppler. And you're giving concerts. Aren't you ashamed to sing at markets like an old beggar?'

'Ashamed?' the bard said, astonished. 'What matters is *what* and *how* one sings, and not *where*. Besides, I'm hungry, and the stallholder promised me lunch. As far as the doppler is concerned, look for it yourselves. I'm not cut out for chases, brawls or mob law. I'm a poet.'

'You would do better not to attract attention, O poet. Your fiancée is here. There could be trouble.'

'Fiancée?' Dandelion blinked nervously. 'Which one do you mean? I have several.'

Vespula, clutching a copper frying pan, had forced her way through the audience with the momentum of a charging aurochs. Dandelion jumped up from the stall and darted away, nimbly leaping over some baskets of carrots. Vespula turned towards the Witcher, dilating her nostrils. Geralt stepped backwards, his back coming up against the hard resistance of the stall's wall.

'Geralt!' Dainty Biberveldt shouted, jumping from the crowd and bumping into Vespula. 'Quickly, quickly! I've seen him! Look, there, he's getting away!'

'I'll get you yet, you lechers!' Vespula screamed, trying to regain her balance. 'I'll catch up with the whole of your debauched gang! A fine company! A pheasant, a scruff and a midget with hairy heels! You'll be sorry!'

'This way, Geralt!' Dainty yelled as he ran, jostling a small group of schoolboys intently playing the shell game. 'There, there, he's scarpered between those wagons! Steal up on him from the left! Quick!'

They rushed off in pursuit, the curses of the stallholders and customers they had knocked over ringing in their ears. By a miracle Geralt avoided tripping over a snot-nosed tot caught up in his legs. He jumped over it, but knocked over two barrels of herrings, for which an enraged fisherman lashed him across the back with a live eel, which he was showing to some customers at that moment.

They saw the doppler trying to flee past a sheep pen.

'From the other side!' Dainty yelled. 'Cut him off from the other side, Geralt!'

The doppler shot like an arrow along the fence, green waistcoat flashing. It was becoming clear why he was not changing into anybody else. No one could rival a halfling's agility. No one. Apart from another halfling. Or a witcher.

Geralt saw the doppler suddenly changing direction, kicking up a cloud of dust, and nimbly ducking into a hole in the fence surrounding a large tent serving as a slaughterhouse and a shambles. Dainty also saw it. The doppler jumped between the palings and began to force his way between the flock of bleating sheep crowded into the enclosure. It was clear he would not make it. Geralt turned and rushed after him between the palings. He felt a sudden tug, heard the crack of leather tearing, and the leather suddenly became very loose under his other arm.

The Witcher stopped. Swore. Spat. And swore again.

Dainty rushed into the tent after the doppler. From inside came screaming, the noise of blows, cursing and an awful banging noise.

The Witcher swore a third time, extremely obscenely, then gnashed his teeth, raised his hand and formed his fingers into the Aard Sign, aiming it straight at the tent. The tent billowed up like a sail during a gale, and from the inside reverberated a hellish howling, clattering and lowing of oxen. The tent collapsed.

The doppler, crawling on its belly, darted out from beneath the canvas and dashed towards another, smaller tent, probably the cold store. Right away, Geralt pointed his hand towards him and jabbed him in the back with the Sign. The doppler tumbled to the ground as though struck by lightning, turned a somersault, but immediately sprang up and rushed into the tent. The Witcher was hot on his heels.

It stank of meat inside the tent. And it was dark.

Tellico Lunngrevink Letorte was standing there, breathing heavily, clinging with both hands onto a side of pork hanging on a pole.

173

There was no other way out of the tent, the canvas firmly fastened to the ground with numerous pegs.

'It's a pleasure to meet you again, mimic,' Geralt said coldly.

The doppler was breathing heavily and hoarsely.

'Leave me alone,' it finally grunted. 'Why are you tormenting me, Witcher?'

'Tellico,' Geralt said, 'You're asking foolish questions. In order to come into possession of Biberveldt's horses and identity, you cut his head open and abandoned him in the wilds. You're still making use of his personality and ignoring the problems you are causing him. The Devil only knows what else you're planning, but I shall confuse those plans, in any event. I don't want to kill you or turn you over to the authorities, but you must leave the city. I'll see to it that you do.'

'And if I don't want to?'

'I'll carry you out in a sack on a handcart.'

The doppler swelled up abruptly, and then suddenly became thinner and began to grow, his curly, chestnut hair turning white and straightening, reaching his shoulders. The halfling's green waistcoat shone like oil, becoming black leather, and silver studs sparkled on the shoulders and sleeves. The chubby, ruddy face elongated and paled.

The hilt of a sword extended above its right shoulder.

'Don't come any closer,' the second Witcher said huskily and smiled. 'Don't come any nearer, Geralt. I won't let you lay hands on me.'

What a hideous smile I have, Geralt thought, reaching for his sword. What a hideous face I have. And how hideously I squint. So is that what I look like? Damn.

The hands of the doppler and the Witcher simultaneously touched their sword hilts, and both swords simultaneously sprang from their scabbards. Both witchers simultaneously took two quick, soft steps; one to the front, the other to the side. Both of them simultaneously raised their swords and swung them in a short, hissing moulinet.

Simultaneously, they both stopped dead, frozen in position.

'You cannot defeat me,' the doppler snarled. 'Because I am you, Geralt.'

'You are mistaken, Tellico,' the Witcher said softly. 'Drop your sword and resume Biberveldt's form. Otherwise you'll regret it, I warn you.'

'I am you,' the doppler repeated. 'You will not gain an advantage over me. You cannot defeat me, because I am you!'

'You cannot have any idea what it means to be me, mimic.'

Tellico lowered the hand gripping the sword.

'I am you,' he repeated.

'No,' the Witcher countered, 'you are not. And do you know why? Because you're a poor, little, good-natured doppler. A doppler who, after all, could have killed Biberveldt and buried his body in the undergrowth, by so doing gaining total safety and utter certainty that he would not be unmasked, ever, by anybody, including the half-ling's spouse, the famous Gardenia Biberveldt. But you didn't kill him, Tellico, because you didn't have the courage. Because you're a poor, little, good-natured doppler, whose close friends call him Dudu. And whoever you might change into you'll always be the same. You only know how to copy what is good in us, because you don't understand the bad in us. That's what you are, doppler.'

Tellico moved backwards, pressing his back against the tent's canvas.

'Which is why,' Geralt continued, 'you will now turn back into Biberveldt and hold your hands out nicely to be tied up. You aren't capable of defying me, because I am what you are unable of copying. You are absolutely aware of this, Dudu. Because you took over my thoughts for a moment.'

Tellico straightened up abruptly. His face's features, still those of the Witcher, blurred and spread out, and his white hair curled and began to darken.

'You're right, Geralt,' he said indistinctly, because his lips had begun to change shape. 'I took over your thoughts. Only briefly, but it was sufficient. Do you know what I'm going to do now?'

The leather witcher jacket took on a glossy, cornflower blue colour. The doppler smiled, straightened his plum bonnet with its egret's feather, and tightened the strap of the lute slung over his shoulder. The lute which had been a sword a moment ago.

'I'll tell you what I'm going to do, Witcher,' he said, with the rippling laughter characteristic of Dandelion. 'I'll go on my way, squeeze my way into the crowd and change quietly into any-old-body, even a beggar. Because I prefer being a beggar in Novigrad to being a doppler in the wilds. Novigrad owes me something, Geralt. The building of a city here tainted a land we could have lived in; lived in in our natural form. We have been exterminated, hunted down like rabid dogs. I'm one of the few to survive. I want to survive and I will survive. Long ago, when wolves pursued me in the winter, I turned into a wolf and ran with the pack for several weeks. And survived. Now I'll do that again, because I don't want to roam about through wildernesses and be forced to winter beneath fallen trees. I don't want to be forever hungry, I don't want to serve as target practice all the time. Here, in Novigrad, it's warm, there's grub, I can make money and very seldom do people shoot arrows at each other. Novigrad is a pack of wolves. I'll join that pack and survive. Understand?'

Geralt nodded reluctantly.

'You gave dwarves, halflings, gnomes and even elves,' the doppler continued, twisting his mouth in an insolent, Dandelion smile, 'the modest possibility of assimilation. Why should I be any worse off? Why am I denied that right? What do I have to do to be able to live in this city? Turn into a she-elf with doe eyes, silky hair and long legs? Well? In what way is a she-elf better than me? Only that at the sight of the she-elf you pick up speed, and at the sight of me you want to puke? You know where you can stuff an argument like that. I'll survive anyway. I know how to. As a wolf I ran, I howled and I fought without others over a she-wolf. As a resident of Novigrad I'll trade, weave wicker baskets, beg or steal; as one of you I'll do what one of you usually does. Who knows, perhaps I'll even take a wife.'

The Witcher said nothing.

'Yes, as I said,' Tellico continued calmly. 'I'm going. And you, Geralt, will not even try to stop me. Because I, Geralt, knew your thoughts for a moment. Including the ones you don't want to admit to, the ones you even hide from yourself. Because to stop me you'd have to kill me. And the thought of killing me in cold blood fills you with disgust. Doesn't it?'

The Witcher said nothing.

Tellico adjusted the strap of the lute again, turned away and walked towards the exit. He walked confidently, but Geralt saw him hunch his neck and shoulders in expectation of the whistle of a sword blade. He put his sword in its scabbard. The doppler stopped in mid-step, and looked around.

'Farewell, Geralt,' he said. 'Thank you.'

'Farewell, Dudu,' the Witcher replied. 'Good luck.'

The doppler turned away and headed towards the crowded bazaar, with Dandelion's sprightly, cheerful, swinging gait. Like Dandelion, he swung his left arm vigorously and just like Dandelion he grinned at the wenches as he passed them. Geralt set off slowly after him. Slowly.

Tellico seized his lute in full stride; after slowing his pace he played two chords, and then dextrously played a tune Geralt knew. Turning away slightly, he sang.

Exactly like Dandelion.

Spring will return, on the road the rain will fall
Hearts will be warmed by the heat of the sun
It must be thus, for fire still smoulders in us all
An eternal fire, hope for each one.

'Pass that on to Dandelion, if you remember,' he called, 'and tell him that *Winter* is a lousy title. The ballad should be called *The Eternal Fire*. Farewell, Witcher!'

'Hey!' suddenly resounded. 'You, pheasant!'

Tellico turned around in astonishment. From behind a stall emerged Vespula, her breast heaving violently, raking him up with a foreboding gaze.

'Eyeing up tarts, you cad?' she hissed, breast heaving more and more enticingly. 'Singing your little songs, are you, you knave?'

Tellico took off his bonnet and bowed, broadly smiling Dandelion's characteristic smile.

177

'Vespula, my dear,' he said ingratiatingly, 'how glad I am to see you. Forgive me, my sweet. I owe you—'

'Oh, you do, you do,' Vespula interrupted loudly. 'And what you owe me you will now pay me! Take that!'

An enormous copper frying pan flashed in the sun and with a deep, loud clang smacked into the doppler's head. Tellico staggered and fell with an indescribably stupid expression frozen on his face, arms spread out, and his physiognomy suddenly began to change, melt and lose its similarity to anything at all. Seeing it, the Witcher leaped towards him, in full flight snatching a large kilim from a stall. Having unfurled the kilim on the ground, he sent the doppler onto it with two kicks and rolled it up in it quickly but tightly.

Sitting down on the bundle, he wiped his forehead with a sleeve. Vespula, gripping the frying pan, looked at him malevolently, and the crowd closed in all around.

'He's sick,' the Witcher said and smiled affectedly. 'It's for his own good. Don't crowd, good people, the poor thing needs air.'

'Did you hear?' Chappelle asked calmly but resonantly, suddenly pushing his way through the throng. 'Please do not form a public gathering here! Please disperse! Public gatherings are forbidden. Punishable by a fine!'

In the blink of an eye the crowd scattered to the sides, only to reveal Dandelion, approaching swiftly, to the sounds of his lute. On seeing him, Vespula let out an ear-splitting scream, dropped the frying pan and fled across the square.

'What happened?' Dandelion asked. 'Did she see the Devil?'

Geralt stood up, holding the bundle, which had begun to move weakly. Chappelle slowly approached. He was alone and his personal guard was nowhere to be seen.

'I wouldn't come any closer,' Geralt said quietly. 'If I were you, Lord Chappelle, sir, I wouldn't come any closer.'

'You wouldn't?' Chappelle tightened his thin lips, looking at him coldly.

'If I were you, Lord Chappelle, I would pretend I never saw anything.'

'Yes, no doubt,' Chappelle said. 'But you are not me.'

Dainty Biberveldt ran up from behind the tent, out of breath and sweaty. On seeing Chappelle he stopped, began to whistle, held his hands behind his back and pretended to be admiring the roof of the granary.

Chappelle went over and stood by Geralt, very close. The Witcher did not move, but only narrowed his eyes. For a moment they looked at each other and then Chappelle leaned over the bundle.

'Dudu,' he said to Dandelion's strangely deformed cordovan boots sticking out of the rolled-up kilim. 'Copy Biberveldt, and quickly.'

'What?' Dainty yelled, stopping staring at the granary. 'What's that?'

'Be quiet,' Chappelle said. 'Well, Dudu, are things coming along?'

'I'm just,' a muffled grunting issued from the kilim. 'I'm . . . Just a moment . . .'

The cordovan boots sticking out of the kilim stretched, became blurred and changed into the halfling's bare, hairy feet.

'Get out, Dudu,' Chappelle said. 'And you, Dainty, be quiet. All halflings look the same, don't they?'

Dainty mumbled something indistinctly. Geralt, eyes still narrowed, looked at Chappelle suspiciously. The minister, however, straightened up and looked all around, and all that remained of any gawkers who were still in the vicinity was the clacking of wooden clogs dying away in the distance.

The second Dainty Biberveldt scrambled and rolled out of the bundle, sneezed, sat up and rubbed his eyes and nose. Dandelion perched himself on a trunk lying alongside, and strummed away on his lute with an expression of moderate interest on his face.

'Who do you think that is, Dainty?' Chappelle asked mildly. 'Very similar to you, don't you think?'

'He's my cousin,' the halfling shot back and grinned. 'A close relative. Dudu Biberveldt of Knotgrass Meadow, an astute business-man. I've actually just decided . . .'

'Yes, Dainty?'

'I've decided to appoint him my factor in Novigrad. What do you say to that, cousin?'

'Oh, thank you, cousin,' his close relative, the pride of the

Biberveldt clan, and an astute businessman, smiled broadly. Chappelle also smiled.

'Has your dream about life in the city come true?' Geralt muttered. 'What do you see in this city, Dudu . . . and you, Chappelle?'

'Had you lived on the moors,' Chappelle muttered back, 'and eaten roots, got soaked and frozen, you'd know. We also deserve something from life, Geralt. We aren't inferior to you.'

'Very true,' Geralt nodded. 'You aren't. Perhaps it even happens that you're better. What happened to the real Chappelle?'

'Popped his clogs,' the second Chappelle whispered. 'Two months ago now. Apoplexy. May the earth lie lightly on him, and may the Eternal Fire light his way. I happened to be in the vicinity . . . No one noticed . . . Geralt? You aren't going to—'

'What didn't anyone notice?' the Witcher asked, with an inscrutable expression.

'Thank you,' Chappelle muttered.

'Are there more of you?'

'Is it important?'

'No,' agreed the Witcher, 'it isn't.'

A two-cubit-tall figure in a green cap and spotted coney fur coat dashed out from behind the wagons and stalls and trotted over.

'Mr Biberveldt,' the gnome panted and stammered, looking around and sweeping his eyes from one halfling to the other.

'I presume, shorty,' Dainty said, 'that you have a matter for my cousin, Dudu Biberveldt, to deal with. Speak. Speak. That is him.'

'Sorrel reports that everything has gone,' the gnome said and smiled broadly, showing small, pointed teeth, 'for four crowns apiece.'

'I think I know what it's about,' Dainty said. 'Pity Vivaldi's not here, he would have calculated the profit in no time.'

'If I may, cousin,' Tellico Lunngrevink Letorte, Penstock for short, Dudu to his close friends, and for the whole of Novigrad a member of the large Biberveldt family, spoke up. 'If I may, I'll calculate it. I have an infallible memory for figures. As well as for other things.'

'By all means,' Dainty gave a bow. 'By all means, cousin.'

'The costs,' the doppler frowned, 'were low. Eighteen for the oil, eight-fifty for the cod liver oil, hmm . . . Altogether, including the string, forty-five crowns. Takings: six hundred at four crowns, makes two thousand four hundred. No commission, because there weren't any middlemen . . .'

'Please do not forget about the tax,' the second Chappelle reminded him. 'Please do not forget that standing before you is a representative of the city authorities and the temple, who treats his duties gravely and conscientiously.'

'It's exempt from tax,' Dudu Biberveldt declared. 'Because it was sold in a sacred cause.'

'Hey?'

'The cod liver oil, wax and oil dyed with a little cochineal,' the doppler explained, 'need only be poured into earthenware bowls with a piece of string dipped into it. The string, when lit, gives a beautiful, red flame, which burns for a long time and doesn't smell. The Eternal Fire. The priests needed vigil lights for the altars of the Eternal Fire. Now they don't need them.'

'Bloody hell . . .' Chappelle muttered. 'You're right. They needed vigil lights . . . Dudu, you're brilliant.'

'I take after my mother,' Tellico said modestly.

'Yes, indeed, the spitting image of his mother,' Dainty agreed. 'Just look into those intelligent eyes. Begonia Biberveldt, my darling aunt, as I live and breathe.'

'Geralt,' Dandelion groaned. 'He's earned more in three days than I've earned in my whole life by singing!'

'In your place,' the Witcher said gravely, 'I'd quit singing and take up commerce. Ask him, he may take you on as an apprentice.'

'Witcher,' Tellico said, tugging him by the sleeve. 'Tell me how I could . . . repay you . . . ?'

'Twenty-two crowns.'

'What?'

'For a new jacket. Look what's left of mine.'

'Do you know what?' Dandelion suddenly yelled. 'Let's all go to the house of ill repute! To Passiflora! The Biberveldts are paying!'

'Do they admit halflings?' Dainty asked with concern.

'Just let them try not to,' Chappelle put on a menacing expression. 'Just let them try and I'll accuse their entire bordello of heresy.'

'Right,' Dandelion called. 'Very satisfactory. Geralt? Are you coming?'

The Witcher laughed softly.

'Do you know what, Dandelion?' he said. 'I'll come with pleasure.'

A LITTLE SACRIFICE

I

The mermaid emerged to waist-height from the water and splashed her hands violently and hard against the surface. Geralt saw that she had gorgeous, utterly perfect breasts. Only the colour spoiled the effect; the nipples were dark green and the areolae around them were only a little lighter. Nimbly aligning herself with an approaching wave, the mermaid arched gracefully, shook her wet, willow-green hair and sang melodiously.

'What?' The duke leaned over the side of the cog. 'What is she saying?'

'She's declining,' Geralt said. 'She says she doesn't want to.'

'Have you explained that I love her? That I can't imagine life without her? That I want to wed her? Only her, no other?'

'Yes, I have.'

'And?'

'And nothing.'

'Say it again.'

The Witcher touched his lips and produced a quavering warble. Struggling to find the words and the intonation, he began to translate the duke's avowal.

The mermaid, lying back on the water, interrupted.

'Don't translate, don't tire yourself,' she sang. 'I understand. When he says he loves me he always puts on such a foolish expression. Did he say anything definite?'

'Not really.'

'Pity,' the mermaid said, before she flapped in the water and dived under, flexing her tail powerfully and making the sea foam with her notched flukes, which resembled the tail of a mullet.

'What? What did she say?' the duke asked.

'That it's a shame.'

'What's a shame? What does she mean, "shame"?'

'I'd say she turned you down.'

'Nobody refuses me!' the duke roared, denying the obvious facts.

'My Lord,' the skipper of the cog muttered, walking over to them. 'The nets are ready, all we need do is cast them and she will be yours . . .'

'I wouldn't advise it,' Geralt said softly. 'She's not alone. There are more of them beneath the waves, and there may be a kraken deeper down there.'

The skipper quaked, blanched and seized his backside with both hands, in a nonsensical gesture.

'A kra— kraken?'

'Yes, a kraken,' the Witcher repeated. 'I don't advise fooling around with nets. All she need do is scream, and all that'll be left of this tub will be a few floating planks. They'd drown us like kittens. Besides, Agloval, you should decide whether you want to wed her or catch her in a net and keep her in a barrel.'

'I love her,' Agloval said firmly. 'I want her for my wife. But for that she must have legs and not a scaly tail. And it's feasible, since I bought a magical elixir with a full guarantee, for two pounds of exquisite pearls. After drinking it she'll grow legs. She'll just suffer a little, for three days, no more. Call her, Witcher, tell her again.'

'I've already told her twice. She said absolutely no, she doesn't consent. But she added that she knows a witch, a sea witch, who is prepared to cast a spell to turn your legs into a handsome tail. Painlessly.'

'She must be insane! She thinks I would have a fishy tail? Not a chance! Call her, Geralt!'

The Witcher leaned far out over the side. The water in the boat's shadow was green and seemed as thick as jelly. He did not have to call. The mermaid suddenly shot out above the surface in a fountain of water. For a moment she literally stood on her tail, then dived

184

down into the waves and turned on her back, revealing her attributes in all their glory. Geralt swallowed.

'Hey!' she sang. 'Will this take much longer? My skin's getting chapped from the sun! White Hair, ask him if he consents.'

'He does not,' the Witcher sang back. 'Sh'eenaz, understand, he cannot have a tail, cannot live beneath the water. You can breathe air, but he cannot breathe underwater!'

'I knew it!' the mermaid screamed shrilly. 'I knew it! Excuses, foolish, naive excuses, not a bit of sacrifice! Whoever loves makes sacrifices! I made sacrifices for him, every day I hauled myself out onto the rocks for him, I wore out the scales on my bottom, frayed my fins; I caught colds for him! And he will not sacrifice those two hideous pegs for me? Love doesn't just mean taking, one also has to be able to give up things, to make sacrifices! Tell him that!'

'Sh'eenaz!' Geralt called. 'Don't you understand? He cannot survive in the water!'

'I don't accept stupid excuses! I . . . I like him too and want to have his fry, but how can I, if he doesn't want to be a spawner? Where should I deposit my eggs, hey? In his cap?'

'What is she saying?' the duke yelled. 'Geralt! I didn't bring you here to chat with her—'

'She's digging her heels in. She's angry.'

'Cast those nets!' Agloval roared. 'I'll keep her in a pool for a month and then she'll—'

'Shove it!' the skipper yelled back, demonstrating what he was to shove with his middle finger. 'There might be a kraken beneath us! Ever seen a kraken, My Lord? Hop into the water, if that is your will, and catch her with your hands! I'm not getting involved. I make my living by fishing from this cog!'

'You make your living by my goodwill, you scoundrel! Cast your net or I'll order you strung up!'

'Kiss a dog's arse! I'm in charge on this cog!'

'Be quiet, both of you!' Geralt shouted irately. 'She's saying something, it's a difficult dialect, I need to concentrate!'

'I've had enough!' Sh'eenaz yelled melodiously. 'I'm hungry! Well, White Hair, he must decide, decide at once. Tell him just one thing: I will not be made a laughing stock of any longer or associate with him if he's going to look like a four-armed starfish. Tell him I have girlfriends who are much better at those frolics he was suggesting on the rocks! But I consider them immature games, fit for children before they shed their scales. I'm a normal, healthy mermaid—'

'Sh'eenaz—'

'Don't interrupt! I haven't finished yet! I'm healthy, normal and ripe for spawning, and if he really desires me, he must have a tail, fins and everything a normal merman has. Otherwise I don't want to know him!'

Geralt translated quickly, trying not to be vulgar. He was not very successful. The duke flushed and swore foully.

'The brazen hussy!' he yelled. 'The frigid mackerel! Let her find herself a cod!'

'What did he say?' Sh'eenaz asked curiously, swimming over.

'That he doesn't want a tail!'

'Then tell him . . . Tell him to dry up!'

'What did she say?'

'She told you,' the Witcher translated, 'to go drown yourself.'

II

'Ah well,' Dandelion said. 'Pity I couldn't sail with you, but what could I do? Sailing makes me puke like nobody's business. But you know what, I've never spoken to a mermaid. It's a shame, dammit.'

'I know you,' Geralt said, fastening his saddle bags. 'You'll write a ballad anyway.'

'Never fear. I already have the first stanzas. In my ballad the mermaid will sacrifice herself for the duke, she'll exchange her fishtail for slender legs, but will pay for it by losing her voice. The duke will betray her, abandon her, and then she'll perish from grief, and turn into foam, when the first rays of sunshine . . .'

'Who'd believe such rot?'

'It doesn't matter,' Dandelion snorted. 'Ballads aren't written to be believed. They are written to move their audience. But why am I talking to you about this, when you know bugger all about it? You'd better tell me how much Agloval paid you.'

'He didn't pay me anything. He claimed I had failed to carry out the task. That he had expected something else, and he pays for results, not good intentions.'

Dandelion shook his head, took off his bonnet and looked at the Witcher with a forlorn grimace on his mouth.

'You mean we still don't have any money?'

'So it would seem.'

Dandelion made an even more forlorn face.

'It's all my fault,' he moaned. 'I'm to blame for it all. Geralt, are you angry at me?'

No, the Witcher wasn't angry at Dandelion. Not at all.

There was no doubt Dandelion was to blame for what had befallen them. He had insisted they went to the fair at Four Maples. Organising festivities, the poet argued, satisfied people's profound and natural needs. From time to time, the bard maintained, a chap has to meet other people in a place where he can have a laugh and a singsong, gorge himself on kebabs and pierogis, drink beer, listen to music and squeeze a girl as he swung her around in the dance. If every chap wanted to satisfy those needs, Dandelion argued, individually, periodically and randomly, an indescribable mess would arise. For that reason holidays and festivities were invented. And since holidays and festivities exist, a chap ought to frequent them.

Geralt did not challenge this, although taking part in festivities occupied a very low position on the list of his own profound and natural needs. Nonetheless, he agreed to accompany Dandelion, for he was counting on obtaining information from the gathered concentration of people about a possible mission or job; he'd had no work for a long time and his cash reserves had shrunk alarmingly.

The Witcher did not bear Dandelion a grudge for provoking the Rangers of the Forest. He was not innocent either; for he could have intervened and held the bard back. He did not, however, for he could not stand the infamous Guardians of the Forest, known as the Rangers, a volunteer force whose mission was to eradicate non-humans. It had annoyed him to hear their boasts about elves, spriggans and eerie wives bristling with arrows, butchered or hanged. Dandelion, though, who after travelling for some time with the Witcher had become convinced of his impunity from retaliation, had surpassed himself. Initially, the Rangers had not reacted to his mockery, taunts or filthy suggestions, which aroused the thunderous laughter of the watching villagers. When, however, Dandelion sang a hastily-composed obscene and abusive couplet, ending with the words: 'If you want to be a nothing, be a Ranger,' an argument and then a fierce, mass punch-up broke out. The shed serving as the dancehall went up in smoke. Intervention came in the form of a squad of men belonging to Castellan Budibog, also known as the Emptyheaded, on whose estates lay Four Maples. The Rangers, Dandelion and Geralt were found jointly guilty of all the damage and offences, which included the seduction of a red-headed and mute girl, who was found in the bushes behind the barn following the incident, blushing and grinning foolishly, with her shift torn up to her armpits. Fortunately, Castellan Budibog knew Dandelion, so it ended with a fine being paid, which nonetheless ate up all the money they had. They also had to flee from Four Maples as fast as they could ride, because the Rangers, who had been chased out of the village, were threatening revenge, and an entire squad of them, numbering over forty men, was hunting rusalkas in the neighbouring forests. Geralt did not have the slightest desire to be hit by one of the Rangers' arrows, whose heads were barbed like harpoons and inflicted dreadful injuries.

So they had to abandon their original plan, which had involved doing the rounds of the villages on the edge of the forest, where the Witcher had reasonable prospects of work. Instead they rode to Bremervoord, on the coast. Unfortunately, apart from the love affair between Duke Agloval and the mermaid Sh'eenaz, which offered small chances of success, the Witcher had failed to find a job. They had already sold Geralt's gold signet for food, and an alexandrite brooch the troubadour had once been given as a souvenir by one of his numerous paramours. Things were tight. But no, the Witcher was not angry with Dandelion.

'No, Dandelion,' he said. 'I'm not angry with you.'

Dandelion did not believe him, which was quite apparent by the fact that he kept quiet. Dandelion was seldom quiet. He patted his horse's neck, and fished around in his saddlebags for the umpteenth time. Geralt knew he would not find anything there they could sell. The smell of food, borne on a breeze from a nearby tavern, was becoming unbearable.

'Master?' somebody shouted. 'Hey, master!'

'Yes?' Geralt said, turning around. A big-bellied, well-built man in felt boots and a heavy fur-lined, wolf-skin coat clambered out of a cart pulled by a pair of onagers which had just stopped alongside.

'Erm . . . that is,' the paunchy man said, embarrassed, walking over, 'I didn't mean you, sir, I meant . . . I meant Master Dandelion . . .'

'It is I.' The poet proudly sat up straight, adjusting his bonnet bearing an egret feather. 'What is your need, my good man?'

'Begging your pardon,' the paunchy man said. 'I am Teleri

Drouhard, spice merchant and dean of our local Guild. My son, Gaspard, has just plighted his troth to Dalia, the daughter of Mestvin, the cog skipper.'

'Ha,' Dandelion said, maintaining a haughty air. 'I offer my congratulations and extend my wishes of happiness to the betrothed couple. How may I be of help? Does it concern *jus primae noctis*? I never decline that.'

'Hey? No . . . that is . . . You see, the betrothal banquet and ball are this evening. Since it got out that you, master, have come to Bremervoord, my wife won't let up – just like a woman. Listen, she says, Teleri, we'll show everybody we aren't churls like them, that we stand for culture and art. That when we have a feast, it's refined, and not an excuse to get pissed and throw up. I says to her, silly moo, but we've already hired one bard, won't that suffice? And she says one is too few, ho-ho, Master Dandelion, well, I never, such a celebrity, that'll be one in the eye for our neighbours. Master? Do us the honour . . . I'm prepared to give five-and-twenty talars, as a gesture, naturally – to show my support for the arts—'

'Do my ears deceive me?' Dandelion drawled. 'I, I am to be the second bard? An appendix to some other musician? I? I have not sunk so low, my dear sir, as to *accompany* somebody!'

Drouhard blushed.

'Forgive me, master,' he gibbered. 'That isn't what I meant . . . It was my wife . . . Forgive me . . . Do us the honour . . .'

'Dandelion,' Geralt hissed softly, 'don't put on airs. We need those few pennies.'

'Don't try to teach me!' the poet yelled. 'Me, putting on airs? Me? Look at him! What should I say about you, who rejects a lucrative proposition every other day? You won't kill hirikkas, because they're an endangered species, or mecopterans, because they're harmless, or night spirits, because they're sweet, or dragons, because your code forbids it. I, just imagine it, also have my self-respect! I also have a code!'

'Dandelion, please, do it for me. A little sacrifice, friend, nothing more. I swear, I won't turn my nose up at the next job that comes along. Come on, Dandelion . . .'

The troubadour looked down at the ground and scratched his chin, which was covered in soft, fair bristles. Drouhard, mouth gaping, moved closer.

'Master . . . Do us this honour. My wife won't forgive me if I don't invite you. Now then . . . I'll make it thirty.'

'Thirty-five,' Dandelion said firmly.

Geralt smiled and hopefully breathed in the scent of food wafting from the tavern.

'Agreed, master, agreed,' Teleri Drouhard said quickly, so quickly it was evident he would have given forty, had the need arisen. 'And now . . . My home, if you desire to groom yourself and rest, is your home. And you, sir . . . What do they call you?'

'Geralt of Rivia.'

'And I invite you too, sir, of course. For a bite to eat and something to drink . . .'

'Certainly, with pleasure,' Dandelion said. 'Show us the way, my dear sir. And just between us, who is the other bard?'

'The honourable Miss Essi Daven.'

III

Geralt rubbed a sleeve over the silver studs of his jacket and his belt buckle one more time, smoothed down his hair, which was held down with a clean headband, and polished his boots by rubbing one leg against the other.

'Dandelion?'

'Mm?' The bard smoothed the egret feather pinned to his bonnet, and straightened and pulled down his jerkin. The two of them had spent half the day cleaning their garments and tidying them up. 'What, Geralt?'

'Behave in such a way as they throw us out after supper and not before.'

'You must be joking,' the poet said indignantly. 'Watch your manners yourself. Shall we go in?'

'We shall. Do you hear? Somebody's singing. A woman.'

'Have you only just noticed? That's Essi Daven, known as Little Eye. What, have you never met a female troubadour? True, I forgot you steer clear of places where art flourishes. Little Eye is a gifted poet and singer, though not without her flaws, among which impertinence, so I hear, is not the least. What she is singing now happens to be one of my ballads. She will soon hear a piece of my mind which will make that little eye of hers water.'

'Dandelion, have mercy. They'll throw us out.'

'Don't interfere. These are professional issues. Let's go in.'

'Dandelion?'

'Hey?'

'Why Little Eye?'

'You'll see.'

The banquet was being held in a huge storeroom, emptied of barrels of herrings and cod liver oil. The smell had been killed – though not entirely – by hanging up bunches of mistletoe and heather decorated with coloured ribbons wherever possible. Here and there, as is customary, were also hung plaits of garlic meant to frighten off vampires.

The tables and benches, which had been pushed towards the walls, had been covered with white linen, and in a corner there was a large makeshift hearth and spit. It was crowded but not noisy. More than four dozen people of various estates and professions, not to mention the pimply youth and his snub-nosed fiancée, with her eyes fixed on her husband-to-be, were listening reverentially to a sonorous and melodious ballad sung by a young woman in a demure blue frock, sitting on a platform with a lute resting on her knee. The woman could not have been older than eighteen, and was very slim. Her long, luxuriant hair was the colour of dark gold. They entered as the girl finished the song and thanked the audience for the thunderous applause with a nod of her head, which shook her hair gently.

'Greetings, master, greetings,' Drouhard, dressed in his best clothes, leapt briskly over to them and pulled them towards the centre of the storeroom. 'Greetings to you, too, Gerard, sir . . . I am honoured . . . Yes . . . Come here . . . Noble ladies, noble gentlemen! Here is our honoured guest, who gave us this honour and honoured us . . . Master Dandelion, the celebrated singer and poetast . . . poet, I mean, has honoured us with this great honour . . . Thus honoured, we . . .'

Cheers and applause resounded, and just in time, for it was looking as though Drouhard would honour and stammer himself to death. Dandelion, blushing with pride, assumed a superior air and bowed carelessly, then waved a hand at a row of girls sitting on a long bench, like hens on a roost, being chaperoned by older matrons. The girls were sitting stiffly, giving the impression they had been stuck to the bench with carpenter's glue or some other powerful adhesive. Without exception they were holding their hands on tightly-clenched knees and their mouths were half-open.

'And presently,' Drouhard called. 'Come forth, help yourself to beer, fellows, and to the vittles! Prithee, prithee! Avail yourselves . . .'

The girl in the blue dress forced her way through the crowd, which had crashed onto the food-laden tables like a sea wave.

'Greetings, Dandelion,' she said.

Geralt considered the expression 'eyes like stars' banal and hackneyed, particularly since he had begun travelling with Dandelion, as the troubadour was inclined to throw that compliment about freely, usually, indeed, undeservedly. However, with regard to Essi Daven, even somebody as little susceptible to poetry as the Witcher had to concede the aptness of her nickname. For in her agreeable and pretty, but otherwise unremarkable, little face shone a huge, beautiful, shining, dark blue eye, which riveted the gaze. Essi Daven's other eye was largely covered and obscured by a golden curl, which fell onto her cheek. From time to time Essi flung the curl away with a toss of her head or a puff, at which point it turned out that Little Eye's other little eye was in every way the equal of the first.

'Greetings, Little Eye,' Dandelion said, grimacing. 'That was a pretty ballad you just sang. You've improved your repertoire considerably. I've always maintained that if one is incapable of writing poetry oneself one should borrow other people's. Have you borrowed many of them?'

'A few,' Essi Daven retorted at once and smiled, revealing little white teeth. 'Two or three. I wanted to use more, but it wasn't possible. Dreadful gibberish, and the tunes, though pleasant and unpretentious in their simplicity – not to say primitivism – are not what my audiences expect. Have you written anything new, Dandelion? I don't seem to be aware of it.'

'Small wonder,' the bard sighed. 'I sing my ballads in places to which only the gifted and renowned are invited, and you don't frequent such locations, after all.'

Essi blushed slightly and blew the lock of hair aside.

'Very true,' she said. 'I don't frequent bordellos, as the atmosphere depresses me. I sympathise with you that you have to sing in places like that. But well, that's the way it is. If one has no talent, one can't choose one's audiences.'

Now Dandelion visibly blushed. Little Eye, however, laughed

194

joyously, flung an arm around his neck all of a sudden and kissed him on the cheek. The Witcher was taken aback, but not too greatly. A professional colleague of Dandelion's could not, indeed, differ much from him in terms of predictability.

'Dandelion, you old bugger,' Essi said, still hugging the bard's neck. 'I'm glad to see you again, in good health and in full possession of your mental faculties.'

'Pshaw, Poppet.' Dandelion seized the girl around the waist, picked her up and spun her around so that her dress billowed around her. 'You were magnificent, by the Gods, I haven't heard such marvellous spitefulness for ages. You bicker even more captivatingly than you sing! And you look simply stunning!'

'I've asked you so many times,' Essi said, blowing her lock of hair away and glancing at Geralt, 'not to call me Poppet, Dandelion. Besides, I think it's high time you introduced me to your companion. I see he doesn't belong to our guild.'

'Save us, O Gods,' the troubadour laughed. 'He, Poppet, has no voice or ear, and can only rhyme "rear" with "beer". This is Geralt of Rivia, a member of the guild of witchers. Come closer, Geralt, and kiss Little Eye's hand.'

The Witcher approached, not really knowing what to do. One usually only kissed ladies of the rank of duchess and higher on the hand, or the ring, and one was supposed to kneel. Regarding women of lower standing that gesture, here, in the South, was considered erotically unambiguous and as such tended to be reserved only for close couples.

Little Eye dispelled his doubts, however, by willingly holding her hand out high with the fingers facing downwards. He grasped it clumsily and feigned a kiss. Essi, her beautiful eye still popping out of her head, blushed.

'Geralt of Rivia,' she said. 'What company you keep, Dandelion.'

'It is an honour for me,' the Witcher muttered, aware he was rivalling Drouhard in eloquence. 'Madam—'

'Damn it,' Dandelion snorted. 'Don't abash Little Eye with all that stammering and titling. She's Essi, he's Geralt. End of introductions. Let's get to the point, Poppet.'

'If you call me Poppet once more you'll get a slap. What point do we have to get to?'

'We have to agree on how we're going to sing. I suggest one after the other, a few ballads each. For the effect. Of course, singing our own ballads.'

'Suits me.'

'How much is Drouhard paying you?'

'None of your business. Who goes first?'

'You.'

'Agreed. Hey, look who's joined us. The Most Noble Duke of Agloval. He's just coming in, look.'

'Well, well,' Dandelion said gleefully. 'The audience is going up-market. Although, on the other hand, we oughtn't to count on him. He's a skinflint. Geralt can confirm it. The local duke bloody hates paying. He hires, admittedly. But he's not so good at paying.'

'I've heard a few things about him.' Essi, looking at Geralt, tossed the lock of hair back from her cheek. 'They were talking about it in the harbour and by the jetty. The famous Sh'eenaz, right?'

Agloval responded to the deep bows of the two rows by the door with a brief nod, and then almost immediately went over to Drouhard and drew him away into a corner, giving a sign that he was not expecting deference or ceremony in the centre of the storehouse. Geralt watched them out of the corner of his eye. They spoke softly, but it was apparent that they were both agitated. Drouhard kept wiping his forehead with a sleeve, shaking his head, and scratching his neck. He was asking questions which the duke, surly and dour, was responding to by shrugging.

'His Grace,' Essi said quietly, moving closer to Geralt, 'looks pre-occupied. Affairs of the heart again? The misunderstanding from earlier today with his famous mermaid? Hey, Witcher?'

'Perhaps,' Geralt answered, looking askance at the poet, astonished and strangely annoyed by her question. 'Well, everybody has some personal problems. However, not everybody likes them to be sung about from the rooftops.'

Little Eye blanched slightly, blew away her lock of hair and looked at him defiantly.

'By saying that did you mean to offend or only tease me?'

'Neither one nor the other. I merely wanted to forestall further questions about the problems between Agloval and the mermaid. Questions I do not feel entitled to answer.'

'I understand.' Essi Daven's gorgeous eye narrowed slightly. 'I won't burden you with a similar dilemma. I shall not ask you any of the questions I meant to ask, and which, if I'm to be frank, I treated only as a prelude and invitation to a pleasant conversation. Very well, that conversation will not come to pass, then, and you need fear not that the content will be sung from some rooftop. It has been my pleasure.'

She turned on her heel and walked off towards the tables, where she was immediately greeted with respect. Dandelion shifted his weight from foot to foot and coughed tellingly.

'I won't say that was exquisitely courteous of you, Geralt.'

'It came out wrongly,' the Witcher agreed. 'I hurt her, quite unintentionally. Perhaps I should follow her and apologise?'

'Drop it,' the bard said and added aphoristically, 'There is never a second opportunity to make a first impression. Come on, let's have a beer instead.'

They did not make it to the beer. Drouhard pushed his way through a garrulous group of merchants.

'Gerard, sir,' he said. 'Please step this way. His Grace would like to talk to you.'

'Very well.'

'Geralt,' Dandelion seized him by the sleeve. 'Don't forget.'

'Forget what?'

'You promised to agree to any task, without complaint. I shall hold you to it. What was it you said? A little sacrifice?'

'Very well, Dandelion.'

He went off with Drouhard into the corner of the storeroom, away from the guests. Agloval was sitting at a low table. He was accompanied by a colourfully dressed, weather-beaten man with a short, black beard whom Geralt had not noticed earlier.

'We meet again, Witcher,' the duke said. 'Although this morning I swore I didn't want to see you again. But I do not have another

197

witcher to hand, so you will have to do. Meet Zelest, my bailiff and pearl diving steward. Speak, Zelest.'

'This morning,' said the weather-beaten individual in a low voice, 'we planned to go diving outside the usual grounds. One boat went further westwards, beyond the headland, towards the Dragons Fangs.'

'The Dragons Fangs,' Agloval cut in, 'are two volcanic reefs at the end of the headland. They can be seen from our coast.'

'Aye,' Zelest confirmed. 'People don't usually sail there, for there are whirlpools and rocks, it's dangerous to dive there. But there's fewer and fewer pearls by the coast. Aye, one boat went there. A crew of seven souls, two sailors and five divers, including one woman. When they hadn't returned by the eventide we began to fret, although the sea was calm, as if oil had been poured on it. I sent a few swift skiffs there and we soon found the boat drifting on the sea. There was no one in it, not a living soul. Vanished into thin air. We know not what happened. But there must have been fighting there, a veritable massacre. There were signs . . .'

'What signs?' the Witcher squinted.

'Well, the whole deck was spattered in blood.'

Drouhard hissed and looked around anxiously. Zelest lowered his voice.

'It was as I said,' he repeated, clenching his jaw. 'The boat was spattered in gore, length and breadth. No question but a veritable massacre took place on board. Something killed those people. They say it was a sea monster. No doubt, a sea monster.'

'Not pirates?' asked Geralt softly. 'Or pearl diving competition? Do you rule out a normal knife fight?'

'We do,' said the duke. 'There are no pirates here, no competition. And knife fights don't result in everybody – to the last man – disappearing. No, Geralt. Zelest is right. It was a sea monster, and nothing else. Listen, now no one dares go to sea, not even to the nearby and familiar fishing grounds. The people are scared stiff and the harbour is paralysed. Even the cogs and galleys aren't setting out. Do you see, Witcher?'

'I see,' Geralt nodded. 'Who will show me this place?'

'Ha,' Agloval placed a hand on the table and drummed his fingers. 'I like that. That's witcher talk. Getting to the point at once, without unnecessary chatter. Yes, I like that. Do you see, Drouhard? I told you, a hungry witcher is a good witcher. Well, Geralt? After all, were it not for your musical companion you would have gone to bed without your supper again. My information is correct, is it not?'

Drouhard lowered his head. Zelest stared vacantly ahead.

'Who'll show me the place?' Geralt repeated, looking coldly at Agloval.

'Zelest,' said the duke, his smile fading. 'Zelest will show you the Dragons Fangs and the route to them. When will you start work?'

'First thing tomorrow morning. Be at the harbour, Mr Zelest.'

'Very well, Master Witcher.'

'Excellent.' The duke rubbed his hands and smiled mockingly again. 'Geralt, I'm relying on you to do better with this monster than you did with the Sh'eenaz situation. I really am. Aha, one more thing. I forbid any gossiping about this incident; I don't want any more panic than we already have on our hands. Do you understand, Drouhard? I'll order your tongue torn out if you breathe a word.'

'I understand, Your Grace.'

'Good,' Agloval said, getting up. 'Then I shall go, I shall not interfere with the ball, nor provoke any rumours. Farewell, Drouhard. Wish the betrothed couple happiness on my behalf.'

'My thanks, Duke.'

Essi Daven, who was sitting on a low stool surrounded by a dense crowd of listeners, was singing a melodious and wistful ballad about the woeful fate of a betrayed lover. Dandelion, leaning against a post, was muttering something under his breath and counting bars and syllables on his fingers.

'Well?' he asked. 'Do you have a job, Geralt?'

'Yes,' the Witcher answered, not going into details, which in any case did not concern the bard.

'I told you I smelt a rat – and money. Good, very good. I'll make some money, you will too, we'll be able to afford to revel. We'll go to Cidaris, in time for the grape harvest festival. And now, if you'll excuse me, I've spotted something interesting on the bench over there.'

Geralt followed the poet's gaze, but aside from about a dozen girls with half-open mouths he saw nothing interesting. Dandelion pulled down his jerkin, set his bonnet over his right ear and approached the bench in long swinging strides. Having passed the matrons guarding the maidens with a deft flanking manoeuvre, he began his customary ritual of flashing a broad smile.

Essi Daven finished her ballad, and was rewarded with applause, a small purse and a large bouquet of pretty – though somewhat withered – chrysanthemums.

The Witcher circulated among the guests, looking for an opportunity to finally occupy a seat at the table, which was laden with vittles. He gazed longingly at the rapidly vanishing pickled herrings, stuffed cabbage leaves, boiled cod heads and mutton chops, at the rings of sausage and capons being torn into pieces, and the smoked salmon and hams being chopped up with knives. The problem was that there were no vacant seats at the table.

The maidens and matrons, somewhat livened up, surrounded Dandelion, calling squeakily for a performance. Dandelion smiled falsely and made excuses, ineffectually feigning modesty.

Geralt, overcoming his embarrassment, virtually forced his way to the table. An elderly gentleman, smelling strongly of vinegar, moved aside surprisingly courteously and willingly, almost knocking off several guests sitting alongside him. Geralt got down to eating without delay and in a flash had cleared the only dish he could reach. The gentleman smelling of vinegar passed him another. In gratitude, the Witcher listened attentively to the elderly gentleman's long tirade concerning the present times and the youth of today. The elderly gentleman stubbornly described sexual freedom as 'laxity', so Geralt had some difficulty keeping a straight face.

Essi stood by the wall, beneath bunches of mistletoe, alone, tuning her lute. The Witcher saw a young man in a brocaded waisted kaftan approaching and saying something to the poet, smiling wanly the while. Essi looked at the young man, her pretty mouth sneering slightly, and said several quick words. The young man cowered and walked hurriedly away, and his ears, as red as beetroots, glowed in the semi-darkness for a long time afterwards.

'. . . abomination, shame and disgrace,' the elderly gentleman smelling of vinegar continued. 'One enormous laxity, sir.'

'Indeed,' Geralt nodded tentatively, wiping his plate with a hunk of bread.

'May I request silence, noble ladies, noble lords,' Drouhard called, walking into the middle of the room. 'The celebrated Master Dandelion, in spite of being a little bodily indisposed and weary, shall now sing for us his celebrated ballad about Queen Marienn and the Black Raven! He shall do it at the urgent plea of Miss Veverka, the miller's daughter, whom, he said, he may not refuse.'

Miss Veverka, one of the less comely girls on the bench, became beautified in the blink of an eye. Uproar and applause erupted, drowning out further laxity from the elderly gentleman smelling of vinegar. Dandelion waited for total silence, played a striking prelude on his lute, after which he began to sing, without taking his eyes off Miss Veverka, who was growing more beautiful with each verse. Indeed, Geralt thought, that whoreson is more effective than all the magical oils and creams Yennefer sells in her little shop in Vengerberg.

He saw Essi steal behind the crowded semicircle of Dandelion's audience and cautiously vanish through the door to the terrace. Driven by a strange impulse, he slipped nimbly out from behind the table and followed her.

She stood, leaning forward, resting her elbows on the railing of the jetty, head drawn into her delicate, upraised shoulders. She was gazing at the rippling sea, glistening from the light of the moon and the fires burning in the harbour. A board creaked beneath Geralt's foot. Essi straightened up.

'I'm sorry, I didn't mean to disturb you,' he said, stiffly, searching for that sudden grimace on her lips to which she had treated the young man in brocade a moment earlier.

'You aren't disturbing me,' she replied, smiling and tossing back her lock of hair. 'I'm not seeking solitude here, but fresh air. Was all that smoke and airlessness bothering you too?'

'A little. But I'm more bothered by knowing that I offended you. I came here to apologise, Essi, to try to regain the chance of a pleasant conversation.'

'You deserve my apology,' she said, pressing her hands down on the railing. 'I reacted too impetuously. I always react too impetuously, I don't know how to control myself. Excuse me and give me another chance. For a conversation.'

He approached and leaned on the railing beside her. He felt the warmth emanating from her, and the faint scent of verbena. He liked the scent of verbena, although the scent of verbena was not the scent of lilac and gooseberry.

'What do you connect with the sea, Geralt?' she asked suddenly.

'Unease,' he answered, almost without thinking.

'Interesting. And you seem so calm and composed.'

'I didn't say I feel unease. You asked for associations.'

'Associations are the image of the soul. I know what I'm talking about, I'm a poet.'

'And what do you associate with the sea, Essi?' he asked quickly, to put an end to discussions about the unease he was feeling.

'With constant movement,' she answered after a pause. 'With change. And with riddles, with mystery, with something I cannot grasp, which I might be able to describe in a thousand different ways, in a thousand poems, never actually reaching the core, the heart of the matter. Yes, that's it.'

'And so,' he said, feeling the verbena affecting him more and more strongly. 'What you feel is also unease. And you seem so calm and composed.'

She turned towards him, tossing back her golden curl and fixing her gorgeous eyes on him.

'I'm not calm or composed, Geralt.'

It happened suddenly, utterly unexpectedly. The movement he made, which was supposed to have been just a touch, a gentle touch of her arms, turned into a powerful grasp of both hands around her very slender waist, into a rapid, though not rough, pulling of her closer, and into a sudden, passionate contact of their bodies. Essi stiffened suddenly, straightened, bent her torso powerfully backwards, pressed her hands down on his, firmly, as though she wanted to pull away and push his hands from her waist, but instead of that she seized them tightly, tipped her head forward, parted her lips and hesitated.

'Why . . . Why this?' she whispered. Her eye was wide open, her golden curl had fallen onto her cheek.

Calmly and slowly he tipped his head forward, brought his face closer and suddenly and quickly pursed his lips into a kiss. Essi, however, even then, did not release his hands grasping her waist and still powerfully arched her back, avoiding bodily contact. Remaining like that they turned around slowly, as though in a dance. She kissed him eagerly, expertly. For a long time.

Then she nimbly and effortlessly freed herself from his embrace, turned away, once again leaned on the railing, and drew her head into her shoulders. Geralt suddenly felt dreadfully, indescribably stupid. The feeling stopped him from approaching her, from putting an arm around her hunched back.

'Why?' she asked coolly, without turning around. 'Why did you do that?'

She glanced at him out of the corner of her eye and the Witcher suddenly understood he had made a mistake. He suddenly knew that insincerity, lies, pretence and bravado would lead him straight into a swamp, where only a springy, matted layer of grass and moss, liable to yield, tear or break at any moment, separated him from the abyss below.

'Why?' she repeated.

He did not answer.

'Are you looking for a woman for the night?'

He did not reply. Essi turned slowly and touched his arm.

'Let's go back in,' she said easily, but he was not deceived by her manner, sensing how tense she was. 'Don't make that face. It was nothing. And the fact that I'm not looking for a man for tonight isn't your fault. Is it?'

'Essi . . .'

'Let's go back, Geralt. Dandelion has played three encores. It's my turn. Come on, I'll sing . . .'

She glanced at him strangely and blew her lock of hair away from her eye.

'I'll sing for you.'

IV

'Oho,' the Witcher said, feigning surprise. 'So you're here? I thought you wouldn't be back tonight.'

Dandelion locked the door with the hasp, hung up his lute and his bonnet with the egret's feather on a peg, took off his jerkin, brushed it down and laid it on some sacks lying in the corner of the small room. Apart from the sacks, a wooden pail and a huge palliasse stuffed with dried bean stalks there was no furniture in the attic room – even the candle stood on the floor in a hardened pool of wax. Drouhard admired Dandelion, but clearly not enough to give him the run of a chamber or even a boxroom.

'And why,' asked Dandelion, removing his boots, 'did you think I wouldn't be back tonight?'

'I thought,' the Witcher lifted himself up on an elbow, crunching bean straw, 'you'd go and sing serenades beneath the window of Miss Veverka, at whom your tongue has been hanging out the whole evening like a pointer at the sight of a bitch.'

'Ha, ha,' the bard laughed. 'But you're so oafishly stupid. You didn't understand anything. Veverka? I don't care about Veverka. I simply wanted to stab Miss Akeretta with jealousy, as I shall make a pass at her tomorrow. Move over.'

Dandelion collapsed on the palliasse and pulled the blanket off Geralt. Geralt, feeling a strange anger, turned his head towards the tiny window, through which, had it not been for some industrious spiders, he would have seen the starry sky.

'Why so huffy?' the poet asked. 'Does it bother you that I make advances to girls? Since when? Perhaps you've become a druid and taken a vow of chastity? Or perhaps . . .'

'Don't go on. I'm tired. Have you not noticed that for the first time in two weeks we have a palliasse and a roof over our heads?

Doesn't it gladden you that the rain won't be dripping on us in the wee small hours?'

'For me,' Dandelion fantasised, 'a palliasse without a girl isn't a palliasse. It's incomplete happiness, and what is incomplete happiness?'

Geralt groaned softly, as usual when Dandelion was assailed by nocturnal talkativeness.

'Incomplete happiness,' the bard continued, engrossed in his own voice, 'is like . . . a kiss interrupted . . . Why are you grinding your teeth, if I may ask?'

'You're incredibly boring, Dandelion. Nothing but palliasses, girls, bums, tits, incomplete happiness and kisses interrupted by dogs set on you by your lovers' parents. Why, you clearly can't behave any differently. Clearly only easy lewdness, not to say uncritical promiscuity, allows you musicians to compose ballads, write poems and sing. That is clearly – write it down – the dark side of your talent.'

He had said too much and had not cooled his voiced sufficiently. And Dandelion saw through him effortlessly and unerringly.

'Aha,' he said calmly. 'Essi Daven, also known as Little Eye. The alluring little eye of Little Eye fixed its gaze on the Witcher and caused confusion in the Witcher. The Witcher behaved like a little schoolboy before a queen. And rather than blame himself he is blaming her and searching for her dark side.'

'You're talking rubbish, Dandelion.'

'No, my dear. Essi made an impression on you, you can't hide it. I don't see anything wrong with that, actually. But beware, and don't make a mistake. She is not what you think. If her talent has its dark sides, they certainly aren't what you imagine.'

'I conjecture,' said the Witcher, trying to control his voice, 'that you know her very well.'

'Quite well. But not in the way you think. Not like that.'

'Quite original for you, you'll admit.'

'You're stupid,' the bard said, stretching and placing both hands under his neck. 'I've known Poppet almost since she was a child. To me she's like . . . well . . . like a younger sister. So I repeat, don't

206

make any silly mistakes about her. You'd be harming her greatly, because you also made an impression on her. Admit it, you desire her?'

'Even if I did, unlike you I'm not accustomed to talking about it,' Geralt said sharply. 'Or writing songs about it. I thank you for your words about her, because perhaps you have indeed saved me from a stupid mistake. But let that be an end to it. I regard the subject as exhausted.'

Dandelion lay motionless for a moment, saying nothing, but Geralt knew him too well.

'I know,' the poet said at last. 'Now I know everything.'

'You know fuck all, Dandelion.'

'Do you know what your problem is, Geralt? You think you're different. You flaunt your otherness, what you consider abnormal. You aggressively impose that abnormality on others, not understanding that for people who think clear-headedly you're the most normal man under the sun, and they all wish that everybody was so normal. What of it that you have quicker reflexes than most and vertical pupils in sunlight? That you can see in the dark like a cat? That you know a few spells? Big deal. I, my dear, once knew an innkeeper who could fart for ten minutes without stopping, playing the tune to the psalm *Greet us, greet us, O, Morning Star.* Heedless of his – let's face it – unusual talent, that innkeeper was the most normal among the normal; he had a wife, children and a grandmother afflicted by palsy—'

'What does that have to do with Essi Daven? Could you explain?'

'Of course. You wrongfully thought, Geralt, that Little Eye was interested in you out of morbid, downright perverted curiosity, that she looks at you as though you were a queer fish, a two-headed calf or a salamander in a menagerie. And you immediately became annoyed, gave her a rude, undeserved reprimand at the first opportunity, struck back at a blow she hadn't dealt. I witnessed it, after all. I didn't witness the further course of events, of course, but I noticed your flight from the room and saw her glowing cheeks when you returned. Yes, Geralt. I'm alerting you to a mistake, and you have already made it. You wanted to take revenge on her for – in

207

your opinion – her morbid curiosity. You decided to exploit that curiosity.'

'You're talking rubbish.'

'You tried,' the bard continued, unmoved, 'to learn if it was possible to bed her in the hay, if she was curious to find out what it's like to make love with a misfit, with a witcher. Fortunately, Essi turned out to be smarter than you and generously took pity on your stupidity, having understood its cause. I conclude this from the fact you did not return from the jetty with a fat lip.'

'Have you finished?'

'Yes, I have.'

'Goodnight, then.'

'I know why you're furious and gnashing your teeth.'

'No doubt. You know everything.'

'I know who warped you like that, who left you unable to understand a normal woman. Oh, but that Yennefer of yours was a troublemaker; I'm damned if I know what you see in her.'

'Drop it, Dandelion.'

'Do you really not prefer normal girls like Essi? What do sorceresses have that Essi doesn't? Age, perhaps? Little Eye may not be the youngest, but she's as old as she looks. And do you know what Yennefer once confessed to me after a few stiff drinks? Ha, ha . . . she told me that the first time she did it with a man it was exactly a year after the invention of the two-furrow plough.'

'You're lying. Yennefer loathes you like the plague and would never confide in you.'

'All right, I was lying, I confess.'

'You don't have to. I know you.'

'You only think you know me. Don't forget: I'm complicated by nature.'

'Dandelion,' the Witcher sighed, now genuinely tired. 'You're a cynic, a lecher, a womaniser and a liar. And there's nothing, believe me, nothing complicated about that. Goodnight.'

'Goodnight, Geralt.'

V

'You rise early, Essi.'

The poet smiled, holding down her hair, which was being blown around by the wind. She stepped gingerly onto the jetty, avoiding the holes and rotten planks.

'I couldn't miss the chance of watching the Witcher at work. Will you think me nosey again, Geralt? Why, I don't deny it, I really am nosey. How goes it?'

'How goes what?'

'Oh, Geralt,' she said. 'You underestimate my curiosity, and my talent for gathering and interpreting information. I know everything about the case of the pearl divers, I know the details of your agreement with Agloval. I know you're looking for a sailor willing to sail there, towards the Dragons Fangs. Did you find one?'

He looked at her searchingly for a moment, and then suddenly decided.

'No,' he replied, 'I didn't. Not one.'

'Are they afraid?'

'Yes, they are.'

'How, then, do you intend to carry out an exploration if you can't go to sea? How, without sailing, do you plan to get at the monster that killed the pearl divers?'

He took her by the hand and led her from the jetty. They walked slowly along the edge of the sea, across the pebbly beach, beside the launches pulled up on the shore, among the rows of nets hung up on stilts, among the curtains of split, drying fish being blown by the wind. Geralt unexpectedly found that the poet's company did not bother him at all, that it was not wearisome or intrusive. Apart from that, he hoped that a calm and matter-of-fact conversation would erase the results of that stupid kiss on the terrace. The fact that Essi had come to the jetty filled him with the hope that she did not bear him a grudge. He was content.

'"Get at the monster",' he muttered, repeating her words. 'If only I knew how. I know very little about sea monsters.'

'Interesting. From what I know, there are many more monsters in the sea than there are on land, both in terms of number and variety of species. It would seem, thus, that the sea ought to be a great opportunity for witchers to show what they can do.'

'Well, it isn't.'

'Why?'

'The expansion of people onto the sea,' he said, clearing his throat and turning his face away, 'hasn't lasted very long. Witchers were needed long ago, on the land, during the first phase of colonisation. We aren't cut out to fight sea-dwelling creatures, although you are right, the sea is full of all sorts of aggressive filth. But our witcher abilities are insufficient against sea monsters. Those creatures are either too big for us, or are too well armoured, or are too sure in their element. Or all three.'

'And the monster that killed the pearl divers? You have no idea what it was?'

'A kraken, perhaps?'

'No. A kraken would have wrecked the boat, but it was intact. And, as they said, totally full of blood,' Little Eye swallowed and visibly paled. 'Don't think I'm being a know-all. I grew up by the sea, and I've seen a few things.'

'In that case what could it have been? A giant squid? It might have dragged those people from the deck . . .'

'There wouldn't have been any blood. It wasn't a squid, Geralt, or a killer whale, or a dracoturtle, because whatever it was didn't destroy or capsize the boat. Whatever it was went on board and carried out the slaughter there. Perhaps you're making a mistake looking for it in the sea?'

The Witcher pondered.

'I'm beginning to admire you, Essi,' he said. The poet blushed. 'You're right. It may have attacked from the air. It may have been an ornithodracon, a gryphon, a wyvern, a flying drake or a forktail. Possibly even a roc—'

'Excuse me,' Essi said, 'Look who's coming.'

Agloval was approaching along the shore, alone, his clothes sopping wet. He was visibly angry, and flushed with rage on seeing them.

Essi curtseyed slightly, Geralt bent his head, pressing his fist to his chest. Agloval spat.

'I sat on the rocks for three hours, almost from daybreak,' he snarled. 'She didn't even make an appearance. Three hours, like an ass, on rocks swept by the waves.'

'I'm sorry . . .' the Witcher muttered.

'You're sorry?' the duke exploded. 'Sorry? It's your fault. You fouled everything up. You spoiled everything.'

'What did I spoil? I was only working as an interpreter—'

'To hell with work like that,' Agloval interrupted angrily, showing off his profile. His profile was indeed kingly, worthy of being struck on coinage. 'Verily, it would have been better not to hire you. It sounds paradoxical, but while we didn't have an interpreter we understood each other better, Sh'eenaz and I, if you know what I mean. But now – do you know what they're saying in town? Rumours are spreading that the pearl divers perished because I enraged the mermaid. That it's her revenge.'

'Nonsense,' the Witcher commented coldly.

'How am I to know that it's nonsense?' the duke growled. 'How do I know you didn't tell her something? Do I really know what she's capable of? What monsters she chums around with down in the depths? By all means prove to me that it's nonsense. Bring me the head of the beast that killed the pearl divers. Get to work, instead of flirting on the beach—'

'To work?' Geralt reacted angrily. 'How? Am I to go out to sea straddling a barrel? Your Zelest threatened the sailors with torture and the noose, but in spite of that no one wants to sail out with me. Zelest himself isn't too keen either. So how—?'

'What does it bother me how?' Agloval yelled, interrupting. 'That's your problem! What are witchers for if not so that decent

211

folk don't have to wrack their brains about how to rid themselves of monsters? I've hired you to do the job and I demand you carry it out. If not, get out of here before I drive you to the borders of my realm with my whip!'

'Calm down, Your Grace,' Little Eye said softly, but her paleness and trembling hands betrayed her irritation. 'And please don't threaten Geralt. It so happens that Dandelion and I have several friends. King Ethain of Cidaris, to mention but one, likes us and our ballads very much. King Ethain is an enlightened monarch and always says that our ballads aren't just lively music and rhymes, but a way of spreading news, that they are a chronicle of humankind. Do you wish, Your Grace, to be written into the chronicle of humankind? I can have it arranged.'

Agloval looked at her for a while with a cold, contemptuous gaze.

'The pearl divers who died had wives and children,' he finally said, much more quietly and calmly. 'When hunger afflicts the remaining ones they will put to sea again. Pearl, sponge and oyster divers, lobster fishers, fishermen; all of them. Now they are afraid, but hunger will overcome their fear. They will go to sea. But will they return? What do you say to that, Geralt? Miss Daven? I'd be interested to hear the ballad which will sing of that. A ballad about a witcher standing idly on the shore looking at the blood-spattered decks of boats and weeping children.'

Essi blanched even more, but raised her head proudly, blew away the lock of hair and was just preparing a riposte, when Geralt seized her hand and squeezed it, stopping her words.

'That is enough,' he said. 'In this entire flood of words only one has true significance. You hired me, Agloval. I accepted the task and shall accomplish it, if it is feasible.'

'I'm relying on it,' the duke said curtly. 'Then goodbye. My respects, Miss Daven.'

Essi did not curtsey, she only tilted her head. Agloval hauled up his wet trousers and headed off towards the harbour, walking unsteadily over the pebbles. Only then did Geralt notice he was still holding the poet's hand, but she was not trying to free herself at all.

212

He released her hand. Essi, slowly returning to her normal colours, turned her face towards his.

'It's easy to make you take a risk,' she said. 'All it takes is a few words about women and children. And so much is said about how unfeeling you witchers are. Geralt, Agloval doesn't give a hoot about women, children or the elderly. He wants the pearl fishing to begin again because he's losing money every day they don't come back with a catch. He's taking you for a ride with those starving children, and you're ready to risk your life—'

'Essi,' he interrupted. 'I'm a witcher. It's my trade to risk my life. Children have nothing to do with it.'

'You can't fool me.'

'Why the assumption that I mean to?'

'Perhaps because if you were the heartless professional you pretend to be, you would have tried to push up the price. But you didn't say a word about your fee. Oh, never mind, enough of all that. Are we going back?'

'Let's walk on a little.'

'Gladly. Geralt?'

'Yes.'

'I told you I grew up by the sea. I know how to steer a boat and—'

'Put that out of your head.'

'Why?'

'Put that out of your head,' he repeated sharply.

'You might,' she said, 'have phrased that more politely.'

'I might have. But you would have taken it as . . . the Devil only knows what. And I *am* an unfeeling witcher and heartless professional. I risk my life. Not other people's.'

Essi fell silent. He saw her purse her lips and toss her head. A gust of wind ruffled her hair again, and her face was covered for a moment by a confusion of golden curls.

'I only wanted to help you,' she said.

'I know. Thank you.'

'Geralt?'

'Yes.'

'What if there is something behind the rumours Agloval was talking about? You know well that mermaids aren't always friendly. There have been cases—'

'I don't believe them.'

'Sea witches,' Little Eye continued, pensively. 'Nereids, mermen, sea nymphs. Who knows what they're capable of. And Sh'eenaz . . . she had reason—'

'I don't believe it,' he interrupted.

'You don't believe or you don't want to believe?'

He did not reply.

'And you want to appear the cold professional?' she asked with a strange smile. 'Someone who thinks with his sword hilt? If you want, I'll tell you what you really are.'

'I know what I really am.'

'You're sensitive,' she said softly. 'Deep in your angst-filled soul. Your stony face and cold voice don't deceive me. You are sensitive, and your sensitivity makes you fear that whatever you are going to face with sword in hand may have its own arguments, may have the moral advantage over you . . .'

'No, Essi,' he said slowly. 'Don't try to make me the subject of a moving ballad, a ballad about a witcher with inner conflicts. Perhaps I'd like it to be the case, but it isn't. My moral dilemmas are resolved for me by my code and education. By my training.'

'Don't talk like that,' she said in annoyance. 'I don't understand why you try to—'

'Essi,' he interrupted her again. 'I don't want you to pick up false notions about me. I'm not a knight errant.'

'You aren't a cold and unthinking killer either.'

'No,' he agreed calmly. 'I'm not, although there are some who think differently. For it isn't my sensitivity and personal qualities that place me higher, but the vain and arrogant pride of a professional convinced of his value. A specialist, in whom it was instilled that the code of his profession and cold routine is more legitimate than emotion, that they protect him against making a mistake, which could be made should he become entangled in the dilemmas of Good and Evil, of Order and Chaos. No, Essi. It's not *I* that am sensitive, but you. After all, your profession demands that, doesn't it? It's you who became alarmed by the thought that an apparently pleasant mermaid attacked the pearl divers in an act of desperate revenge after being insulted. You immediately look for an excuse for the mermaid, extenuating circumstances; you balk at the thought that a witcher, hired by the duke, will murder an exquisite mermaid just because she dared to yield to emotion. But the Witcher, Essi, is free of such dilemmas. And of emotion. Even if it turns out that it *was* the mermaid, the Witcher won't kill the mermaid, because the code forbids him. The code solves the dilemma for the Witcher.'

Little Eye looked at him, abruptly lifting up her head.

'All dilemmas?' she asked quickly.

She knows about Yennefer, he thought. She knows. Dandelion, you bloody gossip . . .

They looked at one another.

What is concealed in your deep blue eyes, Essi? Curiosity? Fascination with otherness? What are the dark sides of your talent, Little Eye?

'I apologise,' she said. 'The question was foolish. And naive. It hinted that I believed what you were saying. Let's go back. That wind chills to the marrow. Look how rough the sea is.'

'It is. Do you know what's fascinating, Essi?'

'What?'

'I was certain the rock where Agloval met his mermaid was nearer the shore and bigger. And now it's not visible.'

'It's the tide,' Essi said shortly. 'The water will soon reach all the way to the cliff.'

'All that way?'

'Yes. The water rises and falls here considerably, well over ten cubits, because here in the strait and the mouth of the river there are so-called tidal echoes, as the sailors call them.'

Geralt looked towards the headland, at the Dragons Fangs, biting into a roaring, foaming breaker.

'Essi,' he asked. 'And when the tide starts going out?'

'What?'

'How far back does the sea go?'

'But what . . . ? Ah, I get it. Yes, you're right. It goes back to the line of the shelf.'

'The line of the what?'

'Well, it's like a shelf – flat shallows – forming the seabed, which ends with a lip at the edge of the deep waters.'

'And the Dragons Fangs . . .'

'Are right on that lip.'

'And they are reachable by wading? How long would I have?'

'I don't know,' Little Eye frowned. 'You'd have to ask the locals. But I don't think it would be a good idea. Look, there are rocks between the land and the Fangs, the entire shore is scored with bays and fjords. When the tide starts going out, gorges and basins full of water are formed there. I don't know if—'

From the direction of the sea and the barely visible rocks came a splash. And a loud, melodic cry.

'White Hair!' the mermaid called, gracefully leaping over the crest of a wave, threshing the water with short, elegant strokes of her tail.

'Sh'eenaz!' he called back, waving a hand.

The mermaid swam over to the rocks, stood erect in the foaming, green water and used both hands to fling back her hair, at the same time revealing her torso with all its charms. Geralt glanced at Essi. The girl blushed slightly and with an expression of regret and embarrassment on her face looked for a moment at her own charms, which barely protruded beneath her dress.

'Where is my man?' Sh'eenaz sang, swimming closer. 'He was meant to have come.'

'He did. He waited for three hours and then left.'

'He left?' the mermaid said in a high trill of astonishment. 'He didn't wait? He could not endure three meagre hours? Just as I thought. Not a scrap of sacrifice! Not a scrap! Despicable, despicable, despicable! And what are you doing here, White Hair? Did you come here for a walk with your beloved? You'd make a pretty couple, were you not marred by your legs.'

'She is not my beloved. We barely know each other.'

'Yes?' Sh'eenaz said in astonishment. 'Pity. You suit each other, you look lovely together. Who is it?'

'I'm Essi Daven, poet,' Little Eye sang with an accent and melody beside which the Witcher's voice sounded like the cawing of a crow. 'Nice to meet you, Sh'eenaz.'

The mermaid slapped her hands on the water and laughed brightly.

'How gorgeous!' she cried. 'You know our tongue! Upon my word, you astonish me, you humans. Verily, not nearly as much divides us as people say.'

The Witcher was no less astonished than the mermaid, although he might have guessed that the educated and well-read Essi would know the Elder Speech better than him. It was the language of the elves, a euphonious version of which was used by mermaids, sea witches and nereids. It also ought to have been clear to him that the melodiousness and complicated intonation pattern of the mermaids' speech, which for him was a handicap, made it easier for Little Eye.

'Sh'eenaz!' he called. 'A few things divide us, nevertheless, and what occasionally divides us is spilled blood! Who ... who killed the pearl divers, over there, by the two rocks? Tell me!'

The mermaid dived down, churning the water. A moment later she spurted back out onto the surface again, and her pretty little face was contracted and drawn into an ugly grimace.

'Don't you dare!' she screamed, piercingly shrilly. 'Don't you dare go near the steps! It is not for you! Don't fall foul of them! It is not for you!'

'What? What isn't for us?'

'Not for you!' Sh'eenaz yelled, falling onto her back on the waves.

Splashes of water shot high up. For just a moment longer they saw her forked, finned tail flapping over the waves. Then she vanished under the water.

Little Eye tidied her hair, which had been ruffled by the wind. She stood motionless with her head bowed.

'I didn't know,' Geralt said, clearing his throat, 'that you knew the Elder Speech so well, Essi.'

'You couldn't have known,' she said with a distinct bitterness in her voice. 'After all ... after all, you barely know me.'

217

VI

'Geralt,' Dandelion said, looking around and sniffing like a hound. 'It stinks terribly here, don't you think?'

'Does it?' the Witcher sniffed. 'I've been in places where it smelled worse. It's only the smell of the sea.'

The bard turned his head away and spat between two rocks. The water bubbled in the rocky clefts, foaming and soughing, exposing gorges full of sea-worn pebbles.

'Look how nicely it's dried out, Geralt. Where has the water gone? What is it with those bloody tides? Where do they come from? Haven't you ever thought about it?'

'No. I've had other concerns.'

'I think,' Dandelion said, trembling slightly, 'that down there in the depths, at the very bottom of this bloody ocean, crouches a huge monster, a fat, scaly beast, a toad with horns on its vile head. And from time to time it draws water into its belly, and with the water everything that lives and can be eaten: fish, seals, turtles – everything. And then, having devoured its prey, it pukes up the water and we have the tide. What do you think about that?'

'I think you're a fool. Yennefer once told me that the moon causes the tides.'

Dandelion cackled.

'What bloody rubbish! What does the moon have to do with the sea? Only dogs howl at the moon. She was having you on, Geralt, that little liar of yours, she put one over on you. Not for the first time either, I'd say.'

The Witcher did not comment. He looked at the boulders glistening with water in the ravines exposed by the tide. The water was still exploding and foaming in them, but it looked as though they would get through.

'Very well, let's get to work,' he said, standing and adjusting his sword on his back. 'We can't wait any longer, or we won't make it back before the tide comes in. Do you still insist on coming with me?'

'Yes. Subjects for ballads aren't fir cones, you don't find them under a tree. Aside from that, it's Poppet's birthday tomorrow.'

'I don't see the link.'

'Pity. There exists the custom among we – normal – people of giving one another presents on birthdays. I can't afford to buy her anything. So I shall find something for her on the seabed.'

'A herring? Or a cuttlefish?'

'Dolt. I'll find some amber, perhaps a seahorse, or maybe a pretty conch. The point is it's a symbol, a sign of concern and affection. I like Little Eye and I want to please her. Don't you understand? I thought not. Let's go. You first, because there might be a monster down there.'

'Right.' The Witcher slid down from the cliff onto the slippery rocks, covered with algae. 'I'll go first, in order to protect you if needs be. As a sign of my concern and affection. Just remember, if I shout, run like hell and don't get tangled up in my sword. We aren't going to gather seahorses. We're going to deal with a monster that murders people.'

They set off downwards, into the rifts of the exposed seabed, in some places wading through the water still swirling in the rocky vents. They splashed around in hollows lined with sand and bladder wrack. To make matters worse it began to rain, so they were soon soaked from head to foot. Dandelion kept stopping and digging around in the pebbles and tangles of seaweed.

'Oh, look, Geralt, a little fish. It's all red, by the Devil. And here, look, a little eel. And this? What is it? It looks like a great big, transparent flea. And this . . . Oh, mother! Geraaalt!'

The Witcher turned around at once, with his hand on his sword.

It was a human skull, white, worn smooth by the rocks, jammed into a rocky crevice, full of sand. But not only sand. Dandelion, seeing a lugworm writhing in the eye socket, shuddered and made an unpleasant noise. The Witcher shrugged and headed towards the rocky plain exposed by the sea, in the direction of the two jagged reefs, known as the Dragons Fangs, which now looked like mountains. He moved cautiously. The seabed was strewn with sea cucumbers, shells and piles of bladder wrack. Large jellyfish swayed and brittle stars whirled in the rock pools and hollows. Small crabs, as colourful as hummingbirds, fled from them, creeping sideways, their legs scurrying busily.

Geralt noticed a corpse some way off, wedged between the rocks. The drowned man's chest could be seen moving beneath his shirt and the seaweed, though in principle there was no longer anything to move it. It was teeming with crabs, outside and inside. The body could not have been in the water longer than a day, but the crabs had picked it so clean it was pointless examining it closer. The Witcher changed direction without a word, giving the corpse a wide berth. Dandelion did not notice anything.

'Why, but it stinks of rot here,' he swore, trying to catch up with Geralt. He spat and shook water from his bonnet. 'And it's tipping down and I'm cold. I'll catch a chill and lose my bloody voice . . .'

'Stop moaning. If you want to go back you know the way.'

Right beyond the base of the Dragons Fangs stretched out a flat, rocky shelf, and beyond it was deep water, the calmly rippling sea. The limit of the tide.

'Ha, Geralt,' Dandelion said, looking around. 'I think that monster of yours had enough sense to withdraw to the high sea with the tide. And I guess you thought it'd be lazing about here somewhere, waiting for you to hack it to pieces?'

'Be quiet.'

The Witcher approached the edge of the shelf and knelt down, cautiously resting his hands on the sharp shells clinging to the rocks. He could not see anything. The water was dark, and the surface was cloudy, dulled by the drizzle.

Dandelion searched the recesses of the reefs, kicking the more aggressive crabs from his legs, examining and feeling the dripping rocks bearded with sagging seaweed and specked with coarse colonies of crustaceans and molluscs.

'Hey, Geralt!'

'What?'

'Look at those shells. They're pearl oysters, aren't they?'

'No.'

'Know anything about them?'

'No.'

'So keep your opinions to yourself until you do know something. They are pearl oysters, I'm certain. I'll start collecting pearls, at least there'll be some profit from this expedition, not just a cold. Shall I begin, Geralt?'

'Go ahead. The monster attacks pearl divers. Pearl collectors probably fall into the same category.'

'Am I to be bait?'

'Start collecting. Take the bigger ones, because if you don't find any pearls we can make soup out of them.'

'Forget it. I'll just collect pearls; fuck the shells. Dammit . . . Bitch . . . How do you . . . bloody . . . open it? Do you have a knife, Geralt?'

'Haven't you even brought a knife?'

'I'm a poet, not some knifer. Oh, to hell with it, I'll put them in a bag and we'll get the pearls out later. Hey, you! Scram!'

He kicked off a crab, which flew over Geralt's head and splashed into the water. The Witcher walked slowly along the edge of the shelf, eyes fixed on the black, impenetrable water. He heard the rhythmic tapping of the stone Dandelion was using to dislodge the shells from the rock.

'Dandelion! Come and look!'

The jagged, cracked shelf suddenly ended in a level, sharp edge, which fell downwards at an acute angle. Immense, angular, regular blocks of white marble, overgrown with seaweed, molluscs and sea anemones swaying in the water like flowers in the breeze, could clearly be seen beneath the surface of the water.

'What is it? They look like – like steps.'

'Because they *are* steps,' Dandelion whispered in awe. 'Ooo, they're steps leading to an underwater city. To the legendary Ys, which was swallowed up by the sea. Have you heard the legend of the city of the chasm, about Ys-Beneath-The-Waves? I shall write such a ballad the competition won't know what's hit them. I have to see it up close . . . Look, there's some kind of mosaic, something is engraved or carved there . . . Some kind of writing? Move away, Geralt.'

'Dandelion! That's a trench! You'll slip off . . .'

'Never mind. I'm wet anyway. See, it's shallow here, barely waist-deep on this first step. And as wide as a ballroom. Oh, bloody hell . . .'

Geralt jumped very quickly into the water and grabbed the bard, who had fallen in up to his neck.

'I tripped on that shit,' Dandelion said, gasping for air, recovering himself and lifting a large, flat mollusc dripping water from its cobalt blue shell, overgrown with threads of algae. 'There's loads of these on the steps. It's a pretty colour, don't you think? Grab it and shove it into your bag, mine's already full.'

'Get out of there,' the Witcher snapped, annoyed. 'Get back on the shelf this minute, Dandelion. This isn't a game.'

'Quiet. Did you hear that? What was it?'

Geralt heard it. The sound was coming from below, from under the water. Dull and deep, although simultaneously faint, soft, brief, broken off. The sound of a bell.

'It's a bloody bell,' Dandelion whispered, clambering out onto the shelf. 'I was right, Geralt. It's the bell of the sunken Ys, the bell of the city of monsters muffled by the weight of the depths. It's the damned reminding us . . .'

'Will you shut up?'

The sound repeated. Considerably closer.

'. . . reminding us,' the bard continued, squeezing out the soaking tail of his jerkin, 'of its dreadful fate. That bell is a warning . . .'

The Witcher stopped paying attention to Dandelion's voice and concentrated on his other senses. He sensed. He sensed something.

'It's a warning,' Dandelion said, sticking the tip of his tongue out, as was his custom when he was concentrating. 'A warning, because . . . hmm . . . So we would not forget . . . hmm . . . hmmm . . . I've got it!

The heart of the bell sounds softly, it sings a song of death

Of death, which can be born more easily than oblivion . . .'

The water right next to the Witcher exploded. Dandelion screamed. The goggle-eyed monster emerging from the foam aimed a broad, serrated, scythe-like blade at Geralt. Geralt's sword was already in his hand, from the moment the water had begun to swell, so now he merely twisted confidently at the hips and slashed the monster across its drooping, scaly dewlap. He immediately turned the other way, where another creature was churning up the water. It was wearing a bizarre helmet and something resembling a suit of armour made of tarnished copper. The Witcher parried the blade of the short spear being thrust towards him with a broad sweep of his sword and with the momentum the parry gave him struck across the ichthyoid-reptilian toothy muzzle. He leapt aside towards the edge of the shelf, splashing water.

'Fly, Dandelion!'

'Give me your hand!'

'Fly, dammit!'

Another creature emerged from the water, the curved sword whistling in its rough green hands. The Witcher thrust his back against the edge of the shellfish-covered rock, assumed a fighting position, but the fish-eyed creature did not approach. It was the same height as Geralt. The water also reached to its waist, but the impressively puffed-up comb on its head and its dilated gills gave the impression of greater size. The grimace distorting the broad maw armed with teeth was deceptively similar to a cruel smile.

The creature, paying no attention to the two twitching bodies floating in the red water, raised its sword, gripping the long hilt without a cross guard in both hands. Puffing up its comb and gills even more, it deftly spun the blade in the air. Geralt heard the light blade hiss and whirr.

The creature took a pace forward, sending a wave towards the Witcher. Geralt took a swing and whirled his sword in response. And also took a step, taking up the challenge.

The fish-eyed creature deftly twisted its long clawed fingers on the hilt and slowly lowered its arms, which were protected by tortoiseshell and copper, and plunged them up to its elbows, concealing

223

the weapon beneath the water. The Witcher grasped his sword in both hands; his right hand just below the cross guard, his left by the pommel, and lifted the weapon up and a little to the side, above his right shoulder. He looked into the monster's eyes, but they were the iridescent eyes of a fish, eyes with spherical irises, glistening coldly and metallically. Eyes which neither expressed nor betrayed anything. Nothing that might warn of an attack.

From the depths at the bottom of the steps, disappearing into the black chasm, came the sound of a bell. Closer and closer, more and more distinct.

The fish-eyed creature lunged forward, pulling its blade from under the water, attacking as swiftly as a thought, with a montante thrust. Geralt was simply lucky; he had expected the blow to be dealt from the right. He parried with his blade directed downwards, powerfully twisting his body, and rotated his sword, meeting the monster's sword flat. Now everything depended on which of them would twist their fingers more quickly on the hilt, who would be first to move from the flat, static impasse of the blades to a blow, a blow whose force was now being generated by both of them, by shifting their bodyweight to the appropriate leg. Geralt already knew they were as fast as each other.

But the fish-eyed creature had longer fingers.

The Witcher struck it in the side, above the hips, twisted into a half-turn, smote, pressing down on the blade, and easily dodged a wide, chaotic, desperate and clumsy blow. The monster, noiselessly opening its ichthyoid mouth, disappeared beneath the water, which was pulsating with crimson clouds.

'Give me your hand! Quickly!' Dandelion yelled. 'They're coming, a whole gang of them! I can see them!'

The Witcher seized the bard's right hand and hauled him out of the water onto the rocky shelf. A broad wave splashed behind him.

The tide had turned.

They fled swiftly, pursued by the swelling wave. Geralt looked back and saw numerous other fish-like creatures bursting from the water, saw them giving chase, leaping nimbly on their muscular legs. Without a word he speeded up.

Dandelion was panting, running heavily and splashing around the now knee-high water. He suddenly stumbled and fell, sloshing among the bladder wrack, supporting himself on trembling arms. Geralt caught him by the belt and hauled him out of the foam, now seething all around them.

'Run!' he cried. 'I'll hold them back!'

'Geralt—'

'Run, Dandelion! The water's about to fill the rift and then we won't get out of here! Run for your life!'

Dandelion groaned and ran. The Witcher ran after him, hoping the monsters would become strung out in the chase. He knew he had no chance taking on the entire group.

They chased him just beside the rift, because the water there was deep enough for them to swim, while he was clambering the slippery rocks with difficulty, wallowing in the foam. In the rift, however, it was too tight for them to assail him from all sides. He stopped in the basin where Dandelion had found the skull.

He stopped and turned around. And calmed down.

He struck the first with the very tip of his sword, where the temple would have been on a man. He split open the belly of the next one, which was armed with something resembling a short battle-axe. A third fled.

The Witcher rushed up the gorge, but at the same time a surging wave boomed, erupting in foam, seethed in an eddy in the vent, tore him off the rocks and dragged him downwards, into the boiling water. He collided with a fishy creature flapping about in the eddy, and thrust it away with a kick. Something caught him by his legs and pulled him down, towards the seafloor. He hit the rock on his back, opened his eyes just in time to see the dark shapes of the creatures, two swift blurs. He parried the first blur with his sword, and instinctively protected himself from the second by raising his left arm. He felt a blow, pain, and immediately afterwards the sharp sting of salt. He pushed off from the bottom with his feet, splashed upwards towards the surface, formed his fingers together and released a Sign. The explosion was dull and stabbed his ears with a brief paroxysm of pain. If I get out of this, he thought, beating the water with his arms and legs, if I get out of this, I'll ride to Yen in Vengerberg and I'll try again . . . If I get out of this . . .

He thought he could hear the booming of a trumpet. Or a horn.

The tidal wave, exploding again in the chimney, lifted him up and tossed him out on his belly onto a large rock. Now he could clearly hear a booming horn and Dandelion's cries, seemingly coming from all sides at once. He snorted the saltwater from his nose and looked around, tossing his wet hair from his face.

He was on the shore, right where they had set out from. He was lying belly-down on the rocks, and a breaker was seething white foam around him.

Behind him, in the gorge – now a narrow bay – a large grey dolphin danced on the waves. On its back, tossing her wet, willow-green hair, sat the mermaid. She still had beautiful breasts.

'White Hair!' she sang, waving a hand which was holding a large, conical, spirally twisting conch. 'Are you in one piece?'

'Yes,' the Witcher said in amazement. The foam around him had become pink. His left arm had stiffened and was stinging from the salt. His jacket sleeve was cut, straight and evenly, and blood was gushing from the cut. I got out of it, he thought, I pulled it off again. But no, I'm not going anywhere.

He saw Dandelion, who was running towards him, stumbling over the wet pebbles.

'I've held them back!' the mermaid sang, and sounded the conch again. 'But not for long! Flee and return here no more, White Hair! The sea . . . is not for you!'

'I know!' he shouted back. 'I know. Thank you, Sh'eenaz!'

VII

'Dandelion,' Little Eye said, tearing the end of the bandage with her teeth and tying a knot on Geralt's wrist. 'Explain to me how a pile of snail shells ended up at the bottom of the stairs? Drouhard's wife is clearing them up right now and is making it clear what she thinks of you two.'

'Shells?' Dandelion asked. 'What shells? I have no idea. Perhaps some passing ducks dropped them?'

Geralt smiled, turning his head toward the shadow. He smiled at the memory of Dandelion's curses; he had spent the entire afternoon opening shells and rummaging around in the slippery flesh, during which process he had nicked himself and soiled his shirt, but hadn't found a single pearl. And no small wonder, as they weren't pearl oysters at all, but ordinary scallops and mussels. They abandoned the idea of making soup from the shellfish when Dandelion opened the first shell; the mollusc looked unappealing and stank to high heaven.

Little Eye finished bandaging him and sat down on an upturned tub. The Witcher thanked her, examining his neatly bandaged arm. The wound was deep and quite long, extending as far as the elbow, and intensely painful when he moved it. She had put on a makeshift dressing by the seashore, but before they had got back it had begun to bleed again. Just before the girl arrived, Geralt had poured a coagulating elixir onto his mutilated forearm, and boosted it with an anaesthetic elixir, and Essi had caught them just as he and Dandelion were suturing the wound using a fishing line tied to a hook. Little Eye swore at them and got down to making a dressing herself, while Dandelion regaled her with a colourful tale of the fight, several times reserving himself the exclusive right to compose a ballad about the whole incident. Essi, naturally, flooded Geralt with an avalanche of questions, which he was unable to answer. She

227

took that badly, and evidently had the impression he was concealing something from her. She became sullen and ceased her questioning.

'Agloval already knows,' she said. 'You were seen returning, and Mrs Drouhard ran off to spread the word when she saw the blood on the stairs. The people dashed towards the rocks, hoping the sea would toss something out. They're still hanging around there, but haven't found anything, from what I know.'

'Nor will they,' the Witcher said. 'I shall visit Agloval tomorrow, but ask him, if you would, to forbid people from hanging around the Dragons Fangs. Just not a word, please, about those steps or Dandelion's fantasies about the city of Ys. Treasure and sensation hunters would immediately go, and there'll be further deaths—'

'I'm not a gossip,' Essi said sulkily, sharply tossing her lock from her forehead. 'If I ask you something it isn't in order to dash off to the well at once and blab it to the washerwomen.'

'I'm sorry.'

'I must go,' Dandelion suddenly said. 'I've got a rendezvous with Akeretta. Geralt, I'm taking your jerkin, because mine is incredibly filthy and wet.'

'Everything here is wet,' Little Eye said sneeringly, nudging the articles of clothing strewn around with the tip of her shoe in disgust. 'How can you? They need to be hung up and properly dried . . . You're dreadful.'

'It'll dry off by itself,' Dandelion pulled on Geralt's damp jacket and examined the silver studs on the sleeves with delight.

'Don't talk rubbish. And what's this? Oh, no, that bag is still full of sludge and seaweed! And this – what's this? Yuck!'

Geralt and Dandelion silently observed the cobalt blue shell Essi was holding between two fingers. They had forgotten. The mollusc was slightly open and clearly reeked.

'It's a present,' the troubadour said, moving back towards the door. 'It's your birthday tomorrow, isn't it, Poppet? Well, that's a present for you.'

'This?'

'Pretty, isn't it?' Dandelion sniffed it and added quickly. 'It's from Geralt. He chose it for you. Oh, is that the time? Farewell . . .'

Little Eye was quiet for a moment after he had gone. The Witcher looked at the stinking shellfish and felt ashamed. Of Dandelion and of himself.

'Did you remember my birthday?' Essi asked slowly, holding the shell at arm's length. 'Really?'

'Give it to me,' he said sharply. He got up from the palliasse, protecting his bandaged arm. 'I apologise for that idiot . . .'

'No,' she protested, removing a small knife from a sheath at her belt. 'It really is a pretty shell, I'll keep it as a memento. It only needs cleaning, after I've got rid of the . . . contents. I'll throw them out of the window, the cats can eat them.'

Something clattered on the floor and rolled away. Geralt widened his pupils and saw what it was long before Essi.

It was a pearl. An exquisitely iridescent and shimmering pearl of faintly blue colour, as big as a swollen pea.

'By the Gods.' Little Eye had also caught sight of it. 'Geralt . . . A pearl!'

'A pearl,' he laughed. 'And so you did get a present, Essi. I'm glad.'

'Geralt, I can't accept it. That pearl is worth . . .'

'It's yours,' he interrupted. 'Dandelion, though he plays the fool, really did remember your birthday. He really wanted to please you. He talked about it, talked aloud about it. Well, fate heard him and did what had to be done.'

'And you, Geralt?'

'Me?'

'Did you . . . also want to please me? That pearl is so beautiful . . . It must be hugely valuable – don't you regret it?'

'I'm pleased you like it. And if I regret anything, it's that there was only one. And that . . .'

'Yes?'

'That I haven't known you as long as Dandelion, long enough to be able to know and remember your birthday. To be able to give you presents and please you. To be able to call you Poppet.'

She moved closer and suddenly threw her arms around his neck. He nimbly and swiftly anticipated her movement, dodged her lips and kissed her coldly on the cheek, embracing her with his unin-jured arm, clumsily, with reserve, gently. He felt the girl stiffen and slowly move back, but only to the length of her arms, which were still resting on his shoulders. He knew what she was waiting for, but did not do it. He did not draw her towards him.

Essi let him go and turned towards the open, dirty little window.

'Of course,' she said suddenly. 'You barely know me. I forgot that you barely know me.'

'Essi,' he said after a moment's silence. 'I—'

'I barely know you either,' she blurted, interrupting him. 'What of it? I love you. I can't help it. Not at all.'

'Essi!'

'Yes. I love you, Geralt. I don't care what you think. I've loved you from the moment I saw you at that engagement party . . .'

She broke off, lowering her head.

She stood before him and Geralt regretted it was her and not the fish-eyed creature with a sword who had been hidden beneath the water. He had stood a chance against that creature. But against her he had none.

'You aren't saying anything,' she said. 'Nothing, not a word.'

I'm tired, he thought, and bloody weak. I need to sit down, I'm feeling dizzy, I've lost some blood and haven't eaten anything . . . I have to sit down. Damned little attic, he thought, I hope it gets struck by lightning and burns down during the next storm. And there's no bloody furniture, not even two stupid chairs and a table, which divides you, across which you can so easily and safely talk; you can even hold hands. But I have to sit down on the palliasse, have to ask her to sit down beside me. And the palliasse stuffed with bean stalks is dangerous, you can't escape from it, take evasive action.

'Sit beside me, Essi.'

She sat down. Reluctantly. Tactfully. Far away. Too close.

'When I found out,' she whispered, interrupting the long silence, 'when I heard that Dandelion had dragged you onto the beach, bleeding, I ran out of the house like a mad thing, rushed blindly, paying no attention to anything. And then . . . Do you know what

I thought? That it was magic, that you had cast a spell on me, that you had secretly, treacherously bewitched me, spellbound me, with your wolfish medallion, with the evil eye. That's what I thought, but I didn't stop, kept running, because I understood that I desire . . . I desire to fall under your spell. And the reality turned out to be more awful. You didn't cast any spell on me, you didn't use any charms. Why, Geralt? Why didn't you bewitch me?'

He was silent.

'If it had been magic,' she said, 'it would all be so simple and easy. I would have succumbed to your power and I'd be happy. But this . . . I must . . . I don't know what's happening to me . . .'

Dammit, he thought, if Yennefer feels like I do now when she's with me, I feel sorry for her. And I shall never be astonished again. I will never hate her again . . . Never again.

Because perhaps Yennefer feels what I'm feeling now, feels a profound certainty that I ought to fulfil what it is impossible to fulfil, even more impossible to fulfil than the relationship between Agloval and Sh'eenaz. Certainty that a little sacrifice isn't enough here; you'd have to sacrifice everything, and there'd still be no way of knowing if that would be enough. No, I won't continue to hate Yennefer for not being able and not wanting to give me more than a little sacrifice. Now I know that a little sacrifice is a hell of a lot.

'Geralt,' Little Eye moaned, drawing her head into her shoulders. 'I'm so ashamed. I'm ashamed of what I'm feeling, it's like an accursed infirmity, like malaria, like being unable to breathe . . .'

He was silent.

'I always thought it was a beautiful and noble state of mind, noble and dignified, even if it makes one unhappy. After all, I've composed so many ballads about it. And it is organic, Geralt, meanly and heartbreakingly organic. Someone who is ill or who has drunk poison might feel like this. Because like someone who has drunk poison, one is prepared to do anything in exchange for an antidote. Anything. Even be humiliated.'

'Essi. Please . . .'

'Yes. I feel humiliated, humiliated by having confessed everything to you, disregarding the dignity that demands one suffers in silence.

231

By the fact that my confession caused you embarrassment. I feel humiliated by the fact that you're embarrassed. But I couldn't have behaved any differently. I'm powerless. At your mercy, like someone who's bedridden. I've always been afraid of illness, of being weak, helpless, hopeless and alone. I've always been afraid of sickness, always believing it the worst thing that could befall me . . .'

He was silent.

'I know,' she groaned again. 'I know I ought to be grateful to you for . . . for not taking advantage of the situation. But I'm not grateful to you. And I'm ashamed of it. For I hate your silence, your terrified eyes. I hate you. For staying silent. For not lying, for not . . . And I hate her, that sorceress of yours, I'd happily stab her for . . . I hate her. Make me go, Geralt. Order me to leave here. For of my own free will I cannot, but I want to get out of here, go to the city, to a tavern . . . I want to have my revenge on you for my shame, for the humiliation, I'll go to the first man I find . . .'

Dammit, he thought, hearing her voice dropping like a rag ball rolling down the stairs. She'll burst into tears, he thought, there's no doubt, she'll burst into tears. What to do, what to bloody do?

Essi's hunched up shoulders were trembling hard. The girl turned her head away and began to weep, crying softly, dreadfully calmly and unrelentingly.

I don't feel anything, he noticed with horror, nothing, not the smallest emotion. That fact that I will embrace her is a deliberate, measured response, not a spontaneous one. I'll hug her, for I feel as though I ought to, not because I want to. I feel nothing.

When he embraced her, she stopped crying immediately, wiped away her tears, shaking her head forcefully and turning away so that he could not see her face. And then she pressed herself to him firmly, burying her head in his chest.

A little sacrifice, he thought, just a little sacrifice. For this will calm her, a hug, a kiss, calm caresses. She doesn't want anything more. And even if she did, what of it? For a little sacrifice, a very little sacrifice, is beautiful and worth . . . Were she to want more . . . It would calm her. A quiet, calm, gentle act of love. And I . . .

Why, it doesn't matter, because Essi smells of verbena, not lilac and gooseberry, doesn't have cool, electrifying skin. Essi's hair is not a black tornado of gleaming curls, Essi's eyes are gorgeous, soft, warm and cornflower blue; they don't blaze with a cold, unemotional, deep violet. Essi will fall asleep afterwards, turn her head away, open her mouth slightly, Essi will not smile in triumph. For Essi . . .

Essi is not Yennefer.

And that is why I cannot. I cannot find that little sacrifice inside myself.

'Please, Essi, don't cry.'

'I won't,' she said, moving very slowly away from him. 'I won't. I understand. It cannot be any other way.'

They said nothing, sitting beside each other on the palliasse stuffed with bean stalks. Evening was approaching.

'Geralt,' she suddenly said, and her voice trembled. 'But perhaps . . . Perhaps it would be like it was with that shell, with that curious gift? Perhaps we could find a pearl? Later? When some time has passed?'

'I can see that pearl,' he said with effort, 'set in silver, in a little silver flower with intricate petals. I see it around your neck, on a delicate silver chain, worn like I wear my medallion. That will be your talisman, Essi. A talisman, which will protect you from all evil.'

'My talisman,' she repeated, lowering her head. 'My pearl, which I shall set in silver, and from which I shall never part. My jewel, which I was given instead of . . . Can a talisman like that bring me luck?'

'Yes, Essi. Be sure of it.'

'Can I stay here a little longer? With you?'

'You may.'

Twilight was approaching and dusk falling, and they were sitting on a palliasse stuffed with bean stalks, in the garret, where there was no furniture, where there was only a wooden tub and an unlit candle on the floor, in a puddle of hardened wax.

They sat in utter silence for a very long time. And then Dandelion came. They heard him approaching, strumming his lute and humming to himself. Dandelion entered, saw them and did not say anything, not a word. Essi also said nothing, stood up and went out without looking at them.

Dandelion did not say a word. But the Witcher saw in his eyes the words that remained unsaid.

VIII

'An intelligent race,' Agloval repeated pensively, resting an elbow on the armrest, and his fist on his chin. 'An underwater civilisation. Fishlike people living on the seabed. Steps leading to the depths. Geralt, you take me for a bloody gullible duke.'

Little Eye, standing beside Dandelion, snarled angrily. Dandelion shook his head in disbelief. Geralt was not in the least bothered.

'It makes no difference to me,' he said quietly, 'if you believe me or not. It is, however, my duty to warn you. Any boat that sails towards the Dragons Fangs, or people who appear there when the tide is out, are in danger. Mortal danger. If you want to find out if it's true, if you want to risk it, that's your business. I'm simply warning you.'

'Ha,' the steward Zelest, who was sitting in a window seat behind Agloval, suddenly said. 'If they are monsters the like of elves or other goblins, we don't need to worry. We feared it was something worse, or, God save us, something magical. From what the Witcher says, they are some kind of sea drowners or other sea monsters. There are ways of dealing with drowners. I heard tell that one sorcerer gave some drowners short shrift in Lake Mokva. He poured a small barrel of magical philtre into the water and did for the fuckers. Didn't leave a trace.'

'That's true,' Drouhard said, who up to then had been silent. 'There wasn't a trace. Nor a trace of bream, pike, crayfish or mussels. Even the waterweed on the lake floor rotted away and the alders on the bank withered.'

'Capital,' Agloval said derisively. 'Thank you for that excellent suggestion, Zelest. Do you have any more?'

'Aye, fair enough,' the steward said, blushing. 'The wizard overdid it a mite with his wand, waved it about a jot too much. But we

235

ought to manage without wizards too, Your Grace. The Witcher says that one can fight those monsters and also kill 'em. That's war, sire. Like the old days. Nothing new there, eh? Werelynxes lived in the mountains, and where are they now? Wild elves and eerie wives still roam the forests, but there'll soon be an end to that. We'll secure what is ours. As our granddaddies . . .'

'And only my grandchildren will see the pearls?' The duke grimaced. 'It is too long to wait, Zelest.'

'Well, it won't be that bad. Seems to me it's like this: two boats of archers to each boat of divers. We'll soon learn those monsters some sense. Learn them some fear. Am I right, Witcher, sir?'

Geralt looked coldly at him, but did not respond.

Agloval turned his head away, showing his noble profile, and bit his lip. Then he looked at the Witcher, narrowing his eyes and frowning.

'You didn't complete your task, Geralt,' he said. 'You fouled things up again. You had good intentions, I can't deny that. But I don't pay for good intentions. I pay for results. For the effect. And the effect, excuse the expression, is shitty. So you earn shit.'

'Marvellous, Your Grace,' Dandelion jibed. 'Pity you weren't with us at the Dragons Fangs. The Witcher and I might have given you the opportunity for an encounter with one of those from the sea, sword in hand. Perhaps then you would understand what this is about, and stop bickering about payment—'

'Like a fishwife,' Little Eye interjected.

'I am not accustomed to bickering, bargaining or discussing,' Agloval said calmly. 'I said I shall not pay you a penny, Geralt. The agreement ran: remove the danger, remove the threat, enable the fishing of pearls without any risk to people. But you? You come and tell me about an intelligent race from the seabed. You advise me to stay away from the place which brings me profit. What did you do? You reputedly killed . . . How many?'

'It matters not how many,' Geralt said, blanching slightly. 'At least, not to you, Agloval.'

'Precisely. Particularly since there is no proof. If you had at least brought the right hands of those fish-toads, who knows, perhaps I would have splashed out on the normal fee my forester takes for a pair of wolf's ears.'

'Well,' the Witcher said coldly. 'I'm left with no choice but to say farewell.'

'You are mistaken,' the duke said. 'Something does remain. Permanent work for quite decent coin and lodgings. The position and ticket of skipper of my armed guard, which from now on will accompany the divers. It does not have to be forever, but only until your reputed intelligent race gains enough good sense to keep well away from my boats, to avoid them like the plague. What do you say?'

'No thank you, I decline,' the Witcher grimaced. 'A job like that doesn't suit me. I consider waging war against other races idiocy. Perhaps it's excellent sport for bored and jaded dukes. But not for me.'

'Oh, how proud,' Agloval smiled. 'How haughty. You reject offers in a way some kings wouldn't be ashamed of. You give up decent money with the air of a wealthy man after a lavish dinner. Geralt? Did you have lunch today? No? And tomorrow? And the day after? I see little chance, Witcher, very little. It's difficult for you to find work normally and now, with your arm in a sling—'

'How dare you!' Little Eye cried shrilly. 'How dare you speak like that to him, Agloval! The arm he now carries in a sling was cut carrying out your mission! How can you be so base—'

'Stop it,' Geralt said. 'Stop, Essi. There's no point.'

'Not true,' she said angrily. 'There *is* a point. Someone has to tell it straight to this self-appointed duke, who took advantage of the fact that no one was challenging him for the title deed to rule this scrap of rocky coastline, and who now thinks he has the right to insult other people.'

Agloval flushed and tightened his lips, but said nothing and did not move.

'Yes, Agloval,' Essi continued, clenching her shaking hands into fists. 'The opportunity to insult other people amuses and pleases you. You delight in the contempt you can show the Witcher, who is prepared to risk his neck for your money. You should know the

Witcher mocks your contempt and slights, that they do not make the faintest impression on him. He doesn't even notice them. No, the Witcher does not even feel what your servants and subjects, Zelest and Drouhard, feel, and they feel shame, deep, burning shame. The Witcher doesn't feel what Dandelion and I feel, and we feel revulsion. Do you know why that is, Agloval? I'll tell you. The Witcher knows he is superior. He is worthier than you. And that gives him his strength.'

Essi fell silent and lowered her head, but not quickly enough for Geralt not to see the tear which sparkled in the corner of her gorgeous eye. The girl touched the little flower with silver petals hanging around her neck, the flower in the centre of which nestled a large, sky blue pearl. The little flower had intricate, plaited petals, executed in masterly fashion. Drouhard, the Witcher thought, had come up trumps. The craftsman he had recommended did a good job. And had not taken a penny from them. Drouhard had paid for everything.

'So, Your Grace,' Little Eye continued, raising her head, 'don't make a fool of yourself by offering the Witcher the role of a mercenary in an army you plan to field against the ocean. Don't expose yourself to ridicule, for your suggestion could only prompt mirth. Don't you understand yet? You can pay the Witcher for carrying out a task, you can hire him to protect people from evil, to remove the danger that threatens them. But you cannot buy the Witcher, you cannot use him to your own ends. Because the Witcher – even wounded and hungry – is better than you. Has more worth. That is why he scorns your meagre offer. Do you understand?'

'No, Miss Daven,' Agloval said coldly. 'I do not understand. On the contrary, I understand less and less. And the fundamental thing I indeed do not understand is why I have not yet ordered your entire trio hanged, after having you thrashed with a scourge and scorched with red-hot irons. You, Miss Daven, are endeavouring to give the impression of somebody who knows everything. Tell me, then, why I do not do that.'

'As you please,' the poet shot back at once. 'You do not do that, Agloval, because somewhere, deep inside, glimmers in you a little spark of decency, a scrap of honour, not yet stifled by the vainglory of a nouveau riche and petty trader. Inside, Agloval. At the bottom of your heart. A heart which, after all, is capable of loving a mermaid.'

Agloval went as white as a sheet and gripped the armrests of his chair. Bravo, the Witcher thought, bravo, Essi, wonderful. He was proud of her. But at the same time he felt sorrow, tremendous sorrow.

'Go away,' Agloval said softly. 'Go away. Wherever you wish. Leave me in peace.'

'Farewell, duke,' Essi said. 'And on parting accept some good advice. Advice which the Witcher ought to be giving you; but I don't want him to stoop to giving you advice. So I'll do it for him.'

'Very well.'

'The ocean is immense, Agloval. No one has explored what lies beyond the horizon, if anything is there at all. The ocean is bigger than any wilderness, deep into which you have driven the elves. It is less accessible than any mountains or ravines where you have massacred werelynxes. And on the floor of the ocean dwells a race which uses weapons and knows the arcana of metalworking. Beware, Agloval. If archers begin to sail with the pearl divers, you will begin a war with something you don't understand. What you mean to disturb may turn out to be a hornets' nest. I advise you, leave them the sea, for the sea is not for you. You don't know and will never know whither lead those steps, which go down to the bottom of the Dragons Fangs.'

'You are mistaken, Miss Daven,' Agloval said calmly. 'We shall learn whither lead those steps. Further, we shall descend those steps. We shall find out what is on that side of the ocean, if there is anything there at all. And we shall draw from the ocean everything we can. And if not we, then our grandsons will do it, or our grandsons' grandsons. It is just a matter of time. Yes, we shall do it, though the ocean will run red with blood. And you know it, Essi, O wise Essi, who writes the chronicles of humanity in your ballads. Life is not a ballad, O poor, little gorgeous-eyed poet, lost among her fine words. Life is a battle. And we were taught that struggle by these witchers, whose worth is greater than ours. It was they who

239

showed us the way, who paved the way for us. They strewed the path with the corpses of those who stood in the way of humans, and defended that world from us. We, Essi, are only continuing that battle. It is we, not your ballads, who create the chronicles of humanity. And we no longer need witchers, and now nothing will stop us. Nothing.'

Essi blanched, blew her lock away and tossed her head.

'Nothing, Agloval?'

'Nothing, Essi.'

The poet smiled.

A sudden noise, shouts and stamping, came from the anterooms. Pages and guards rushed into the chamber. They knelt or bowed by the door in two rows. Sh'eenaz stood in the doorway.

Her willow-green hair was elaborately coiffured, pinned up with a marvellous circlet encrusted with coral and pearls. She was in a gown the colour of seawater, with frills as white as foam. The gown had a plunging neckline, so that the mermaid's charms, though partly concealed and decorated with a necklace of nephrite and lapis lazuli, still earned the highest admiration.

'Sh'eenaz . . .' Agloval groaned, dropping to his knees. 'My . . . Sh'eenaz . . .'

The mermaid slowly came closer and her gait was soft and graceful, as fluid as an approaching wave.

She stopped in front of the duke, flashed her delicate, white, little teeth in a smile, then quickly gathered her gown in her small hands and lifted it, quite high, high enough for everyone to be able to judge the quality of the marine sorceress, the sea witch. Geralt swallowed. There was no doubt: the sea witch knew what shapely legs were and how to make them.

'Ha!' Dandelion cried. 'My ballad . . . It is just like in my ballad . . . She has gained legs for him, but has lost her voice!'

'I have lost nothing,' Sh'eenaz said melodiously in the purest Common Speech. 'For the moment. I am as good as new after the operation.'

'You speak our tongue?'

'What, mayn't I? How are you, White Hair? Oh, and your

240

beloved one, Essi Daven, if I recall, is here. Do you know her better or still barely?'

'Sh'eenaz . . .' Agloval groaned heartrendingly, moving towards her on his knees. 'My love! My beloved . . . my only . . . And so, at last. At last, Sh'eenaz!'

With a graceful movement the mermaid proffered her hand to be kissed.

'Indeed. Because I love you too, you loon. And what kind of love would it be if the one who loves were not capable of a little sacrifice?'

IX

They left Bremervoord early on a cool morning, among fog which dulled the intensity of the red sun rolling out from below the horizon. They rode as a threesome, as they had agreed. They did not talk about it, they were making no plans – they simply wanted to be together. For some time.

They left the rocky headland, bade farewell to the precipitous, jagged cliffs above the beaches, the fantastic limestone formations carved out by the sea and gales. But as they rode into the green, flower-strewn valley of Dol Adalatte, they still had the scent of the sea in their nostrils, and in their ears the roar of breakers and the piercing, urgent cries of seagulls.

Dandelion talked ceaselessly, hopping from one subject to another and virtually not finishing any. He talked about the Land of Barsa, where a stupid custom required girls to guard their chastity until marriage; about the iron birds of the island of Inis Porhoet; about living water and dead water; about the taste and curious properties of the sapphire wine called 'cill'; and about the royal quadruplets of Ebbing – dreadful, exasperating brats called Putzi, Gritzi, Mitzi and Juan Pablo Vassermiller. He talked about new trends in poetry promoted by his rivals, which were, in Dandelion's opinion, phantoms simulating the movements of the living.

Geralt remained silent. Essi also said nothing or replied in monosyllables. The Witcher felt her gaze on him. He avoided her eyes.

They crossed the River Adalatte on the ferry, having to pull the ropes themselves, since the ferryman happened to be in a pathetic drunken state of deathly white, rigid-trembling, gazing-into-the-abyss pallor, unable to let go of the pillar in his porch, which he was clinging to with both hands, and answering every question they asked him with a single word, which sounded like 'voorg'.

The Witcher had taken a liking to the country on the far side of the Adalatte; the riverside villages were mainly surrounded by palisades, which portended a certain likelihood of finding work.

Little Eye walked over to him while they were watering the horses in the early afternoon, taking advantage of the fact that Dandelion had wandered off. The Witcher was not quick enough. She surprised him.

'Geralt,' she said softly. 'I can't . . . I can't bear this. I don't have the strength.'

He tried to avoid the necessity of looking her in the eye, but she would not let him. She stood in front of him, toying with the sky blue pearl set in a small, silver flower hanging around her neck. She stood like that and he wished again that it was the fish-eyed creature with its sword hidden beneath the water in front of him.

'Geralt . . . We have to do something about this, don't we?'

She waited for his answer. For some words. For a little sacrifice. But the Witcher had nothing he could sacrifice and he knew it. He did not want to lie. And he truly did not have it in him, because he could not find the courage to cause her pain.

The situation was saved by the sudden appearance of Dandelion, dependable Dandelion. Dandelion with his dependable tact.

'Of course!' he yelled and heaved into the water the stick he had been using to part the rushes and the huge, riverside nettles. 'And of course you have to do something about it, it's high time! I have no wish to watch what is going on between you any longer! What do you expect from him, Poppet? The impossible? And you, Geralt, what are you hoping for? That Little Eye will read your thoughts like . . . like the other one? And she will settle for that, and you will conveniently stay quiet, not having to explain, declare or deny anything? And not have to reveal yourself? How much time, how many facts do you both need, to understand? And when you'll want to recall it in a few years, in your memories? I mean we have to part tomorrow, dammit!

'I've had enough, by the Gods, I'm up to here with you, up to here! Very well, listen: I'm going to break myself off a hazel rod and go fishing, and you will have some time to yourselves, you'll be able to tell each other everything. Tell each other everything, try to understand each other. It is not as difficult as you think. And after that, by the Gods, do it. Do it with him, Poppet. Do it with her, Geralt, and be good to her. And then, you'll either bloody get over it, or . . .'

Dandelion turned around rapidly and walked away, breaking reeds and cursing. He made a rod from a hazel branch and horsehair and fished until dusk fell.

After he had walked off, Geralt and Essi stood for a long time, leaning against a misshapen willow tree bent over the water. They stood, holding hands. Then the Witcher spoke, spoke softly for a long time, and Little Eye's little eye was full of tears.

And then, by the Gods, they did it, she and he.

And everything was all right.

X

The next day they organised something of a ceremonial supper. Essi and Geralt bought a dressed lamb in a village they passed through. While they were haggling, Dandelion surreptitiously stole some garlic, onions and carrots from the vegetable patch behind the cottage. As they were riding away they also swiped a pot from the fence behind the smithy. The pot was a little leaky, but the Witcher soldered it using the Igni Sign.

The supper took place in a clearing deep in the forest. The fire crackled merrily and the pot bubbled. Geralt carefully stirred the stew with a star-shaped stirrer made from the top of a spruce tree stripped of bark. Dandelion peeled the onions and carrots. Little Eye, who had no idea about cooking, made the time more pleasant by playing the lute and singing racy couplets.

It was a ceremonial supper. For they were going to part in the morning. In the morning each of them was going to go their own way; in search of something they already had. But they did not know they had it, they could not even imagine it. They could not imagine where the roads they were meant to set off on the next morning would lead. Each of them travelling separately.

After they had eaten, and drunk the beer Drouhard had given them, they gossiped and laughed, and Dandelion and Essi held a singing contest. Geralt lay on a makeshift bed of spruce branches with his hands under his head and thought he had never heard such beautiful voices or such beautiful ballads. He thought about Yennefer. He thought about Essi, too. He had a presentiment that . . .

At the end, Little Eye and Dandelion sang the celebrated duet of Cynthia and Vertvern, a wonderful song of love, beginning with the words: *'Many tears have I shed . . .'* It seemed to Geralt that even the trees bent down to listen to the two of them.

Then Little Eye, smelling of verbena, lay down beside him, squeezed in under his arm, wriggled her head onto his chest, sighed maybe once or twice and fell peacefully asleep. The Witcher fell asleep, much, much later.

Dandelion, staring into the dying embers, sat much longer, alone, quietly strumming his lute.

It began with a few bars, from which an elegant, soothing melody emerged. The lyric suited the melody, and came into being simultaneously with it, the words blending into the music, becoming set in it like insects in translucent, golden lumps of amber.

The ballad told of a certain witcher and a certain poet. About how the witcher and the poet met on the seashore, among the crying of seagulls, and how they fell in love at first sight. About how beautiful and powerful was their love. About how nothing – not even death – was able to destroy that love and part them.

Dandelion knew that few would believe the story told by the ballad, but he was not concerned. He knew ballads were not written to be believed, but to move their audience.

Several years later, Dandelion could have changed the contents of the ballad and written about what had really occurred. He did not. For the true story would not have moved anyone. Who would have wanted to hear that the Witcher and Little Eye parted and never, ever, saw each other again? About how four years later Little Eye died of the smallpox during an epidemic raging in Vizima? About how he, Dandelion, had carried her out in his arms between corpses being cremated on funeral pyres and had buried her far from the city, in the forest, alone and peaceful, and, as she had asked, buried two things with her: her lute and her sky blue pearl. The pearl from which she was never parted.

No, Dandelion stuck with his first version. And he never sang it. Never. To no one.

Right before the dawn, while it was still dark, a hungry, vicious werewolf crept up to their camp, but saw that it was Dandelion, so he listened for a moment and then went on his way.

THE SWORD OF DESTINY

I

He found the first body around noon.

The sight of victims of violent death seldom shocked the Witcher; much more often he looked at corpses with total indifference. This time he was not indifferent.

The boy was around fifteen. He was lying on his back, legs sprawled, his face frozen in a grimace of terror. In spite of that Geralt knew the boy had died at once, had not suffered, and probably had not even known he was dying. The arrow had struck him in the eye and was driven deep into the skull, through the occipital bone. The arrow was fletched with striped, pheasant flight feathers dyed yellow. The shaft stuck up above the tufts of grass.

Geralt looked around, and quickly and easily found what he was hunting for. A second, identical arrow, lodged in the trunk of a pine tree, around six paces behind the corpse. He knew what had happened. The boy had not understood the warning, and hearing the whistle and thud of the arrow had panicked and begun to run the wrong way. Towards the one who had ordered him to stop and withdraw at once. The hissing, venomous, feathered whistle and the short thud of the arrowhead cutting into the wood. *Not a step further, man*, said that whistle and that thud. *Begone, man, get out of Brokilon at once. You have captured the whole world, man, you are everywhere. Everywhere you introduce what you call modernity, the era of change, what you call progress. But we want neither you nor your progress here. We do not desire the changes you bring. We do not desire anything you bring. A whistle and a thud. Get out of Brokilon!*

Get out of Brokilon, thought Geralt. *Man.* No matter that you are fifteen and struggling through the forest, insane with fear, unable to find your way home. No matter that you are seventy and have to gather brushwood, because otherwise they will drive you from the cottage for being useless, they will stop giving you food. No matter that you are six and you were lured by a carpet of little blue flowers in a sunny clearing. *Get out of Brokilon!* A whistle and a thud.

Long ago, thought Geralt, before they shot to kill, they gave two warnings. Even three.

Long ago, he thought, continuing on his way. Long ago.

Well, that's progress.

The forest did not seem to deserve the dreadful notoriety it enjoyed. It was terribly wild and arduous to march through, but it was the commonplace arduousness of a dense forest, where every gap, every patch of sunlight filtered by the boughs and leafy branches of huge trees, was immediately exploited by dozens of young birches, alders and hornbeams, by brambles, junipers and ferns, their tangle of shoots covering the crumbly mire of rotten wood, dry branches and decayed trunks of the oldest trees, the ones that had lost the fight, the ones that had lived out their lifespan. The thicket, however, did not generate the ominous, weighty silence which would have suited the place more. No, Brokilon was alive. Insects buzzed, lizards rustled the grass underfoot, iridescent beetles scuttled, thousands of spiders tugged webs glistening with drops of water, woodpeckers thumped tree trunks with sharp series of raps and jays screeched.

Brokilon was alive.

But the Witcher did not let himself be deceived. He knew where he was. He remembered the boy with the arrow in his eye. He had occasionally seen white bones with red ants crawling over them among the moss and pine needles.

He walked on, cautiously but swiftly. The trail was fresh. He hoped to reach and send back the men walking in front of him. He deluded himself that it was not too late.

But it was.

He would not have noticed the next corpse had it not been for the sunlight reflecting on the blade of the short sword it was gripping.

It was a grown man. His simple clothing, coloured a practical dun, indicated his lowly status. His garments – not counting the blood stains surrounding the two feathers sticking into his chest – were clean and new, so he could not have been a common servant.

Geralt looked around and saw a third body, dressed in a leather jacket and short, green cape. The ground around the dead man's legs was churned up, the moss and pine needles were furrowed right down to the sand. There was no doubt; this man had taken a long time to die.

He heard a groan.

He quickly parted the juniper bushes and saw the deep tree throw they were concealing. A powerfully built man, with black, curly hair and beard contrasting with the dreadful, downright deathly pallor of his face, was lying in the hollow on the exposed roots of the pine. His pale, deerskin kaftan was red with blood.

The Witcher jumped into the hollow. The wounded man opened his eyes.

'Geralt . . .' he groaned. 'O, ye Gods . . . I must be dreaming . . .'

'Frexinet?' the Witcher asked in astonishment. 'You, here?'

'Yes, me . . . Ooooow . . .'

'Don't move,' Geralt said, kneeling beside him. 'Where were you hit? I can't see the arrow . . .'

'It passed . . . right through. I broke off the arrowhead and pulled it out . . . Listen Geralt—'

'Be quiet, Frexinet, or you'll choke on your blood. You have a punctured lung. A pox on it, I have to get you out of here. What the bloody hell were you doing in Brokilon? It's dryad territory, their sanctuary, no one gets out of here alive. I can't believe you didn't know that.'

'Later . . .' Frexinet groaned and spat blood. 'I'll tell you later . . . Now get me out. Oh, a pox on it. Have a care . . . Oooooow . . .'

'I can't do it,' Geralt said, straightening up and looking around. 'You're too heavy.'

'Leave me,' the wounded man grunted. 'Leave me, too bad . . . But save her . . . by the Gods, save her . . .'

'Who?'

'The princess . . . Oh . . . Find her, Geralt.'

'Lie still, dammit! I'll knock something up and haul you out.'

Frexinet coughed hard and spat again; a viscous, stretching thread of blood hung from his chin. The Witcher cursed, vaulted out of the hollow and looked around. He needed two young saplings. He moved quickly towards the edge of the clearing, where he had seen a clump of alders.

A whistle and thud.

Geralt froze to the spot. The arrow, buried in a tree trunk at head height, had hawk feather fletchings. He looked at the angle of the ashen shaft and knew where it had been shot from. About four dozen paces away there was another hollow, a fallen tree, and a tangle of roots sticking up in the air, still tightly gripping a huge lump of sandy earth. There was a dark mass of blackthorn there amid the lighter stripes of birches. He could not see anyone. He knew he would not.

He raised both hands, very slowly.

'Ceádmil! Vá an Eithné meáth e Duén Canell! Esseá Gwynbleidd!'

This time he heard the soft twang of the bowstring and saw the arrow, for it had been shot for him to see. Powerfully. He watched it soar upwards, saw it reach its apex and then fall in a curve. He did not move. The arrow plunged into the moss almost vertically, two paces from him. Almost immediately a second lodged next to the first, at exactly the same angle. He was afraid he might not see the next one.

'Meáth Eithné!' he called again. 'Esseá Gwynbleidd!'

'Gláeddyv vort!' A voice like a breath of wind. A voice, not an arrow. He was alive. He slowly unfastened his belt buckle, drew his sword well away from himself and threw it down. A second dryad emerged noiselessly from behind a fir trunk wrapped around with juniper bushes, no more than ten paces from him. Although she was small and very slim, the trunk seemed thinner. He had no idea how he had not seen her as he approached. Perhaps her outfit had disguised her; a patchwork which accentuated her shapely form, sewn weirdly from scraps of fabric in numerous shades of green and brown, strewn with leaves and pieces of bark. Her hair, tied with a black scarf around her forehead, was olive green and her face was criss-crossed with stripes painted using walnut-shell dye.

Naturally, her bowstring was taut and she was aiming an arrow at him.

'Eithné . . .' he began.

'Tháess aep!'

He obediently fell silent, standing motionless, holding his arms away from his trunk. The dryad did not lower her bow.

'Dunca!' she cried. 'Braenn! Caemm vort!'

The one who had shot the arrows earlier darted out from the blackthorn and slipped over the upturned trunk, nimbly clearing the depression. Although there was a pile of dry branches in it Geralt did not hear even one snap beneath her feet. He heard a faint murmur close behind, something like the rustling of leaves in the wind. He knew there was a third.

It was that one, dashing out from behind him, who picked up his sword. Her hair was the colour of honey and was tied up with a band of bulrush fibres. A quiver full of arrows swung on her back.

The furthest one approached the tree throw swiftly. Her outfit was identical to that of her companions. She wore a garland woven from clover and heather on her dull, brick-red hair. She was holding a bow, not bent, but with an arrow nocked.

'T'en thesse in meáth aep Eithné llev?' she asked, coming over. Her voice was extremely melodious and her eyes huge and black. 'Ess' Gwynbleidd?'

'Aé . . . aesseá . . .' he began, but the words in the Brokilon dialect, which sounded like singing in the dryad's mouth, stuck in his throat and made his lips itchy. 'Do none of you know the Common Speech? I don't speak your—'

'An' váill. Vort llinge,' she cut him off.

'I am Gwynbleidd. White Wolf. Lady Eithné knows me. I am travelling to her as an envoy. I have been in Brokilon before. In Duén Canell.'

'Gwynbleidd.' The redhead narrowed her eyes. 'Vatt'ghern?'

'Yes,' he confirmed. 'The Witcher.'

The olive-haired one snorted angrily, but lowered her bow. The red-haired one looked at him with eyes wide open, but her face – smeared with green stripes – was quite motionless, expressionless, like that of a statue. The immobility meant her face could not be categorised as pretty or ugly. Instead of such classification, a thought came to him about indifference and heartlessness, not to say cruelty. Geralt reproached himself for that judgement, catching himself mistakenly humanising the dryad. He ought to have known, after all, that she was older than the other two. In spite of appearances she was much, much older than them.

They stood in indecisive silence. Geralt heard Frexinet moaning, groaning and coughing. The red-haired one must also have heard, but her face did not even twitch. The Witcher rested his hands on his hips.

'There's a wounded man over there in the tree hole,' he said calmly. 'He will die if he doesn't receive aid.'

'Tháess aep!' the olive-haired one snapped, bending her bow and aiming the arrowhead straight at his face.

'Will you let him die like a dog?' he said, not raising his voice. 'Will you leave him to drown slowly in his own blood? In that case better to put him out of his misery.'

'Be silent!' the dryad barked, switching to the Common Speech. But she lowered her bow and released the tension on the bowstring. She looked at the other questioningly. The red-haired one nodded, indicating the tree hollow. The olive-haired one ran over, quickly and silently.

'I want to see Lady Eithné,' Geralt repeated. 'I'm on a diplomatic mission . . .'

'She,' the red-haired one pointed to the honey-haired one, 'will lead you to Duén Canell. Go.'

'Frex . . . And the wounded man?'

The dryad looked at him, squinting. She was still fiddling with the nocked arrow.

'Do not worry,' she said. 'Go. She will lead you there.'

'But . . .'

'Va'en vort!' She cut him off, her lips tightening.

He shrugged and turned towards the one with the hair the colour of honey. She seemed the youngest of the three, but he might have been mistaken. He noticed she had blue eyes.

'Then let us go.'

'Yes,' the honey-coloured haired one said softly. After a short moment of hesitation she handed him his sword. 'Let us go.'

'What is your name?' he asked.

'Be silent.'

She moved very swiftly through the dense forest, not looking back. Geralt had to exert himself to keep up with her. He knew the dryad was doing it deliberately, knew that she wanted the man following her to get stuck, groaning, in the undergrowth, or to fall to the ground exhausted, incapable of going on. She did not know, of course, that she was dealing with a witcher, not a man. She was too young to know what a witcher was.

The young woman – Geralt now knew she was not a pure-blood dryad – suddenly stopped and turned around. He saw her chest heaving powerfully beneath her short, dappled jacket, saw that she was having difficulty stopping herself from breathing through her mouth.

'Shall we slow down?' he suggested with a smile.

'Yeá.' She looked at him with hostility. 'Aeén esseáth Sidh?'

'No, I'm not an elf. What is your name?'

'Braenn,' she answered, marching on, but now at a slower pace, not trying to outdistance him. They walked alongside each other, close. He smelled the scent of her sweat, the ordinary sweat of a young woman. The sweat of dryads carried the scent of delicate willow leaves crushed in the hands.

'And what were you called before?'

She glanced at him and suddenly grimaced; he thought she would become annoyed or order him to be silent. She did not.

'I don't remember,' she said reluctantly. He did not think it was true.

She did not look older than sixteen and she could not have been in Brokilon for more than six or seven years. Had she come earlier, as a very young child or simply a baby, he would not now be able to see the human in her. Blue eyes and naturally fair hair did occur among dryads. Dryad children, conceived in ritual mating with elves or humans, inherited organic traits exclusively from their mothers, and were always girls. Extremely infrequently, as a rule, in a subsequent generation a child would nonetheless occasionally be born with the eyes or hair of its anonymous male progenitor. But Geralt was certain that Braenn did not have a single drop of dryad blood. And anyway, it was not especially important. Blood or not, she was now a dryad.

'And what,' she looked askance at him, 'do they call you?'

'Gwynbleidd.'

She nodded.

'Then we shall go . . . Gwynbleidd.'

They walked more slowly than before, but still briskly. Braenn, of course, knew Brokilon; had he been alone, Geralt would have been unable to maintain the pace or the right direction. Braenn stole through the barricade of dense forest using winding, concealed paths, clearing gorges, running nimbly across fallen trees as though they were bridges, confidently splashing through glistening stretches of swamp, green from duckweed, which the Witcher would not have dared to tread on. He would have lost hours, if not days, skirting around.

Braenn's presence did not only protect him from the savagery of the forest; there were places where the dryad slowed down, walking extremely cautiously, feeling the path with her foot and holding him by the hand. He knew the reason. Brokilon's traps were legendary; people talked about pits full of sharpened stakes, about booby-trapped bows, about falling trees, about the terrible urchin – a spiked ball on a rope, which, falling suddenly, swept the path clear. There were also places where Braenn would stop and whistle melodiously, and answering whistles would come from the undergrowth. There were other places where she would stop with her hand on the arrows in her quiver, signalling for him to be silent, and wait, tense, until whatever was rustling in the thicket moved away.

In spite of their fast pace, they had to stop for the night. Braenn chose an excellent spot; a hill onto which thermal updrafts carried gusts of warm air. They slept on dried bracken, very close to one another, in dryad custom. In the middle of the night Braenn hugged him close. And nothing more. He hugged her back. And nothing more. She was a dryad. The point was to keep warm.

They set off again at daybreak, while it was still almost dark.

II

They passed through a belt of sparsely forested hills, creeping cautiously across small valleys full of mist, moving through broad, grassy glades, and across clearings of wind-felled trees.

Braenn stopped once again and looked around. She had apparently lost her way, but Geralt knew that was impossible. Taking advantage of a break in the march, however, he sat down on a fallen tree.

And then he heard a scream. Shrill. High-pitched. Desperate.

Braenn knelt down in a flash, at once drawing two arrows from her quiver. She seized one in her teeth and nocked the other, bent her bow, taking aim blindly through the bushes towards the sound of the voice.

'Don't shoot!' he cried.

He leaped over the tree trunk and forced his way through the brush.

A small creature in a short grey jacket was standing in a small clearing, at the foot of a rocky cliff, with its back pressed against the trunk of a withered hornbeam. Something was moving slowly about five paces in front of it, parting the grass. That thing was about twelve feet long and was dark brown. At first Geralt thought it was a snake. But then he noticed the wriggling, yellow, hooked limbs and flat segments of the long thorax and realised it was not a snake. It was something much more sinister.

The creature hugging the tree cried out shrilly. The immense myriapod raised above the grass long, twitching feelers with which it sensed odours and warmth.

'Don't move!' The Witcher yelled and stamped to attract the scolopendromorph's attention. But the myriapod did not react, for its feelers had already caught the scent of the nearer victim. The

256

monster wriggled its limbs, coiled itself up like an 'S' and moved forward. Its bright yellow limbs rippled through grass, evenly, like the oars of a galley.

'Yghern!' Braenn yelled.

Geralt hurtled into the clearing in two bounds, jerking his sword from its scabbard on his back as he ran, and in full flight struck the petrified creature beneath the tree with his hip, shoving it aside into some brambles. The scolopendromorph rustled the grass, wriggled its legs and attacked, raising its anterior segments, its venom-dripping pincers chattering. Geralt danced, leaped over the flat body and slashed it with his sword from a half-turn, aiming at a vulnerable spot between the armoured plates on its body.

The monster was too swift, however, and the sword struck the chitinous shell, without cutting through it; the thick carpet of moss absorbed the blow. Geralt dodged, but not deftly enough. The scolopendromorph wound the posterior part of its body around his legs with enormous strength. The Witcher fell, rolled over and tried to pull himself free. In vain.

The myriapod flexed and turned around to reach him with its pincers, and at the same time fiercely dug its claws into the tree and wrapped itself around it. Right then an arrow hissed above Geralt's head, penetrating the armour with a crack, pinning the creature to the trunk. The scolopendromorph writhed, broke the arrow and freed itself, but was struck at once by two more. The Witcher kicked the thrashing abdomen off and rolled away to the side.

Braenn, kneeling, was shooting at an astonishing rate, sending arrow after arrow into the scolopendromorph. The myriapod was breaking the shafts to free itself, but each successive arrow would pin it to the trunk again. The creature snapped its flat, shiny, dark-red maw and clanged its pincers by the places which had been pierced by the arrows, instinctively trying to reach the enemy which was wounding it.

Geralt leaped at it from the side, took a big swing and hacked with his sword, ending the fight with one blow. The tree acted like an executioner's block.

Braenn approached slowly, an arrow nocked, kicked the body

writing in the grass, its limbs thrashing around, and spat on it.

'Thanks,' the Witcher said, crushing the beast's severed head with blows of his heel.

'Eh?'

'You saved my life.'

The dryad looked at him. There was neither understanding nor emotion in her expression.

'Yghern,' she said, nudging the writhing body with a boot. 'It broke my arrows.'

'You saved my life and that little dryad's,' Geralt repeated. 'Where the bloody hell is she?'

Braenn deftly brushed aside the bramble thicket and plunged an arm among the thorny shoots.

'As I thought,' she said, pulling the little creature in the grey jacket from the thicket. 'See for yourself, Gwynbleidd.'

It was not a dryad. Neither was it an elf, sylph, puck or halfling. It was a quite ordinary little human girl. In the centre of Brokilon, it was the most extraordinary place to come across an ordinary, human little girl.

She had fair, mousy hair and huge, glaringly green eyes. She could not have been more than ten years old.

'Who are you?' he asked. 'How did you get here?'

She did not reply. Where have I seen her before? he wondered. I've seen her before somewhere. Either her or someone very similar to her.

'Don't be afraid,' he said, hesitantly.

'I'm not afraid,' she mumbled indistinctly. She clearly had a cold.

'Let us get out of here,' Braenn suddenly said, looking all around. 'Where there is one yghern, you can usually expect another. And I have few arrows now.'

The girl looked at her, opened her mouth and wiped it with the back of her hand, smearing dust over her face.

'Who the hell are you?' Geralt asked again, leaning forward. 'What are you doing . . . in this forest? How did you get here?'

The girl lowered her head and sniffed loudly.

'Cat got your tongue? Who are you, I said? What's your name?'

'Ciri,' she said, sniffing.

Geralt turned around. Braenn, examining her bow, glanced at him.

'Listen, Braenn . . .'

'What?'

'Is it possible . . . Is it possible she . . . has escaped from Duén Canell?'

'Eh?'

'Don't play dumb,' he said, annoyed. 'I know you abduct little girls. And you? What, did you fall from the sky into Brokilon? I'm asking if it's possible . . .'

'No,' the dryad cut him off. 'I have never seen her before.'

Geralt looked at the little girl. Her ashen-grey hair was dishevelled, full of pine needles and small leaves, but smelled of cleanliness, not smoke, nor the cowshed, nor tallow. Her hands, although incredibly dirty, were small and delicate, without scars or calluses. The boy's clothes, the jacket with a red hood she had on, did not indicate anything, but her high boots were made of soft, expensive calfskin. No, she was certainly not a village child. Frexinet, the Witcher suddenly thought. This was the one that Frexinet was looking for. He'd followed her into Brokilon.

'Where are you from? I'm asking you, you scamp.'

'How dare you talk to me like that!' The little girl lifted her head haughtily and stamped her foot. The soft moss completely spoiled the effect.

'Ha,' the Witcher said, and smiled. 'A princess, indeed. At least in speech, for your appearance is wretched. You're from Verden, aren't you? Do you know you're being looked for? Don't worry, I'll deliver you home. Listen, Braenn . . .'

The moment he looked away the girl turned very quickly on her heel and ran off through the forest, across the gentle hillside.

'Bloede dungh!' the dryad yelled, reaching for her quiver. 'Caemm aere!'

The little girl, stumbling, rushed blindly through the forest, crunching over dry branches.

'Stop!' shouted Geralt. 'Where are you bloody going!?'

Braenn bent her bow in a flash. The arrow hissed venomously, describing a flat parabola, and the arrowhead thudded into the tree trunk, almost brushing the little girl's hair. The girl cringed and flattened herself to the ground.

'You bloody fool,' the Witcher hissed, hurrying over to the dryad. Braenn deftly drew another arrow from her quiver. 'You might have killed her!'

'This is Brokilon,' she said proudly.

'But she's only a child!'

'What of it?'

He looked at the arrow's shaft. It had striped fletchings made from a pheasant's flight feathers dyed yellow in a decoction of tree bark. He did not say a word. He turned around and went quickly into the forest. The little girl was lying beneath the tree, cowering, cautiously raising her head and looking at the arrow stuck into the tree. She heard his steps and leaped to her feet, but he reached her with a single bound and seized her by the red hood of her jacket. She turned her head and looked at him, then at his hand, holding her hood. He released her.

'Why did you run away?'

'None of your business,' she sniffed. 'Leave me alone, you, you—'

'Foolish brat,' he hissed furiously. 'This is Brokilon. Wasn't the myriapod enough? You wouldn't last till morning in this forest. Haven't you got it yet?'

'Don't touch me!' she yelled. 'You peasant! I am a princess, so you'd better be careful!'

'You're a foolish imp.'

'I'm a princess!'

'Princesses don't roam through forests alone. Princesses have clean noses.'

'I'll have you beheaded! And her too!' The girl wiped her nose with her hand and glared at the approaching dryad. Braenn snorted with laughter.

'Alright, enough of this,' the Witcher cut her off. 'Why were you running away, Your Highness? And where to? What were you afraid of?'

She said nothing, and sniffed.

'Very well, as you wish,' he winked at the dryad. '*We're* going. If you want to stay alone in the forest, that's your choice. But the next time a yghern attacks you, don't yell. It doesn't befit a princess. A princess dies without even a squeal, having first wiped her snotty nose. Let's go, Braenn. Farewell, Your Highness.'

'W . . . wait.'

'Aha?'

'I'm coming with you.'

'We are greatly honoured. Aren't we, Braenn?'

'But you won't take me to Kistrin again? Do you swear?'

'Who is—?' he began. 'Oh, dammit. Kistrin. Prince Kistrin? The son of King Ervyll of Verden?'

The little girl pouted her little lips, sniffed and turned away.

'Enough of these trifles,' said Braenn grimly. 'Let us march on.'

'Hold on, hold on.' The Witcher straightened up and looked down at the dryad. 'Our plans are changing somewhat, my comely archer.'

'Eh?' Braenn said, raising her eyebrows.

'Lady Eithné can wait. I have to take the little one home. To Verden.'

The dryad squinted and reached for her quiver.

'You're not going anywhere. Nor is she.'

The Witcher smiled hideously.

'Be careful, Braenn,' he said. 'I'm not that pup whose eye you speared with an arrow from the undergrowth. I can look after myself.'

'Bloede arss!' she hissed, raising her bow. 'You're going to Duén Canell, and so is she! Not to Verden!'

'No. Not to Verden!' the mousy-haired girl said, throwing herself at the dryad and pressing herself against her slim thigh. 'I'm going with you! And he can go to Verden by himself, to silly old Kistrin, if he wants!'

Braenn did not even look at her, did not take her eyes off Geralt. But she lowered her bow.

'Ess dungh!' she said, spitting at his feet. 'Very well! Then go on your way! We'll see how you fare. You'll kiss an arrow before you leave Brokilon.'

She's right, thought Geralt. I don't have a chance. Without her I won't get out of Brokilon nor reach Duén Canell. Too bad, we shall see. Perhaps I'll manage to persuade Eithné . . .

'Very well, Braenn,' he said placatingly, and smiled. 'Don't be furious, fair one. Very well, have it your way. We shall all go to Duén Canell. To Lady Eithné.'

The dryad muttered something under her breath and unnocked the arrow.

'To the road, then,' she said, straightening her hairband. 'We have tarried too long.'

'Ooow . . .' the little girl yelped as she took a step.

'What's the matter?'

'I've done something . . . To my leg.'

'Wait, Braenn! Come here, scamp, I'll carry you pick-a-back.'

She was warm and smelt like a wet sparrow.

'What's your name, princess? I've forgotten.'

'Ciri.'

'And your estates, where do they lie, if I may ask?'

'I won't tell,' she grunted. 'I won't tell, and that's that.'

'I'll get by. Don't wriggle or sniff right by my ear. What were you doing in Brokilon? Did you get lost? Did you lose your way?'

'Not a chance! I never get lost.'

'Don't wriggle. Did you run away from Kistrin? From Nastrog Castle? Before or after the wedding?'

'How did you know?' She sniffed, intent.

'I'm staggeringly intelligent. Why did you run away to Brokilon, of all places? Weren't there any safer directions?'

'I couldn't control my stupid horse.'

'You're lying, princess. Looking at your size, the most you could ride is a cat. And a gentle one at that.'

'I was riding with Marck. Sir Voymir's esquire. But the horse fell in the forest and broke its leg. And we lost our way.'

'You said that never happens to you.'

'He got lost, not me. It was foggy. And we lost our way.'

You got lost, thought Geralt. Sir Voymir's poor esquire, who had the misfortune to happen upon Braenn and her companions. A young stripling, who had probably never known a woman, helped the green-eyed scamp escape, because he'd heard a lot of knightly stories about virgins being forced to marry. He helped her escape, to fall to a dryad's dyed arrow – one who probably hasn't known a man herself. But already knows how to kill.

'I asked you if you bolted from Nastrog Castle before or after the wedding?'

'I just scarpered and it's none of your business,' she grunted. 'Grandmamma told me I had to go there and meet him. That Kistrin. Just meet him. But that father of his, that big-bellied king . . .'

'Ervyll.'

' . . . kept on: "the wedding, the wedding". But I don't want him. That Kistrin. Grandmamma said—'

'Is Prince Kistrin so revolting?'

'I don't want him,' Ciri proudly declared, sniffing loudly. 'He's fat, stupid and his breath smells. Before I went there they showed me a painting, but he wasn't fat in the painting. I don't want a husband like that. I don't want a husband at all.'

'Ciri,' the Witcher said hesitantly. 'Kistrin is still a child, like you. In a few years he might turn into a handsome young man.'

'Then they can send me another painting, in a few years,' she snorted. 'And him too. Because he told me that I was much prettier in the painting they showed him. And he confessed that he loves Alvina, a lady-in-waiting and he wants to be a knight. See? He doesn't want me and I don't want him. So what use is a wedding?'

'Ciri,' the Witcher muttered, 'he's a prince and you're a princess. Princes and princesses marry like that, that's how it is. That's the custom.'

'You sound like all the rest. You think that just because I'm small you can lie to me.'

'I'm not lying.'

'Yes you are.'

Geralt said nothing. Braenn, walking in front of them, turned around, probably surprised by the silence. She shrugged and set off.

'Which way are we going?' Ciri asked glumly. 'I want to know!'

Geralt said nothing.

'Answer, when I ask a question!' she said menacingly, backing up the order with a loud sniff. 'Do you know . . . who's sitting on you?'

He didn't react.

'I'll bite you in the ear!' she yelled.

The Witcher had had enough. He pulled the girl off his back and put her on the ground.

'Now listen, you brat,' he said harshly, struggling with his belt buckle. 'In a minute I'll put you across my knee, pull down your britches and tan your backside. No one will stop me doing it, because this isn't the royal court, and I'm not your flunkey or servant. You'll soon regret you didn't stay in Nastrog. You'll soon see it's better being a princess than a snot-nosed kid who got lost in the forest. Because, it's true, a princess is allowed to act obnoxiously. And no one thrashes a princess's backside with a belt. At most her husband, the prince, might with his own hand.'

Ciri cowered and sniffed a few times. Braenn watched dispassionately, leaning against a tree.

'Well?' the Witcher asked, wrapping his belt around his wrist. 'Are we going to behave with dignity and temperance? If not, we shall set about tanning Her Majesty's hide. Well? What's it to be?'

The little girl snivelled and sniffed, then eagerly nodded.

'Are you going to be good, princess?'

'Yes,' she mumbled.

'Gloaming will soon fall,' the dryad said. 'Let us make haste, Gwynbleidd.'

The forest thinned out. They walked through a sandy young forest, across moors, and through fog-cloaked meadows with herds of red deer grazing. It was growing cooler.

'Noble lord . . .' Ciri began after a long, long silence.

'My name is Geralt. What's the matter?'

'I'm awffy, awffy hungry.'

'We'll stop in a moment. It'll be dark soon.'

'I can't go on,' she snivelled. 'I haven't eaten since—'

'Stop whining.' He reached into a saddlebag and took out a piece of fatback, a small round of white cheese and two apples. 'Have that.'

'What's that yellow stuff?'

'Fatback.'

'I won't eat that,' she grunted.

'That's fine,' he said indistinctly, stuffing the fatback into his mouth. 'Eat the cheese. And an apple. Just one.'

'Why only one.'

'Don't wriggle. Have both.'

'Geralt?'

'Mhm?'

'Thank you.'

'Don't mention it. Food'll do you good.'

'I didn't . . . Not for that. That too, but . . . You saved me from that centipede . . . Ugh . . . I almost died of fright.'

'You almost died,' he confirmed seriously. You almost died in an extremely painful and hideous way, he thought. 'But you ought to thank Braenn.'

'What is she?'

'A dryad.'

'An eerie wife?'

'Yes.'

'So she's . . . They kidnap children! She's kidnapped us? Hey, but you aren't small. But why does she speak so strangely?'

'That's just her way, it's not important. What's important is how she shoots. Don't forget to thank her when we stop.'

'I won't forget,' she sniffed.

'Don't wriggle, future Princess of Verden, ma'am.'

'I'm not going to be a princess,' she muttered.

'Very well, very well. You won't be a princess. You'll become a hamster and live in a burrow.'

'No I won't! You don't know anything!'

'Don't squeak in my ear. And don't forget about the strap!'

'I'm not going to be a princess. I'm going to be . . .'

'Yes? What?'

'It's a secret.'

'Oh, yes, a secret. Splendid.' He raised his head. 'What is it, Braenn?'

The dryad had stopped. She shrugged and looked at the sky.

'I cannot go on,' she said softly. 'Neither can you, I warrant, with her on your back, Gwynbleidd. We shall stop here. It will darken soon.'

III

'Ciri?'

'Mhm?' the little girl sniffed and rustled the branches she was lying on.

'Aren't you cold?'

'No,' she sighed. 'It's warm today. Yesterday ... Yesterday I froze awffy, oh my, how I did.'

'It is a marvel,' Braenn said, loosening the straps of her long, soft boots. 'A tiny little moppet, but she has covered a long stride of forest. And she got past the lookouts, through the bog and the thicket. She is robust, healthy and stout. Truly, she would come in useful. To us.'

Geralt glanced quickly at the dryad, at her eyes shining in the semi-darkness. Braenn leaned back against a tree, removed her hairband and let her hair down with a shake of her head.

'She entered Brokilon,' she muttered, forestalling his comment. 'She is ours, Gwynbleidd. We are marching to Duén Canell.'

'Lady Eithné will decide,' he responded tartly. But he knew Braenn was right.

Pity, he thought, looking at the little girl wriggling on the green bed. She's such a determined rascal! Where have I seen her before? Never mind. But it's a pity. The world is so big and so beautiful. And Brokilon will now be her world, until the end of her days. And there may not be many. Perhaps only until the day she falls in the bracken, amidst cries and the whistles of arrows, fighting in this senseless battle for the forest. On the side of those who will lose. Who have to lose. Sooner or later.

'Ciri?'

'Yes?'

'Where do your parents live?'

'I don't have any parents,' she sniffed. 'They drowned at sea when I was tiny.'

Yes, he thought, that explains a lot. A princess, the child of a deceased royal couple. Who knows if she isn't the third daughter following four sons? A title which in practice means less than that of chamberlain or equerry. A mousy-haired, green-eyed thing hanging around the court, who ought to be shoved out as quickly as possible and married off. As quickly as possible, before she matures and becomes a young woman and brings the threat of scandal, misalliance or incest, which would not be difficult in a shared castle bedchamber.

Her escape did not surprise the Witcher. He had frequently met princesses – and even queens – roaming around with troupes of wandering players, happy to have escaped some decrepit king still desirous of an heir. He had seen princes, preferring the uncertain fate of a soldier of fortune to marriage to a lame or pockmarked princess – chosen by their father – whose withered or doubtful virginity was to be the price of an alliance or dynastic coalition.

He lay down beside the little girl and covered her with his jacket.

'Sleep,' he said. 'Sleep, little orphan.'

'Orphan? Humph!' she growled. 'I'm a princess, not an orphan. And I have a grandmamma. And my grandmamma is a queen, so you'd better be careful. When I tell her you wanted to give me the strap, my grandmamma will order your head chopped off, you'll see.'

'Ghastly! Ciri, have mercy!'

'Not a chance!'

'But you're a good little girl. And beheading hurts awfully. You won't say anything, will you?'

'I will.'

'Ciri.'

'I will, I will, I will! Afraid, are you?'

'Dreadfully. You know, Ciri, you can die from having your head cut off.'

'Are you mocking me?'

'I wouldn't dream of it.'

'She'll put you in your place, you'll see. No one takes liberties with my grandmamma. When she stamps her foot the greatest knights and warriors kneel before her; I've seen it myself. And if one of them is disobedient, then it's "chop" and off with his head.'

'Dreadful. Ciri?'

'Uh-huh?'

'I think they'll cut off your head.'

'*My* head?'

'Naturally. After all, your grandmamma, the queen, arranged a marriage with Kistrin and sent you to Nastrog Castle in Verden. You were disobedient. As soon as you return . . . it'll be "chop!" and off with *your* head.'

The little girl fell silent. She even stopped fidgeting. He heard her smacking her lips, biting her lower lip and sniffing.

'You're wrong,' she said. 'Grandmamma won't let anyone chop off my head, because . . . Because she's my grandmamma, isn't she? Oh, at most I'll get . . .'

'Aha,' Geralt laughed. 'There's no taking liberties with grandmamma, is there? The switch has come out, hasn't it?'

Ciri snorted angrily.

'Do you know what?' he said. 'We'll tell your grandmamma that I've already whipped you, and you can't be punished twice for the same crime. Is it a deal?'

'You must be silly!' Ciri raised herself on her elbows, making the branches rustle. 'When grandmamma hears that you thrashed me, they'll chop your head off just like that!'

'So you are worried for my head then?'

The little girl fell silent and sniffed again.

'Geralt . . .'

'What, Ciri?'

'Grandmamma knows I have to go home. I can't be a princess or the wife of that stupid Kistrin. I have to go home, and that's that.'

You do, he thought. Regrettably, it doesn't depend on you or on your grandmamma. It depends on the mood of old Eithné. And on my persuasive abilities.

'Grandmamma knows,' Ciri continued. 'Because I . . . Geralt,

269

promise you won't tell anybody. It's a terrible secret. Dreadful, I'm serious. Swear.'

'I swear.'

'Very well, I'll tell you. My mama was a witch, so you'd better watch your step. And my papa was enchanted, too. It was all told to me by one of my nannies, and when grandmamma found out about it, there was a dreadful to-do. Because I'm destined, you know?'

'To do what?'

'I don't know,' Ciri said intently. 'But I'm destined. That's what my nanny said. And grandmamma said she won't let anyone . . . that the whole ruddy castle will collapse first. Do you understand? And nanny said that nothing, nothing at all, can help with destiny. Ha! And then nanny wept and grandmamma yelled. Do you see? I'm destined. I won't be the wife of that silly Kistrin. Geralt?'

'Go to sleep,' he yawned, so that his jaw creaked. 'Go to sleep, Ciri.'

'Tell me a story.'

'What?'

'Tell me a story,' she snorted. 'How am I supposed to sleep without a story? I mean, really!'

'I don't know any damned stories. Go to sleep.'

'You're lying. You do. What, no one told you stories when you were little? What are you laughing about?'

'Nothing. I just recalled something.'

'Aha! You see. Go on.'

'What?'

'Tell me a story.'

He laughed again, put his hands under his head and looked up at the stars twinkling beyond the branches above their heads.

'There was once . . . a cat,' he began. 'An ordinary, tabby mouser. And one day that cat went off, all by itself, on a long journey to a terrible, dark forest. He walked . . . And he walked . . . And he walked . . .'

'Don't think,' Ciri mumbled, cuddling up to him, 'that I'll fall asleep before he gets there.'

'Keep quiet, rascal. So . . . he walked and he walked until he came across a fox. A red fox.'

Braenn sighed and lay down beside the Witcher, on the other side, and also snuggled up a little.

'Very well,' Ciri sniffed. 'Say what happened next.'

'The fox looked at the cat. "Who are you?" he asked. "I'm a cat," said the cat. "Ha," said the fox. "But aren't you afraid, cat, to be roaming the forest alone? What will you do if the king comes a-hunting? With hounds and mounted hunters and beaters? I tell you, cat," said the fox, "the chase is a dreadful hardship to creatures like you and I. You have a pelt, I have a pelt, and hunters never spare creatures like us, because hunters have sweethearts and lovers, and their little hands and necks get cold, so they make muffs and collars for those strumpets to wear".'

'What are muffs?' Ciri asked.

'Don't interrupt. And the fox went on. "I, cat, know how to outwit them; I have one thousand, two hundred and eighty-six ways to outfox those hunters, so cunning am I. And you, cat, how many ways do you have?"'

'Oh, what a fine tale,' Ciri said, cuddling more tightly to the Witcher. 'What did the cat say?'

'Aye,' whispered Braenn from the other side. 'What did the cat say?'

The Witcher turned his head. The dryad's eyes were sparkling, her mouth was half-open and she was running her tongue over her lips. He could understand. Little dryads were hungry for tales. Just like little witchers. Because both of them were seldom told bedtime stories. Little dryads fell asleep listening raptly to the wind blowing in the trees. Little witchers fell asleep listening raptly to their aching arms and legs. Our eyes also shone like Braenn's when we listened to the tales of Vesemir in Kaer Morhen. But that was long ago . . . So long ago . . .

'Well,' Ciri said impatiently. 'What then?'

'The cat said: "I, fox, don't have any ways. I only know one thing; up a tree as quick as can be. That ought to be enough, oughtn't it?" The fox burst out laughing. "Hah," he said. "What a goose you are!

271

Flourish your stripy tail and flee, for you'll perish if the hunters trap you." And suddenly, from nowhere, the horns began to sound! And the hunters leaped out from the bushes. And they saw the cat and the fox. And they were upon them!'

'Oh!' Ciri sniffed, and the dryad shifted suddenly.

'Quiet. And they were upon them, yelling: "Have them, skin them! We'll make muffs out of them, muffs!" And they set the hounds on the fox and the cat. And the cat darted up a tree, like every cat does. Right to the very top. But the hounds seized the fox! And before Reynard had time to use any of his cunning ways, he'd been made into a collar. And the cat meowed from the top of the tree and hissed at the hunters, but they couldn't do anything to him, because the tree was as high as hell. They stood at the foot of the tree, swearing like troopers, but they had to go away empty-handed. And then the cat climbed down from the tree and slunk calmly home.'

'What happened then?'

'Nothing. That's the end.'

'What about the moral?' Ciri asked. 'Tales always have a moral, don't they?'

'Hey?' Braenn said, hugging Geralt even harder. 'What's a moral?'

'A good story has a moral and a bad one doesn't,' Ciri sniffed with conviction.

'That was a good one,' the dryad yawned. 'So it has what it ought to have. You, moppet, should have scurried up a tree from that yghern, like that canny tomcat. Not pondered, but scurried up the tree without a thought. And that is all the wisdom in it. To survive. Not to be caught.'

The Witcher laughed softly.

'Weren't there any trees in the castle grounds, Ciri? In Nastrog? Instead of coming to Brokilon you could have skinned up a tree and stayed there, at the very top, until Kistrin's desire to wed had waned.'

'Are you mocking me?'

'Uh-huh.'

'Know what? I can't stand you.'

'That's dreadful. Ciri, you've stabbed me in the very heart.'

272

'I know,' she nodded gravely, sniffing, and then clung tightly to him.

'Sleep well, Ciri,' he muttered, breathing in her pleasant, sparrow scent. 'Sleep well. Goodnight, Braenn.'

'Deárme, Gwynbleidd.'

Above their heads a billion Brokilon branches soughed and hundreds of billions of Brokilon leaves rustled.

IV

The next day they reached the Trees. Braenn knelt down and bent her head. Geralt felt the need to do the same. Ciri heaved a sigh of awe.

The Trees – chiefly oaks, yews and hickories – had girths of over a hundred feet, some much more. It was impossible to say how high their crowns were. The places where the mighty, twisted roots joined the vertical trunks were high above their heads, however. They could have walked more quickly, as the giants grew slowly and no other vegetation could survive in their shadows; there was only a carpet of decaying leaves.

They could have walked more quickly. But they walked slowly. In silence. With bowed heads. Among the Trees they were small, insignificant, irrelevant. Unimportant. Even Ciri kept quiet – she did not speak for almost half an hour.

And after an hour's walk they passed the belt of Trees and once again plunged deep into ravines and wet beechwood forests.

Ciri's cold was troubling her more and more. Geralt did not have a handkerchief, and having had enough of her incessant sniffing, taught her to clear her nose directly onto the ground. The little girl was delighted by it. Looking at her smirk and shining eyes, the Witcher was deeply convinced that she was savouring the thought of showing off her new trick at court, during a ceremonial banquet or an audience with a foreign ambassador.

Braenn suddenly stopped and turned around.

'Gwynbleidd,' she said, unwinding a green scarf wrapped around her elbow. 'Come here. I will blindfold you. I must.'

'I know.'

'I will lead you. Give me your hand.'

'No,' protested Ciri. 'I'll lead him. May I, Braenn?'

'Very well, moppet.'

'Geralt?'

'Uh-huh?'

'What does "Gwyn . . . bleidd" mean?'

'White Wolf. The dryads call me that.'

'Beware, there's a root. Don't trip! Do they call you that because you have white hair?'

'Yes . . . Blast!'

'I said there was a root.'

They walked on. Slowly. It was slippery under their feet from fallen leaves. He felt warmth on his face, the sunlight shining through the blindfold.

'Oh, Geralt,' he heard Ciri's voice. 'How delightful it is here . . . Pity you can't see. There are so many flowers. And birds. Can you hear them singing? Oh, there's so many of them. Heaps. Oh, and squirrels. Careful, we're going to cross a stream, over a stone bridge. Don't fall in. Oh, so many little fishes! Hundreds. They're swimming in the water, you know. So many little animals, oh my. There can't be so many anywhere else.'

'There can't,' he muttered. 'Nowhere else. This is Brokilon.'

'What?'

'Brokilon. The Last Place.'

'I don't understand.'

'No one understands. No one wants to understand.'

V

'You can take off the blindfold now, Gwynbleidd. We have arrived.'

Braenn stood up to her knees in a dense carpet of fog.

'Duén Canell,' she said, pointing.

Duén Canell, the Place of the Oak. The Heart of Brokilon.

Geralt had already been there. Twice. But he had never told anyone about it. No one would have believed him.

A basin enclosed by the crowns of mighty green trees. Bathed in fog and mist rising from the earth, the rocks and the hot springs. A basin . . .

The medallion around his neck vibrated slightly.

A basin bathed in magic. Duén Canell. The Heart of Brokilon.

Braenn lifted her head and adjusted the quiver on her back.

'We must go. Give me your little hand, moppet.'

At first, the valley seemed to be lifeless. Deserted. But not for long. A loud, modulated whistling rang out, and a slender, dark-haired dryad, dressed, like all of them, in dappled, camouflaged attire slid nimbly down barely perceptible steps of bracket mushrooms winding around the nearest trunk.

'Ceád, Braenn.'

'Ceád, Sirssa. Va'n vort meáth Eithné á?'

'Neén, aefder,' the dark-haired dryad answered, sweeping her gaze up and down the Witcher. 'Ess' ae'n Sidh?'

She smiled, flashing white teeth. She was incredibly comely, even according to human standards. Geralt felt uncertain and foolish, aware that the dryad was inspecting him uninhibitedly.

'Neén,' Braenn shook her head. 'Ess' vatt'ghern, Gwynbleidd, á váen meáth Eithné va, a'ss.'

'Gwynbleidd?' the beautiful dryad said, grimacing. 'Bloede caérme! Aen'ne caen n'wedd vort! T'ess foile!'

Braenn sniggered.

'What is it?' the Witcher asked, growing angry.

'Nothing,' Braenn sniggered again. 'Nothing. Let us be moving.'

'Oh,' Ciri said in delight. 'Look at those funny cottages, Geralt!'

Duén Canell really began deep in the valley; the 'funny cottages', resembling huge bunches of mistletoe in shape, clung to the trunks and bows at various heights, both low, just above the ground, and high, occasionally very high, right beneath the very crowns. Geralt also saw several larger constructions on the ground, shelters made of woven branches, still covered in leaves. He saw movements in the openings to the shelters, but the dryads themselves could barely be made out. There were far fewer than there had been the last time he was there.

'Geralt,' Ciri whispered. 'Those cottages are living. They've got little leaves!'

'They're made of living wood,' the Witcher nodded. 'That's how dryads live, that's how they build their houses. No dryad will ever harm a tree by chopping or sawing it. They love trees. However, they can make the branches grow to form those dwellings.'

'How sweet. I'd like to have a little house like that on our estate.'

Braenn stopped in front of one of the larger shelters.

'Enter, Gwynbleidd,' she said. 'You will wait here for Lady Eithné. Vá fáill, moppet.'

'What?'

'That was a farewell, Ciri. She said "goodbye".'

'Oh. Goodbye, Braenn.'

They went inside. The interior of the 'cottage' twinkled like a kaleidoscope, from the patches of sunlight filtered and diffused through the roof structure.

'Geralt!'

'Frexinet!'

'You're alive, by the Devil!' the wounded man said, flashing his teeth, raising himself up on a makeshift bed of spruce. He saw Ciri clinging to the Witcher's thigh and his eyes widened, a flush rushing to his face.

'You little beast!' he yelled. 'I almost lost my life thanks to you! Oh, you're fortunate I cannot stand, for I'd tan your hide!'

Ciri pouted.

'You're the second person,' she said, wrinkling her nose comically, 'to want to thrash me. I'm a little girl and little girls can't be beaten!'

'I'd soon show you . . . what's allowed and what isn't,' Frexinet coughed. 'You little wretch! Ervyll is beside himself . . . He's sending out word, terrified that your grandmother's army is marching on him. Who will believe that you bolted? Everyone knows what Ervyll's like and what his pleasures are. Everyone thinks he . . . did something to you in his cups, and then had you drowned in the fishpond! War with Nilfgaard is looming, and because of you the treaty and the alliance with your grandmother have gone up in smoke! See what you've done?'

'Don't excite yourself,' the Witcher warned, 'for you might open your wounds. How did you get here so swiftly?'

'The Devil only knows, I've been lying half-dead most of the time. They poured something revolting down my throat. By force. They held my nose and . . . What a damned disgrace . . .'

'You're alive thanks to what they poured down your throat. Did they bring you here?'

'They dragged me here on a sledge. I asked after you but they said nothing. I was certain you'd caught an arrow. You vanished so suddenly . . . But you're hale and hearty, not even in fetters, and not only that, prithee, you rescued Princess Cirilla . . . A pox on it, you get by everywhere, Geralt, and you always fall on your feet.'

The Witcher smiled but did not respond. Frexinet hacked, turned his head away and spat out saliva tinged pink.

'Well,' he added. 'And you're sure to be the reason they didn't finish me off. They know you, bloody eerie wives. That's the second time you've got me out of trouble.'

'Oh, come on, baron.'

Frexinet, moaning, tried to sit up, but abandoned the attempt.

'Bollocks to my barony,' he panted. 'I was a baron back in Hamm. Now I'm something like a governor at Ervyll's court in Verden. I mean I was. Even if I get out of this forest somehow, there's no place for me in Verden now, apart from on the scaffold. This little weasel, Cirilla, slipped out of my hands and my protection. Do you think the three of us went to Brokilon for the hell of it? No, Geralt, I was fleeing too, and could only count on Ervyll's mercy if I brought her back. And then I happened on those accursed eerie wives . . . If not for you I'd have expired in that hollow. You've rescued me again. It's destiny, that's as clear as day.'

'You're exaggerating.'

Frexinet shook his head.

'It's destiny,' he repeated. 'It must have been written up there that we'd meet again, Witcher. That you'd save my skin again. Remember, people talked about it in Hamm after you lifted that bird curse from me.'

'Chance,' Geralt said coldly. 'Pure chance, Frexinet.'

'What chance? Dammit, if it hadn't been for you, I'd probably still be a cormorant—'

'You were a cormorant?' Ciri cried in excitement. 'A real cormorant? A bird?'

'I was,' the baron grinned. 'I was cursed by . . . by a bitch . . . Damn her . . . for revenge.'

'I bet you didn't give her a fur,' Ciri said, wrinkling up her nose. 'For a, you know . . . muff.'

'There was another reason,' Frexinet blushed slightly, then glowered angrily at the little girl. 'But what business is it of yours, you tyke!'

Ciri looked offended and turned her head away.

'Yes,' Frexinet coughed. 'Where was I . . . Aha, when I was cursed in Hamm. Were it not for you, Geralt, I would have remained a cormorant till the end of my days, I would be flying around the lake, shitting on tree branches, deluding myself that the shirt made of nettle fibres stubbornly woven by my dear sister would save me. Dammit, when I recall that shirt of hers, I feel like kicking somebody. That idiot—'

'Don't say that,' the Witcher smiled. 'She had the best of intentions. She was badly informed, that's all. Lots of nonsensical myths

279

circulate about undoing curses. You were lucky, anyway, Frexinet. She might have ordered you to dive into a barrel of boiling milk. I've heard of a case like that. Donning a nettle shirt, if you think about it, isn't very harmful to the health, even if it doesn't help much.'

'Ha, perhaps you're right. Perhaps I expect too much of her. Eliza was always stupid, from a child she was stupid and lovely, as a matter of fact; splendid material for a king's wife.'

'What is lovely material?' Ciri asked. 'And why for a wife?'

'Don't interfere, you tyke, I said. Yes, Geralt, I was lucky you turned up in Hamm then. And that my brother-in-law king was ready to spend the few ducats you demanded for lifting the spell.'

'You know, Frexinet,' Geralt said, smiling even more broadly, 'that news of the incident spread far and wide?'

'The true version?'

'I wouldn't say that. To begin with, they gave you ten more brothers.'

'Oh no!' The baron raised himself on an elbow and coughed. 'And so, counting Eliza, there were said to be twelve of us? What bloody idiocy! My mama wasn't a rabbit!'

'That's not all. It was agreed that cormorants aren't romantic enough.'

'Because they aren't! There's nothing romantic about them!' The baron grimaced, feeling his chest, wrapped in bast and sheets of birch bark. 'What was I turned into, according to the tale?'

'A swan. I mean swans. There were eleven of you, don't forget.'

'And how is a swan more romantic than a cormorant?'

'I don't know.'

'I don't either. But I'll bet that in the story Eliza lifted the curse from me with the help of her gruesome nettle blouse?'

'You win. How is Eliza?'

'She has consumption, poor thing. She won't last long.'

'That's sad.'

'It is,' Frexinet agreed dispassionately, looking away.

'Coming back to the curse . . .' Geralt leaned back against a wall made of woven, springy switches. 'You don't have any recurrences? You don't sprout feathers?'

'No, may the Gods be praised,' the baron sighed. 'Everything is in good order. The one thing that I was left with from those times is a taste for fish. There are no better vittles for me, Geralt, than fish. Occasionally I go down to the fishermen on the jetty early in the morning, and before they find me something more refined, I gobble down a handful or two of bleak straight from the holding cage, a few minnows, dace or chub . . . It's pure bliss, not food.'

'He was a cormorant,' Ciri said slowly, looking at Geralt. 'And you lifted the curse from him. You can do magic!'

'I think it's obvious,' Frexinet said, 'that he can. Every witcher can.'

'Wi . . . witcher?'

'Didn't you know he was a witcher? The famous Geralt Riv? True enough, how is a little tyke like you to know what a witcher is? Things aren't what they used to be. Now there are very few witchers. You'd have a job finding one. You've probably never seen a witcher before?'

Ciri shook her head slowly, not taking her eyes off Geralt.

'A witcher, little tyke, is a . . .' Frexinet broke off and paled, seeing Braenn entering the cottage. 'No, I don't want it! I won't let you pour any more of it down my throat, never, never again! Geralt! Tell her—'

'Calm down.'

Braenn did not grace Frexinet with anything more than a fleeting glance. She walked over to Ciri, who was squatting beside the Witcher.

'Come,' she said. 'Come, moppet.'

'Where to?' Ciri grimaced. 'I'm not going. I want to be with Geralt.'

'Go,' the Witcher managed a smile. 'You can play with Braenn and the young dryads. They'll show you Duén Canell . . .'

'She didn't blindfold me,' Ciri said very slowly. 'She didn't blindfold me while we were walking here. She blindfolded you. So you couldn't find your way back here when you leave. That means . . .'

Geralt looked at Braenn. The dryad shrugged and then hugged the little girl tightly.

'That means . . .' Ciri's voice suddenly cracked. 'That means I'm not leaving here. Doesn't it?'

'No one can escape their destiny.'

All heads turned at the sound of that voice. Quiet, but sonorous, hard and decisive. A voice demanding obedience, which brooked no argument. Braenn bowed. Geralt went down on one knee.

'Lady Eithné.'

The ruler of Brokilon was wearing a flowing, gauzy, light-green gown. Like most dryads she was small and slender, but her proudly raised head, grave, sharp-featured face and resolute mouth made her seem taller and more powerful. Her hair and eyes were the colour of molten silver.

She entered the shelter escorted by two younger dryads armed with bows. Without a word she nodded towards Braenn, who immediately took Ciri by the hand and pulled her towards the door, bowing her head low. Ciri trod stiffly and clumsily, pale and speechless. When they passed Eithné, the silver-haired dryad seized her swiftly beneath the chin, lifted it and looked long in the girl's eyes. Geralt could see that Ciri was trembling.

'Go,' Eithné finally said. 'Go, my child. Fear naught. Nothing is capable of changing your destiny. You are in Brokilon.'

Ciri followed Braenn obediently. In the doorway she turned around. The Witcher noticed that her mouth was quivering, and her green eyes were misty with tears. He didn't say a word.

He continued to kneel, head bowed.

'Get up, Gwynbleidd. Welcome.'

'Greetings, Eithné, Lady of Brokilon.'

'I have the pleasure to host you in my Forest once again. Although you come here without my knowledge or permission. Entering Brokilon without my knowledge or permission is perilous, White Wolf. Even for you.'

'I come on a mission.'

'Ah . . .' the dryad smiled slightly. 'That explains your boldness, which I shall not describe using other, more blunt words. Geralt, the inviolability of envoys is a custom observed by humans. I do not recognise it. I recognise nothing human. This is Brokilon.'

'Eithné—'

'Be silent,' she interrupted, without raising her voice. 'I ordered you to be spared. You will leave Brokilon alive. Not because you are an envoy. For other reasons.'

'Are you not curious whose envoy I am? Where I come from, on whose behalf?'

'Frankly speaking, no. This is Brokilon. You come here from the outside, from a world that concerns me not. Why then would I waste time listening to supplications? What could some kind of proposal, some kind of ultimatum, devised by someone who thinks and feels differently to me, mean to me? What could I care what King Venzlav thinks?'

Geralt shook his head in astonishment.

'How do you know I come from Venzlav?'

'For it is obvious,' the dryad said with a smile. 'Ekkehard is too stupid. Ervyll and Viraxas detest me too much. No other realms border Brokilon.'

'You know a great deal about what happens beyond Brokilon, Eithné.'

'I know much, White Wolf. It is a privilege of my age. Now, though, if you permit, I would like to deal with a confidential matter. That man with the appearance of a bear,' the dryad stopped smiling and looked at Frexinet. 'Is he your friend?'

'We are acquainted. I once removed a curse from him.'

'The problem is,' Eithné said coldly, 'that I don't know what to do with him. I cannot, after all, order him put to death. I have permitted him to recover his health, but he represents a threat. He does not look like a fanatic. Thus he must be a scalp-hunter. I know that Ervyll pays for every dryad scalp. I do not recall how much. In any case, the price rises as the value of money falls.'

'You are in error. He is not a scalp-hunter.'

'Why then did he enter Brokilon?'

'To seek the girl-child whose care he was entrusted with. He risked his life to find her.'

'Most foolish,' Eithné said coldly. 'Difficult to call it even a risk. He was heading for certain death. The fact that he lives at all he owes

283

entirely to his iron constitution and endurance. As far as the child is concerned, it also survived by chance. My girls did not shoot, for they thought it was a puck or a leprechaun.'

She looked once again at Frexinet, and Geralt saw that her mouth had lost its unpleasant hardness.

'Very well. Let us celebrate this day in some way.'

She walked over to the bed of branches. The two dryads accompanying her also approached. Frexinet blanched and cowered, without becoming any smaller.

Eithné looked at him for a while, narrowing her eyes a little.

'Have you children?' she finally asked. 'I am talking to you, blockhead.'

'Eh?'

'I trust I express myself clearly.'

'I'm not . . .' Frexinet hemmed and coughed. 'I'm not married.'

'Your marital status is of little concern to me. What interests me is whether you are capable of mustering anything from your suety loins. By the Great Tree! Have you ever made a woman with child?'

'Errr . . . Yes . . . Yes, my lady, but—'

Eithné waved a hand carelessly and turned towards Geralt.

'He shall stay in Brokilon,' she said, 'until he is fully healed and then a little longer. Afterwards . . . He may go whither he so wish.'

'Thank you, Eithné,' the Witcher bowed.' And . . . the little girl? What about her?'

'Why do you ask?' The dryad looked at him with a cold glint in her silver eyes. 'You know.'

'She is not an ordinary, village child. She is a princess.'

'That makes no impression on me. Nor makes any difference.'

'Listen . . .'

'Not another word, Gwynbleidd.'

He fell silent and bit his lip.

'What about my petition?'

'I shall listen to it,' the dryad sighed. 'No, not out of curiosity. I shall do it for you, that you might distinguish yourself before Venzlav and collect the fee he probably promised you for reaching me. But not now, now I shall be busy. Come to my Tree this evening.'

When she had gone, Frexinet raised himself on an elbow, groaned, coughed and spat on his hand.

'What is it all about, Geralt? Why am I to stay here? And what did she mean about those children? What have you got me mixed up in, eh?'

The Witcher sat down.

'You'll save your hide, Frexinet,' he said in a weary voice. 'You'll become one of the few to get out of here alive, at least recently. And you'll become the father of a little dryad. Several, perhaps.'

'What the . . . ? Am I to be . . . a stud?'

'Call it what you will. You have limited choices.'

'I get it,' the baron winked and grinned lewdly. 'Why, I've seen captives working in mines and digging canals. It could be worse . . . Just as long as my strength suffices. There's quite a few of them here . . .'

'Stop smiling foolishly,' Geralt grimaced, 'and daydreaming. Don't imagine adoration, music, wine, fans and swarms of adoring dryads. There'll be one, perhaps two. And there won't be any adoration. They will treat the entire matter very practically. And you even more so.'

'Doesn't it give them pleasure? It can't cause them any harm?'

'Don't be a child. In this respect they don't differ in any way from women. Physically, at least.'

'What do you mean?'

'It depends on you whether it'll be agreeable or disagreeable. But that doesn't change the fact that the only thing that interests her is the result. You are of minor importance. Don't expect any gratitude. Aha, and under no circumstances try anything on your own initiative.'

'My own what?'

'Should you meet her in the morning,' the Witcher explained patiently, 'bow, but without any damned smirks or winks. For a dryad it is a deadly serious matter. Should she smile or approach you, you can talk to her. About trees, ideally. If you don't know much about trees, then about the weather. But should she pretend not to see you, stay well away from her. And stay well away from

285

other dryads, and watch your hands. Those matters do not exist to a dryad who is not ready. If you touch her she'll stab you, because she won't understand your intentions.'

'You're familiar,' Frexinet smiled, 'with their mating habits. Has it ever befallen you?'

The Witcher did not reply. Before his eyes was the beautiful, slender dryad and her impudent smile. *Vatt'ghern, bloede caérme.* A witcher, dammit. Why did you bring him here, Braenn? What use is he to us? No benefit from a witcher . . .

'Geralt?'

'What?'

'And Princess Cirilla?'

'Forget about her. They'll turn her into a dryad. In two or three years she'd shoot an arrow in her own brother's eye, were he to try to enter Brokilon.'

'Dammit,' Frexinet swore, scowling. 'Ervyll will be furious. Geralt? Couldn't I—?'

'No,' the Witcher cut him off. 'Don't even try. You wouldn't get out of Duén Canell alive.'

'That means the lass is lost.'

'To you, yes.'

VI

Eithné's Tree was, naturally, an oak, but it was actually three oaks fused together, still green, not betraying any signs of age, although Geralt reckoned they were at least three hundred years old. The trees were hollow inside and the cavity had the dimensions of a large chamber with a high ceiling narrowing into a cone. The interior was lit by a cresset which did not smoke, and it had been modestly – but not crudely – transformed into comfortable living quarters.

Eithné was kneeling inside on something like a fibrous mat. Ciri sat cross-legged before her, erect and motionless, as though petrified. She had been bathed and cured of her cold, and her huge, emerald eyes were wide open. The Witcher noticed that her little face, now that the dirt and the grimace of a spiteful little devil had vanished from it, was quite pretty.

Eithné was combing the little girl's long hair, slowly and tenderly.

'Enter, Gwynbleidd. Be seated.'

He sat down, after first ceremonially going down on one knee.

'Are you rested?' the dryad asked, not looking at him, and continuing to comb. 'When can you embark on your return journey? What would you say to tomorrow morn?'

'When you give the order,' he said coldly. 'O Lady of Brokilon. One word from you will suffice for me to stop vexing you with my presence in Duén Canell.'

'Geralt,' Eithné slowly turned her head. 'Do not misunderstand me. I know and respect you. I know you have never harmed a dryad, rusalka, sylph or nymph; quite the opposite, you have been known to act in their defence, to save their lives. But that changes nothing. Too much divides us. We belong to different worlds. I neither want nor am able to make exceptions. For anybody. I shall not ask if you understand, for I know it is thus. I ask whether you accept it.'

287

'What does it change?'

'Nothing. But I want to know.'

'I do,' he confirmed. 'But what about her? What about Ciri? She also belongs to another world.'

Ciri glanced at him timidly and then upwards at the dryad. Eithné smiled.

'But not for long,' she said.

'Eithné, please. First think it over.'

'What for?'

'Give her to me. Let her return with me. To the world she belongs to.'

'No, White Wolf,' the dryad plunged the comb into the little girl's mousy hair again. 'I shall not. You of all people ought to understand.'

'Me?'

'Yes, you. Certain tidings from the world even reach Brokilon. Tidings about a certain witcher, who for services rendered occasionally demanded curious vows. "You will give me what you do not expect to find at home." "You will give me what you already have, but about which you do not know." Does that sound familiar? After all, for some time you witchers have been trying in this way to direct fate, you have been seeking boys designated by fate to be your successors, wishing to protect yourself from extinction and oblivion. From nihilism. Why, then, are you surprised at me? I care for the fate of the dryads. Surely that is just? A young human girl for each dryad killed by humans.'

'By keeping her here, you will arouse hostility and the desire for vengeance, Eithné. You will arouse a consuming hatred.'

'Human hatred is nothing new to me. No, Geralt. I shall not give her up. Particularly since she is hale. That has been uncommon recently.'

'Uncommon?'

The dryad fixed her huge, silver eyes on him.

'They abandon sick little girls with me. Diphtheria, scarlet fever, croup, recently even smallpox. They think we are not immune, that the epidemic will annihilate or at least decimate us. We disappoint them, Geralt. We have something more than immunity. Brokilon cares for its children.'

She fell silent, leaning over, carefully combing out a lock of Ciri's tangled hair, using her other hand to help.

'May I,' the Witcher cleared his throat, 'turn to the petition, with which King Venzlav has sent me?'

'Is it not a waste of time?' Eithné lifted her head. 'Why bother? I know perfectly well what King Venzlav wants. For that, I do not need prophetic gifts at all. He wants me to give him Brokilon, probably as far as the River Vda, which, I gather, he considers – or would like to consider – the natural border between Brugge and Verden. In exchange, I presume, he is offering me a small and untamed corner of the forest. And probably gives his kingly word and offers kingly protection that that small, untamed corner, that scrap of forest, will belong to me forever and ever and that no one will dare to disturb the dryads there. That the dryads there will be able to live in peace. So what, Geralt? Venzlav would like to put an end to the war over Brokilon, which has lasted two centuries. And in order to end it, the dryads would have to give up what they have been dying in the defence of for two hundred years? Simply hand it over? Give up Brokilon?'

Geralt was silent. He had nothing to add. The dryad smiled.

'Did the royal proposal run thus, Gwynbleidd? Or perhaps it was more blunt, saying: "Don't put on airs, you sylvan monster, beast of the wilderness, relict of the past, but listen to what I, King Venzlav, want. I want cedar, oak and hickory, mahogany and golden birch, yew for bows and pine for masts, because Brokilon is close at hand, and otherwise I have to bring wood from beyond the mountains. I want the iron and copper that are beneath the earth. I want the gold that lies on Craag An. I want to fell and saw, and dig in the earth, without having to listen to the whistling of arrows. And most importantly; I want at last to be a king, one to whom everything bows down in his kingdom. I do not wish for some Brokilon in our kingdom, for a forest I cannot enter. Such a forest affronts me, rouses me to wrath and affords me sleepless nights, for I am a man, we rule over the world. We may, if we wish, tolerate a few elves, dryads or

289

rusalkas in this world. If they are not too insolent. Submit to my will, O Witch of Brokilon. Or perish."'

'Eithné, you admitted yourself that Venzlav is not a fool or a fanatic. You know, I am certain, that he is a just and peace-loving king. The blood shed here pains and troubles him . . .'

'If he stays away from Brokilon not a single drop of blood shall be shed.'

'You well know . . .' Geralt raised his head.' You well know it is not thus. People have been killed in Burnt Stump, in Eight-Mile, in the Owl Hills. People have been killed in Brugge and on the left bank of the Ribbon. Beyond Brokilon.'

'The places you have mentioned,' the dryad responded calmly, 'are Brokilon. I do not recognise human maps or borders.'

'But the forest was cleared there a hundred summers ago!'

'What is a hundred summers to Brokilon? Or a hundred winters?'

Geralt fell silent.

The dryad put down the comb and stroked Ciri's mousy hair.

'Agree to Venzlav's proposal, Eithné.'

The dryad looked at him coldly.

'How shall we profit by that? We, the children of Brokilon?'

'With the chance of survival. No, Eithné, do not interrupt. I know what you would say. I understand your pride in Brokilon's sovereignty. Nonetheless, the world is changing. Something is ending. Whether you like it or not, man's dominion over this world is a fact. Only those who assimilate with humans will survive. The rest will perish. Eithné, there are forests where dryads, rusalkas and elves live peacefully, having come to agreement with humans. We are so close to each other, after all. Men can be the fathers of your children. What will you gain through this war you are waging? The potential fathers of your children are perishing from your arrows. And what is the result? How many of Brokilon's dryads are pure-blood? How many of them are abducted human girls you have modified? You even have to make use of Frexinet, because you have no choice. I seem to see few tiny dryads, Eithné. I see only her; a little human girl, terrified, dulled by narcotics, paralysed by fear—'

'I'm not afraid at all!' Ciri suddenly cried, assuming her little devil

290

face for a moment. 'And I'm not parrotised! So you'd better watch your step! Nothing can happen to me here. Be sure! I'm not afraid. My grandmamma says that dryads aren't evil, and my grandmamma is the wisest woman in the world! My grandmamma . . . My grandmamma says there should be more forests like this one . . .'

She fell silent and lowered her head. Eithné laughed.

'A Child of the Elder Blood,' she said. 'Yes, Geralt. There are still being born Children of the Elder Blood, of whom the prophesies speak. And you tell me that something is ending . . . You worry whether we shall survive—'

'The scamp was supposed to marry Kistrin of Verden,' Geralt interrupted. 'It's a pity it will not be. Kistrin will one day succeed Ervyll, and were he influenced by a wife with such views, perhaps he would cease raids on Brokilon?'

'I don't want that Kistrin!' the little girl screamed shrilly, and something flashed in her green eyes. 'Kistrin can go and find some gorgeous, stupid material! I'm not material! I won't be a princess!'

'Soft, Child of the Elder Blood,' the dryad said, hugging Ciri. 'Don't shout. Of course you will not be a princess—'

'Of course,' the Witcher interjected caustically. 'You, Eithné, and I well know what she will be. I see it has already been decided. So it goes. What answer should I take to King Venzlav, O Lady of Brokilon?'

'None.'

'What do you mean, "none"?'

'None. He will understand. Long ago, long, long ago, before Venzlav was in the world, heralds rode up to Brokilon's borders. Horns and trumpets blared, armour glinted, and pennants and standards fluttered. "Humble yourself, Brokilon!" they cried. "King Goat Tooth, king of Bald Hillock and Marshy Meadow, orders you to humble yourself, Brokilon!" And Brokilon's answer was always the same. As you are leaving my Forest, Gwynbleidd, turn around and listen. In the rustle of the leaves you will hear Brokilon's answer. Pass it on to Venzlav and add that he will never hear another while the oaks still stand in Duén Canell. Not while a single tree still grows or a single dryad still lives here.'

Geralt was silent.

'You say something is ending,' Eithné slowly went on. 'Not true. There are things that never end. You talk of survival? I am fighting to survive. Brokilon endures thanks to my fight, for trees live longer than men, as long as they are protected from your axes. You talk to me of kings and princes. Who are they? Those whom I know are white skeletons lying in the necropolises of Craag An, deep in the forest. In marble tombs, on piles of yellow metal and shining gems. But Brokilon endures, the trees sough above the ruins of palaces, their roots break up the marble. Does your Venzlav recall those kings? Do you, Gwynbleidd? And if not, how can you claim that something is ending? How do you know whose destiny is destruction and whose eternity? What entitles you to speak of destiny? Do you actually know what it is?'

'No,' the Witcher agreed, 'I do not. But—'

'If you know not,' she interrupted, 'there is no place for any "but". You know not. You simply know not.'

She was silent, touched her forehead with her hand and turned her face away.

'When you came here the first time, years ago,' she said, 'you did not know either. And Morénn . . . My daughter . . . Geralt, Morénn is dead. She fell by the Ribbon, defending Brokilon. I did not recognise her when they brought her to me. Her face had been crushed by the hooves of your horses. Destiny? And today, you, Witcher, who could not give Morénn a child, bring her – the Child of the Elder Blood – to me. A little girl who knows what destiny is. No, it is not knowledge which would suit you, knowledge which you could accept. She simply believes. Say it again, Ciri, repeat what you told me before the Witcher, Geralt of Rivia, White Wolf, entered. That witcher who does not know. Say it again, Child of the Elder Blood.'

'Your Maj . . . Venerable lady,' Ciri said in a voice that cracked. 'Do not keep me here. I cannot . . . I want to go . . . home. I want to return home with Geralt. I must go . . . With him . . .'

'Why with him?'

'For he . . . is my fate.'

Eithné turned away. She was very pale.

292

'What do you say to that, Geralt?'

He did not reply. Eithné clapped her hands. Braenn entered the oak tree, emerging like a ghost from the night outside, holding a large, silver goblet in both hands. The medallion around the Witcher's neck began vibrating rapidly and rhythmically.

'What do you say to that?' repeated the silver-haired dryad, standing up. 'She does not want to remain in Brokilon! She does not wish to be a dryad! She does not want to replace Morénn, she wants to leave, walk away from her fate! Is that right, Child of the Elder Blood? Is that what you actually want?'

Ciri nodded her bowed head. Her shoulders were trembling. The Witcher had had enough.

'Why are you bullying the child, Eithné? We both know you will soon give her the Water of Brokilon and what she wants will cease to mean anything. Why are you doing this? Why are you doing it in my presence?'

'I want to show you what destiny is. I want to prove to you that nothing is ending. That everything is only beginning.'

'No, Eithné,' he said, standing up. 'I'm sorry if I'm spoiling this display for you, but I have no intention of watching it. You have gone too far, Lady of Brokilon, desirous to stress the chasm dividing us. You, the Elder Folk, like to say that hatred is alien to you, that it is a feeling known only to humans. But it is not true. You know what hatred is and are capable of hating, you merely evince it a little differently, more wisely and less savagely. But because of that it may be more cruel. I accept your hatred, Eithné, on behalf of all humankind. I deserve it. I am sorry about Morénn.'

The dryad did not respond.

'And that is precisely Brokilon's answer, which I am to communicate to Venzlav of Brugge, isn't it? A warning and a challenge? Clear proof of the hatred and Power slumbering among these trees, by whose will a human child will soon drink poison which will destroy its memory, taking it from the arms of another human child whose psyche and memory have already been annihilated? And that answer is to be carried to Venzlav by a witcher who knows and feels affection for both children? The witcher who is guilty of your daughter's

293

death? Very well, Eithné, let it be in accordance with your will. Venzlav will hear your answer, will hear my voice, will see my eyes and read everything in them. But I do not have to look on what is to occur here. And I do not want to.'

Eithné still said nothing.

'Farewell, Ciri,' Geralt knelt down and hugged the little girl. Ciri's shoulders were trembling powerfully.

'Don't cry. Nothing evil can happen to you here.'

Ciri sniffed. The Witcher stood up.

'Farewell, Braenn,' he said to the younger dryad. 'Good health and take care. Survive, Braenn; live as long as your tree. Like Brokilon. And one more thing . . .'

'Yes, Gwynbleidd?' Braenn lifted her head and something wet glistened in her eyes.

'It is easy to kill with a bow, girl. How easy it is to release the bow-string and think, it is not I, not I, it is the arrow. The blood of that boy is not on my hands. The arrow killed him, not I. But the arrow does not dream anything in the night. May you dream nothing in the night either, blue-eyed dryad. Farewell, Braenn.'

'Mona . . .' Braenn said indistinctly. The goblet she was holding shuddered and the transparent liquid filling it rippled.

'What?'

'Mona!' she wailed. 'I am Mona! Lady Eithné! I—'

'Enough of this,' Eithné said sharply. 'Enough. Control yourself, Braenn.'

Geralt laughed drily.

'There you have your destiny, Lady of the Forest. I respect your doggedness and your fight. But I know that soon you will be fighting alone. The last dryad of Brokilon sending dryads – who nonetheless still remember their real names – to their deaths. In spite of everything I wish you fortune, Eithné. Farewell.'

'Geralt . . .' Ciri whispered, still sitting motionless, with her head lowered. 'Don't leave me . . . all by myself . . .'

'White Wolf,' Eithné said, embracing the little girl's hunched back. 'Did you have to wait until she asked you? Not to abandon her? To remain with her until the end? Why do you wish to abandon

294

her at this moment? To leave her all alone? Where do you wish to flee to, Gwynbleidd? And from what?'

Ciri's head slumped further down. But she did not cry.

'Until the end,' the Witcher said, nodding. 'Very well, Ciri. You will not be alone. I will be with you. Do not fear anything.'

Eithné took the goblet from Braenn's trembling hands and raised it up.

'Can you read Old Runes, White Wolf?'

'Yes, I can.'

'Read what is engraved on the goblet. It is from Craag An. It was drunk from by kings whom no one now remembers.'

'Duettaeánn aef cirrán Cáerme Gláeddyv. Yn á esseáth.'

'Do you know what that means?'

'The Sword of Destiny has two blades ... You are one of them.'

'Stand up, Child of the Elder Blood.' The dryad's voice clanged like steel in an order which could not be defied, a will which had to be yielded to. 'Drink. It is the Water of Brokilon.'

Geralt bit his lips and stared at Eithné's silver eyes. He did not look at Ciri, who was slowly bringing her lips to the edge of the goblet. He had seen it before, once, long ago. The convulsions, the tremors; the incredible, horrifying, slowly dwindling cry. And the emptiness, torpor and apathy in the slowly opening eyes. He had seen it before.

Ciri drank. A tear rolled slowly down Braenn's unmoving face.

'That will do,' Eithné took the goblet away, placed it on the ground, and stroked the little girl's hair, which fell onto her shoulders in mousy waves.

'O Child of the Elder Blood,' she said. 'Choose. Do you wish to remain in Brokilon, or do you follow your destiny?'

The Witcher shook his head in disbelief. Ciri was flushed and breathing a little more quickly. And nothing else. Nothing.

'I wish to follow my destiny,' she said brightly, looking the dryad in the eyes.

'Then let it be,' Eithné said, coldly and tersely. Braenn sighed aloud.

'I wish to be alone,' Eithné said, turning her back on them. 'Please leave.'

Braenn took hold of Ciri and touched Geralt's arm, but the Witcher pushed her arm away.

'Thank you, Eithné,' he said. The dryad slowly turned to face him.

'What are you thanking me for?'

'For destiny,' he smiled. 'For your decision. For that was not the Water of Brokilon, was it? It was Ciri's destiny to return home. But you, Eithné, played the role of destiny. And for that I thank you.'

'How little you know of destiny,' the dryad said bitterly. 'How little you know, Witcher. How little you see. How little you understand. You thank me? You thank me for the role I have played? For a vulgar spectacle? For a trick, a deception, a hoax? For the sword of destiny being made, as you judge, of wood dipped in gold paint? Then go further; do not thank, but expose me. Have it your own way. Prove that the arguments are in your favour. Fling your truth in my face, show me the triumph of sober, human truth, thanks to which, in your opinion, you gain mastery of the world. This is the Water of Brokilon. A little still remains. Dare you? O conqueror of the world?'

Geralt, although annoyed by her words, hesitated, but only for a moment. The Water of Brokilon, even if it were authentic, would have no effect on him. He was completely immune to the toxic, hallucinogenic tannins. But there was no way it could have been the Water of Brokilon; Ciri had drunk it and nothing had happened. He reached for the goblet with both hands and looked into the dryad's silver eyes.

The ground rushed from under his feet all at once and hurled him on his back. The powerful oak tree whirled around and shook. He fumbled all around himself with his numb arms and opened his eyes with difficulty; it was as though he were throwing off a marble tombstone. He saw above him Braenn's tiny face, and beyond her Eithné's eyes, shining like quicksilver. And other eyes; as green as emeralds. No; brighter. Like spring grass. The medallion around his neck was quivering, vibrating.

'Gwynbleidd,' he heard. 'Watch carefully. No, closing your eyes will not help you at all. Look, look at your destiny.'

'Do you remember?'

A sudden explosion of light rending a curtain of smoke, huge candelabras heavy with candles, dripping garlands of wax. Stone walls, a steep staircase. Descending the staircase, a green-eyed, mousy-haired girl in a small circlet with an intricately carved gemstone, in a silver-blue gown with a train held up by a page in a short, scarlet jacket.

'Do you remember?'

His own voice speaking . . . speaking . . .

I shall return in six years . . .

A bower, warmth, the scent of flowers, the intense, monotonous hum of bees. He, alone, on his knees, giving a rose to a woman with mousy locks spilling from beneath a narrow, gold band. Rings set with emeralds – large, green cabochons – on the fingers taking the rose from his hand.

'Return here,' the woman said. 'Return here, should you change your mind. Your destiny will be waiting.'

I shall never return here, he thought. I never . . . went back there. I never returned to . . .

Whither?

Mousy hair. Green eyes.

His voice again in the darkness, in a gloom in which everything was engulfed. There are only fires, fires all the way to the horizon. A cloud of sparks in the purple smoke. Beltane! May Day Eve! Dark, violet eyes, shining in a pale, triangular face veiled by a black, rippling shock of curls, look out from the clouds of smoke.

Yennefer!

'Too little,' the apparition's thin lips suddenly twist, a tear rolls down the pale cheek, quickly, quicker and quicker, like a drop of wax down a candle.

'Too little. Something more is needed.'

'Yennefer!'

'Nothingness for nothingness,' the apparition says in Eithné's voice.

'The nothingness and void in you, conqueror of the world, who is unable even to win the woman he loves. Who walks away and flees, when his destiny is within reach. The sword of destiny has two blades. You are one of them. But what is the other, White Wolf?'

'There is no destiny,' his own voice. 'There is none. None. It does not exist. The only thing that everyone is destined for is death.'

'That is the truth,' says the woman with the mousy hair and the mysterious smile. 'That is the truth, Geralt.'

The woman is wearing a silvery suit of armour, bloody, dented and punctured by the points of pikes or halberds. Blood drips in a thin stream from the corner of her mysteriously and hideously smiling mouth.

'You sneer at destiny,' she says, still smiling. 'You sneer at it, trifle with it. The sword of destiny has two blades. You are one of them. Is the second . . . death? But it is we who die, die because of you. Death cannot catch up with you, so it must settle for us. Death dogs your footsteps, White Wolf. But others die. Because of you. Do you remember me?'

'Ca . . . Calanthe!'

'You can save him,' the voice of Eithné, from behind the curtain of smoke. 'You can save him, Child of the Elder Blood. Before he plunges into the nothingness which he has come to love. Into the black forest which has no end.'

Eyes, as green as spring grass. A touch. Voices, crying in chorus, incomprehensibly. Faces.

He could no longer see anything. He was plummeting into the chasm, into the void, into darkness. The last thing he heard was Eithné's voice.

'Let it be so.'

VII

'Geralt! Wake up! Please wake up!'

He opened his eyes and saw the sun, a golden ducat with distinct edges, high up above the treetops, beyond the turbid veil of the morning mist. He was lying on damp, spongy moss and a hard root was digging into his back.

Ciri was kneeling beside him, tugging at his jacket.

'Curses . . .' He cleared his throat and looked around. 'Where am I? How did I end up here?'

'I don't know,' she answered. 'I woke up a moment ago, here, beside you, awffy frozen. I can't remember how . . . Do you know what? It's magic!'

'You're probably right,' he said, sitting up and pulling pine needles from his collar. 'You're probably right, Ciri. Bloody Water of Brokilon . . . Looks like the dryads were enjoying themselves at our expense.'

He stood up, picked up his sword, which was lying alongside him and slung the strap across his back.

'Ciri?'

'Uh-huh?'

'You were also enjoying yourself at my expense.'

'Me?'

'You're the daughter of Pavetta and the granddaughter of Calanthe of Cintra. You knew who I was from the very beginning, didn't you?'

'No,' she blushed. 'Not from the beginning. You lifted the curse from my daddy, didn't you?'

'That's not true,' he said, shaking his head. 'Your mama did. And your grandmamma. I only helped.'

'But my nanny said . . . She said that I'm destined. Because I'm a Surprise. A Child of Surprise. Geralt?'

'Ciri,' he looked at her, shaking his head and smiling. 'Believe me, you're the greatest surprise I could have come across.'

'Ha!' The little girl's face brightened up. 'It's true! I'm destined. My nanny said a witcher would come who would have white hair and would take me away. But grandmamma yelled . . . Oh, never mind! Tell me where you're taking me.'

'Back home. To Cintra.'

'Ah . . . But I thought you . . . ?'

'You'll have time to think on the way. Let's go, Ciri, we must leave Brokilon. It isn't a safe place.'

'I'm not afraid!'

'But I am.'

'Grandmamma said that witchers aren't afraid of anything.'

'Grandmamma overstated the facts. Let's go, Ciri. If I only knew where we . . .'

He looked up at the sun.

'Right, let's risk it . . . We'll go this way.'

'No.' Ciri wrinkled her nose and pointed in the opposite direction. 'That way. Over there.'

'And how do you know, may I ask?'

'I just know,' she shrugged and gave him a helpless, surprised, emerald look. 'Somehow . . . Somewhere, over there . . . I don't know . . .'

Pavetta's daughter, he thought. A Child . . . A Child of the Elder Blood? She might have inherited something from her mother.

'Ciri.' He tugged open his shirt and drew out his medallion. 'Touch this.'

'Oh,' she said, opening her mouth. 'What a dreadful wolf. What fangs he has . . .'

'Touch it.'

'Oh, my!'

The Witcher smiled. He had also felt the sudden vibration of the medallion, the sharp wave running through the silver chain.

'It moved!' Ciri sighed. 'It moved!'

'I know. Let's go, Ciri. You lead.'

'It's magic, isn't it!'

'Naturally.'

It was as he had expected. The little girl could sense the direction. How, he did not know. But soon – sooner than he had expected – they came out onto a track, onto a forked, three-way junction. It was the border of Brokilon – according to humans, at least. Eithné did not recognise it, he remembered.

Ciri bit her lip, wrinkled her nose and hesitated, looking at the junction, at the sandy, rutted track, furrowed by hooves and cart-wheels. But Geralt now knew where he was and did not want to depend on her uncertain abilities. He set off along the road heading eastwards, towards Brugge. Ciri, still frowning, was looking back towards the west.

'That leads to Nastrog Castle,' he jibed. 'Are you missing Kistrin?'

The little girl grunted and followed him obediently, but looked back several times.

'What is it, Ciri?'

'I don't know,' she whispered. 'But we're going the wrong way, Geralt.'

'Why? We're going to Brugge, to King Venzlav, who lives in a splendid castle. We shall take baths and sleep on a feather bed . . .'

'It's a bad road,' she said. 'A bad road.'

'That's true, I've seen better. Don't be sniffy, Ciri. Let's go. With a will.'

They went around an overgrown bend. And it turned out Ciri had been right.

They were suddenly, quickly, surrounded, from all sides. Men in conical helmets, chainmail and dark-blue tunics with the gold and black chequered pattern of Verden on their chests. They encircled the pair, but none of the men approached or reached for a weapon.

'Whence and whither?' barked a thickset individual in worn-out, green apparel, standing before Geralt with bandy legs set wide apart. His face was as swarthy and wrinkled as a prune. A bow and white-fletched arrows protruded behind him, high above his head.

'We've come from Burnt Stump,' the Witcher lied effortlessly, squeezing Ciri's little hand knowingly. 'And we're going home to Brugge. What's happening?'

'Royal service,' the dark-faced individual said courteously, as though he had only then noticed the sword on Geralt's back. 'We . . .'

'Bring 'im 'ere, Junghans!' yelled someone standing further down the road. The mercenaries parted.

'Don't look, Ciri,' Geralt said quickly. 'Avert your eyes. Don't look.'

A fallen tree lay on the road, blocking the way with a tangle of boughs. Long white splinters radiated from the partly-hacked and broken trunk standing in the roadside thicket. A loaded wagon covered with a tarpaulin stood before the tree. Two small, shaggy horses, stuck with arrows and exposing yellow teeth, were lying on the ground caught up in in the shafts and halters. One was still alive and was snorting heavily and kicking.

There were also people lying in dark patches of blood soaked into the sand, hanging over the side of the wagon and hunched over the wheels.

Two men slowly emerged from among the armed men gathered around the wagon, to be joined by a third. The others – there were around ten of them – stood motionless, holding their horses.

'What happened?' the Witcher asked, standing so as to block out Ciri's view of the massacre.

A beady-eyed man in a short coat of mail and high boots gave him a searching look and audibly rubbed his bristly chin. He had a worn, shiny leather bracer of the kind archers use on his left forearm.

'Ambush,' he said curtly. 'Eerie wives did for these merchants. We're looking into it.'

'Eerie wives? Ambushing merchants?'

'You can see for yourself,' the beady-eyed man pointed. 'Stuck with arrows like urchins. On the highway! They're becoming more and more impudent, those forest hags. You can't just not venture into the forest now, you can't even travel the road by the forest.'

'And you,' the Witcher asked, squinting. 'Who are you?'

'Ervyll's men. From the Nastrog squads. We were serving under Baron Frexinet. But the baron was lost in Brokilon.'

Ciri opened her mouth, but Geralt squeezed her hand hard, ordering her to stay quiet.

'Blood for blood, I say!' roared the beady-eyed man's companion, a giant in a brass-studded kaftan. 'Blood for blood! You can't let that go. First Frexinet and the kidnapped princess from Cintra, and now merchants. By the Gods, vengeance, vengeance, I say! For if not, you'll see, tomorrow or the next day they'll start killing people on their own thresholds!'

'Brick's right,' the beady-eyed one said. 'Isn't he? And you, fellow, where are you from?'

'From Brugge,' the Witcher lied.

'And the girl? Your daughter?'

'Aye,' Geralt squeezed Ciri's hand again.

'From Brugge,' Brick frowned. 'So I'll tell you, fellow, that your king, Venzlav, is emboldening the monstrosities right now. He doesn't want to join forces with Ervyll, nor with Viraxas of Kerack. But if we marched on Brokilon from three sides, we'd finally destroy that scum . . .'

'How did the slaughter happen?' Geralt asked slowly. 'Does anybody know? Did any of the merchants survive?'

'There aren't any witnesses,' the beady-eyed one said. 'But we know what happened. Junghans, a forester, can read spoors like a book. Tell him, Junghans.'

'Well,' said the one with the wrinkled face, 'it were like this: the merchants were travelling along the highway. And their way were blocked. You see, sir, that fallen pine lying across the road, freshly felled. There are tracks in the thicket, want to see? Well, when the merchants stopped to clear away the tree, they were shot, just like that. Over there, from the bushes by that crooked birch. There are tracks there too. And the arrows, mark you, all dryad work, fletchings stuck on with resin, shafts bound with bast . . .'

'I see,' the Witcher interrupted, looking at the bodies. 'Some of them, I think, survived the arrows and had their throats cut. With knives.'

One more man emerged from behind the group of mercenaries standing in front of him. He was skinny and short, in an elk-hide kaftan. He had black, short hair, and his cheeks were blue from closely-shaved, black beard growth. One glance at the small, narrow hands in short, black, fingerless gloves, at the pale, fish-like eyes, at his sword and at the hafts of the daggers stuck into his belt and down his left boot was all the Witcher needed. Geralt had seen too many murderers not to recognise one more instantly.

'You've a keen eye,' said the black-haired man, extremely slowly. 'Indeed, you see much.'

'And well he does,' said the beady-eyed man. 'Let him tell his king what he saw. Venzlav still swears eerie wives shouldn't be killed, because they are agreeable and good. I'll bet he visits them on May Day and ruts them. Perhaps they're good for that. We'll find out for ourselves if we take one alive.'

'Or even half-dead,' Brick cackled. 'Hi, where's that bloody druid? Almost noon, but no sign of him. We must off.'

'What do you mean to do?' Geralt asked, without releasing Ciri's hand.

'What business is it of yours?' the black-haired man hissed.

'Oh, why so sharp right away, Levecque?' the beady-eyed one asked, smiling foully. 'We're honest men, we have no secrets. Ervyll is sending us a druid, a great magician, who can even talk with trees. Him'll guide us into the forest to avenge Frexinet and try and rescue the princess. We aren't out for a picnic, fellow, but on a punitive ex— ex—'

'Expedition,' the black-haired man, Levecque, prompted.

'Aye. Took the words out of me mouth. So then go on your way, fellow, for it may get hot here anon.'

'Aaaye,' Levecque drawled, looking at Ciri. ''Twill be dangerous here, particularly with a young 'un. Eerie wives are just desperate for girls like that. Hey, little maid? Is your mama at home waiting?'

Ciri, trembling, nodded.

''Twould be disastrous,' the black-haired one continued, not taking his eye off her, 'were you not to make it home. She would surely race to King Venzlav and say: "You were lax with the dryads, king, and now you have my daughter and husband on your conscience." Who knows, perhaps Venzlav would weigh up an alliance with Ervyll once more?'

'Leave them, Mr Levecque,' Junghans snarled, and his wrinkled face wrinkled up even more. 'Let them go.'

'Farewell, little maid,' Levecque said and held out his hand to stroke Ciri on the head. Ciri shuddered and withdrew.

'What is it? Are you afraid?'

'You have blood on your hand,' the Witcher said softly.

'Ah,' Levecque said, raising his hand. 'Indeed. It's their blood. The merchants. I checked to see if any of them had survived. But alas, the eerie wives shoot accurately.'

'Eerie wives?' said Ciri in a trembling voice, not reacting to the Witcher's squeeze of her hand. 'Oh, noble knights, you are mistaken. It could not be dryads!'

'What are you squeaking about, little maid?' The pale eyes of the black-haired man narrowed. Geralt glanced to the right and left, estimating the distances.

'It wasn't dryads, sir knight,' Ciri repeated. 'It's obvious!'

'Ay?'

'I mean, that tree . . . That tree was chopped down! With an axe! But no dryad would ever chop a tree down, would they?'

'Indeed,' Levecque said and glanced at the beady-eyed man. 'Oh, what a clever little girl, you are. Too clever.'

The Witcher had already seen his thin, gloved hands creeping like a black spider towards the haft of his dagger. Although Levecque had not taken his eyes off Ciri, Geralt knew the blow would be aimed at him. He waited for the moment when Levecque touched his weapon, while the beady-eyed man held his breath.

Three movements. Just three. His silver-studded forearm slammed into the side of the black-haired man's head. Before he fell, the Witcher was standing between Junghans and the beady-eyed man, and his sword, hissing out of the scabbard, whined in the air, slashing open the temple of Brick, the giant in the brass-studded kaftan.

'Run, Ciri!'

305

The beady-eyed man, who was drawing his sword, leaped, but was not fast enough. The Witcher slashed him across his chest, diagonally, downwards, and immediately, taking advantage of the blow's momentum, upwards, from a kneeling position, cutting the mercenary open in a bloody 'X'.

'Men!' Junghans yelled at the rest, who were frozen in astonishment. 'Over here!'

Ciri leaped into a crooked beech tree and scampered like a squirrel up the branches, disappearing among the foliage. The forester sent an arrow after her but missed. The remaining men ran over, breaking up into a semi-circle, pulling out bows and arrows from quivers. Geralt, still kneeling, put his fingers together and struck with the Aard Sign, not at the bowmen, for they were too far away, but at the sandy road in front of them, spraying them in a cloud of sand.

Junghans, leaping aside, nimbly drew another arrow from his quiver.

'No!' Levecque yelled, springing up from the ground with his sword in his right hand and a dagger in his left. 'Leave him, Junghans!'

The Witcher spun around smoothly, turning to face him.

'He's mine,' Levecque said, shaking his head and wiping his cheek and mouth with his forearm. 'Leave him to me!'

Geralt, crouching, started to circle, but Levecque did not, instead attacking at once, leaping forward in two strides.

He's good, the Witcher thought, working hard to connect with the killer's blade with a short moulinet, avoiding the dagger's jab with a half-turn. He intentionally did not reply, but leaped back, counting on Levecque trying to reach him with a long, extended thrust and losing his balance. But the killer was no novice. He dropped into a crouch and also moved around in a semi-circle with soft, feline steps. He unexpectedly bounded forward, swung his sword and whirled, shortening the distance. The Witcher did not meet him halfway, but restricted himself to a swift, high feint which forced the killer to dodge. Levecque stooped over, offered a quarte, hiding the hand with the dagger behind his back. The Witcher did not attack this time either, did not move in, but described a semi-circle again, skirting around him.

'Aha,' Levecque drawled, straightening up. 'Shall we prolong the game? Why not? You can never have too much amusement!'

He leaped, spun, struck, once, twice, thrice, in a rapid rhythm; a cut from above with his sword and immediately from the left with a flat, scything blow of his dagger. The Witcher did not disturb the rhythm; parried, leaped back and once again circled, forcing the killer to move around. Levecque suddenly drew back, circling in the opposite direction.

'Every game,' he hissed through clenched teeth, 'must have its end. What would you say to a single blow, trickster? A single blow and then we'll shoot your little brat down from the tree. How about that?'

Geralt saw that Levecque was watching his shadow, waiting for it to reach his opponent, indicating that he had the sun in his eyes. Geralt stopped circling to make the killer's job easier.

And narrowed his pupils into vertical slits, two narrow lines.

In order to maintain the illusion, he screwed his eyes up a little, pretending to be blinded.

Levecque leaped, spun, keeping his balance by extending his dagger hand out sideways, and struck with a simply impossible bend of his wrist, upwards, aiming at the Witcher's crotch. Geralt shot forward, spun, deflected the blow, bending his arm and wrist equally impossibly, throwing the killer backwards with the momentum of the parry and slashing him across his left cheek with the tip of his blade. Levecque staggered, grabbing his face. The Witcher twisted into a half-turn, shifted his bodyweight onto his left leg and cleaved open his opponent's carotid artery with a short blow. Levecque curled up, bleeding profusely, dropped to his knees, bent over and fell headfirst onto the sand.

Geralt slowly turned towards Junghans. Junghans, contorting his wrinkled face in a furious grimace, took aim with his bow. The Witcher crouched, gripping his sword in both hands. The remaining mercenaries also raised their bows, in dead silence.

307

'What are you waiting for?' the forester roared. 'Shoot! Shoot hi—' He stumbled, staggered, tottered forwards and fell on his face with an arrow sticking out of his back. The arrow's shaft had striped fletchings made from a pheasant's flight feathers, dyed yellow in a concoction of tree bark.

The arrows flew with a whistle and hiss in long, flat parabolas from the black wall of the forest. They flew apparently slowly and calmly, their fletchings sighing, and it seemed as though they picked up speed and force as they struck their targets. And they struck unerringly, scything down the Nastrog mercenaries, knocking them over into the sand, inert and mown down, like sunflowers hit with a stick.

The ones who survived rushed towards the horses, jostling one another. The arrows continued to whistle, catching up with them as they ran, hitting them as they sat in the saddle. Only three managed to rouse their horses to a gallop and ride off, yelling, their spurs bloodying their mounts' flanks. But not even they got far.

The forest closed up, blocking the way. Suddenly the sandy highway, bathed in sunlight, disappeared. It was now a dense, impenetrable wall of black tree trunks.

The mercenaries, terrified and stupefied, spurred their horses, but the arrows flew unceasingly. And hit them, knocking them from their saddles among the hoof-falls and neighing of the horses, and screams.

And afterwards a silence fell.

The wall of trees blocking the highway shimmered, became blurred, shone brightly and vanished. The road could be seen again and on it stood a grey horse and on the grey horse sat a rider – mighty, with a flaxen, fan-shaped beard, in a jerkin of sealskin with a tartan, woollen sash.

The grey horse, turning its head away and champing at the bit, moved forward, lifting its fore hooves high, snorting and becoming agitated by the corpses and the smell of blood. The rider, upright in the saddle, raised a hand and a sudden gust of wind struck the trees' branches.

From the undergrowth on the distant edge of the forest emerged small shapes in tight-fitting garments patched green and brown, with faces streaked with walnut-shell dye.

'Ceádmil, Wedd Brokiloéne!' the rider called. 'Fáill, Aná Woedwedd!'

'Fáill!' replied a voice from the forest like a gust of wind.

The green and brown shapes began to disappear, one after the other, melting into the thicket of the forest. Only one remained, with flowing hair the colour of honey. She took several steps and approached.

'Vá fáill, Gwynbleidd!' she called, coming even closer.

'Farewell, Mona,' the Witcher said. 'I will not forget you.'

'Forget me,' she responded firmly, adjusting her quiver on her back. 'There is no Mona. Mona was a dream. I am Braenn. Braenn of Brokilon!'

She waved at him once more. And disappeared.

The Witcher turned around.

'Mousesack,' he said, looking at the rider on the grey horse.

'Geralt,' the rider nodded, eyeing him up and down coldly. 'An interesting encounter. But let us begin with the most important things. Where is Ciri?'

'Here!' the girl yelled from the foliage. 'Can I come down yet?'

'Yes, you may,' the Witcher said.

'But I don't know how!'

'The same way as you climbed up, just the other way around.'

'I'm afraid! I'm right at the very top!'

'Get down, I said! We need to have a serious conversation, young lady!'

'What about?'

'About why the bloody hell you climbed up there instead of running into the forest? I would have followed you instead of . . . Oh, blow it. Get down!'

'I did what the cat in the story did! Whatever I do it's always wrong! Why, I'd like to know.'

'I would too,' the druid said, dismounting. 'I would also like to know. And your grandmamma, Queen Calanthe, would like to know, too. Come on, climb down, princess.'

Leaves and dry branches fell from the tree. Then there was a sharp crack of tearing material, and finally Ciri appeared, sliding astride the trunk. She had picturesque shreds instead of a hood on her jacket.

'Uncle Mousesack!'

'In person.' The druid embraced and cuddled the little girl.

'Did grandmamma send you? Uncle? Is she very worried?'

'Not very,' Mousesack smiled. 'She is too busy soaking her switch. The way to Cintra, Ciri, will take us some time. Devote it to thinking up an explanation for your deeds. It ought to be, if you want to benefit from my counsel, a very short and matter-of-fact explanation. One which can be given very, very quickly. For in any case I judge you will be screaming at the end of it, princess. Very, very loudly.'

Ciri grimaced painfully, wrinkled up her nose, snorted softly, and her hands involuntarily went towards the endangered place.

'Let's go,' Geralt said, looking around. 'Let's go, Mousesack.'

VIII

'No,' the druid said. 'Calanthe has changed her plans, she does not want the marriage of Ciri and Kistrin to go ahead now. She has her reasons. Additionally, I presume I don't have to explain that following that dreadful scandal with the sham ambush on the merchants, King Ervyll has gone down a long way in my estimation, and my estimation matters in the kingdom. No, we won't even stop off at Nastrog. I'll take the lass straight to Cintra. Ride with us, Geralt.'

'What for?' The Witcher glanced at Ciri, who was now slumbering beneath a tree, wrapped in Mousesack's jerkin.

'You well know what for. That child, Geralt, is linked to you by destiny. For the third time, yes, the third, your paths have crossed. Metaphorically, of course, particularly as regards the previous two occasions. You surely can't call it coincidence?'

'What does it matter what I call it?' The Witcher smiled wryly. 'The essence is not in the name, Mousesack. Why ought I to ride to Cintra? I have already been to Cintra; I have already, as you described it, crossed paths. What of it?'

'Geralt, you demanded a vow from Calanthe, then from Pavetta and her husband. The vow has been kept. Ciri is the Child of Destiny. Destiny demands . . .'

'That I take the child and turn her into a witcher? A little girl? Take a good look at me, Mousesack. Can you imagine me as a comely lass?'

'To hell with witchering,' the druid said, annoyed. 'What are you talking about? What has the one to do with the other? No, Geralt, I see that you understand nothing, I shall have to use simple words. Listen, any fool, including you, may demand a vow, may exact a promise, and will not become remarkable because of it. It is the child who is extraordinary. And the bond which comes into being when

311

the child is born is extraordinary. Need I be more clear? Very well, Geralt. From the moment Ciri was born, what you wanted and what you planned to do ceased to matter, and what you don't want and what you mean to give up doesn't make any difference either. You don't bloody matter! Don't you understand?'

'Don't shout, you'll wake her up. Our destiny is asleep. And when she awakes . . . Mousesack, one must occasionally give up . . . Even the most extraordinary things.'

'But you know,' the druid looked at him coldly, 'you will never have a child of your own.'

'Yes.'

'And you're still giving her up?'

'Yes, I am. I'm surely permitted to, aren't I?'

'You are,' Mousesack said. 'Indeed. But it is risky. There is an old prophecy saying that the sword of destiny . . .'

' . . . has two blades,' Geralt completed the sentence. 'I've heard it.'

'Oh, do as you think fit,' the druid turned his head away and spat. 'Just think, I was prepared to stick my neck out for you . . .'

'You?'

'Me. Unlike you, I believe in destiny. And I knew that it is hazardous to trifle with a two-edged sword. Don't trifle with it, Geralt. Take advantage of the chance which is presenting itself. Turn what connects you to Ciri into the normal, healthy bond of a child with its guardian. For if you do not . . . Then that bond may manifest itself differently. More terribly. In a negative and destructive way. I want to protect you both from that. If you wanted to take her, I would not protest. I would take upon myself the risk of explaining why to Calanthe.'

'How do you know Ciri would want to go with me? Because of some old prophecies?'

'No,' Mousesack said gravely. 'Because she only fell asleep after you cuddled her. Because she mutters your name and searches for your hand in her sleep.'

'Enough,' Geralt got up, 'because I'm liable to get emotional. Farewell, bearded one. My compliments to Calanthe. And think something up . . . For Ciri's sake.'

'You will not escape, Geralt.'

'From destiny?' The Witcher tightened the girth of the captured horse.

'No,' the druid said, looking at the sleeping child. 'From her.'

The Witcher nodded and jumped into the saddle. Mousesack sat motionless, poking a stick into the dying campfire.

He rode slowly away, through heather as high as his stirrups, across the hillside leading into the valley, towards the black forest.

'Geraaalt!'

He turned around. Ciri was standing on the brow of the hill, a tiny, grey figure with windblown, mousy hair.

'Don't go!'

She waved.

'Don't go!'

She yelled shrilly.

'Don't goooo!'

I have to, he thought. I have to, Ciri. Because . . . I always do.

'You won't get away!' she cried. 'Don't go thinking that! You can't run away! I'm your destiny, do you hear?'

There is no destiny, he thought. It does not exist. The only thing that everyone is destined for is death. Death is the other blade of the two-edged sword. I am the first blade. And the second is death, which dogs my footsteps. I cannot, I may not expose you to that, Ciri.

'I am your destiny!'

The words reached his ears from the hilltop, more softly, more despairingly.

He nudged the horse with his heel and rode straight ahead, heading deep into the black, cold and boggy forest, as though into an abyss, into the pleasant, familiar shade, into the gloom which seemed to have no end.

SOMETHING MORE

When hooves suddenly rapped on the timbers of the bridge, Yurga did not even raise his head; he just howled softly, released the wheel rim he was grappling with and crawled under the cart as quickly as he could. Flattened, scraping his back against the rough manure and mud caked onto the underside of the vehicle, he whined and trembled with fear.

The horse moved slowly towards the cart. Yurga saw it place its hooves cautiously on the rotted, moss-covered timbers.

'Get out,' the unseen horseman said. Yurga's teeth chattered and he pulled his head into his shoulders. The horse snorted and stamped.

'Easy, Roach,' the horseman said. Yurga heard him pat his mount on the neck. 'Get out from under there, fellow. I won't do you any harm.'

The merchant did not believe the stranger's declaration in the slightest. There was something calming and at the same time intriguing in his voice, however, though it was by no means a voice which could be described as pleasant. Yurga, mumbling prayers to a dozen deities all at once, timidly stuck his head out from under the cart.

The horseman had hair as white as milk, tied back from his forehead with a leather band, and a black, woollen cloak falling over the rump of the chestnut mare. He did not look at Yurga. Leaning from his saddle, he was examining the cartwheel, sunk up to the hub between the bridge's broken beams. He suddenly raised his head, flicked a gaze over the merchant and observed the undergrowth above the banks of the ravine.

Yurga scrambled out, blinked and rubbed his nose with a hand, smearing wood tar from the wheel hub over his face. The horseman fixed dark, narrowed, piercing eyes, as sharp as a spear tip, on him. Yurga was silent.

'The two of us won't be able to pull it out,' said the stranger finally, pointing at the stuck wheel. 'Were you travelling alone?'

'There were three of us,' Yurga stammered. 'Servants, sir. But they fled, the scoundrels . . .'

'I'm not surprised,' said the horseman, looking under the bridge towards the bottom of the ravine. 'I'm not surprised at all. I think you ought to do the same. Time is short.'

Yurga did not follow the stranger's gaze. He did not want to look at the mass of skulls, ribs and shinbones scattered among the rocks, peeping out from the burdock and nettles covering the bottom of the dried-up stream. He was afraid that with just one more glance, one more glimpse of the black eye sockets, grinning teeth and cracked bones, something would snap in him, the remains of his desperate courage would escape like air from a fish's bladder, and he would dash back up the highway, stifling a scream, just as the carter and his lad had less than an hour before.

'What are you waiting for?' the horseman asked softly, reining his horse around. 'For nightfall? It'll be too late then. They'll come for you as soon as it begins to get dark. Or maybe even sooner. Let's go, jump up behind me. Let's both get out of here as quick as we can.'

'But the cart, sir?' Yurga howled at the top of his voice, not knowing if from fear, despair or rage. 'And my goods? That's a whole year's work! I'd rather drop dead! I'm not leaving it!'

'I think you still don't know where the bloody hell you are, friend,' the stranger said calmly, extending a hand towards the ghastly graveyard beneath the bridge. 'Won't leave your cart, you say? I tell you, when darkness falls not even King Dezmod's treasury will save you, never mind your lousy cart. What the hell came over you to take a shortcut through this wilderness? Don't you know what has infested this place since the war?'

Yurga shook his head.

'You don't know,' nodded the stranger. 'But you've seen what's down there? It'd be difficult not to notice. That's all the other men who took a shortcut through here. And you say you won't leave your cart. And what, I wonder, do you have in your cart?'

Yurga did not reply, but glowered at the horseman, trying to choose between 'oakum' and 'old rags'.

The horseman did not seem particularly interested in the answer. He reassured his chestnut, who was chewing its bit and tossing its head.

'Please, sir . . .' the merchant finally muttered. 'Help me. Save me. My eternal gratitude . . . Don't leave . . . I'll give you whatever you want, whatever you ask . . . Save me, sir!'

The stranger, resting both hands on the pommel of his saddle, suddenly turned his head towards him.

'What did you say?'

Yurga opened his mouth but said nothing.

'You'll give me whatever I ask for? Say it again.'

Yurga smacked his lips, closed his mouth and wished he was agile enough to kick himself in the arse. His head was spinning with fantastic theories as to the reward that this weird stranger might demand. Most of them, including the privilege of weekly use of his rosy-cheeked young wife, did not seem as awful as the prospect of losing the cart, and certainly not as macabre as the possibility of ending up at the bottom of the canyon as one more bleached skeleton. His merchant's experience forced him into some rapid calculations. The horseman, although he did not resemble a typical ruffian, tramp or marauder – of which there were plenty on the roads after the war – surely wasn't a magnate or governor either, nor one of those proud little knights with a high opinion of themselves who derive pleasure from robbing the shirt off their neighbours' backs. Yurga reckoned him at no more than twenty pieces of gold. However, his commercial instincts stopped him from naming a price. So he limited himself to mumbling something about 'lifelong gratitude'.

'I asked you,' the stranger calmly reminded him, after waiting for the merchant to be quiet, 'if you'll give me whatever I ask for?'

There was no way out. Yurga swallowed, bowed his head and nodded his agreement. The stranger, in spite of Yurga's expectations, did not laugh portentously; quite the opposite, he did not show any sign of being delighted by his victory in the negotiations. Leaning over in the saddle, he spat into the ravine.

'What am I doing?' he said grimly. 'What the fuck am I doing? Well, so be it. I'll try to get you out of this, though I don't know that it won't finish disastrously for us both. But if I succeed, in exchange you will . . .'

Yurga curled up, close to tears.

'You will give me,' the horseman in the black cloak suddenly and quickly recited, 'whatever you come across at home on your return, but did not expect. Do you swear?'

Yurga groaned and nodded quickly.

'Good,' the stranger grimaced. 'And now stand aside. It would be best if you got back under the cart. The sun is about to set.'

He dismounted and took his cloak from his shoulders. Yurga saw that the stranger was carrying a sword on his back, on a belt slung diagonally across his chest. He had a vague sense he had once heard of people with a similar way of carrying a weapon. The black, leather, hip-length jacket with long sleeves sparkling with silver studs might have indicated that the stranger came from Novigrad or the surroundings, but the fashion for such dress had recently become widespread, particularly among youngsters. Although this stranger was no youngster.

After removing his saddlebags from his mount the horseman turned around. A round medallion hung on a silver chain around his neck. He was holding a small, metal-bound chest and an oblong parcel wrapped in skins and fastened with a strap under one arm.

'Aren't you under the cart yet?' he asked, approaching. Yurga saw that a wolf's head with open jaws and armed with fangs was depicted on the medallion. He suddenly recalled.

'Would you be . . . a witcher? Sir?'

The stranger shrugged.

'You guess right. A witcher. Now move away. To the other side

318

of the cart. Don't come out from there and be silent. I must be alone for a while.'

Yurga obeyed. He hunkered down by the wheel, wrapped in a mantle. He didn't want to look at what the stranger was doing on the other side of the cart, even less at the bones at the bottom of the ravine. So he looked at his boots and at the green, star-shaped shoots of moss growing on the bridge's rotten timbers.

A witcher.

The sun was setting.

He heard footsteps.

Slowly, very slowly, the stranger moved out from behind the cart, into the centre of the bridge. He had his back to Yurga, who saw that the sword on his back was not the sword he had seen earlier. Now it was a splendid weapon; the hilt, crossguard and fittings of the scabbard shone like stars. Even in the gathering darkness they reflected light, although there was almost none; not even the golden-purple glow which a short while earlier had been hanging over the forest.

'Sir—'

The stranger turned his head. Yurga barely stifled a scream.

The stranger's face was white – white and porous, like cheese drained and unwrapped from a cloth. And his eyes . . . Ye Gods, something howled inside Yurga. His eyes . . .

'Behind the cart. Now,' the stranger rasped. It was not the voice Yurga had heard before. The merchant suddenly felt his full bladder troubling him terribly. The stranger turned and walked further along the bridge.

A witcher.

The horse tied to the cart's rack snorted, neighed, and stamped its hooves dully on the beams.

A mosquito buzzed above Yurga's ear. The merchant did not even move a hand to shoo it away. A second one joined it. Whole clouds of mosquitoes were buzzing in the thicket on the far side of the ravine. Buzzing.

And howling.

Yurga, clenching his teeth till they hurt, realised they were not mosquitoes.

319

From the thickening darkness on the overgrown side of the ravine emerged some small, misshapen forms – less than four feet tall, horribly gaunt, like skeletons. They stepped onto the bridge with a peculiar, heron-like gait, feet high, making staccato, jerky movements as they lifted their bony knees. Their eyes, beneath flat, dirty foreheads, shone yellow, and pointed little fangs gleamed white in wide, frog-like maws. They came closer, hissing.

The stranger, as still as a statue in the centre of the bridge, suddenly raised his right hand, making a bizarre shape with his fingers. The monstrous little beasts retreated, hissing loudly, before once again moving forwards, quickly, quicker and quicker, on their long, spindly, taloned forefeet.

Claws scraped on the timbers to the left, as another monster jumped out from under the bridge, and the remaining ones on the bank rushed forwards in bewildering leaps. The stranger spun around on the spot and the sword, which had suddenly appeared in his hand, flashed. The head of the creature scrambling onto the bridge flew two yards up into the air, trailing a ribbon of blood behind it. Then the white-haired man fell on a group of them and whirled, slashing swiftly all around him. The monsters, flailing their arms and wailing, attacked him from all sides, ignoring the luminous blade cutting them like a razor. Yurga cowered, hugging the cart.

Something fell right at his feet, bespattering him with gore. It was a long, bony hand, four-clawed and scaly, like a chicken's foot.

The merchant screamed.

He sensed something flitting past him. He cowered, intending to dive under the cart, just as something landed on his neck, and a scaly hand seized him by the temple and cheek. He covered his eyes, howling and jerking his head, leaped to his feet and staggered into the middle of the bridge, stumbling over the corpses sprawled across the timbers. A battle was raging there – but Yurga could not see anything apart from a furious swarm, a mass, within which the silver blade kept flashing.

'Help meeeee!' he howled, feeling the sharp fangs penetrating the felt of his hood and digging into the back of his head.

'Duck!'

He pressed his chin down onto his chest, looking out for the flash of the blade. It whined in the air and grazed his hood. Yurga heard a hideous, wet crunching sound and then a hot liquid gushed down his back. He fell to his knees, dragged down by the now inert weight hanging from his neck.

He watched as three more monsters scuttled out from under the bridge. Leaping like bizarre grasshoppers, they latched onto the stranger's thighs. One of them, slashed with a short blow across its toadlike muzzle, took a few steps upright and fell onto the timbers. Another, struck with the very tip of the sword, collapsed in squirming convulsions. The remaining ones swarmed like ants over the white-haired man, pushing him towards the edge of the bridge. One flew out of the swarm bent backwards, spurting blood, quivering and howling, and right then the entire seething mass staggered over the edge and plummeted into the ravine. Yurga fell to the ground, covering his head with his hands.

From below the bridge he heard the monsters' triumphant squeals, suddenly transforming into howls of pain, those howls silenced by the whistling of the blade. Then from the darkness came the rattle of stones and the crunch of skeletons being trodden on and crushed, and then once again came the whistle of a falling sword and a despairing, bloodcurdling shriek which suddenly broke off.

And then there was only silence, interrupted by the sudden cry of a terrified bird, deep in the forest among the towering trees. And then the bird fell silent too.

Yurga swallowed, raised his head and stood up with difficulty. It was still quiet; not even the leaves rustled, the entire forest seemed to be dumbstruck with terror. Ragged clouds obscured the sky.

'Hey . . .'

He turned around, involuntarily protecting himself with raised arms. The Witcher stood before him, motionless, black, with the shining sword in his lowered hand. Yurga noticed he was standing somehow crookedly, leaning over to one side.

'What's the matter, sir?'

The Witcher did not reply. He took a step, clumsily and heavily,

321

limping on his left leg. He held out a hand and grasped the cart. Yurga saw blood, black and shining, dripping onto the timbers.

'You're wounded, sir!'

The Witcher did not reply. Looking straight into the merchant's eyes, he fell against the cart's box and slowly collapsed onto the bridge.

II

'Careful, easy does it . . . Under his head . . . One of you support his head!'

'Here, here, onto the cart!'

'Ye Gods, he'll bleed to death . . . Mr Yurga, the blood's seeping through the dressing—'

'Quiet! Drive on, Pokvit, make haste! Wrap him in a sheepskin, Vell, can't you see how he shivers?'

'Shall I pour some vodka down his throat?'

'Can't you see he's unconscious? You astonish me, Vell. But give me that vodka, I need a drink . . . You dogs, you scoundrels, you rotten cowards! Scarpering like that and leaving me all alone!'

'Mr Yurga! He said something!'

'What? What's he saying?'

'Err, can't make it out . . . seems to be a name . . .'

'What name?'

'Yennefer . . .'

III

'Where am I?'

'Lie still, sir, don't move, or everything will tear open again. Those vile creatures bit your thigh down to the bone, you've lost a deal of blood . . . Don't you know me? It's Yurga! You saved me on the bridge, do you recall?'

'Aha . . .'

'Do you have a thirst?'

'A hell of one . . .'

'Drink, sir, drink. You're burning with fever.'

'Yurga . . . Where are we?'

'We're riding in my cart. Don't say anything, sir, don't move. We had to venture out of the forest towards human settlements. We must find someone with healing powers. What we've wrapped round your leg may be insufficient. The blood won't stop coming—'

'Yurga . . .'

'Yes, sir?'

'In my chest . . . A flacon . . . With green sealing wax. Strip off the seal and give it to me . . . In a bowl. Wash the bowl well, don't let a soul touch the flacon . . . If you value your life . . . Swiftly, Yurga. Dammit, how this cart shakes . . . The flacon, Yurga . . .'

'I have it . . . Drink, sir.'

'Thanks . . . Now pay attention. I'll soon fall asleep. I'll thrash around and rave, then lie as though dead. It's nothing, don't be afeared . . .'

'Lie still, sir, or the wound will open and you'll lose blood.'

He fell back onto the skins, turned his head and felt the merchant drape him in a sheepskin and a blanket stinking of horse sweat. The cart shook and with each jolt pangs of fierce pain shot through his

324

thigh and hip. Geralt clenched his teeth. He saw above him

billions
of stars. So close it seemed he could reach out and touch them. Right
above his head, just above the treetops.

As he walked he picked his way in order to stay away from the
light, away from the glow of bonfires, in order to remain within the
compass of rippling shadow. It was not easy – pyres of fir logs were
burning all around, sending into the sky a red glow shot with the
flashes of sparks, marking the darkness with brighter pennants of
smoke, crackling, exploding in a blaze among the figures dancing all
around.

Geralt stopped to let through a frenzied procession, boisterous
and wild, which was barring his way and lurching towards him.
Someone tugged him by the arm, trying to shove into his hand a
wooden beer mug, dripping with foam. He declined and gently but
firmly pushed away the man, who was staggering and splashing
beer all around from the small cask he was carrying under one arm.
Geralt did not want to drink.

Not on a night like this.

Close by – on a frame of birch poles towering above a huge fire –
the fair-haired May King, dressed in a wreath and coarse britches,
was kissing the red-haired May Queen, groping her breasts through
her thin, sweat-soaked blouse. The monarch was more than a little
drunk and tottered, trying to keep his balance, as he hugged the
queen, pressing a fist clamped onto a mug of beer against her back.
The queen, also far from sober, wearing a wreath which had slipped
down over her eyes, hung on the king's neck and leaned close against
him in anticipation. The throng was dancing beneath the frame,
singing, yelling and shaking poles festooned with garlands of foliage
and blossom.

'Beltane!' screamed a short, young woman right in Geralt's ear.
Pulling him by the sleeve, she forced him to turn around among the
procession encircling them. She cavorted by him, fluttering her skirt
and shaking her hair, which was full of flowers. He let her spin him
in the dance and whirled around, nimbly avoiding the other couples.

'Beltane! May Day Eve!'

Besides them there was a struggle, a squealing and the nervous laugh of another young woman, feigning a fight and resistance, being carried off by a young man into the darkness, beyond the circle of light. The procession, hooting, snaked between the burning pyres. Someone stumbled and fell, breaking the chain of hands, rending the procession apart into smaller groups.

The young woman, looking at Geralt from under the leaves decorating her brow, came closer and pressed herself urgently against him, encircling him with her arms and panting. He grabbed her more roughly than he had intended and felt the hot dampness of her body, perceptible on his hands through the thin linen pressing against her back. She raised her head. Her eyes were closed and her teeth flashed from beneath her raised, twisted upper lip. She smelled of sweat and sweet grass, smoke and lust.

Why not? he thought, crumpling her dress and kneading her back with his hands, enjoying the damp, steaming warmth on his fingers. The woman was not his type. She was too small and too plump – under his hand he felt the line where the too-tight bodice of her dress was cutting into her body, dividing her back into two distinctly perceptible curves, where he should not have been able to feel them. Why not? he thought, on a night like this, after all . . . It means nothing.

Beltane . . . Fires as far as the horizon. Beltane, May Day Eve.

The nearest pyre devoured the dry, outstretched pine branches being thrown onto it with a crack, erupted in a golden flash, lighting everything up. The young woman's eyes opened wide, looking up into his face. He heard her suck air in, felt her tense up and violently push her hands against his chest. He released her at once. She hesitated. Tilted her trunk away to the length of her almost straightened arms, but she did not peel her hips away from his thighs. She lowered her head, then withdrew her hands and drew away, looking to the side.

They stood motionless for a moment until the returning procession barged into them, shook and jostled them again. The young woman quickly turned and fled, clumsily trying to join the dancers. She looked back. Just once.

Beltane . . .

What am I doing here?

A star shone in the dark, sparkling, drawing his gaze. The medallion around the Witcher's neck vibrated. Geralt involuntarily dilated his pupils, his vision effortlessly penetrating the obscurity.

She was not a peasant woman. Peasant women did not wear black velvet cloaks. Peasant women – carried or dragged into the bushes by men – screamed, giggled, squirmed and tensed their bodies like trout being pulled out of the water. None of them gave the impression that it was *they* who were leading their tall, fair-haired swains with gaping shirts into the gloom.

Peasant women never wore velvet ribbons or diamond-encrusted stars of obsidian around their necks.

'Yennefer.'

Wide-open, violet eyes blazing in a pale, triangular face.

'Geralt . . .'

She released the hand of the fair-haired cherub whose breast was shiny as a sheet of copper with sweat. The lad staggered, tottered, fell to his knees, rolled his head, looked around and blinked. He stood up slowly, glanced at them uncomprehending and embarrassed, and then lurched off towards the bonfires. The sorceress did not even glance at him. She looked intently at the Witcher, and her hand tightly clenched the edge of her cloak.

'Nice to see you,' he said easily. He immediately sensed the tension which had formed between them falling away.

'Indeed,' she smiled. He seemed to detect something affected in the smile, but he could not be certain. 'Quite a pleasant surprise, I don't deny. What are you doing here, Geralt? Oh . . . Excuse me, forgive my indiscretion. Of course, we're doing the same thing. It's Beltane, after all. Only you caught me, so to speak, in flagrante delicto.'

'I interrupted you.'

'I'll survive,' she laughed. 'The night is young. I'll enchant another if the fancy takes me.'

'Pity I'm unable to do that,' he said trying hard to affect indifference. 'A moment ago a girl saw my eyes in the light and fled.'

'At dawn,' she said, smiling more and more falsely, 'when they really let themselves go, they won't pay any attention. You'll find another, just you wait . . .'

'Yen—' The rest of the words stuck in his throat. They looked at one another for a long, long time, and the red reflection of fire flickered on their faces. Yennefer suddenly sighed, veiling her eyes with her eyelashes.

'Geralt, no. Don't let's start—'

'It's Beltane,' he interrupted. 'Have you forgotten?'

She moved slowly closer, placed her hands on his arms, and slowly and cautiously snuggled against him, touching his chest with her forehead. He stroked her raven-black hair, strewn in locks coiled like snakes.

'Believe me,' she whispered, lifting her head. 'I wouldn't think twice, if it were only to be . . . But it's senseless. Everything will start again and finish like last time. It would be senseless if we were to—'

'Does everything have to make sense? It's Beltane.'

'Beltane,' she turned her head. 'What of it? Something drew us to these bonfires, to these people enjoying themselves. We meant to dance, abandon ourselves, get a little intoxicated and take advantage of the annual loosening of morals which is inextricably linked to the celebration of the endless natural cycle. And, prithee, we run right into each other after . . . How long has passed since . . . A year?'

'One year, two months and eighteen days.'

'How touching. Was that deliberate?'

'It was. Yen—'

'Geralt,' she interrupted, suddenly moving away and tossing her head. 'Let me make things perfectly clear. I don't want to.'

He nodded to indicate that was sufficiently clear.

Yennefer threw her cloak back over one shoulder. Beneath her cloak she had on a very thin, white blouse and a black skirt girdled with a belt of silver links.

'I don't want,' she repeated, 'to start again. And the thought of doing with you . . . what I meant to do with that young blond boy . . .

328

According to the same rules . . . The thought, Geralt, seems to me somewhat improper. An affront to both of us. Do you understand?'

He nodded once more. She looked at him from beneath lowered eyelashes.

'Will you go?'

'No.'

She was silent for a moment, fidgeting nervously.

'Are you angry?'

'No.'

'Right, come on, let's sit down somewhere, away from this hubbub, let's talk for a while. Because, as you can see, I'm glad we've met. Truly. Let's sit together for a while. Alright?'

'Let us, Yen.'

They headed off into the gloom, far onto the moors, towards the black wall of trees, avoiding couples locked in embraces. They had to go a long way in order to find a secluded spot. A dry hilltop marked by a juniper bush, as slender as a cypress.

The sorceress unfastened the brooch from her cloak, shook it out and spread it on the ground. He sat down beside her. He wanted to embrace her very much, but contrariness stopped him. Yennefer tidied up her deeply unbuttoned blouse, looked at him penetratingly, sighed and embraced him. He might have expected it. She had to make an effort to read his mind, but sensed his intentions involuntarily.

They said nothing.

'Oh, dammit,' she suddenly said, pulling away. She raised her hand and cried out a spell. Red and green spheres flew above their heads, breaking up high in the air, forming colourful, fluffy flowers. Laughter and joyous cries drifted up from the bonfires.

'Beltane . . . ' she said bitterly. 'May Day Eve . . . The cycle repeats. Let them enjoy themselves . . . if they can.'

There were other sorcerers in the vicinity. In the distance, three orange lightning bolts shot into the sky and away over by the forest a veritable geyser of rainbow-coloured, whirling meteors exploded. The people by the bonfires gave awe-struck gasps and cried out. Geralt, tense, stroked Yennefer's curls and breathed in the scent of lilac and gooseberry they gave off. If I desire her too intensely, he thought, she'll sense it and she'll be put off. Her hackles will rise, she'll bristle and spurn me. I'll ask her calmly how she's doing . . .

'Nothing to report,' she said, and something in her voice quavered. 'Nothing worth mentioning.'

'Don't do that to me, Yen. Don't read me. It unsettles me.'

'Forgive me. It's automatic. And what's new with you, Geralt?'

'Nothing. Nothing worth mentioning.'

They said nothing.

'Beltane!' she suddenly snapped, and he felt the arm she was pressing against his chest stiffen and tauten. 'They're enjoying themselves. They're celebrating the eternal cycle of nature regenerating itself. And us? What are we doing here? We, relics, doomed to obliteration, to extinction and oblivion? Nature is born again, the cycle repeats itself. But not for us, Geralt. We cannot reproduce ourselves. We were deprived of that potential. We were given the ability to do extraordinary things with nature, occasionally literally against her. And at the same time what is most natural and simple in nature was taken from us. What if we live longer than them? After our winter will come the spring, and we shall not be reborn; what finishes will finish along with us. But both you and I are drawn to those bonfires, though our presence here is a wicked, blasphemous mockery of this world.'

He was silent. He didn't like it when she fell into a mood like this, the origin of which he knew only too well. Once again, he thought, once again it's beginning to torment her. There was a time when it seemed she had forgotten, that she had become reconciled to it like the others. He embraced her, hugged her, rocked her very gently like a child. She let him. It didn't surprise him. He knew she needed it.

'You know, Geralt,' she suddenly said, now composed. 'I miss your silence the most.'

He touched her hair and ear with his mouth. I desire you, Yen, he thought, I desire you, but you know that. You know that, don't you, Yen?

'Yes, I do,' she whispered.

'Yen . . .'

She sighed again.

'Just today,' she said, looking at him with eyes wide open. 'Just this night, which will soon slip away. Let it be our Beltane. We shall part in the morning. Don't expect any more; I cannot, I could not . . . Forgive me. If I have hurt you, kiss me and go away.'

'If I kiss you I won't go away.'

'I was counting on that.'

She tilted her head. He touched her parted lips with his own. Tentatively. First the upper, then the lower. He entwined his fingers in her winding locks, touched her ear, her diamond earring, her neck. Yennefer, returning the kiss, clung to him, and her nimble fingers quickly and surely unfastened the buckles of his jacket.

She fell back onto her cloak, spread out on the soft moss. He pressed his mouth to her breast and felt the nipple harden and press against the very fine stuff of her blouse. She was breathing shallowly.

'Yen . . .'

'Don't say anything . . . Please . . .'

The touch of her naked, smooth, cool skin electrified his fingers and his palms. A shiver down his back being pricked by her fingernails. From the bonfires screams, singing, a whistle; a far, distant cloud of sparks in purple smoke. Caresses and touches. He touching her. She touching him. A shiver. And impatience. The gliding skin of her slim thighs gripping his hips, drawing closed like a clasp.

Beltane!

Breathing, riven into gasps. Flashes beneath their eyelids, the scent of lilac and gooseberry. The May Queen and May King? A blasphemous mockery? Oblivion?

Beltane! May Day Eve!

A moan. Hers? His? Black curls on his eyes, on his mouth. Intertwined fingers, quivering hands. A cry. Hers? Black eyelashes. A moan. His?

Silence. All eternity in the silence.

Beltane . . . Fires all the way to the horizon . . .

'Yen?'

'Oh, Geralt . . .'

'Yen . . . Are you weeping?'

331

'No!'

'Yen . . .'

'I promised myself . . . I promised . . .'

'Don't say anything. There's no need. Aren't you cold?'

'Yes, I am.'

'And now?'

'Now I'm warmer.'

The sky grew lighter at an alarming rate, the contours of the black wall of trees becoming more prominent, the distinct, serrated line of the treetops emerging from the shapeless gloom. The blue foretoken of dawn creeping up from behind it spread along the horizon, extinguishing the lamps of the stars. It had grown cooler. He hugged her more tightly and covered her with his cloak.

'Geralt?'

'Mhm?'

'It'll soon be dawn.'

'I know.'

'Have I hurt you?'

'A little.'

'Will it begin again?'

'It never ended.'

'Please . . . You make me feel . . .'

'Don't say anything. Everything is all right.'

The smell of smoke creeping among the heather. The scent of lilac and gooseberry.

'Geralt?'

'Yes?'

'Do you remember when we met in the Owl Mountains? And that golden dragon . . . What was he called?'

'Three Jackdaws. Yes, I do.'

'He told us . . .'

'I remember, Yen.'

She kissed him where the neck becomes the collarbone and then nuzzled her head in, tickling him with her hair.

'We're made for each other,' she whispered. 'Perhaps we're destined for each other? But nothing will come of it. It's a pity, but when dawn breaks, we shall part. It cannot be any other way. We have to part so as not to hurt one another. We two, destined for each other. Created for each other. Pity. The one or ones who created us for each other ought to have made more of an effort. Destiny alone is insufficient, it's too little. Something more is needed. Forgive me. I had to tell you.'

'I know.'

'I knew it was senseless for us to make love.'

'You're wrong. It wasn't. In spite of everything.'

'Ride to Cintra, Geralt.'

'What?'

'Ride to Cintra. Ride there and this time don't give up. Don't do what you did then . . . When you were there . . .'

'How did you know?'

'I know everything about you. Have you forgotten? Ride to Cintra, go there as fast as you can. Fell times are approaching, Geralt. Very fell. You cannot be late . . .'

'Yen . . .'

'Please don't say anything.'

It was cooler. Cooler and cooler. And lighter and lighter.

'Don't go yet. Let's wait until the dawn . . .'

'Yes, let's.'

IV

'Don't move, sir. I must change your dressing. The wound is getting messy and your leg is swelling something terrible. Ye Gods, it looks hideous . . . We must find a doctor as fast as we can . . .'

'Fuck the doctor,' the Witcher groaned. 'Hand me the chest, Yurga. Yes, that flacon there . . . Pour it straight onto the wound. Oh, bloody hell! It's nothing, nothing, keep pouring . . . Oooow! Right. Bandage it up well and cover me . . .'

'It's swollen, sir, the whole thigh. And you're burning with fever—'

'Fuck the fever. Yurga?'

'Yes, sir?'

'I forgot to thank you . . .'

'It's not you who should be doing the thanking, sir, but me. You saved my life, you suffered an injury in my defence. And me? What did I do? I bandaged a wounded man, who'd fainted away, and put him on my cart and didn't leave him to expire. It's an ordinary matter, Witcher, sir.'

'It's not so ordinary, Yurga. I've been left . . . in similar situations . . . Like a dog . . .'

The merchant, lowering his head, said nothing.

'Well, what can I say, it's a base world,' he finally muttered. 'But that's no reason for us all to become despicable. What we need is kindness. My father taught me that and I teach it to my sons.'

The Witcher was silent, and observed the branches of the trees above the road, sliding past as the cart went on. His thigh throbbed. He felt no pain.

'Where are we?'

'We've forded the River Trava, now we're in the Groundcherry Forests. It's no longer Temeria, but Sodden. You were asleep when we crossed the border, when the customs officers were rummaging in the cart. I'll tell you, though, they were astonished by you. But their senior officer knew you and ordered us through without delay.'

'He knew me?'

'Aye, there's no doubt. He called you Geralt. That's what he said; Geralt of Rivia. Is that your name?'

'It is . . .'

'And he promised to send a man ahead with the tidings that a doctor is needed. And I gave him a little something so as he wouldn't forget.'

'Thank you, Yurga.'

'No, Witcher, sir. I've already said, it's me as thanks you. And not just that. I'm also in your debt. We have an agreement . . . What is it, sir? Are you feeling faint?'

'Yurga . . . The flacon with the green seal . . .'

'Sir . . . You'll start . . . You were calling out dreadfully in your sleep . . .'

'I must, Yurga . . .'

'As you wish. Wait, I'll pour it into a bowl right away . . . By the Gods, we need a doctor as quickly as possible, otherwise . . .'

The Witcher turned his head away. He heard

the cries of children playing in a dried-up, inner moat surrounding the castle grounds. There were around ten of them. The youngsters were making an ear-splitting din, outshouting each other in shrill, excited voices which kept breaking into falsetto. They were running to and fro along the bottom of the moat, like a shoal of swift little fishes, unexpectedly and very quickly changing direction, but always staying together. As usual, behind the screeching older boys, as skinny as scarecrows, ran a little child, panting and quite incapable of catching up.

'There are plenty of them,' the Witcher observed.

Mousesack smiled sourly, tugging at his beard, and shrugged.

'Aye, plenty.'

'And which of them . . . Which of these boys is the celebrated Child of Destiny?'

The druid looked away.

'I am forbidden, Geralt . . .'

'Calanthe?'

'Of course. You cannot have deluded yourself that she would give the child up so easily? You have met her, after all. She is a woman of iron. I shall tell you something, something I ought not to say, in the hope that you'll understand. I hope too, that you will not betray me before her.'

'Speak.'

'When the child was born six years ago she summoned me and ordered me to cheat you. And kill it.'

'You refused.'

'No one refuses Calanthe,' Mousesack said, looking him straight in the eyes. 'I was prepared to take to the road when she summoned me once again. She retracted the order, without a word of explanation. Be cautious when you talk to her.'

'I shall. Mousesack, tell me, what happened to Duny and Pavetta?'

'They were sailing from Skellige to Cintra. They were surprised by a storm. Not a single splinter was found of the ship. Geralt . . . That the child was not with them then is an incredibly queer matter. Inexplicable. They were meant to take it with them but at the last moment did not. No one knows why, Pavetta could never be parted from—'

'How did Calanthe bear it?'

'What do you think?'

'Of course.'

Shrieking like a band of goblins, the boys hurtled upwards and flashed beside them. Geralt noticed that not far behind the head of the rushing herd hurried a little girl, as thin and clamorous as the boys, only with a fair plait waving behind her. Howling wildly, the band spilled down the moat's steep slope again. At least half of them, including the girl, slid down on their behinds. The smallest one, still unable to keep up, fell over, rolled down to the bottom and began crying loudly, clutching a grazed knee. The other boys surrounded him, jeering and mocking, and then ran on. The little girl knelt by the little boy, hugged him and wiped away his tears, smudging dust and dirt over his face.

'Let us go, Geralt. The queen awaits.'

'Let's go, Mousesack.'

Calanthe was sitting on a large bench suspended on chains from the bough of a huge linden tree. She appeared to be dozing, but that was belied by an occasional push of her foot to swing the bench every now and again. There were three young women with her. One of them was sitting on the grass beside the swing, her spread-out dress shining bright white against the green like a patch of snow. The other two were not far away, chatting as they cautiously pulled apart the branches on some raspberry bushes.

'Ma'am,' Mousesack bowed.

The queen raised her head. Geralt went down on one knee.

'Witcher,' she said drily.

As in the past she was decorated with emeralds, which matched her green dress. And the colour of her eyes. As in the past, she was wearing a narrow, gold band on her mousy hair. But her hands, which he remembered as white and slender, were less slender now. She had gained weight.

'Greetings, Calanthe of Cintra.'

'Welcome, Geralt of Rivia. Rise. I've been waiting for you. Mousesack, my friend, escort the young ladies back to the castle.'

'At your behest, Your Majesty.'

They were left alone.

'Six years,' began Calanthe unsmilingly. 'You are horrifyingly punctual, Witcher.'

He did not comment.

'There were moments – what am I saying – years, when I convinced myself that you would forget. Or that other reasons would prevent you from coming. No, I did not in principle wish misfortune on you, but I had to take into consideration the none-too-safe nature of your profession. They say that death dogs your footsteps, Geralt of Rivia, but that you never look back. And later . . . When Pavetta . . . Do you know?'

'I do,' Geralt bowed his head. 'I sympathise with all my heart—'

'No,' she interrupted. 'It was long ago. I no longer wear mourning, as you see. I did, for long enough. Pavetta and Duny . . . Destined for each other. Until the very end. How can one not believe in the power of destiny?'

They were both silent. Calanthe moved her foot and set the swing in motion again.

'And so the Witcher has returned after six years, as agreed,' she said slowly, and a strange smile bloomed on her face. 'He has returned and demands the fulfilment of the oath. Do you think, Geralt, that storytellers will tell of our meeting in this way, when a hundred years have passed? I think so. Except they will probably colour the tale, tug on heart strings, play on the emotions. Yes, they know how. I can imagine it. Please listen. And the cruel Witcher spake thus: "Fulfil your vow, O Queen, or my curse shall fall on you". And the queen, weeping fulsomely, fell on her knees before the Witcher, crying: "Have mercy! Do not take the child from me! It is all I have left!".'

'Calanthe—'

'Don't interrupt,' she said sharply. 'I am telling a story, haven't you noticed? Listen on. The evil, cruel Witcher stamped his foot, waved his arms and cried: "Beware, faithless one, beware of fate's vengeance. If you do not keep your vow you will never escape punishment". And the queen replied: "Very well, Witcher. Let it be as fate wishes it. Look over there, where ten children are frolicking. Choose the one destined to you, and you shall take it as your own and leave me with a broken heart".'

The Witcher said nothing.

'In the story,' Calanthe's smile became more and more ugly, 'the queen, I presume, would let the Witcher guess thrice. But we aren't in a story, Geralt. We are here in reality, you and I, and our problem. And our destiny. It isn't a fairy story, it's real life. Lousy, evil, onerous, not sparing of errors, harm, sorrow, disappointments or misfortunes; not sparing of anyone, neither witchers, nor queens. Which is why, Geralt of Rivia, you will only have one guess.'

The Witcher still said nothing.

'Just one, single attempt,' Calanthe repeated. 'But as I said, this is not a fairy tale but life, which we must fill with moments of happiness for ourselves, for, as you know, we cannot count on fate to smile on us. Which is why, irrespective of the result of your choice, you will not leave here with nothing. You will take one child. The one you choose. A child you will turn into a witcher. Assuming the child survives the Trial of the Grasses, naturally.'

Geralt jerked up his head. The queen smiled. He knew that smile, hideous and evil, contemptuous because it did not conceal its artificiality.

'You are astonished,' she stated. 'Well, I've studied a little. Since Pavetta's child has the chance of becoming a witcher, I went to great pains. My sources, Geralt, reveal nothing, however, regarding how many children in ten withstand the Trial of the Grasses. Would you like to satisfy my curiosity in this regard?'

'O Queen,' Geralt said, clearing his throat. 'You certainly went to sufficient pains in your studies to know that the code and my oath forbid me from even uttering that name, much less discussing it.'

Calanthe stopped the swing abruptly by jabbing a heel into the ground.

'Three, at most four in ten,' she said, nodding her head in feigned pensiveness. 'A stringent selection, very stringent, I'd say, and at every stage. First the Choice and then the Trials. And then the Changes. How many youngsters ultimately receive medallions and silver swords? One in ten? One in twenty?'

The Witcher said nothing.

'I've pondered long over this,' Calanthe continued, now without a smile. 'And I've come to the conclusion that the selection of the children at the stage of the Choice has scant significance. What difference does it make, in the end, Geralt, which child dies or goes insane, stuffed full of narcotics? What difference does it make whose brain bursts from hallucinations, whose eyes rupture and gush forth, instead of becoming cats' eyes? What difference does it make whether the child destiny chose or an utterly chance one dies in its own blood and puke? Answer me.'

The Witcher folded his arms on his chest, in order to control their trembling.

'What's the point of this?' he asked. 'Are you expecting an answer?'

'You're right, I'm not,' the queen smiled again. 'As usual you are quite correct in your deductions. Who knows, perhaps even though I'm not expecting an answer I would like benignly to devote a little attention to your frank words, freely volunteered? Words, which, who knows, perhaps you would like to unburden yourself of, and along with them whatever is oppressing your soul? But if not, too bad. Come on, let's get down to business, we must supply the story-tellers with material. Let's go and choose a child, Witcher.'

'Calanthe,' he said, looking her in the eyes. 'It's not worth wor-rying about storytellers. If they don't have enough material they'll make things up anyway. And if they do have authentic material at their disposal, they'll distort it. As you correctly observed, this isn't a fairy tale, it's life. Lousy and evil. And so, damn it all, let's live it decently and well. Let's keep the amount of harm done to others to the absolute minimum. In a fairy tale, I grant you, the queen has to beg the witcher and the witcher can demand what's his and stamp his foot. In real life the queen can simply say: "Please don't take the child". And the Witcher can reply: "Since you ask – I shall not". And go off into the setting sun. Such is life. But the storyteller wouldn't get a penny from his listeners for an ending to a fairy tale like that. At most they'd get a kick up the arse. Because it's dull.'

Calanthe stopped smiling and something he had seen once before flashed in her eyes.

'What?' she hissed.

'Let's not beat about the bush, Calanthe. You know what I mean. As I came here, so I shall leave. Should I choose a child? Why would I need one? Do you think it matters so much to me? That I came here to Cintra, driven by an obsession to take your grandchild away from you? No, Calanthe. I wanted, perhaps, to see this child, look destiny in the eyes . . . For I don't know myself . . . But don't be afraid. I shan't take it, all you have to do is ask—'

Calanthe sprang up from the bench and a green flame blazed in her eyes.

'Ask?' she hissed furiously. 'Me, afraid? Of you? I should be afraid of you, you accursed sorcerer? How dare you fling your scornful pity in my face? Revile me with your compassion? Accuse me of cowardice, challenge my will? My overfamiliarity has emboldened you! Beware!'

The Witcher decided not to shrug, concluding it would be safer to genuflect and bow his head. He was not mistaken.

'Well,' Calanthe hissed, standing over him. Her hands were lowered, clenched into fists bristling with rings. 'Well, at last. That is the right response. One answers a queen from such a position, when a queen asks one a question. And if it is not a question, but an order, one bows one's head even lower and goes off to carry it out, without a moment's delay. Is that clear?'

'Yes, O Queen.'

'Splendid. Now stand up.'

He stood up. She gazed at him and bit her lip.

'Did my outburst offend you very much? I refer to the form, not the content.'

'Not especially.'

'Good. I shall try not to flare up again. And so, as I was saying, ten children are playing in the moat. You will choose the one you regard as the most suitable, you will take it, and by the Gods, make a witcher of it, because that is what destiny expects. And if not destiny, then know that I expect it.'

He looked her in the eyes and bowed low.

'O Queen,' he said. 'Six years ago I proved to you that some things are more powerful than a queen's will. By the Gods – if such exist – I shall prove that to you one more time. You will not compel me to make a choice I do not wish to make. I apologise for the form, but not the content.'

'I have deep dungeons beneath the castle. I warn you, one second more, one word more and you will rot in them.'

'None of the children playing in the moat is fit to be a witcher,' he said slowly. 'And Pavetta's son is not among them.'

Calanthe squinted her eyes. He did not even shudder.

'Come,' she finally said, turning on her heel.

He followed her among rows of flowering shrubs, among flower-beds and hedges. The queen entered an openwork summerhouse. Four large wicker chairs stood around a malachite table. A pitcher and two silver goblets stood on the veined table top supported by four legs in the shape of gryphons.

'Be seated. And pour.'

She drank to him, vigorously, lustily. Like a man. He responded in kind, remaining standing.

'Be seated,' she repeated. 'I wish to talk.'

'Yes, ma'am.'

'How did you know Pavetta's son is not among the children in the moat?'

'I didn't,' Geralt decided to be frank. 'It was a shot in the dark.'

'Aha. I might have guessed. And that none of them is fit to be a witcher? Is that true? And how were you able to tell that? Were you aided by magic?'

'Calanthe,' he said softly. 'I did not have to state it or find it out. What you said earlier contained the whole truth. Every child is fit. Selection decides. Later.'

'By the Gods of the Sea, as my permanently absent husband would say!' she laughed. 'So nothing is true? The whole Law of Surprise? Those legends about children that somebody was not expecting and about the ones who were first encountered? I suspected as much! It's a game! A game with chance, a game with destiny! But it's an awfully dangerous game, Geralt.'

'I know.'

'A game based on somebody's suffering. Why then, answer me, are parents or guardians forced to make such difficult and burden-some vows? Why are children taken from them? After all, there are plenty of children around who don't need to be taken away from anybody. Entire packs of homeless children and orphans roam the roads. One can buy a child cheaply enough in any village; every peasant is happy to sell one during the hungry gap, for why worry when he can easily sire another? Why then? Why did you force an oath on Duny, on Pavetta and on me? Why have you turned up here exactly six years after the birth of the child? And why, dammit, don't you want one, why do you say it's of no use?'

He was silent. Calanthe nodded.

'You do not reply,' she said, leaning back in her chair. 'Let's ponder on the reason for your silence. Logic is the mother of all knowledge. And what does she hint at? What do we have here? A witcher searching for destiny concealed in the strange and doubtful Law of Surprise. The witcher finds his destiny. And suddenly gives it up. He claims not to want the Child of Destiny. His face is stony; ice and metal in his voice. He judges that a queen – a woman when all's said and done – may be tricked, deceived by the appearances of hard maleness. No, Geralt, I shall not spare you. I know why you are declining the choice of a child. You are quitting because you do not believe in destiny. Because you are not certain. And you, when you are not certain . . . you begin to fear. Yes, Geralt. What leads you is fear. You are afraid. Deny that.'

He slowly put the goblet down on the table. Slowly, so that the clink of silver against malachite would not betray the uncontrollable shaking of his hand.

'You do not deny it?'

'No.'

She quickly leaned forward and seized his arm. Tightly.

'You have gained in my eyes,' she said. And smiled. It was a pretty smile. Against his will, almost certainly against his will, he responded with a smile.

'How did you arrive at that, Calanthe?'

'I arrived at nothing,' she said, without releasing his arm. 'It was a shot in the dark.'

They both burst out laughing. And then sat in silence among the greenery and the scent of wild cherry blossom, among the warmth and the buzzing of bees.

'Geralt?'

'Yes, Calanthe?'

'Don't you believe in destiny?'

'I don't know if I believe in anything. And as regards . . . I fear it isn't enough. Something more is necessary.'

'I must ask you something. What happened to you? I mean you were reputedly a Child of Destiny yourself. Mousesack claims—'

'No, Calanthe. Mousesack was thinking about something completely different. Mousesack . . . He probably knows. But he uses those convenient myths when it suits him. It's not true that I was an unexpected encounter at home, as a child. That's not how I became a witcher. I'm a commonplace foundling, Calanthe. The unwanted bastard of a woman I don't remember. But I know who she is.'

The queen looked at him penetratingly, but the Witcher did not continue.

'Are all stories about the Law of Surprise myths?'

'Yes. It's hard to call an accident destiny.'

'But you witchers do not stop searching?'

'No, we don't. But it's senseless. Nothing has any point.'

'Do you believe a Child of Destiny would pass through the Trials without danger?'

'We believe such a child would not require the Trials.'

'One question, Geralt. Quite a personal one. May I?'

He nodded.

'There is no better way to pass on hereditary traits than the natural way, as we know. You went through the Trials and survived. So if you need a child with special qualities and endurance . . . Why don't you find a woman who . . . I'm tactless, aren't I? But I think I've guessed, haven't I?'

'As usual,' he said, smiling sadly, 'you are correct in your deductions, Calanthe. You guessed right, of course. What you're suggesting is impossible for me.'

'Forgive me,' she said, and the smile vanished from her face. 'Oh, well, it's a human thing.'

'It isn't human.'

'Ah . . . So, no witcher can—'

'No, none. The Trial of the Grasses, Calanthe, is dreadful. And what is done to boys during the time of the Changes is even worse. And irreversible.'

344

'Don't start feeling sorry for yourself,' she muttered. 'Because it ill behooves you. It doesn't matter what was done to you. I can see the results. Quite satisfactory, if you ask me. If I could assume that Pavetta's child would one day be similar to you I wouldn't hesitate for a moment.'

'The risks are too great,' he said quickly. 'As you said. At most, four out of ten survive.'

'Dammit, is only the Trial of the Grasses hazardous? Do only potential witchers take risks? Life is full of hazards, selection also occurs in life, Geralt. Misfortune, sicknesses and wars also select. Defying destiny may be just as hazardous as succumbing to it. Geralt . . . I would give you the child. But . . . I'm afraid, too.'

'I wouldn't take the child. I couldn't assume the responsibility. I wouldn't agree to burden you with it. I wouldn't want the child to tell you one day . . . As I'm telling you—'

'Do you hate that woman, Geralt?'

'My mother? No, Calanthe. I presume she had a choice . . . Or perhaps she didn't? No, but she did; a suitable spell or elixir would have been sufficient . . . A choice. A choice which should be respected, for it is the holy and irrefutable right of every woman. Emotions are unimportant here. She had the irrefutable right to her decision and she took it. But I think that an encounter with her, the face she would make then . . . Would give me something of a perverse pleasure, if you know what I mean.'

'I know perfectly well what you mean,' she smiled. 'But you have slim chances of enjoying such a pleasure. I cannot judge your age, Witcher, but I suppose you're much, much older than your appearance would indicate. So, that woman—'

'That woman,' he interrupted coldly, 'probably looks much, much younger than I do now.'

'A sorceress?'

'Yes.'

'Interesting. I thought sorceresses couldn't . . . ?'

'She probably thought so too.'

'Yes. But you're right, let's not discuss a woman's right to this

345

decision, because it is a matter beyond debate. Let us return to our problem. You will not take the child? Definitely?'

'Definitely.'

'And if . . . If destiny is not merely a myth? If it really exists, doesn't a fear arise that it may backfire?'

'If it backfires, it'll backfire on me,' he answered placidly. 'For I am the one acting against it. You, after all, have carried out your side of the bargain. For if destiny isn't a myth, I would have to choose the appropriate child among the ones you have shown me. But is Pavetta's child among those children?'

'Yes,' Calanthe slowly nodded her head. 'Would you like to see it? Would you like to gaze into the eyes of destiny?'

'No. No, I don't. I quit, I renounce it. I renounce my right to the boy. I don't want to look destiny in the eyes, because I don't believe in it. Because I know that in order to unite two people, destiny is insufficient. Something more is necessary than destiny. I sneer at such destiny; I won't follow it like a blind man being led by the hand, uncomprehending and naive. This is my irrevocable decision, O Calanthe of Cintra.'

The queen stood up. She smiled. He was unable to guess what lay behind her smile.

'Let it be thus, Geralt of Rivia. Perhaps your destiny was precisely to renounce it and quit? I think that's exactly what it was. For you should know that if you had chosen, chosen correctly, you would see that the destiny you mock has been sneering at you.'

He looked into her glaring green eyes. She smiled. He could not decipher the smile.

There was a rosebush growing beside the summerhouse. He broke a stem and picked a flower, kneeled down, and proffered it to her, holding it in both hands, head bowed.

'Pity I didn't meet you earlier, White Hair,' she murmured, taking the rose from his hands. 'Rise.'

He stood up.

'Should you change your mind,' she said, lifting the rose up to her face. 'Should you decide . . . Come back to Cintra. I shall be waiting.

And your destiny will also be waiting. Perhaps not forever, but certainly for some time longer.'

'Farewell, Calanthe.'

'Farewell, Witcher. Look after yourself. I have . . . A moment ago I had a foreboding . . . A curious foreboding . . . that this is the last time I shall see you.'

'Farewell, O Queen.'

V

He awoke and discovered to his astonishment that the pain gnawing at his thigh had vanished. It also seemed that the throbbing swelling which was stretching the skin had stopped troubling him. He tried to reach it, touch it, but could not move. Before he realised that he was being held fast solely by the weight of the skins covering him, a cold, hideous dread ran down to his belly and dug into his guts like a hawk's talons. He clenched and relaxed his fingers, rhythmically, repeating in his head, no, no, I'm not . . .

Paralysed.

'You have woken.'

A statement, not a question. A quiet, but distinct, soft voice. A woman. Probably young. He turned his head and groaned, trying to raise himself up.

'Don't move. At least not so vigorously. Are you in pain?'

'Nnnn . . .' the coating sticking his lips together broke. 'Nnno. The wound isn't . . . My back . . .'

'Bedsores.' An unemotional, cool statement, which did not suit the soft alto voice. 'I shall remedy it. Here, drink this. Slowly, in small sips.'

The scent and taste of juniper dominated the liquid. An old method, he thought. Juniper or mint; both insignificant additives, only there to disguise the real ingredients. In spite of that he recognised sewant mushrooms, and possibly burdock. Yes, certainly burdock, burdock neutralises toxins, it purifies blood contaminated by gangrene or infection.

'Drink. Drink it all up. Not so fast or you'll choke.'

The medallion around his neck began to vibrate very gently. So there was also magic in the draught. He widened his pupils with difficulty. Now that she had raised his head he could examine her more precisely. She was dainty. She was wearing men's clothing. Her face was small and pale in the darkness.

'Where are we?'

'In a tar makers' clearing.'

Indeed, resin could be smelled in the air. He heard voices coming from the campfire. Someone had just thrown on some brushwood, and flames shot upwards with a crackle. He looked again, making the most of the light. Her hair was tied back with a snakeskin band. Her hair . . .

A suffocating pain in his throat and sternum. Hands tightly clenched into fists.

Her hair was red, flame-red, and when lit by the glow of the bonfire seemed as red as vermilion.

'Are you in pain?' she asked, interpreting the emotion, but wrongly. 'Now . . . Just a moment . . .'

He sensed a sudden impact of warmth emanating from her hands, spreading over his back, flowing downwards to his buttocks.

'We will turn you over,' she said. 'Don't try by yourself. You are very debilitated. Hey, can someone help me?'

Steps from the bonfire, shadows, shapes. Somebody leaned over. It was Yurga.

'How are you feeling, sir? Any better?'

'Help me turn him over on his belly,' said the woman. 'Gently, slowly. That's right . . . Good. Thank you.'

He did not have to look at her anymore. Lying on his belly, he did not have to risk looking her in the eyes. He calmed down and overcame the shaking of his hands. She could sense it. He heard the clasps of her bag clinking, flacons and small porcelain jars knocking against each other. He heard her breath, felt the warmth of her thigh. She was kneeling just beside him.

'Was my wound,' he asked, unable to endure the silence, 'troublesome?'

'It was, a little,' and there was coldness in her voice. 'It can happen with bites. The nastiest kinds of wound. But you must be familiar with it, Witcher.'

She knows. She's digging around in my thoughts. Is she reading them? Probably not. And I know why. She's afraid.

'Yes, you must be familiar with it,' she repeated, clinking the glass vessels again. 'I saw a few scars on you . . . But I coped with them. I am, as you see, a sorceress. And a healer at the same time. It's my specialisation.'

That adds up, he thought. He did not say a word.

'To return to the wound,' she continued calmly, 'you ought to know that you were saved by your pulse; fourfold slower than a normal man's. Otherwise you wouldn't have survived, I can say with complete honesty. I saw what had been tied around your leg. It was meant to be a dressing, but it was a poor attempt.'

He was silent.

'Later,' she continued, pulling his shirt up as far as his neck, 'infection set in, which is usual for bite wounds. It has been arrested. Of course, you took the witcher's elixir? That helped a lot. Though I don't understand why you took hallucinogens at the same time. I was listening to your ravings, Geralt of Rivia.'

She *is* reading my mind, he thought. Or perhaps Yurga told her my name? Perhaps I was talking in my sleep under the influence of the Black Gull? Damned if I know . . . But knowing my name gives her nothing. Nothing. She doesn't know who I am. She has no idea who I am.

He felt her gently massage a cold, soothing ointment with the sharp smell of camphor into his back. Her hands were small and very soft.

'Forgive me for doing it the old way,' she said. 'I could have removed the bedsores using magic, but I strained myself a little treating the wound on your leg and feel none too good. I've bandaged the wound on your leg, as much as I am able, so now you're in no danger. But don't get up for the next few days. Even magically sutured blood vessels tend to burst, and you'd have hideous effusions. A scar will remain, of course. One more for your collection.'

'Thanks . . .' He pressed his cheek against the skins in order to distort his voice, disguise its unnatural sound. 'May I ask . . . Whom should I thank?'

350

She won't say, he thought. Or she'll lie.

'My name is Visenna.'

I know, he thought.

'I'm glad,' he said slowly, with his cheek still against the skins. 'I'm glad our paths have crossed, Visenna.'

'Why, it's chance,' she said coolly, pulling his shirt down over his back and covering him with the sheepskins. 'I received word from the customs officers that I was needed. If I'm needed, I come. It's a curious habit I have. Listen, I'll leave the ointment with the merchant; ask him to rub it on every morning and evening. He claims you saved his life, he can repay you like that.'

'And me? How can I repay you, Visenna?'

'Let's not talk about that. I don't take payment from witchers. Call it solidarity, if you will. Professional solidarity. And affection. As part of that affection some friendly advice or, if you wish, a healer's instructions: stop taking hallucinogens, Geralt. They have no healing power. None at all.'

'Thank you, Visenna. For your help and advice. Thank you . . . for everything.'

He dug his hand out from under the skins and found her knee. She shuddered, put her hand into his and squeezed it lightly. He cautiously released her fingers, and slid his down over her forearm.

Of course. The soft skin of a young woman. She shuddered even more strongly, but did not withdraw her arm. He brought his fingers back to her hand and joined his with hers.

The medallion on his neck vibrated and twitched.

'Thank you, Visenna,' he repeated, trying to control his voice. 'I'm glad our paths crossed.'

'Chance . . .' she said, but this time there was no coolness in her voice.

'Or perhaps destiny?' he asked, astonished, for the excitement and nervousness had suddenly evaporated from him completely. 'Do you believe in destiny, Visenna?'

'Yes,' she replied after a while. 'I do.'

'That people linked by destiny will always find each other?' he continued.

'Yes, I believe that too . . . What are you doing? Don't turn over . . .'

'I want to look into your face . . . Visenna. I want to look into your eyes. And you . . . You must look into mine.'

She made a movement as though about to spring up from her knees. But she remained beside him. He turned over slowly, lips twisting with pain. There was more light, someone had put some more wood on the fire.

She was not moving now. She simply moved her head to the side, offering her profile, but this time he clearly saw her mouth quivering. She tightened her fingers on his hand, powerfully.

He looked.

There was no similarity at all. She had an utterly different profile. A small nose. A narrow chin. She was silent. Then she suddenly leaned over him and looked him straight in the eye. From close up. Without a word.

'How do you like my enhanced eyes?' he asked calmly. 'Unusual, aren't they? Do you know, Visenna, what is done to witchers' eyes to improve them? Do you know it doesn't always work?'

'Stop it,' she said softly. 'Stop it, Geralt.'

'Geralt . . .' he suddenly felt something tearing in him. 'Vesemir gave me that name. Geralt of Rivia! I even learned to imitate a Rivian accent. Probably from an inner need to possess a homeland. Even if it was an invented one. Vesemir . . . gave me my name. Vesemir also revealed yours. Not very willingly.'

'Be quiet, Geralt. Be quiet.'

'You tell me today you believe in destiny. And back then . . . Did you believe back then? Oh, yes, you must have. You must have believed that destiny would bring us together. The fact you did nothing to quicken this encounter ought to be attributed to that.'

She was silent.

'I always wanted . . . I have pondered over what I would say to you, when we finally met. I've thought about the question I would ask you. I thought it would give me some sort of perverse pleasure . . .'

What sparkled on her cheek was a tear. Undoubtedly. He felt his

352

throat constrict until it hurt. He felt fatigue. Drowsiness. Weakness.

'In the light of day . . .' he groaned. 'Tomorrow, in the sunshine, I'll look into your eyes, Visenna . . . And I'll ask you my question. Or perhaps I won't ask you, because it's too late. Destiny? Oh, yes, Yen was right. It's not sufficient to be destined for each other. Something more is needed . . . But tomorrow I'll look into your eyes . . . In the light of the sun . . .'

'No,' she said gently, quietly, velvety, in a voice which gnawed at, racked the layers of memory, memory which no longer existed. Which should never have existed, but had.

'Yes!' he protested. 'Yes. I want to —'

'No. Now you will fall asleep. And when you awake, you'll stop wanting. Why should we look at each other in the sunlight? What will it change? Nothing can now be reversed, nothing changed. What's the purpose of asking me questions, Geralt? Does knowing that I won't be able to answer give you some kind of perverse pleasure? What will mutual hurt give us? No, we won't look at each other in the daylight. Go to sleep, Geralt. And just between us, Vesemir did not give you that name. Although it doesn't change or reverse anything either, I'd like you to know that. Farewell and look after yourself. And don't try to look for me . . .'

'Visenna—'

'No, Geralt. Now you'll fall asleep. And I . . . I was a dream. Farewell.'

'No! Visenna!'

'Sleep.' There was a soft order in her velvety voice, breaking his will, tearing it like cloth. Warmth, suddenly emanating from her hands.

'Sleep.'

He slept.

VI

'Are we in Riverdell yet, Yurga?'

'Have been since yesterday, sir. Soon the River Yaruga and then my homeland. Look, even the horses are walking more jauntily, tossing their heads. They can sense home is near.'

'Home . . . Do you live in the city?'

'No, outside the walls.'

'Interesting,' the Witcher said, looking around. 'There's almost no trace of war damage. I had heard this land was devastated.'

'Well,' Yurga said. 'One thing we're not short of is ruins. Take a closer look – on almost every cottage, in every homestead, you can see the white timber of new joinery. And over there on the far bank, just look, it was even worse, everything was burned right down to the ground . . . Well, war's war, but life must go on. We endured the greatest turmoil when the Black Forces marched through our land. True enough, it looked then as though they'd turn everything here into a wasteland. Many of those who fled then never returned. But fresh people have settled in their place. Life must go on.'

'That's a fact,' Geralt muttered. 'Life must go on. It doesn't matter what happened. Life must go on . . .'

'You're right. Right, there you are, put them on. I've mended your britches, patched them up. They'll be good as new. It's just like this land, sir. It was rent by war, ploughed up as if by the iron of a harrow, ripped up, bloodied. But now it'll be good as new. And it will be even more fertile. Even those who rotted in the ground will serve the good and fertilise the soil. Presently it is hard to plough, because the fields are full of bones and ironware, but the earth can cope with iron too.'

'Are you afraid the Nilfgaardians, the Black Forces, will return? They found a way through the mountains once already . . .'

'Well, we're afeared. And what of it? Do we sit down and weep and tremble? Life must go on. And what will be, will be. What is destined can't be avoided, in any case.'

'Do you believe in destiny?'

'How can I not believe? After what I encountered on the bridge, in the wilderness, when you saved me from death? Oh, Witcher, sir, you'll see, my wife will fall at your feet . . .'

'Oh, come on. Frankly speaking, I have more to be grateful to you for. Back there on the bridge . . . That's my job, after all, Yurga, my trade. I mean, I protect people for money. Not out of the goodness of my heart. Admit it, Yurga, you've heard what people say about witchers. That no one knows who's worse; them or the monsters they kill—'

'That's not true, sir, and I don't know why you talk like that. What, don't I have eyes? You're cut from the same cloth as that healer.'

'Visenna . . .'

'She didn't tell us her name. But she followed right behind us, for she knew she was needed, caught us up in the evening, and took care of you at once, having barely dismounted. You see, sir, she took great pains over your leg, the air was crackling from all that magic, and we fled into the forest out of fear. And then there was blood pouring from her nose. I see it's not a simple thing, working magic. You see, she dressed your wound with such care, truly, like a—'

'Like a mother?' Geralt clenched his teeth.

'Aye. You've said it. And when you fell asleep . . .'

'Yes, Yurga?'

'She could barely stand up, she was as white as a sheet. But she came to check none of us needed any help. She healed the tar maker's hand, which had been crushed by a log. She didn't take a penny, and even left some medicine. No, Geralt, sir, I know what people say about Witchers and sorcerers in the world isn't all good. But not here. We, from Upper Sodden and the people from Riverdell, we know better. We owe too much to sorcerers not to know what they're like. Memories about them here aren't rumours and gossip, but hewn in stone. You'll see for yourself, just wait till we leave the copse. Anyway, you're sure to know better yourself. For that battle was talked about all over the world, and a year has barely passed. You must have heard.'

'I haven't been here for a year,' the Witcher muttered. 'I was in the North. But I heard . . . The second Battle of Sodden . . .'

'Precisely. You'll soon see the hill and the rock. We used to call that hill Kite Top, but now everybody calls it the Sorcerers' Peak or the Mountain of the Fourteen. For twenty-two of them stood on that hill, twenty-two sorcerers fought, and fourteen fell. It was a dreadful battle, sir. The earth reared up, fire poured from the sky like rain and lightning bolts raged . . . Many perished. But the sorcerers overcame the Black Forces, and broke the Power which was leading them. And fourteen of them perished in that battle. Fourteen laid down their lives . . . What, sir? What's the matter?'

'Nothing. Go on, Yurga.'

'The battle was dreadful, oh my, but were it not for those sorcerers on the hill, who knows, perhaps we wouldn't be talking here today, riding homeward, for that home wouldn't exist, nor me, and maybe not you either . . . Yes, it was thanks to the sorcerers. Fourteen of them perished defending us, the people of Sodden and Riverdell. Ha, certainly, others also fought there, soldiers and noblemen, and peasants, too. Whoever could, took up a pitchfork or an axe, or even a club . . . All of them fought valiantly and many fell. But the sorcerers . . . It's no feat for a soldier to fall, for that is his trade, after all, and life is short anyhow. But the sorcerers could have lived, as long they wished. And they didn't waver.'

'They didn't waver,' the Witcher repeated, rubbing his forehead with a hand. 'They didn't waver. And I was in the North . . .'

'What's the matter, sir?'

'Nothing.'

'Yes . . . So now we – everyone from around here – take flowers there, to that hill, and in May, at Beltane, a fire always burns. And it shall burn there forever and a day. And forever shall they be in people's memories, that fourteen. And living like that in memory is . . . is . . . something more! More, Geralt, sir!'

'You're right, Yurga.'

'Every child of ours knows the names of the fourteen, carved in the stone that stands on the top of the hill. Don't you believe me? Listen: Axel Raby, Triss Merigold, Atlan Kerk, Vanielle of Brugge, Dagobert of Vole—'

'Stop, Yurga.'

'What's the matter, sir? You're as pale as death!'

'It's nothing.'

VII

He walked uphill very slowly, cautiously, listening to the creaking of the sinews and muscles around the magically healed wound. Although it seemed to be completely healed, he continued to protect the leg and not risk resting all his body weight on it. It was hot and the scent of grass struck his head, pleasantly intoxicating him.

The obelisk was not standing in the centre of the hill's flat top, but was further back, beyond the circle of angular stones. Had he climbed up there just before sunset the shadow of the menhir falling on the circle would have marked the precise diameter, would have indicated the direction in which the faces of the sorcerers had been turned during the battle. Geralt looked in that direction, towards the boundless, undulating fields. If any bones of the fallen were still there – and there were for certain – they were covered by lush grass. A hawk was circling, describing a calm circle on outspread wings. The single moving point in a landscape transfixed in the searing heat.

The obelisk was wide at the base – five people would have had to link hands in order to encircle it. It was apparent that without the help of magic it could not have been hauled up onto the hill. The surface of the menhir, which was turned towards the stone circle, was smoothly worked; runic letters could be seen engraved on it.

The names of the fourteen who fell.

He moved slowly closer. Yurga had been right. Flowers lay at the foot of the obelisk – ordinary, wild flowers – poppies, lupins, mallows and forget-me-nots.

The names of the fourteen.

He read them slowly, from the top, and before him appeared the faces of those he had known.

The chestnut-haired Triss Merigold, cheerful, giggling for no reason, looking like a teenager. He had liked her. And she had liked him.

Lawdbor of Murivel, with whom he had almost fought in Vizima, when he had caught the sorcerer using delicate telekinesis to tamper with dice in a game.

Lytta Neyd, known as Coral. Her nickname derived from the colour of the lipstick she used. Lytta had once denounced him to King Belohun, so he went to the dungeon for a week. After being released he went to ask her why. When, still without knowing the reason, he had ended up in her bed, he spent another week there.

Old Gorazd, who had offered him a hundred marks to let him dissect his eyes, and a thousand for the chance to carry out a post mortem – 'not necessarily today' – as he had put it then.

Three names remained.

He heard a faint rustling behind him and turned around.

She was barefoot, in a simple, linen dress. She was wearing a garland woven from daisies on long, fair hair, falling freely onto her shoulders and back.

'Greetings,' he said.

She looked up at him with cold, blue eyes, but did not answer.

He noticed she was not suntanned. That was odd, then, at the end of the summer, when country girls were usually tanned bronze. Her face and uncovered shoulders had a slight golden sheen.

'Did you bring flowers?'

She smiled and lowered her eyelashes. He felt a chill. She passed him without a word and knelt at the foot of the menhir, touching the stone with her hand.

'I do not bring flowers,' she said, lifting her head. 'But the ones lying here are for me.'

He looked at her. She knelt so that she was concealing the last name engraved in the stone of the menhir from him. She was bright, unnaturally, luminously bright against the stone.

'Who are you?' he asked slowly.

She smiled and emanated cold.

'Don't you know?'

Yes, I do, he thought, gazing into the cold blue of her eyes. Yes, I think I do.

He was tranquil. He could not be anything else. Not anymore.

'I've always wondered what you look like, my lady.'

'You don't have to address me like that,' she answered softly. 'We've known each other for years, after all.'

'We have,' he agreed. 'They say you dog my footsteps.'

'I do. But you have never looked behind you. Until today. Today, you looked back for the first time.'

He was silent. He had nothing to say. He was weary.

'How ... How will it happen?' he finally asked, cold and emotionless.

'I'll take you by the hand,' she said, looking him directly in the eyes. 'I'll take you by the hand and lead you through the meadow. Into the cold, wet fog.'

'And then? What is there, beyond the fog?'

'Nothing,' she smiled. 'There is nothing more.'

'You dogged my every footstep,' he said. 'But struck down others, those that I passed on my way. Why? I was meant to end up alone, wasn't I? So I would finally begin to be afraid? I'll tell you the truth. I was always afraid of you; always. I never looked behind me out of fear. Out of terror that I'd see you following me. I was always afraid, my life has passed in fear. I was afraid ... until today.'

'Until today?'

'Yes. Until today. We're standing here, face to face, but I don't feel any fear. You've taken everything from me. You've also taken the fear from me.'

'Then why are your eyes full of fear, Geralt of Rivia? Your hands are trembling, you are pale. Why? Do you fear the last – fourteenth – name engraved on the obelisk so much? If you wish I shall speak that name.'

'You don't have to. I know what it is. The circle is closing, the snake is sinking its teeth into its own tail. That is how it must be. You and that name. And the flowers. For her and for me. The four-teenth name engraved in the stone, a name that I have spoken in the

360

middle of the night and in the sunlight, during frosts and heat waves and rain. No, I'm not afraid to speak it now.'

'Then speak it.'

'Yennefer . . . Yennefer of Vengerberg.'

'And the flowers are mine.'

'Let us be done with this,' he said with effort. 'Take . . . Take me by the hand.'

She stood up and came closer, and he felt the coldness radiating from her; a sharp, penetrating cold.

'Not today,' she said. 'One day, yes. But not today.'

'You have taken everything from me—'

'No,' she interrupted. 'I do not take anything. I just take people by the hand. So that no one will be alone at that moment. Alone in the fog . . . We shall meet again, Geralt of Rivia. One day.'

He did not reply. She turned around slowly and walked away. Into the mist, which suddenly enveloped the hilltop, into the fog, which everything vanished into, into the white, wet fog, into which melted the obelisk, the flowers lying at its foot and the fourteen names engraved on it. There was nothing, only the fog and the wet grass under his feet, sparkling from drops of water

which smelled intoxicating, heady, sweet, until his forehead ached, he began to forget and become weary . . .

'Geralt, sir! What's the matter? Did you fall asleep? I told you, you're weak. Why did you climb up to the top?'

'I fell asleep.' He wiped his face with his hand and blinked. 'I fell asleep, dammit . . . It's nothing, Yurga, it's this heat . . .'

'Aye, it's devilish hot . . . We ought to be going, sir. Come along, I'll aid you down the slope.'

'There's nothing wrong with me . . .'

'Nothing, nothing. Then I wonder why you're staggering. Why the hell did you go up the hill in such a heat? Wanted to read their names? I could have told you them all. What's the matter?'

'Nothing . . . Yurga . . . Do you really remember all the names?'

'Certainly.'

'I'll see what your memory's like . . . The last one. The fourteenth. What name is it?'

'What a doubter you are. You don't believe in anything. You want to find out if I'm lying? I told you, didn't I, that every youngster knows those names. The last one, you say? Well, the last one is Yoël Grethen of Carreras. Perhaps you knew him?'

Geralt rubbed his eyelid with his wrist. And he glanced at the menhir. At all the names.

'No,' he said. 'I didn't.'

VIII

'Geralt, sir?'

'Yes, Yurga?'

The merchant lowered his head and said nothing for some time, winding around a finger the remains of the thin strap with which he was repairing the Witcher's saddle. He finally straightened up and gently tapped the servant driving the cart on the back with his fist.

'Mount one of those spare horses, Pokvit. I'll drive. Sit behind me on the box, Geralt, sir. Why are you hanging around the cart, Pokvit? Go on, ride on! We want to talk here, we don't need your eyes!'

Roach, dawdling behind the cart, neighed, tugged at the tether, clearly envious of Pokvit's mare trotting down the highway.

Yurga clicked his tongue and tapped the horses lightly with the reins.

'Well,' he said hesitantly. 'It's like this, sir. I promised you . . . Back then on the bridge . . . I made a promise—'

'You needn't worry,' the Witcher quickly interrupted. 'It's not necessary, Yurga.'

'But it is,' the merchant said curtly. 'It's my word. Whatever I find at home but am not expecting is yours.'

'Give over. I don't want anything from you. We're quits.'

'No, sir. Should I find something like that at home it means it's destiny. For if you mock destiny, if you deceive it, then it will punish you severely.'

I know, thought the Witcher. I know.

'But . . . Geralt, sir . . .'

'What, Yurga?'

'I won't find anything at home I'm not expecting. Nothing, and for certain not what you were hoping for. Witcher, sir, hear this:

after the last child, my woman cannot have any more and whatever you're after, there won't be an infant at home. Seems to me you're out of luck.'

Geralt did not reply.

Yurga said nothing either. Roach snorted again and tossed her head.

'But I have two sons,' Yurga suddenly said quickly, looking ahead, towards the road. 'Two; healthy, strong and smart. I mean, I'll have to get them apprenticed somewhere. One, I thought, would learn to trade with me. But the other . . .'

Geralt said nothing.

'What do you say?' Yurga turned his head away, and looked at him. 'You demanded a promise on the bridge. You had in mind a child for your witcher's apprenticeship, and nothing else, didn't you? Why does that child have to be unexpected? Can it not be expected? I've two, so one of them could go for a witcher. It's a trade like any other. It ain't better or worse.'

'Are you certain,' Geralt said softly, 'it isn't worse?'

Yurga squinted.

'Protecting people, saving their lives, how do you judge that; bad or good? Those fourteen on the hill? You on that there bridge? What were you doing? Good or bad?'

'I don't know,' said Geralt with effort. 'I don't know, Yurga. Sometimes it seems to me that I know. And sometimes I have doubts. Would you like your son to have doubts like that?'

'Why not?' the merchant said gravely. 'He might as well. For it's a human and a good thing.'

'What?'

'Doubts. Only evil, sir, never has any. But no one can escape his destiny.'

The Witcher did not answer.

The highway curved beneath a high bluff, under some crooked birch trees, which by some miracle were hanging onto the vertical hillside. The birches had yellow leaves. Autumn, Geralt thought, it's autumn again. A river sparkled down below, the freshly-cut palisade of a watchtower shone white, the roofs of cottages, hewn stakes of the jetty. A windlass creaked. A ferry

was reaching the
bank, pushing a wave in front of it, shoving the water with its blunt
prow, parting the sluggish straw and leaves in the dirty layer of dust
floating on the surface. The ropes creaked as the ferrymen hauled
them. The people thronged on the bank were clamouring. There
was everything in the din: women screaming, men cursing, children crying, cattle lowing, horses neighing and sheep bleating. The
monotonous, bass music of fear.

'Get away! Get away, get back, dammit!' yelled a horseman, head
bandaged with a bloody rag. His horse, submerged up to its belly,
thrashed around, lifting its fore hooves high and splashing water.
Yelling and cries from the jetty – the shield bearers were brutally
jostling the crowd, hitting out in all directions with the shafts of
their spears.

'Get away from the ferry!' the horseman yelled, swinging his
sword around. 'Soldiers only! Get away, afore I start cracking some
skulls!'

Geralt pulled on his reins, holding back his mare, who was dancing near the edge of the ravine.

Heavily armoured men, weapons and armour clanging, galloped
along the ravine, stirring up clouds of dust which obscured the shield
bearers running in their wake.

'Geraaaalt!'

He looked down. A slim man in a cherry jerkin and a bonnet with
an egret's feather was jumping up and down and waving his arms on
an abandoned cart loaded with cages which had been shoved off the
highway. Chickens and geese fluttered and squawked in the cages.

'Geraaalt! It's me!'

'Dandelion! Come here!'

'Get away, get away from the ferry!' roared the horseman with
the bandaged head on the jetty. 'The ferry's for the army only! If
you want to get to the far bank, scum, seize your axes and get into
the forest, cobble together some rafts! The ferry's just for the army!'

'By the Gods, Geralt,' the poet panted, scrambling up the side of

365

the ravine. His cherry jerkin was dotted, as though by snow, with birds' feathers. 'Do you see what's happening? The Sodden forces have surely lost the battle, and the retreat has begun. What am I saying? What retreat? It's a flight, simply a panicked flight! And we have to scarper, too, Geralt. To the Yaruga's far bank . . .'

'What are you doing here, Dandelion? How did you get here?'

'What am I doing?' the bard yelled. 'You want to know? I'm fleeing like everybody else, I was bumping along on that cart all day! Some whoreson stole my horse in the night! Geralt, I beg you, get me out of this hell! I tell you, the Nilfgaardians could be here any moment! Whoever doesn't get the Yaruga behind them will be slaughtered. Slaughtered, do you understand?'

'Don't panic, Dandelion.'

Below on the jetty, the neighing of horses being pulled onto the ferry by force and the clattering of hooves on the planks. Uproar. A seething mass. The splash of water after a cart was pushed into the river, the lowing of oxen holding their muzzles above the surface. Geralt looked on as the bundles and crates from the cart turned around in the current, banged against the side of the ferry and drifted away. Screaming, curses. In the ravine a cloud of dust, hoof beats.

'One at a time!' yelled the bandaged soldier, driving his horse into the crowd. 'Order, dammit! One at a time!'

'Geralt,' Dandelion groaned, seizing a stirrup. 'Do you see what's happening? We haven't a chance of getting on that ferry. The soldiers will get as many across on it as they can, and then they'll burn it so the Nilfgaardians won't be able to use it. That's how it's normally done, isn't it?'

'Agreed,' the Witcher nodded. 'That's how it's normally done. I don't understand, though, why the panic? What, is this the first war ever, have there never been any others? Just like usual, the kings' forces beat each other up and then the kings reach agreement, sign treaties and get plastered to celebrate. Nothing will really change for those having their ribs crushed on the jetty now. So why all this brutality?'

Dandelion looked at him intently, without releasing the stirrup.

'You must have lousy information, Geralt,' he said. 'Or you're unable to understand its significance. This isn't an ordinary war about succession to a throne or a small scrap of land. It's not a skirmish between two feudal lords, which peasants watch while leaning on their pitchforks.'

'What is it then? Enlighten me, because I really don't know what it's about. Just between you and I, it doesn't actually interest me that much, but please explain.'

'There's never been a war like this,' the bard said gravely. 'The Nilfgaard army are leaving scorched earth and bodies behind them. Entire fields of corpses. This is a war of destruction, total destruction. Nilfgaard against everyone. Cruelty—'

'There is and has never been a war without cruelty,' the Witcher interrupted. 'You're exaggerating, Dandelion. It's like it is by the ferry: that's how it's normally done. A kind of military tradition, I'd say. As long as the world has existed, armies marching through a country kill, plunder, burn and rape; though not necessarily in that order. As long as the world has existed, peasants have hidden in forests with their women and what they can carry, and when everything is over, return—'

'Not in this war, Geralt. After this war there won't be anybody or anything to return to. Nilfgaard is leaving smouldering embers behind it, the army is marching in a row and dragging everybody out. Scaffolds and stakes stretch for miles along the highways, smoke is rising into the sky across the entire horizon. You said there hasn't been anything like this since the world has existed? Well, you were right. Since the world has existed. Our world. For it looks as though the Nilfgaardians have come from beyond the mountains to destroy our world.'

'That makes no sense. Who would want to destroy the world? Wars aren't waged to destroy. Wars are waged for two reasons. One is power and the other is money.'

'Don't philosophise, Geralt! You won't change what's happening with philosophy! Why won't you listen? Why won't you see? Why don't you want to understand? Believe me, the Yaruga won't stop the Nilfgaardians. In the winter, when the river freezes over, they'll march on. I tell you, we must flee, flee to the North; they may not

367

get that far. But even if they don't, our world will never be what it was. Geralt, don't leave me here! I'll never survive by myself! Don't leave me!'

'You must be insane, Dandelion,' the Witcher said, leaning over in the saddle. 'You must be insane with fear, if you could think I'd leave you. Give me your hand and jump up on the horse. There's nothing for you here, nor will you shove your way onto the ferry. I'll take you upstream and then we'll hunt for a boat or a ferry.'

'The Nilfgaardians will capture us! They're close now. Did you see those horsemen? They are clearly coming straight from the fighting. Let's ride downstream towards the mouth of the Ina.'

'Stop looking on the dark side. We'll slip through, you'll see. Crowds of people are heading downstream, it'll be the same at every ferry as it is here, they're sure to have nabbed all the boats too. We'll ride upstream, against the current. Don't worry, I'll get you across on a log if I have to.'

'The far bank's barely visible!'

'Don't whinge. I said I'd get you across.'

'What about you?'

'Hop up onto the horse. We'll talk on the way. Hey, not with that bloody sack! Do you want to break Roach's back?'

'Is it Roach? Roach was a bay, and she's a chestnut.'

'All of my horses are called Roach. You know that perfectly well; don't try to get round me. I said get rid of that sack. What's in it, dammit? Gold?'

'Manuscripts! Poems! And some vittles . . .'

'Throw it into the river. You can write some new poems. And I'll share my food with you.'

Dandelion made a forlorn face, but did not ponder long, and hurled the sack into the water. He jumped onto the horse and wriggled around, making a place for himself on the saddlebags, and grabbed the Witcher's belt.

'Time to go, time to go,' he urged anxiously. 'Let's not waste time, Geralt, we'll disappear into the forest, before—'

'Stop it, Dandelion. That panic of yours is beginning to affect Roach.'

'Don't mock. If you'd seen what I—'

'Shut up, dammit. Let's ride, I'd like to get you across before dusk.'

'Me? What about you?'

'I have matters to deal with on this side of the river.'

'You must be mad, Geralt. Do you have a death wish? What "matters"?'

'None of your business. I'm going to Cintra.'

'To Cintra? Cintra is no more.'

'What do you mean?'

'There is no Cintra. Just smouldering embers and piles of rubble. The Nilfgaardians—'

'Dismount, Dandelion.'

'What?'

'Get off!' The Witcher jerked around. The troubadour looked at his face and leaped from the horse onto the ground, took a step back and stumbled.

Geralt got off slowly. He threw the reins across the mare's head, stood for a moment undecided, and then wiped his face with a gloved hand. He sat down on the edge of a tree hollow, beneath a spreading dogwood bush with blood-red branches.

'Come here, Dandelion,' he said. 'Sit down. And tell me what's happened to Cintra. Everything.'

The poet sat down.

'The Nilfgaardians invaded across the passes,' he began after a moment's silence. 'There were thousands of them. They surrounded the Cintran army in the Marnadal valley. A battle was joined lasting the whole day, from dawn till dusk. The forces of Cintra fought courageously, but were decimated. The king fell, and then their queen—'

'Calanthe.'

'Yes. She headed off a stampede, didn't let them disperse, gathered anyone she was able to around herself and the standard. They fought their way through the encirclement and fell back across the river towards the city. Whoever was able to.'

'And Calanthe?'

369

'She defended the river crossing with a handful of knights, and shielded the retreat. They say she fought like a man, threw herself like a woman possessed into the greatest turmoil. They stabbed her with pikes as she charged the Nilfgaardian foot. She was transported to the city gravely wounded. What's in that canteen, Geralt?'

'Vodka. Want some?'

'What do you think?'

'Speak. Go on, Dandelion. Tell me everything.'

'The city didn't put up a fight. There was no siege, because there was no one to defend the walls. What was left of the knights and their families, the noblemen and the queen . . . They barricaded themselves in the castle. The Nilfgaardians captured the castle at once, their sorcerers pulverised the gate and some of the walls. Only the keep was being defended, clearly protected by spells, because it resisted the Nilfgaardian magic. In spite of that, the Nilfgaardians forced their way inside within four days. They didn't find anyone alive. Not a soul. The women had killed the children, the men had killed the women and then fallen on their swords or . . . What's the matter, Geralt?'

'Speak, Dandelion.'

'Or . . . like Calanthe . . . Headlong from the battlements, from the very top. They say she asked someone to . . . But no one would. So she crawled to the battlements and . . . Headfirst. They say dreadful things were done to her body. I don't want to . . . What's the matter?'

'Nothing. Dandelion . . . In Cintra there was a . . . little girl. Calanthe's granddaughter, she was around ten or eleven. Her name was Ciri. Did you hear anything about her?'

'No. But there was a terrible massacre in the city and the castle and almost no one got out alive. And nobody survived of those who defended the keep, I told you. And most of the women and children from the notable families were there.'

The Witcher said nothing.

'That Calanthe,' Dandelion asked. 'Did you know her?'

'Yes.'

'And the little girl you were asking about? Ciri?'

'I knew her too.'

The wind blew from the river, rippled the water, shook the trees and the leaves fell from the branches in a shimmering shower. Autumn, thought the Witcher, it's autumn again.

He stood up.

'Do you believe in destiny, Dandelion?'

The troubadour raised his head and looked at him with his eyes wide open.

'Why do you ask?'

'Answer.'

'Well . . . yes.'

'But did you know that destiny alone is not enough? That something more is necessary?'

'I don't understand.'

'You're not the only one. But that's how it is. Something more is needed. The problem is that . . . that I won't ever find out what.'

'What's the matter, Geralt?'

'Nothing, Dandelion. Come, get on. Let's go, we're wasting the day. Who knows how long it'll take us to find a boat, and we'll need a big one. I'm not leaving Roach, after all.'

'Are we crossing the river today?' the poet asked, happily.

'Yes. There's nothing for me on this side of the river.'

IX

'Yurga!'

'Darling!'

She ran from the gate – her hair escaping her headscarf, blowing around – stumbling and crying out. Yurga threw the halter to his servant, jumped down from the cart, ran to meet his wife, seized her around the waist, lifted her up and spun her, whirled her around.

'I'm home, my darling! I've returned!'

'Yurga!'

'I'm back! Hey, throw open the gates! The man of the house has returned!'

She was wet, smelling of soap suds. She had clearly been doing the laundry. He stood her on the ground, but she still did not release him, and remained clinging, trembling, warm.

'Lead me inside.'

'By the Gods, you've returned . . . I couldn't sleep at night . . . Yurga . . . I couldn't sleep at night—'

'I've returned. Oh, I've returned! And I've returned with riches! Do you see the cart? Hey, hurry, drive it in! Do you see the cart? I'm carrying enough goods to—'

'Yurga, what are goods to me, or a cart . . . You've returned . . . Healthy . . . In one piece—'

'I've returned wealthy, I tell you. You'll see directly—'

'Yurga? But who's that? That man in black? By the Gods, and with a sword—'

The merchant looked around. The Witcher had dismounted and was standing with his back to them, pretending to be adjusting the girth and saddlebags. He did not look at them, did not approach.

'I'll tell you later. Oh, but if it weren't for him . . . But where are the lads? Hale?'

'Yes, Yurga, they're hale. They went to the fields to shoot at crows, but the neighbours will tell them you're back. They'll soon rush home, the three of them—'

'Three? What do you mean, Goldencheeks? Were you—'

'No . . . But I must tell you something . . . You won't be cross?'

'Me? With you?'

'I've taken a lassie in, Yurga. I took her from the druids, you know, the ones who rescued children after the war? They gathered homeless and stray children in the forests . . . Barely alive . . . Yurga? Are you cross?'

Yurga held a hand to his forehead and looked back. The Witcher was walking slowly behind the cart, leading his horse. He was not looking at them, his head turned away.

'Yurga?'

'O, Gods,' the merchant groaned. 'O, Gods! Something I wasn't expecting! At home!'

'Don't take on, Yurga . . . You'll see, you'll like her. She's a clever lassie, pleasing, hardworking . . . A mite odd. She won't say where she's from, she weeps at once if you ask. So I don't. Yurga, you know I always wished for a daughter . . . What ails you?'

'Nothing,' he said softly. 'Nothing. Destiny. The whole way he was raving in his sleep, delirious ravings, nothing but destiny and destiny . . . By the Gods . . . It's not for the likes of us to understand. We can't mark what people like him think. What they dream about. It's not for us to understand . . .'

'Dad!'

'Nadbor! Sulik! How you've grown, a pair of young bulls! Well, come here, to me! Look alive . . .'

He broke off, seeing a small, very slim, mousy-haired creature walking slowly behind the boys. The little girl looked at him and he saw the huge eyes as green as spring grass, shining like two little stars. He saw the girl suddenly start, run . . . He heard her shrill, piercing cry.

'Geralt!'

The Witcher turned away from his horse with a swift, agile

movement and ran to meet her. Yurga stared open-mouthed. He had never thought a man could move so quickly.

They came together in the centre of the farmyard. The mousy-haired girl in a grey dress. And the white-haired Witcher with a sword on his back, all dressed in black leather, gleaming with silver. The Witcher bounding softly, the girl trotting, the Witcher on his knees, the girl's thin hands around his neck, the mousy hair on his shoulders. Goldencheeks shrieked softly. Yurga hugged his rosy-cheeked wife when she cried out softly, pulling her towards him without a word, and gathered up and hugged both boys.

'Geralt!' the little girl repeated, clinging to the Witcher's chest. 'You found me! I knew you would! I always knew! I knew you'd find me!'

'Ciri,' said the Witcher.

Yurga could not see his face hidden among the mousy hair. He saw hands in black gloves squeezing the girl's back and shoulders.

'You found me! Oh, Geralt! I was waiting all the time! For so very long . . . We'll be together now, won't we? Now we'll be together, won't we? Say it, Geralt! Forever! Say it!'

'Forever, Ciri.'

'It's like they said! Geralt! It's like they said! Am I your destiny? Say it! Am I your destiny?'

Yurga saw the Witcher's eyes. And was very astonished. He heard his wife's soft weeping, felt the trembling of her shoulders. He looked at the Witcher and waited, tensed, for his answer. He knew he would not understand it, but he waited for it. And heard it.

'You're more than that, Ciri. Much more.'

Turn the page for a preview of the next thrilling adventure of Geralt the Witcher:

THE TOWER OF THE SWALLOW

'I can give you everything you desire,' said the fortune-teller. 'Riches, power and influence, fame and a long and happy life. Choose.'

'I wish for neither riches nor fame, neither power nor influence,' rejoined the witcher girl. 'I wish for a horse, as black and swift as a nightly gale. I wish for a sword, as bright and keen as a moonbeam. I wish to overstride the world on my black horse through the black night. I wish to smite the forces of Evil and Darkness with my luminous blade. This I would have.'

'I shall give you a horse, blacker than the night and fleeter than a nightly gale,' vowed the fortune-teller. 'I shall give you a sword, brighter and keener than a moonbeam. But you demand much, witcher girl, thus you must pay me dearly.'

'With what? For I have nothing.'

'With your blood.'

Flourens Delannoy, Fairy Tales and Stories

ONE

As is generally known, the Universe – like life – describes a wheel. A wheel on whose rim eight magical points are etched, making a complete turn; the annual cycle. These points, lying on the rim in pairs directly opposite each other, include Imbolc, or Budding; Lughnasadh, or Mellowing; Beltane, or Blooming; and Samhain, or Dying. Also marked on the wheel are the two Solstices, the winter one called Midinvaerne and Midaëte, for the summer. There are also the two Equinoxes – Birke, in spring, and Velen, in autumn. These dates divide the circle into eight parts – and so in the elven calendar the year is also so divided.

When they landed on the beaches in the vicinity of the Yaruga and the Pontar, humans brought with them their own calendar, based on the moon, which divided the year into twelve months, giving the farmer's annual working cycle – from the beginning, with the markers in January, until the end, when the frost turns the sod into a hard lump. But although people divided up the year and reckoned dates differently, they accepted the elven wheel and the eight points around its rim. Adopted from the elven calendar, Imbolc and Lughnasadh, Samhain and Beltane, both Solstices and both Equinoxes became important holidays, hallowed dates for people. They stood out from the other dates as a lone tree stands out in a meadow.

Those dates are also set apart by magic.

It was not – and is not – a secret that those eight dates are days and nights during which the enchanted aura is greatly intensified. No longer is anyone astonished by the magical phenomena and mysterious occurrences that accompany those eight dates, in particular the Equinoxes and Solstices. Everyone is now accustomed to such phenomena and they seldom evoke a great sensation.

But that year it was different.

That year people had, as usual, celebrated the autumnal Equinox with a solemn family meal, during which all the type of fruits from that year's harvest had to be arrayed on the table, even if only a little of each. Custom dictated it. Having eaten and given thanks to the goddess Melitele for the harvest, the people retired for the night. And then the nightmare began.

Just before midnight a frightful storm got up and a hellish gale blew, in which through the rustling of trees being bent nigh to the ground, the creaking of rafters and the banging of shutters, a ghastly howling, screaming and wailing were heard. The clouds driven across the sky assumed outlandish shapes, among which the most common were silhouettes of galloping horses and unicorns. The gale did not abate for a good hour, and in the sudden silence that followed it the night came alive with the trilling and whirring of the wings of hundreds of goatsucker nightjars, those mysterious fowl which – according to folk tales – gather together to sing a demonic death knell over a dying person. This time the chorus of nightjars was as mighty and loud as if the entire world were about to expire.

The nightjars sang their death knell in clamorous voices while the horizon became shrouded in clouds, quenching the remains of the moonlight. At that moment sounded the howl of the fell beann'shie, the harbinger of imminent and violent death, and across the black sky galloped the Wild Hunt – a procession of fiery-eyed phantoms on skeleton horses, their tattered cloaks and standards fluttering behind them. So it was every few years. The Wild Hunt gathered its harvest, but it had not been this terrible for decades – in Novigrad alone over two dozen people went missing without trace.

After the Hunt had galloped by and the clouds had dispersed, folk saw the moon – on the wane, as was customary during the Equinox. But that night the moon was the colour of blood.

Simple folk had many explanations for these equinoctial phenomena, which tended to differ considerably from each other according to the specifics of local demonology. Astrologers, druids and sorcerers also had their explanations, but they were in the main erroneous and cobbled together haphazardly. Few, very few, people were able to connect the phenomena to real facts.

On the Isles of Skellige, for example, a few very superstitious folk saw in the curious events a harbinger of Tedd Deireadh, the end of the world, preceded by Ragh nar Roog, the last battle between Light and Darkness. The violent storm which rocked the Islands on the night of the Autumn Equinox was regarded by the superstitious as a wave pushed by the prow of the fearsome Naglfar of Morhögg, a longship with sides built of dead men's fingernails and toenails, bearing an army of spectres and demons of Chaos. More enlightened or better informed people, however, linked the turmoil of the heavens with the evil witch Yennefer, and her dreadful death. Others yet – who were even better informed – saw in the churned-up sea a sign that someone was dying, someone in whose veins flowed the blood of the kings of Skellige and Cintra.

The world over, the autumn Equinox was a night of spectres, nightmares and apparitions, a night of sudden, suffocating awakenings, fraught with menace, among sweat-soaked and rumpled sheets. Neither did the most illustrious escape the apparitions and awakenings; Emperor Emhyr var Emreis awoke with a cry in the Golden Towers in Nilfgaard. In the North, in Lan Exeter, King Esterad Thyssen leaped from his bed, waking his spouse, Queen Zuleyka. In Tretogor, arch-spy Dijkstra leaped up and reached for his dagger, waking the wife of the state treasurer. In the huge castle of Montecalvo the sorceress Philippa Eilhart leaped from damask sheets, without waking the Comte de Noailles' wife. The dwarf Yarpen Zigrin in Mahakam, the old witcher Vesemir in the mountain stronghold of Kaer Morhen, the bank clerk Fabio Sachs in the city of Gors Velen and Yarl Crach an Craite on board the longboat *The Ringhorn* all awoke more or less abruptly. The sorceress Fringilla Vigo came awake in Beauclair Castle, as did the priestess Sigrdrifa of the temple of the goddess Freyja on the island of Hindarsfjall. Daniel Etcheverry, Count of Garramone, awoke in the besieged fortress of Maribor. Zyvik, decurion of the Dun Banner, in Ban Gleann fort. The merchant Dominik Bombastus Houvenaghel in the town of Claremont. And many, many others.

381

Few people, though, were capable of connecting all those occurrences and phenomena with an actual, specific fact. Or a specific person. A stroke of luck meant that three such people were spending the night of the autumn Equinox under one roof. They were in the temple of the goddess Melitele in Ellander.

'Lich fowl . . .' groaned the scribe Jarre, staring into the darkness filling the temple grounds. 'There must be thousands of them, whole flocks. They're crying over someone's death. Over her death . . . She's dying . . .'

'Don't talk nonsense!' Triss Merigold spun around, raised a clenched fist, and, for a moment, looked as though she would shove the boy or strike him in the chest. 'Do you believe in foolish superstitions? September is coming to an end and the nightjars are gathering before taking flight! It's quite natural!'

'She's dying . . .'

'No one is dying!' screamed the sorceress, paling in fury. 'No one, do you understand? Stop talking nonsense!'

Young female adepts appeared in the library corridor, aroused by the nocturnal alarm. Their countenances were grave and ashen.

'Jarre.' Triss had calmed down. She placed a hand on the boy's shoulder and squeezed hard. 'You're the only man in the temple. We're all watching you, looking for support and succour from you. You must not fear, you must not panic. Master yourself. Do not let us down.'

Jarre took a deep breath, trying to calm the trembling of his hands and lips.

'It is not fear . . .' he whispered, avoiding the sorceress's gaze. 'I'm not afraid, I'm troubled! About her. I saw her in a dream.'

'I saw her too.' Triss pursed her lips. 'We had the same dream, you, I and Nenneke. Not a word about it.'

'Blood on her face . . . So much blood—'

'Be silent, I say. Nenneke approaches.'

The high priestess joined them. She looked weary. She shook her head in answer to Triss's wordless question. Seeing that Jarre had opened his mouth, she forestalled him.

'Nothing, sadly. When the Wild Hunt was flying over the temple almost all the girls awoke, but none of them had a vision. Not even one as hazy as ours. Go to bed, lad, you cannot help. Back to the dormitory, girls.'

She rubbed her face and eyes with both hands.

'Oh . . . The Equinox! This accursed night . . . Go to bed, Triss. We can do nothing.'

The sorceress clenched her fists. 'This helplessness is driving me to insanity. The thought that somewhere she is suffering, bleeding, that she's in peril . . . If I only knew what to do, dammit!'

Nenneke, high priestess of the temple of Melitele, turned around. 'Have you tried praying?'

In the South, far beyond the mountains of Amell, in Ebbing, in the land called Pereplut, on the vast marshes crisscrossed by the rivers Velda, Lete and Arete, in a place eight hundred miles as the crow flies from the city of Ellander and the temple of Melitele, a nightmare jerked the old hermit Vysogota from sleep. Once awake, Vysogota could not for the life of him recall his dream, but a weird unease prevented him from falling asleep again.

'It's cold, cold, cold,' said Vysogota to himself, as he tramped along a path among the reeds. 'It's cold, cold, brrr.'

Yet another trap was empty. Not a single muskrat. A most unsuccessful night. Vysogota cleaned sludge and duckweed from the trap, muttering curses and sniffing through his frozen nose.

'It's cold, brrr, hooeee!' he said, walking towards the edge of the swamp. 'And September not yet over! It's but four days after the Equinox! Ah, I don't recall such chills at the end of September, not for as long as I've lived. And I've lived a long time!'

The next – and penultimate – trap was also empty. Vysogota didn't even feel like cursing.

'There's no doubt,' he wittered on, as he walked, 'that the climate grows colder with every passing year. And now it looks as though the cooling will progress apace. Ha, the elves predicted that long since, but who believed in elven forecasts?'

Once again small wings whirred, and incredibly swift grey shapes flashed by over the old man's head. Once again the fog over the swamps echoed with the wild, intermittent churring of the goatsucker nightjars and the rapid slapping of their wings. Vysogota paid no attention to the birds. He was not superstitious, and there were always plenty of lich fowl on the bogs, particularly at dawn. The air was so thick with them he feared they would collide with him. Well, perhaps there weren't always as many as there were today, perhaps they didn't always call quite so bloodcurdlingly . . . Ah well, he thought, latterly nature has been playing queer pranks, and it's been one oddity after another, each one queerer than the last.

He was just removing the last – empty – trap from the water when he heard the neighing of a horse. The nightjars suddenly all fell silent.

On the swamps of Pereplut there were tussocks, dry, raised places, with river birch, alder, dogwood and blackthorn growing on them. Most of the tussocks were surrounded so completely by the bogs that it was impossible for a horse or a rider who didn't know the paths to reach them. But the neighing – Vysogota heard it once again – was coming from one of the hillocks.

Curiosity got the better of caution.

Vysogota was no expert on horses and their breeds, but he was an aesthete, and was able to recognise and appreciate beauty. And the black horse he saw framed against the birch trunks, with its coat gleaming like anthracite, was extraordinarily beautiful. It was the sheer quintessence of beauty. It was so beautiful it seemed unreal.

But it *was* real. And quite really caught in a trap, its reins and bridle entangled in the blood-red, clinging branches of a dogwood bush. When Vysogota went closer, the horse put its ears back and stamped so hard the ground shuddered, jerked its shapely head and whirled around. Now it was evident it was a mare. There was something else. Something that made Vysogota's heart begin to pound frantically, and invisible pincers of adrenaline tighten around his throat.

Behind the horse, in a shallow hollow, lay a body.

Vysogota dropped his sack on the ground. And was ashamed of

his first thought; which was to turn tail and run. He went closer, exercising caution, because the black mare was stamping her hooves, flattening her ears, baring her teeth on the bit and just waiting for the opportunity to bite or kick him.

The corpse was that of a teenage boy. He was lying face down, with one arm pinned by his trunk, the other extended to one side with its fingers digging into the sand. The boy was wearing a short suede jacket, tight leather britches and soft knee-high elven boots with buckles.

Vysogota leaned over and just then the corpse gave a loud groan. The black mare gave a long-drawn-out neigh and thumped its hooves against the ground.

The hermit knelt down and cautiously turned over the injured boy. He involuntarily drew back and hissed at the sight of the ghastly mask of dirt and congealed blood the boy had where his face should have been. He delicately picked moss, leaves and sand from the spittle- and mucous-covered lips, and tried to pull away the matted hair stuck to his cheek with blood. The injured boy moaned softly and tensed up. And began to shake. Vysogota peeled the hair away from the boy's face.

'A girl,' he said aloud, unable to believe what was right in front of him. 'It's a girl.'

ABOUT GOLLANCZ

Gollancz is the oldest SF publishing imprint in the world. Since being founded in 1927 Gollancz has continued to publish a focused selection of bestselling and award-winning authors. The front-list includes **Ben Aaronovitch**, **Joe Abercrombie**, **Charlaine Harris**, **Joanne Harris**, **Joe Hill**, **Alastair Reynolds**, **Patrick Rothfuss**, **Nalini Singh** and **Brandon Sanderson**.

As one of the largest Science Fiction and Fantasy imprints in the UK it is no surprise we have one of the most extensive backlists in the world. Find high-quality SF on Gateway written by such authors as **Philip K. Dick**, **Ursula Le Guin**, **Connie Willis**, **Sir Arthur C. Clarke**, **Pat Cadigan**, **Michael Moorcock** and **George R.R. Martin**.

We also have a strand of publishing in translation, which includes French, Polish and Russian authors. Gollancz is home to more award-winning authors than any other imprint, with names including **Aliette de Bodard**, **M. John Harrison**, **Paul McAuley**, **Sarah Pinborough**, **Pierre Pevel**, **Justina Robson** and many more.

The SF Gateway
*More than 3,000 classic, rare and previously
out-of-print SF novels at your fingertips.*
www.sfgateway.com

The Gollancz Blog
*Bringing you news from our worlds to yours. Stories,
interviews, articles and exclusive extracts just for you!*
www.gollancz.co.uk

GOLLANCZ
LONDON